Road Trip
to
Forever

chelsea curto

To the ones out there with brains that are a little bit different from everyone else.
That difference is special.
You are magical. Your ideas are magical.
Never stop chasing your dreams.
And to never being too much, but rather the perfect amount of enough.

Playlist

Green Green Grass by George Ezra

Paper Rings by Taylor Swift

One Headlight by The Wallflowers

Little Bit More by Suriel Hess

Best Friend by Rex Orange County

Starman by David Bowie

Perfect Day by Lou Reed

Love You Still by Tyler Shaw

Until I Found You by Stephen Sanchez and Em Beihold

She's A Rainbow by The Rolling Stones

Hold My Hand by Hootie & The Blowfish

Only Wanna Be with You by Hootie & The Blowfish

Love Me Now by John Legend

Fast Car by Jonas Blue and Dokata

Ho Hey by The Lumineers

Dress by Taylor Swift

Timeless (Taylor's Version) (From The Vault) by Taylor Swift

AUTHOR'S NOTE

Hi, reader.

Thank you for picking up my book. While I hope you laugh and swoon over Patrick and Lola's love story, I do want to share a couple of content warnings with you before you dive in. The majority of this book is happy and fun, but there are a few subjects readers might want to be advised of ahead of time, including:

-multiple open door romance scenes with detailed intimacy
-explicit language
-discussion of ADHD including the use of medicine
-mention of a loved one passing away (brief, no on page depiction)
-an on page migraine
-alcohol consumption (brief and not excessive)

You will see Lola talk about her ADHD (not diagnosed on page) and Patrick suffer from a migraine. These are experiences that many are familiar with, but no two people are the same.

The symptoms and thought processes *you* have might not be completely reflected in this story.

Everyone's individual experience is important and valuable, and just because certain characteristics are highlighted, it does not make them more severe or "real" than others.

Please take care while reading, and know my DMs on Instagram (@authorchelseacurto) are always open if you'd like to chat.

CHARACTER CATCH UP

Me again!

Road Trip to Forever is a standalone romance novel, but it does mention characters from my previous works—including some crossovers!

I know it can be frustrating to pick up a story and feel like you're thrown into multiple plot lines you're not familiar with, so I wanted mention other characters you'll meet in this book. No, you don't have to read the other books to love this one!

Jack Lancaster and Josephine (Jo) Bowen can be found in **An Unexpected Paradise**, which is my debut novel. It features a workplace romance, grumpy (him) x sunshine (her), forced proximity and fake dating. They head to a conference in Key West together and... you guessed it. They end up falling in love.

Henry Dawson and Emma Burns can be found in **The Companion Project**. In their story, Henry needs a date to a family function. He starts communicating online with a woman he's hired to be his girlfriend only to find out it's Emma, his coworker. It's a workplace romance, fake dating, opposites attract story and... you guessed it again. They also end up falling in love.

Noah Reynolds is a friend who does not have his own book. Neil and Rebecca Richardson are married and also do not have their own book.

Bridget Boylston and Theo Gardner (who you meet toward the halfway point of the book) are from **Booked for the Holidays**, the first book in a new small town series.

Jeremiah, the photographer mentioned in chapter forty-two, is a side character from my Valentine's Day novella **Camera Chemistry**.

I hope this answers any questions about who is who. My DMs are always open if you want some more clarification!

Happy reading!

PROLOGUE

Patrick
Ten years old

"IT'S NOT YOUR TURN," I yell.

I stomp my foot on the driveway and fold my arms over my sweaty shirt. Isaac, my older brother, ignores me and shoots the basketball into the hoop. It swishes through the net, and then I charge toward the loose ball, but Isaac gets there first and knocks me out of the way.

"You snooze, you lose, Patrick. Gotta be faster than that, little bro." He laughs and dribbles the ball between his legs.

I grumble and kick the tire of Mom's gray Volvo parked in the driveway. There's a small dent in the hood from where we hit it when we were playing yesterday morning. We haven't told her about the damage yet, but she's definitely going to be mad.

I hear the rumble of a car and as I look toward the sound, I see a minivan driving up the street. Bright red, like a fire truck. I haven't seen it before. It stops two houses down before inching forward and turning into the driveway next to ours.

There was a For Sale sign outside the home about a month

ago. I know Mr. and Mrs. Jenkins moved so they could be closer to their grandkids in Georgia. I've been wondering about our new neighbors. I don't have a lot of friends, so I hope it's a kid my age so I'll have someone to play with.

"Patrick," Isaac says from behind me. "You're up."

I ignore him. I'm too busy watching the car door fly open. The sun is bright and I have to hold my arm over my eyes to see anything because of the glare. A blonde girl tumbles out and falls to the pavement.

I jolt forward, about to ask her if she's okay, but she moves too quickly. She barrel-rolls across the driveway and leaps up. When she's back on two feet, she dusts off her elbows and glances around. She spots me right away, and immediately crosses the grass between our yards. The blades are damp from the humidity in the air, making water droplets stick to her shins.

I hate summer.

It's way too hot.

It doesn't seem to bother her, though. She's smiling.

When she's two feet away, she stops and sticks out a hand for me to shake.

"Hi," she says. Her voice is high and light. It sounds like Mom's when she's trying to make me feel better after I fall off my bike and scrape my knee on the ground. "I'm Lola."

I blink, confused. I've talked to girls before. Sally sits at my lunch table, and sometimes Jenna and I play on the swings together at recess. But none of them ever come up and just *talk* to me.

"Hi," I answer after a minute. "I'm Patrick."

Her hand still hovers between us, and I don't think she's going to drop it until she gets what she wants. I reach out and intertwine our fingers. My palms are sweaty, and there's dirt under my fingernails from playing outside, but hers are clean and soft.

I've never held a girl's hand before. I wonder if she can hear my heart beating in my chest. It's really fast, like when I sprint around the track during P.E. class and it's hard to breathe.

She stares at me with blue eyes. Bright blue, like the ocean. Her head tilts to the side, and I stare back. There are freckles covering her entire nose. Lots of them. They remind me of pencil marks, like someone drew them on her face in art class, one by one, and forgot to erase them. They look really cool.

Her long hair is pulled up in two high pigtails that swish back and forth. There's a Band-Aid on her arm and a barely visible scar above her lip. I can only see it if I squint really hard, and I wonder if anyone else has ever found it.

She's the prettiest girl I've ever seen.

"What are you looking at?" she asks.

"Uh." I point to her arm. "Your Band-Aid."

"It's from falling out of a window. My brother was so mad because *he* couldn't climb down the side of the house, and he didn't think I could either. Girls can do anything boys can do, though; sometimes we can even do things boys can't do. So, I proved him wrong. Scratched my elbows on some rocks at the bottom, but it was worth it."

"Whoa," I breathe out. "That's awesome."

"Thanks." She grins and drops our hands. I forgot we were still holding onto each other. "How old are you?"

"I'm ten. How about you?" I ask.

"Nine. Almost ten. So you're in fifth grade?"

"In September, yeah."

"Maybe we'll be in the same class. Do you go to Redding Elementary School?"

"Yeah. Is that where you're going to go?"

"Mhmm. My parents said it's one of the nicest schools in the area," she says.

"It's okay. Where did you move here from?"

"Illinois. My mom is a flight attendant, and she had to pick between Massachusetts, Utah, or Georgia for work. My dad *hates* the heat, so we came up here to Boston."

"I hate the heat, too," I say. "You made a good choice."

Lola scratches her arm then looks up at the sky and taps her cheek. I don't think she's stopped moving since she got out of her car. "I love flying." She points to an airplane passing through a patch of clouds. "See? Isn't it cool?"

"I've never been on a plane."

"Never?"

"No. We drive everywhere," I say.

"It's fun. They give you snacks, like pretzels and cookies. Sometimes an entire meal."

"That's awesome. Maybe I'll get to go on one someday."

"I bet you would like it." She tilts her chin down to look at me. "We should probably be friends."

I frown. "Who? You and me? Why?"

"Why not? We're neighbors. We should also be friends."

This girl isn't like the others in my class.

When those girls aren't quiet, all they do is giggle or whisper under their breath. Lola isn't quiet at all. She likes to talk, but not in a bad way. I can tell she has a lot to say, and something about her makes me want to listen.

"Okay." I nod. I want to answer her before she changes her mind and takes it back. "That sounds good."

"Good." Lola peers over my shoulder. "Is that your brother?"

"Yeah. That's Isaac. He's thirteen."

"I have an older brother, too. His name is James."

"If we're going to be friends, they should be friends," I say. "They can hang out so I can finally play basketball without fighting Isaac for the ball."

Lola tips her head back and laughs so loudly, it echoes in the summer air. Suddenly, I feel dizzy as my legs wobble and my vision blurs. Isaac and I have been playing outside for three hours already and it's been getting hotter and hotter. I think I need some water, but that means I'd have to go inside, and I want to stay here and keep listening to Lola's laugh.

Her laugh is really nice. Warm and friendly. I like hearing it. I wonder how I can make her laugh again. I need to come up with some funny jokes.

"What else do you like besides basketball?" she asks.

"Anything, really. My dad is teaching me the rules of baseball. I also like to read. What do you like to do for fun?"

"I love to draw. I want to make my own clothes someday. I like to use a lot of color. Green is my favorite." Lola smiles at me again. She's missing a tooth, and I bet if I asked, she'd have a cool story about how she lost it. Maybe she tied a string to a door and pulled it out, or it fell out when she ate a Rice Krispies Treat. "Like the color of your eyes."

"My eyes are your favorite color?" I ask, wanting to make sure I heard her right. No one's ever said something so nice to me before.

"Yeah. My mom taught me how to sew, so I make shirts and put them on my dolls."

"You can sew? Is there anything you can't do?" I ask, impressed. Sometimes I can't even button my shirts right.

"I can't ride my bike with my hands in the air."

"I can do that. I'll teach you. Can you teach me how to draw?"

"Of course. What are friends for?" Lola turns back to her new house. "I should help my parents unpack. They said I can paint my room bright pink tomorrow."

"Pink is cool. Do you know which room is going to be yours?"

"Yeah." She points to the set of windows on the left side of the house, upstairs on the second story. "That one."

"My room is right across from yours. We can wave to each other."

"Maybe we can make a pulley system and pass notes," she says. "I saw that on a TV show once."

"I can fold paper airplanes. If you leave your window open, I'll throw one inside," I say.

"I'd like that. See you later, Patrick. Thanks for being my friend." Lola bounds over to her driveway and grabs a box from her mom.

I stand there for a few minutes and watch the way she moves so easily. It's like she's floating on air. Isaac nudges my shoulder, and I blink out of my trance.

"Who's that?" he asks.

"Lola," I say. "She's our new neighbor."

"Don't you have any guy friends?"

"Not really, no. But who cares? She wants to hang out with me."

"Weirdo."

I grab the basketball from his hands and dribble toward the hoop. Lola grins at me from across the hedges, waves, then disappears inside.

I think I'm lucky she picked me to be her friend.

ONE

LOLA

Present day

I HOIST my heavy suitcases off the conveyor belt at baggage claim with an exhausted grumble.

Logan International Airport is loud and crowded for mid-May, visitors trickling into Boston to see all the city has to offer before summertime officially descends on the Northeast in a couple of weeks. A child wails from a stroller, kicking and screaming with an impressively loud screech for a human that doesn't even know how to walk. His feet flail wildly, and he throws a toy across the tile floor.

I don't blame him. If I don't get some fresh air soon, I might start to wail too.

I brush a few loose pieces of hair out of my eyes and roll my bags toward the exit, recognizing the Border Patrol agent near the automatic double doors that lead out to the terminal. It's the same guy I saw a month ago—and three months before that—checking passports and directing passengers to secondary screenings if necessary. I give him a nod. He nods back, a silent conversation passing between us.

Good to see you again, he's probably thinking, his arms covered in colorful tattoos and a shiny, official-looking badge pinned to his shirt. With a gun holstered at his waist and a bored, indifferent expression on his face, he gestures me forward, approval to proceed to sweet, sweet freedom.

I might be the most sane person you see today, I answer, a chocolate stain on the front of my dress and mascara under my eyes. *A little jet lagged, but not terrible, right?*

Right, he'd say. *I had someone try to smuggle in raw meat an hour ago. A whole ass turkey. I'll take your unbrushed hair over E.coli any day.*

I hold back a laugh.

The doors slide open and I make my way into the arrivals hall, greeted with bright beams of sunlight. The air conditioning is cool on my plane-dry face, and the smell of Dunkin' coffee tickles my nose. Arabica beans, freshly ground. I let out a sigh.

It's good to be home.

I love to travel, love to see the world and meet new people, but there's something so grounding and gratifying about being in a place you know so well. My phone buzzes in my purse and I step to the side to check it, narrowly avoiding getting run over by a family of four and a Pomeranian walking off its leash. A slew of text messages pop up on my screen, all coming in at the same time.

Have a good flight!

Crossword clue this morning: eight letters. A person who boasts loudly or exaggeratedly.

Braggart.

What's a synonym of braggart? Blowhard.

Would've been a much better answer.

Note to self: buy eggs.

And milk.

Took a student to the nurse today because he shoved dry macaroni from an art project up his nose.

Remember when you shoved those glow-in-the-dark beads up your nose to see if you would light up? Hysterical.

You landed. See you soon!

I'm about to type out a response to my best friend of twenty-four years when another text comes through.

You're going to get run over if you don't stop looking at your phone.

My chin jerks up to scan the crowd. It doesn't take long to find him; he's impossible to miss. There, amid a sea of tearful reunions and metal luggage carts, standing a head above everyone else, is Patrick Walker.

He's holding up a sign with the words *Welcome home, Blowhard!* scrawled across the bright red poster board in his messy handwriting. Smiling, like always, a half beam away from splitting at the seams to a wide, vivacious grin.

He looks just like he did when I left town three weeks ago: brown hair tucked neatly under a baseball hat, long limbs, broad shoulders, a six-foot-five frame, the trace of stubble on his jaw, and green eyes that twinkle in the artificial airport lighting. His cheeks have some color to them, like he's spent time out in the sun. Probably a weekend at the pool, lounging in a chair while he thumbed through a book.

A sob of pure delight escapes me as I tug my bags toward him, nearing a full-on sprint as I leap into his outstretched arms. It's ungraceful and I come at him from the side, but Patrick catches me with ease, scooping me out of the air and into his hold.

"What are you doing here?" I ask.

I touch his forehead and then his cheek to make sure he's real. Run my fingers over the little scar below his hairline; seven stitches and a jagged white line left behind after a baseball cleat went flying and hit him straight in the head. His grip around me is tight, secure, and he laughs into the crook of my neck as he spins us around.

Real. So real.

"Surprising you. It would be cruel to make you slum it home on the Silver Line after your eight-hour flight from Rome," he says. "Plus, I couldn't break our tradition of picking you up. Fifteen times in a row. We've got to keep the streak going."

"You've always been superstitious. How many days since an MBTA accident?" I ask.

"Zero. There was a fire yesterday, and people jumped—literally *jumped*—into the Charles River, Lola."

"I leave and this place turns into total anarchy."

He laughs, a low sound in my ear that warms my insides and makes me feel alive and wide-awake. My exhaustion fades the longer I stare at him and categorize every feature of his face I've missed in great detail.

The sharp line of his jaw, the flecks of blue mixed in his eyes. His nose and his neck and the lock of hair slipping out from under the bill of his hat, the wave curling against his forehead in pesky rebellion.

"God I've missed you," Patrick says.

"I've missed you too." I squeeze his arm, and he sets me down. "Where's the Jeep?"

"Double parked outside, so we better hightail it out of here. Let me take your bags."

"I can handle them," I say.

"Of course you can, but I want to help." He reaches for the bigger one before I can argue, the handle jammed and the zipper on the large pocket halfway undone. He gives it a firm yank, and it pops to its full height. "How was your flight? Did you have the chicken or pasta? What movie did you watch? How was your seatmate? And the classes in Italy? Tell me everything."

"Long but bearable. Chicken, since I've practically turned into a plate of gnocchi in my time away."

"I would've picked the same. Nothing says fine dining like poorly reheated meat on an airplane."

"*Legally Blonde*, then *Miss Congeniality*."

"You can never go wrong with a classic romcom."

"My seatmate crocheted me a dinosaur, and I cried when they gave it to me. Look how cute it is." I pull the trinket out of my purse and show him the purple and pink gift, complete with a scarf wrapped around its neck.

"That's cute as hell. I'm so jealous. I've only ever gotten stuck next to people who like to steal my armrest."

"The sewing class was great. The instructor liked my needle-work," I say.

"Not surprising. You're a creative marvel."

Patrick slings the bags into the back of his Jeep like they don't weigh twelve pounds over the checked baggage allowance, accruing me an oversized-luggage charge at Fiumicino Airport earlier this morning. He opens the passenger side door and ushers me inside, ignoring the incessant honking coming from the car behind us. A white paper bag sits on the floorboard and I recognize the logo instantly, snatching it up with greedy hands.

"You brought me donuts?" I ask. "You tall, wonderful, thoughtful creature, you."

"They come with a caveat."

He slides into the driver's seat and turns down the radio, a hit song from the early 2000s quieting through the speakers. Chocolate glazed is the first flavor I pull out and I sink my teeth into it, a murmur of ecstasy working its way from my mouth.

"Don't care what it is," I say around a second bite, crumbs spewing from my lips and landing on the dashboard. Patrick likes to keep his belongings clean, and I guiltily brush the mess away with a rogue napkin I find in the cup holder. "I'll do whatever it takes to get another one of these."

"Finish applying for the fashion show."

I groan. "Noooo. I take it back. I'd do anything for love, but I won't do that."

"Okay, Meatloaf," Patrick says. He flicks on his turn signal and merges into the steady stream of cars making their way toward the city. "Give me three reasons you shouldn't apply. *Good* reasons, not bullshit excuses."

I pop the last piece of donut into my mouth and wash it down with a sip of water. "I could get rejected."

"You could also get accepted," he counters.

I narrow my eyes in his direction and he ignores my gaze, attention trained firmly on the road.

He planned this bombardment, buttering me up with sugary sweets. I bet he's considered all the angles of my replies, a spreadsheet drawn up of my rebuttals, ranked in order from most likely to use as an argument to the least.

Dammit.

This is going to be harder than I thought.

"I don't know what designs I would bring," I say, grasping for anything that sounds mildly believable.

"You have a hundred outfits in your storage unit, half of which have never seen the light of—"

"The deadline is tonight."

"Then it's a good thing it's only two in the afternoon and I'm taking you straight home."

I stare out the window and let out a huff, feeling like a moody teenager not getting her way. "I hate when you're logical. Fine. *Fine*. I'll finish applying."

"You know I'm going to come upstairs with you and make sure you actually submit the application, right?"

"Right," I grumble, resigned.

"You've done scarier stuff than this, Lola. You've been skydiving, for heaven's sake," Patrick says.

"Yes, and the possibility of death by jumping out of a metal tube was more appealing than the possibility of rejection, so that should tell you something," I say.

The Friday afternoon traffic is light, making the drive to my apartment quick. Patrick parks in the visitor's spot near the front of my building and helps me haul my bags into the elevator. He taps his foot to the jazz melody playing and I stifle a yawn as I unlock my door, keys jangling when I push it open with my foot.

"Tired?" he asks.

"Exhausted." I step into the foyer and pull out my laptop, dropping my purse to the floor. I kick off my shoes and nudge them against the wall, next to a pair of leather sandals Patrick left in my kitchen before my trip. "Don't worry about the bags. I'll deal with them later."

Patrick shudders and rubs his palms over his navy-blue shorts. His fingers twitch, ready to shove clothes into a dresser or the laundry hamper, and I can *see* the revolt in his eyes at having to wait to put things in their proper place.

"How you can just live your life without unpacking immediately after a trip is mind-boggling to me," he finally says.

"Pick your battles, Walker. Unpacked suitcases or a submitted application. You can't have it all."

"Application," he says like a kid in a candy shop, eagerness for me to get started evident with the clap of his hands and the guidance to my sofa.

I plop onto the couch I scored from a garage sale last spring—green velvet with antique wooden legs and three square cushions. A steal for the price I paid, almost highway robbery. I balance my computer on top of my knees and type in my password, pulling up the website that's been taunting me for weeks.

Spurred on by a brief bout of spontaneity somewhere over the Atlantic Ocean after two glasses of red wine and a bowl of chocolate mousse, I started the application for the Florida Fashion Show the night I left on my trip. I hit a roadblock when the plane touched down in Italy though, the wheels on the tarmac a screech of pessimism ringing in my ears, a puncture to my inspiration. Every time I tried to talk about my experiences as a designer, they never sounded *remarkable*.

Good? Yes.

But impressive enough to earn a coveted spot in the Southeast's largest show? To be determined.

Patrick takes the seat next to me and taps my hand twice. He lifts his chin toward the computer screen and I nod, his gesture not requiring any words.

With over two decades of friendship, that's how in sync we are.

He thinks it and I understand it, our minds working as one.

I fill in the parts of the application I've been reluctant to finish. The letter of intent and the highlights of my resume condensed into a handful of paragraphs with a grammatical error or two. Sentences about creative vision and industry role models. Where I see myself in five years.

It's awkward to talk about myself, to boast my strengths and accomplishments and argue why I should be chosen over thousands of other talented designers who are just as deserving, but I forge on, fresh enthusiasm behind my typing with my best friend by my side.

I add in the links to my social media accounts, upload sample photos of my design style, and attach a lopsided headshot of myself, inwardly cringing at the image of me boasting a cheesy smile and half-closed eyes.

Patrick took that picture in his living room with a cracked iPhone and a white sheet covering the window behind me to block out the setting sun. He committed to the task, getting on his hands and knees and bruising his shins on the hardwood floor so he could find the perfect angle with the best lighting.

I could never bring myself to tell him it was crooked.

After I input all of the required information being asked of me, I stare at the completed form. The cursor hovers near a small box at the bottom of the website, six letters big and bold.

SUBMIT.

"You can do this, Lola," Patrick says.

The words are gentle. An assurance, not a demand, and the encouragement dances over my ears and works its way to the tips of my toes. It takes root, blossoming from a seed of doubt into a bountiful tree of hope and belief in a mythical world where I really *can* do anything.

A deep breath in, a deep breath out, and I click the button that might change my life forever, channeling courage and optimism.

A new window pops up. Animated confetti springs from the page, a digital celebration, and the slow realization of doing the thing I was terrified of settles in.

"Done. Happy?" I ask him. My legs knock against his chest and he folds his hand over the curve of my knee, just below the spot where my dress ends. Warmth erupts under the tips of his fingers.

"Doesn't matter if I'm happy. Are *you* happy?"

"Yeah," I say. "I am happy."

I tilt my chin and look at him. He's grinning, and the dual dimples etched on his cheeks are as dazzling as twinkling stars in a cloudless night sky.

"Then I'm happy too," he says. "Come here, Lo."

I don't hesitate. I shove my laptop onto the coffee table next to the candle I like to light in the evenings when I open the windows and let a breeze billow through the living room. Maine Summers, it's called, the scents of ocean spray and sand cherry lingering on the wick and in the surrounding air. For the second time in an hour, I launch myself into his embrace.

One of my favorite things about Patrick is how he hugs. He hugs with his whole being, pouring every part of himself into the places where our bodies connect. Chest, shoulders, arms looped around the small of my back.

It's careful. Soft. Bone-crushingly perfect.

Of all the cities I've traveled to and all the countries I've visited, *this* is my favorite place in the entire world. A chin on top of my head. Warm breath tickling my forehead. Fingers drifting down my back, then up, calming me in a way only a lifelong friend knows how to do.

It's like home.

Familiar.

Comfortable.

The spot you can come back to again and again, and not a single thing has changed.

If I could, I'd bottle up this feeling of belonging and carry it in the back pocket of my jeans to save for a rainy day when I'm lonely and missing home. Enjoy it for a little while longer before it slips away and becomes nothing but sand in an hourglass, flashes of memories left behind.

"Thank you for making me apply," I say into the stitching of Patrick's shirt.

It smells like lime and coffee and his favorite laundry detergent—a rare impulse buy after falling victim to fifteen Facebook ads. All scents synonymous with *him*, a gentle reminder that no matter how long I'm gone, no matter how far I go, when I'm nestled here in his hold, it's like I never left.

"When you say that," he murmurs into my hair, "it sounds like I tied you to a chair and refused to let you leave."

"Stockholm Syndrome," I murmur back. "You bribed me with donuts. It's the same thing."

"Will you write to me when I go to jail?"

"I'll cut out the comics and send them to you. The crossword puzzles, too."

"A true friend," he says. "How're you feeling about finally hitting submit?"

"Even if I don't get accepted, this is the first fashion show I've ever entered," I say. "And doing something new is really freaking cool, isn't it?"

"Cool doesn't even scratch the surface."

"Really freaking groovy, isn't it?"

"Now you're trying too hard. Quit while you're ahead," he jokes.

"A for effort?"

"B minus at best. I'm so proud of you, Lola."

Proud.

What a wonderful word.

Five little letters that wedge themselves into the center of my chest, loop around my heart, and pull tight. It's nice for your hard work to be acknowledged, to be recognized and appreciated.

It's even better when it's by someone you care about so very much, who's been there on your journey with you every step of the way.

"I couldn't have done it without you," I say.

"I didn't do anything. This was all you," Patrick answers.

We pull apart, and as he rests his elbows on his thighs, the tattoo that takes up six inches of space on his left arm sneaks out from under his sleeve.

I grin at the sight.

A slice of pepperoni pizza he got three years ago, the result of too much tequila and an unseasonably warm winter night.

We were four drinks deep, giddy as we stumbled down the sidewalk and home from the bar after being out with our friends. Not quite drunk, but well past sober, that pleasant place where everything is funny and wonderful and seems like a good idea. There was no destination in mind, and we were content to stroll until we found somewhere we wanted to be.

He slung his arm over my shoulder, slouching down to compensate for our nine-inch height difference and mumbling about how short I was, even in a pair of cute leather boots. I buried my face in his jacket and called him vertically gifted. *Patrick and the Beanstalk*, I said as we jumped over a square of pavement to avoid a pile of melting snow, and then he tapped my nose while asking if I had any magic beans.

Bursts of uncontrollable laughter slipped out of us like popped champagne bottles at the stroke of midnight. We were two idiots, no reason for the jubilation besides simply being thankful to be alive and with such lovely company.

And aren't those some of the best snapshots in life? The moments that make you so grateful you want to shout for joy because you're with a person who makes you so perfectly happy?

The tattoo started as a joke when I spotted the flickering neon sign and the building with no windows. A dare to see if he'd agree. With a shrug and a mischievous grin, we wandered inside the dimly lit parlor.

The idea of a pizza design came to mind. I blurted it out as I sat on a leather bench in the heated room, swinging my legs back and forth while the world started to spin. I didn't think he'd go along with the suggestion so easily. Patrick is a planner, someone who pays meticulous attention to details and outlines the pros and cons of a purchase before fully committing to it. It once took him a month to decide on new sheets for his bed, reading review after review until settling on the gray cotton set loved by over thirty-thousand customers.

He surprised me by slapping down his credit card for a spur-of-the-moment appointment with the artist at the shop who had a tiger tattooed on the side of his face, and there was nothing I could do to talk him out of the permanent marking.

It was one of the best nights of my life, and I'm lucky to have amassed a treasure trove full of favorites with him. I smile whenever I see the silly thing, the trophy a fuzzy, distant memory forever immortalized on a patch of tan skin.

"How are we celebrating?" Patrick asks, and I drag my eyes away from the inky design. "You need a nap, obviously. You can't even keep your head up."

"I can keep my head up."

"There's drool in the corner of your mouth, Lo."

"That's just water."

"Water. Sure."

"It might be Sprite."

"You don't even drink Sprite."

"I lied. It's drool from the plane."

"I knew it. You can't hide anything from me."

"Maybe I could."

"Don't even try. The gang is going to The Garden tonight. Want to meet up with them later?"

"I can't," I say. "I'm busy."

"Busy?" he repeats. There's a divot between his eyebrows, a waterfall of wrinkles that cascade down to the bridge of his nose. It's his Confused Face, the same one he employs when he can't think of an answer to a difficult crossword puzzle clue or has to pick between chocolate chip cookies or snickerdoodle. I see the wheels turning in his head as he tries to figure out what I mean. "With what?"

TWO
LOLA

"I HAVE A DATE."

I stare at the mark on the wall behind his shoulder as I say it, the spot where the paint is chipping and the drywall is starting to show.

I don't know why I'm afraid to tell him. Patrick knows I go on dates.

He's seen my Tinder profile. One night he stole my phone, joking that he needed to make sure I hadn't written *Live, Laugh, Love* or some other horrifically corny phrase under my name and age. He flipped through my pictures, and the jokes stopped.

His eyes got glassy. His sentences got shorter, the room settling into stifling silence until he quietly told me he would swipe right if he ever came across my profile on the app.

I didn't know what to do with that information, and he never mentioned it again.

It feels weird to tell him about *this* date though, a sharp twinge of uncomfortableness settling in the pit of my stomach as I think about the rest of my evening. After doing something big and important, a monumental step in my career, it's a crash down from a high. We should be celebrating together, right?

Going out with our group of friends who I love dearly, the people that have constantly supported me. Not with a woman named Jade who has an apartment full of plants.

She's nice, a lovely conversationalist who asks about my day and dietary preferences, but I'm not sure she'll understand the scope of my excitement, my reasons for squirming in my seat and checking my inbox every seven minutes, refreshing and refreshing to see if a new message has popped up.

"You've been home an hour and you already have a date? Good for you, Lo," Patrick says.

His voice hitches at the end, almost like he's trying to convince himself of something he doesn't quite believe. Strain laces the edges of the words, and I wonder if he says it three more times, it'll come true.

I don't like it.

It feels like he's keeping something from me, and I like that even less.

Patrick and I don't have any secrets, since having gone from *friends* to *best friends* in the blink of an eye. Our dads built us a treehouse for Christmas when we were eleven, a structure made of maple and a ladder held together by thick rope in the forty-foot oak on the property line between our childhood homes.

It was our spot.

The place where we went every night until the summer we graduated high school, spending hours and hours talking about everything and nothing and anything in between. We laid on the rickety wood held together by rusty nails and contemplated the wonders of the universe.

Up there, we were invincible. No goal unobtainable. No dream too big as we shared every part of ourselves with each other—our deepest fears, our greatest aspirations, and our wildest dreams. Life outside those four walls didn't exist. It was me and it was Patrick and it was perfect.

We were bound forever.

We've been in each other's orbits ever since, a continuous rotation through the whirlwind of life. No matter how unstable things become, no matter how volatile or uncertain the future is, I know from deep within my heart, Patrick will always be by my side.

We had to adjust a bit as we sailed into adulthood.

He got taller.

I got curvier, hips sprouting up almost overnight. I kissed size zero goodbye and embraced my midsized frame.

His voice changed to deep and authoritative, a tone that makes you want to lean in close and listen because you know he's going to say something important.

I dyed my hair. Pink streaks. Blue streaks then pink again.

He started kissing girls. I started kissing everyone.

The years changed, and so did we.

Drastically.

We became less alike, gravitating toward different things and operating in different ways.

Patrick went from a shy boy to popular and well-liked in high school. A star athlete and a Yale graduate. The youngest elementary school principal in Massachusetts history and the leader behind passing a revolutionary state bill that requires cafeteria lunches to be free for all students, regardless of income.

I dropped out of college after a semester. Started a social media account to chronicle my life as a fashion designer trying to get her name out there and opened a small commissions-based online store that earns me enough money to pay my rent each month. I created a video series where I teach people how to sew. It went viral, at the right place on the internet at the right time and earning me thousands of followers.

I make easy, downloadable patterns and walk the viewers

through the sewing process, step by step, until we complete the product together. We've done bucket hats and basic tops. A couple of sundresses. Last week I uploaded a tutorial on how to make your own bathing suit in time for summer over spotty Wi-Fi from my room in an Italian hostel.

Our paths of life also differ.

Patrick craves stability and staying in the same spot. Laying down roots and getting comfortable. Saving up for a mortgage. A kitchen large enough for an island. A fridge with a water dispenser and a garage with bikes.

I can't sit still, always on the hunt for the next adventure. A life of independence. A meager savings account but plenty of plane tickets and passport stamps. Memories money can't buy, like riding through the streets of Paris on the back of a scooter and cliff jumping into the Mediterranean, my skin burning under the summer sun.

He likes to spend time at home. I want to see the world.

We've grown from the little boy and young girl who spent their nights staring at the sky and dreaming on a shooting star, but our friendship *works*. It's strong and sturdy and perfect.

We never fight, and when I'm away, we rely on technology to make sure we're near at risk of drifting apart despite the thousands of miles separating us.

A flurry of text messages from sunrise to sunset. Him calling on his way to work to curse unreliable public transportation. Me FaceTiming from eight time zones away while I hold up a fresh baguette.

A picture of Patrick in bed, lamplight bathing his face in soft hues of yellow and gold. A book in his hands and a smile curving his lips.

All the voice messages I've kept from him because I love to hear his voice when I've been gone for far too long.

Like him bouncing around gift ideas for Teacher Appreciation Day. No more mugs or gift cards, he said firmly, but maybe T-shirts with something witty written on them?

Why red sauce is superior to white sauce on pasta. *Flavor,* he told me, pausing to apologize to someone he ran into on the sidewalk. *It's much heartier, Lola.*

A rant about why dogs shouldn't wear clothes or socks or reindeer antlers at Christmastime.

Cats too, he added, half an hour later as a distracted afterthought.

A six-minute diatribe about which *Star Wars* movie is the best. He gave up after going back and forth with himself to order a burrito and never picked a favorite.

Still, after all these years, we don't have any secrets.

And that's how I know that Patrick is, without a doubt, keeping a secret from me now.

"You're not mad?" I ask, tabling his behavior to dissect later.

"Why would I be mad?"

"Because I'm bailing."

"Lola." Patrick laughs. The deep rumble echoes off the walls and works its way into my bones. It settles there, like a sip of hot cocoa on a cold winter day. A scoop of ice cream in scorching heat on a summer afternoon. Pleasant and nice and a much-needed imaginary hug. "I could never be mad at you for living your life. Where are you going for the date?"

"Dinner at a Mexican restaurant with unlimited chips and queso. It was impossible to say no."

"Food *is* the way to your heart. I'm surprised you aren't already there. Lined up outside, waiting for the clock to strike five," he says.

"I wish I was going with you to The Garden. I miss everyone."

"I'll tell them you say hey, and we'll celebrate with them when you get accepted to the show."

"*If* I get accepted to the show."

"It'll be a whole spectacle. Confetti. Streamers." He waves his hand around, imagining where he'll hang decorations. A poster boasting "**Congratulations!**" and a balloon archway. Bright colors. Glitter too, probably. I can see the steely glint he gets in his eye when he sets his mind to something and fully commits.

"Streamers? Who the hell is going to do all this decorating?" I ask.

"Hell, I'll get those annoying blower things. It'll force Eavesdropping Evan next door to buy earplugs," he says, steamrolling past my question. "Payback for when he stole your new *Vogue* magazine and never gave it back. There will be snacks. Cheetos. Chocolate ice cream. All your favorite foods."

"You say this like it's a sure thing."

"Because, Lola," Patrick says. He reaches out and curls his thumb and pointer finger around the curve of my chin. He eases my head back so I can look at him. I see the fan of his dark eyelashes. The color on his cheeks—he's definitely sunburned. The way his bottom lip bends into a crooked almost-smile. Our gazes hold steady, neither one wanting to be the first to break. "It is a sure thing."

"I'm scared," I admit. "What if I get accepted, go all the way down there, and they hate the designs I've spent hours on? I know criticism is part of the job, but I like to pretend what I do is good."

"What if you go down there and they love your designs?" His smile stretches wider. I see the whites of his teeth. The crinkles around his eyes that have gotten deeper with age. The perfect divots of dimples chiseled in his cheeks. His Hopeful Face. "What if everything goes right?"

"All these unknowns are terrifying," I say. "The fear of rejection sucks, doesn't it?"

"It definitely sucks, but that's why I'm here. You're not alone. *Never* alone. Do you hear me?"

"I hear you," I say. "Never alone."

"I believe in everything you do," he adds, as if he hasn't said enough of the right things this afternoon.

"Thank you." Tears sting my eyes, and I blink the emotion away before they can fall. "I think I'm going to take a nap. You can hang out here if you want. I'd love it if you stayed."

"Sounds good. I have some work I need to catch up on," Patrick says.

"End of the year stuff?"

"Yeah. No one talks about all the paperwork a principal has to do."

"Funny. I thought all you did was paperwork," I say. "Piles and piles of paperwork."

"Don't forget watching macaroni shoot out of noses. I do that too."

"I bet your educational leadership classes didn't prepare you for such an undertaking."

"They did not. I am wildly unqualified for all this responsibility," he says.

I hum and stretch out my legs. My calves end up in his lap, and he drapes a blanket over my lower half. A gag gift he got me for my birthday four years ago, with his face plastered on the fleece three dozen times.

"Will you wake me up in a few hours?" I ask.

"Of course. You're sticking around for a while, right? No other trips planned?"

"Nope. I'll be here for a couple months."

"What are you going to do with your free time? You haven't been home for longer than a week or two in years."

"Get accepted to the fashion show, hopefully. Take on more

commissions. Film some new videos. I'm tired. I've been on the move for so long, I need a break."

"If you're tired," Patrick says, "then you should rest. There's nothing wrong with slowing down."

"I'll be doing lots of resting. I'm also going to find ways to bug you. You'll be downright sick of me soon, Patrick Walker."

"Doubtful. At the very least, maybe the subway system will run smoothly since you're home. Lola Jones: a champion for the people."

"That's a nice campaign slogan." I reach out and thread our hands together, giving his palm a squeeze. "Thank you for picking me up. Thank you for believing in me. Thank you for being here."

"There's nowhere else I'd rather be," he says, squeezing my palm back. "Sweet dreams, Lo. It's good to have you home."

"It's good to be home. I missed you, Patrick," I say.

"More than the donuts?"

"No." I turn on my side and press my face into a decorative pillow. A button makes an imprint on my cheek. "Never more than donuts. But you're a very close second."

"To be fair," he says as I slip away into a dream, "I'd pick the donuts too."

THREE
PATRICK

THE GARDEN IS loud when I walk through the double wood doors.

Bodies press together. Music thumps from speakers mounted to the ceiling. The bass rattles the picture frames nailed to the walls. I feel like I'm at a rave instead of the neighborhood watering hole situated next to an eyeglass store.

Multiple televisions are showing the hockey playoffs and fans in jerseys congregate in small clusters to watch the game. Everyone erupts in cheers when the Bruins score. Someone calls out *free shots*, someone else rings a brass bell, and the crowd goes wild.

I scan the restaurant and spot my friends tucked away in a corner of the room, gathered around a table full of fried food and half-empty glasses. I make a pit stop at the bar on the way over, nodding hello to one of the regular bartenders behind the counter.

"Gin and tonic?" Cleo asks. She reaches for a large metal shaker and fills it with a generous pour of alcohol before she finishes the question.

"Might as well put 'predictable' on my headstone," I say.

She tops the beverage with a lime skewered through a tiny wooden toothpick and slides the glass my way. I pull a ten from my wallet and drop it in the overflowing tip jar.

"Predictability makes my life easier," she says. "If you give me a second, I'll grab a whiskey and ginger ale for your girl."

I take a sip of my drink, a deep pull that has the gin burning my throat and working its way into my bloodstream. "My girl?"

"Lola. I haven't seen her in ages."

"Ah." Another sip, then a third. It makes saying my next words easier. "She's on a date."

Cleo's smile twists into one that's sad. Full of pity, if I had to guess. "Oh. Right. Cool. Enjoy your drink. It's on the house tonight," she says. "Let me know if you want another round."

"Thanks, but you don't need—"

She disappears with a wave before I can argue or attempt to pay my tab. I sigh and push off the counter, dropping a couple of bills behind the bar in a spot I know she'll see so she has no choice but to take the money.

"There he is," Henry Dawson, one of my best friends, says as I approach the table.

He slings his arm around his fiancée's shoulders, and Emma Burns glances up at him with pure adoration etched on her face. I swear the two of them could be out of a cartoon, hearts in their eyes and attention only on the other. The world could go up in flames and they wouldn't notice, too enamored to be distracted.

"Hey." I slide into the booth and take my usual spot at the end of the bench, settling against the leather ripped from years of wear and tear. Noah Reynolds and Neil Richardson, two other buddies, lift their glasses in my direction.

"Where's Lola?" Henry asks.

"On a date with some girl who's a plant enthusiast."

"A plant enthusiast? Huh. That's new."

"Better than the circus performer from last year," I say.

"You're not serious."

"He breathed fire for a living, Henry. I would never joke about such a serious matter." I turn my attention to the women at the table. "Ladies. Plant enthusiast or circus performer? Take your pick."

The ladies in question are Emma, Josephine—Jo—Bowen, who's been dating my friend Jack for a couple years, and Rebecca, Neil's wife. All good people, with witty humor and the ability to put up with their partner's shit, which is a full-time gig. They're genuine friends who care about each other and plan Saturdays down at the Cape or hiking the Blue Hills. They volunteer their time at the local food bank and create a carpool schedule to shuttle Neil and Rebecca's kid, Wyatt, back and forth from preschool.

Lola dragged me to the last remaining Babies 'R Us in the Northeast so we could buy a car seat for my Jeep. The safest one, with all the bells and whistles, that can magically convert into a stroller too. During checkout, the cashier congratulated us and asked how far along we were. Lola grabbed my hand, placed it over her stomach and said, *two months, but he's my brother, so it's a little complicated. Don't tell my husband*, she added, and I shooed her out of the store while she laughed hysterically.

I bet that poor woman still has a look of horror on her face.

"A circus performer is probably pretty proficient with their hands," Jo says.

"The plant enthusiast could be nice," Rebecca counters. "Tender and caring, you know?"

"An ax thrower would be a happy medium. Good with their hands *and* pays attention to detail. Ask her if she's ever gone out with an ax thrower, Patrick," Emma says.

"Lola would never go out with an ax thrower." I squeeze the lime into my drink to make it tart. "She hates flannel."

"Darn." Emma sighs. "I forget how well you two know each other."

I shrug. "Imagine if we had been friends for years and I didn't know her middle name."

"What *is* her middle name?" Henry asks.

"Patricia," I say.

"It is not."

"No. It's not. It's Adeline. Let's move on to someone else's love life," I suggest, turning my attention to Henry and Emma. "What are you doing for your bachelor and bachelorette parties? It's getting close to the big day."

I never thought Henry, the man who claimed relationships weren't for him, would get *married*, yet here we are, a few weeks out from an over-the-top, lavish ceremony at the history museum with a guest list a mile long. Even the governor is invited, an old family friend of Henry's parents.

"Oh." Emma brightens and leans into her husband-to-be, a sturdy pillar by her side. "We wanted to talk to you all about that."

"No parties," Henry says. "And no gifts either. Instead of people spending money on us, guests can donate to charities picked out by you all. Each couple will decide on an organization that's close to your heart."

"Wow," Neil says. "Henry Dawson cares about someone other than himself? I never thought I'd see the day."

"Is it love?" Noah asks. "Or the benefit of being obscenely rich?"

"Both, probably," I say. "Because I'd take the blender and toaster oven."

"If you all are finished," Henry says, irritation ripe in his words, "I'd love to hear your opinions."

"On what? Global warming?" I ask.

"Bitcoin?"

"Electric cars?"

"I hate all of you," Henry grumbles.

"I like the idea," Jack says, the one to stop our merciless teasing. "It's for a good cause."

"Some people get wiser with age. You get less grumpy. I'm proud of you." Jo leans over and taps her boyfriend's cheek. She lets out a squeal when he grabs her hand and presses a kiss to her palm, then the tips of her fingers. Jack's eyes never leave hers as they dissolve into a private moment.

Another couple in love who found each other when they least expected it.

Another happily ever after.

There must be something in the water, a pitcher of Kool-Aid I didn't get a sip of yet. Our circle of friends has multiplied in the last few years, adding significant others and moving on to the next stages of life.

Marriage. Children. Joint bank accounts and talk of a second dog. Swing sets and a wooden sandbox. A lawn perfect for Easter egg hunts and a place in the living room for decorating a Christmas tree in matching pajama sets.

Pain lances through me as I watch Jack and Jo, an ache I've grown to despise as of late. It happens when I see my friends with their partners, a noticeable rush of jealousy and loneliness I've tried to combat and ignore.

It's bone-deep, that longing. A persistent bruise that won't go away. The feeling of wanting another half to make you a whole. It's an awareness of being left out, of being left behind. Of wishing I had someone to look at me the way they all look at their partners.

Like they're a split second away from throwing a net around the moon and tugging it down as an offering of love.

My phone buzzes in my pocket and interrupts the intrusive thoughts creeping in. The prickly sensation in my chest abates, shifting to tolerable and bearable when I see Lola's name on the screen.

> There's someone at the bar doing a Sudoku puzzle.
>
> A printed out sheet of paper and everything.
>
> Oh my god, he has a magnifying glass.
>
> Are you in two places at one time?

I huff out a laugh and take a sip of my drink before answering.

> You're hilarious, Jones.
>
> I only do crossword puzzles in public. Sudoku is too easy.
>
> How's your date?

Three dots appear then disappear. Minutes pass, and I tap my foot while I wait for a response. There are conversations happening around me, but I don't hear them, too busy staring at my phone.

> Two out of ten.
>
> At least she didn't dine and dash.
>
> Or, I hope she didn't. Maybe the bathroom excuse isn't real, and I'm dumb enough to believe it.
>
> The bar is low, isn't it?
>
> The bar is in hell, Patrick.
>
> Gotta run. I'll text you later!

I double tap the message and click my phone closed, setting it face down so I'm not tempted to pick it back up and heckle her with a million questions. Why is the date so bad? Does she want me to come and grab her so her night can take a turn for the better with our friends?

I'd do it if she asked. It wouldn't matter how far I'd have to drive.

Lola prefers flings over long-lasting relationships, not sticking around long enough to learn what side of the bed someone prefers to sleep on or if they take milk or cream with their coffee. It's been like this for years, since we were in our early twenties and she lost her dad to cancer.

It was sudden, barely enough time to say goodbye before he was gone. His death wrecked her. The bright girl I knew faded away and only a shell of herself remained.

And, as if losing the man she admired more than anything in the world wasn't enough, when Lola was at her lowest point, the most vulnerable she's ever been, the guy she was dating—for a year and a fucking half—broke up with her at her father's funeral.

He didn't want to help her through her grief, he told her, patting her shoulder and handing her a bouquet of wilted flowers.

A metaphor of love, I guess.

I punched him in the nose after the service. The bloody knuckles were worth it.

Lola's gotten stronger over the years. Therapy helps, but she still carries an anxiousness with her, the fear of letting anyone get too close, too connected, because they'll leave, too. It's why she enjoys bouncing from place to place, traveling the world without getting settled or reliant on another person. It gives her an out, an escape for when she needs it.

I know how she operates, but I don't understand it.

I *want* commitment. A steady partner. A routine and the same plus-one to all the weddings I'm invited to. Splitting holidays between my family and hers. A life with someone else is *good*. It's fun and it's exciting and I enjoy knowing a person for longer than a week or two. I like learning their habits and what makes them smile.

I've dated women—a couple for a month or two, a few for close to a year. Every relationship has been... okay. Not bad, not great. Amicable breakups and knowing we won't stay in touch down the road. *Almost perfect*, not *totally perfect*. So close, but so, so far.

The only time I feel *totally perfect*, I've learned, is when I'm with Lola.

Eating dinner together. Listening to her talk about her day or watching her with a needle stuck between her teeth as she stitches up a hole in one of her dresses. Saturdays with our friends and picnics in the Common. The time we were driving back from Acadia National Park and got stuck in a hailstorm. We parked under a highway overpass for an hour and talked about the stupidest things: If we would rather read minds or stop time. Who the Zodiac killer might be. If pineapple belongs on pizza. It felt like it did when we saw each other every day as kids, and *god* I've missed those moments.

I'm greedy for her time when she's in town, always looking for opportunities to see her and finding excuses to stay around her a little while longer. A late train. A second piece of cake even though I'm full and might explode with another bite. Watching a movie she's excited about despite already seeing it.

Twice.

My mind has turned cruel over the years. Traitorous and imaginative, looking at my best friend in a way that's going to get me in trouble one day. I've wondered how it would feel to press my lips to her ankle, to her shin, to the top of her knee and further up.

The sounds she would make if I kept going.

If she would beg and say please.

What would Lola look like in my bed, wearing nothing but a smile?

Devastating enough to kill me, probably.

There have been times when we're out with our friends at a place that's too crowded, too hot, and we sit beside each other to get away from the masses of people.

Our thighs press together. Her shoulder knocks against mine. My hand drapes over the back of her chair, close enough where I could play with the ends of her hair if I wanted to. Her lips quirk up, like she *knows* I'm hiding something, and she's determined to figure it out.

A wildfire burns in my chest under her gaze, a raging, unmanageable thing I shove aside, to the place where I keep all my secrets. A hidden compartment deep in the recesses of my brain, somewhere no one can ever find it. It's safe there, a box I only pull out when I'm sad that she's gone and missing her like hell.

Because we're friends.

Just friends.

There's no chance of us ever being anything more.

"Patrick?"

I blink, pulled back to the present. "Yeah?"

"Are you in?"

"Of course I'm in. Anything for the happy couple." I smile and lift my empty glass—*when the hell did that happen?*—toward Henry and Emma.

I'm about to slip out of the booth and fight through the booze-thirsty crowd to get the table another round of drinks and avoid more public displays of affection when a text pops up on my phone.

A photo with dim lighting. A row of bottles lined up under a big mirror and bar stools made of dark leather. Lola's in the center, the pink streaks in her blonde hair looking brighter than usual and a twinkle behind her blue eyes.

Her arm is around an older man. There's a cap on his head and an impressive mustache curling under his nose. They're both giving a thumbs up to the camera, and it looks like they're mid-laugh, caught at the tail end of a joke.

> This is Harold! A look into your future!!!

> No way. Harold is cooler than me. Check out that hat.

> I'm buying you one for Christmas.

> Ask him if he does the NYT puzzles.

> He does. With a pen! You've met your match, Patrick Walker.

I save the photo to my collection of pictures from Lola, right next to the one of her cuddling a stray cat outside the Colosseum. The sun is in her eyes and she's squinting into the camera, but her smile is wide and bright and so *her*.

That grin is lethal, poison around the edges of her mouth that seeps through the screen and makes me dizzy and lightheaded.

I feel that burst of *totally perfect* as I stare at the image, put under her spell.

I can never have Lola.

Not in the way I want her—as mine forever.

I don't care. I keep loving her anyway.

FOUR
LOLA

"DID YOUR DATE GET ANY BETTER?" Patrick asks. He pops the tops off two bottle of beer and puts them on a coaster.

"Nope." I take a seat on his white sectional and pull a blanket over my legs. "I should have gone home with Harold. Probably would've had a better night doing word searches."

I reach for the pizzas sitting on the coffee table and dole out two slices of pepperoni onto each of our paper plates. Before I can take a single bite, Patrick is already finishing his first slice. I look over and see a string of cheese hanging from the corner of his mouth. An unholy moan catches in the back of his throat as he swallows, the noise echoing through the apartment and making my skin flush a vibrant pink.

Patrick has always loved pizza night, and I've always loved that wicked sound.

"This story is going to be good," he says, his knee knocking against mine as he waits, a man made of exasperating patience.

It's been almost a week since I last saw him, and the day I applied to the Florida Fashion Show and my ill-fated outing with Jade, the fiddle-leaf-fig lover, are both nearly forgotten.

He's been busy with end of the year parent-teacher conferences, double checking report cards, and sorting through the lost-and-found bucket he keeps in his office. He sent me a picture yesterday of a single shoe, pink and sparkly with white laces and wrote, *I don't understand kids* underneath the image. *Where'd the other one go?* he added. *Outer space?*

I've kept my phone in the living room while I've been in my home office, bending over the sewing machine I've had for a decade as I rework the same outfit three times—a purple dress that flares at the waist and hits just above my knees. A bow that ties in the back and a scooped neckline that shows off my curves. It's light and flowy, perfect for summer nights with a skirt that will catch in the breeze when I skip down the sidewalk.

"Why?" I ask. "So you can revel in my misery?"

"I need to add it to your bad date list. It's been a while. Time for an update," Patrick says.

"Stop. You do not have a list."

He holds up a grease-covered finger and pulls out his phone, his lock screen boasting a photo of us at Six Flags New England on a fall day. Patrick has a balloon hat on his head and a super-hero cape around his neck. There's face paint on my nose and cheeks, the design of sparkly butterfly wings catching in the autumn sunlight.

"Here," he says, a note titled 'How to Not Piss Off Lola While on a Date' displayed on his screen.

I groan, and the grin on his lips stretches wider. His eyes twinkle with mirth and mischief. He looks younger than his thirty-four years, turning into a rebellious teenager on a quest to tease the shit out of me.

"Asshole," I say. A laugh bursts free, and I throw a crumpled napkin at his head. "Okay, let me read."

I scan the lines, amazed he's remembered so many details from my past. All the times I recanted my horrible dates to him once I had been marked safe from subpar conversion and an

ROAD TRIP TO FOREVER

underwhelming connection are laid out in front of me. He's included his own commentary after each one, and while I'd never admit it to him, that might be my favorite part.

- *Do NOT propose on the first date (Paul is a moron).*
- *Be five minutes early, and don't keep her waiting for half an hour (invest in a watch, John).*
- *Don't tell her you have dinner planned, then take her to your old fraternity house during alumni week for a hotdog eating contest (she's not nineteen).*
- *Own a bed frame (people don't?).*

"I really don't think having a bed frame is asking a lot of someone," I say.

"It's not. It's right up there with wearing pants. Common courtesy, if you ask me. Frankly, I'm still confused why you turned down the proposal. You could've ended up as a Guinness World Record holder, Lola. Shortest engagement ever. They would've given you a plaque."

"He had a ring, Patrick, and made me FaceTime his mom. For someone with a phobia of commitment, sitting through that phone call was like climbing Mount Everest."

"Last week can't be any worse than making a man cry in the middle of a sushi restaurant."

"Oh, it was worse."

"Go on. Tell me what she did so I can add some new material."

I sigh and rub away the ache between my eyes, the embarrassment of having to relive a conversation I want to forget. "According to Jade, my laugh is too loud, and the things I laughed at weren't funny. She didn't like when I interrupted her, and my job—the fashion industry as a whole, apparently—is a joke."

An irritated grumble erupts from deep in Patrick's chest with volcanic intensity. "Where the hell are you meeting these people, Lo?"

"Dating apps I'm going to delete later tonight. That was the last straw. Even if it's just one cup of coffee, I'm not doing it. Single forever. It's better this way."

"You just haven't dated the right person yet."

"I knew you'd say that, Mr. Romantic. The more I think about it, the more I realize they might not be the problem. I am."

He blinks and leans forward to set his plate down, staring at me with unwavering focus. "What are you talking about?"

"I wear my heart on my sleeve, you know? My feelings... I think they might be too big, Patrick. Too much. I laugh too much. I cry too much. My brain is too much, jumbled and disorganized chaos almost all of the time. My whole *being* is too much. I'm a mess. And, it's become abundantly clear through shitty dates at Mexican restaurants that others think that, too."

I don't *want* a relationship. I'm happy without the agony of wondering when someone might walk away and how soon I'll wind up alone. I'm good without having my passions mocked and the traits I loathe about myself prodded and picked apart, displayed for all the world to see. They make me feel *different* when all I want to be is *normal,* and it's exhausting having to defend myself. It makes me want to never socialize again.

I let out a breath. I didn't mean for our night to take a turn. To sour the mood and strip myself bare, letting Patrick see these parts of myself I've been grappling with lately. My inability to focus without medicine. Not letting someone finish their sentence before I jump in, eager to add to the conversation. The hyper-fixation on an activity or food or outfit for three to four days before I'm bored, wanting nothing to do with it ever again. I'm exposed, unwoven. Teetering close to the lines of sadness and loneliness, yet something stops me from completely falling over the precipice.

Him.

"Did someone call you a mess, Lola?" Patrick's voice is low, a vicious undertone to the question. I hear that protectiveness he's always shown, and my heart thaws half a degree. It gives me an ounce of hope that there are good people left in this world, and one of them is sitting right in front of me. "Because I will *kill* them."

"It's a self-diagnosis. A reflection when I'm alone in my hotel room sort of thing. When I'm missing my dad and remembering all the good times we had together."

"Don't do that," he says. The harshness shifts, his words serrated with the altruism I adore about him.

"Do what?" I ask.

"Make yourself small and diminish all your wonderful qualities when you should be proud. Don't think these parts of you are wrong. They aren't. You're so special, Lo. Fuck anyone who thinks otherwise," he says. "So you interrupt people sometimes? Big deal. Your brain works faster than everyone else's. You're not being rude. You're just..." He rolls his lips together, deep in thought. His eyebrows furrow and he takes a minute to find the right words. *Studious Face. Contemplative Face. I'm Going To Find A Way To Make You Feel Better Face.* "You think ahead. That's hardly a crime. And your laugh? Your laugh is one of my favorite things about you."

"You like my laugh?"

"Of course I like your laugh. How could anyone not? It lights up an entire room, like the sun on the first afternoon of spring," he says. "You know what I'm talking about, right? That day after months of bitter cold when you walk outside, look up at the sky, and there's so much warmth. It makes you happy and complete. *That* is what I feel every time you laugh. I feel whole."

My bottom lip wobbles, and the coil in my chest turns snug. I think my heart skips a beat or two. That might be the nicest thing anyone has ever said to me, the single compliment from him worth more than a million from anyone else. "What about when I cry? I do that a lot, too."

Patrick chuckles and opens his arms, an invitation there. I all but shove my forgotten plate to the floor and make my way into his embrace.

"You're keeping people employed," he murmurs in the crevice behind my ear. The small secret sliver of space that turns my insides into molten lava. "The folks at Kleenex thank you for your generous displays of emotion so they can put food on the table for their families. You're doing the world a favor. There's talk of a statue. Or a bench with an inspirational quote: *to all the tears I've yet to cry.*"

I laugh at his ridiculousness. "Isn't that a country song? Or a teen movie?"

"No," he says. "But we should make it one."

"How was The Garden with everyone?"

"It was fine."

"Fine? That's an interesting way to describe a night out with our friends."

I break away from his hold and look down at him. The movement shifts us into a more intimate position. I'm on my knees between his parted thighs. His palm rests on my hip to keep me steady, and his thumb presses into the inch of bare skin between the end of my shirt and the top of my khaki shorts.

Heat pools in my belly and glides through me like oil. Patrick's thumb moves half a millimeter higher to just below my belly button, like that single inch of skin he's touching isn't sufficient and he needs more.

I suck in a breath and stare at his palm. His fingers flex, as if he's holding on to a thread of careful restraint he badly wants to cut with a pair of scissors and sever in two.

We've always been affectionate with each other, a shared love language of physical touch. Long hugs and piggyback rides. Legs squished together on the couch and using one blanket for a scary movie instead of bothering with two.

I've never thought anything of it. That's what best friends *do*. It's what we've always done.

This, though, feels different.

It feels intentional, a purpose to his fingertips pushing deeper into my flesh and the way his eyes hold mine. They're a shade darker than normal as he watches me, a characteristic far from friendly behind the green. His grip tightens, a fleeting flash of pressure on my skin before his hand falls to his side and he clears his throat.

"Henry and Emma are skipping the bachelor and bachelorette parties," he says, the first to break the silence. He glances away, taking a reluctant interest in his shirt.

"And not having a party has you all melancholy?" I ask.

"I am not melancholy." Patrick fiddles with his sleeve, and I think he's trying to break free from the starchy material holding his arms hostage. "They also want people to donate to charities instead of giving them gifts. It's a great idea."

"I don't understand how this makes the night fine," I say. "What a crappy word choice. I remember when you went on a rant about how it's the worst adjective in the English language."

"Because it's too ambiguous. There are so many better words out there begging to be used."

I narrow my eyes and flick his ear. He's deflecting, trying to segue us to a different topic but I refuse to budge. "What aren't you telling me?"

"Hanging out with our friends is more fun when you're

there," he says. "I feel out of place when I'm alone, like I'm the seventh wheel."

"What about Noah?"

"I like you more."

"You know I'm definitely going to use that to get my way one of these days, right?"

"I'd expect nothing less."

"What about Jessica? Was she busy? Also out on a date?" I joke.

Patrick's been dating her for half a year. She's the sister of a teacher at his school, and they met during drop-off one morning. She chased down her niece with forgotten multiplication homework and ran smack dab into Patrick's chest. Pencils went flying. A backpack ended up in the bushes. He caught her before she fell onto the hood of a car. She offered to buy him coffee, and the rest, as they say, is history.

I've met her a few times. She's nice. Quiet, smart. A woman who uses *acrimonious* in casual discussions and goes to yoga on the weekends. She sits on the board of three different charity organizations and when given the choice of what she'd like to read, she'll pick nonfiction every time.

Perfect for the man who has a stack of books that have won the Nobel Prize in Literature on his bedside table.

"Maybe she was," Patrick says. "I don't know. We broke up."

"*What*?" I almost tumble off the couch. "When? Why?"

"A couple months ago. I'm not bent out of shape about it."

"*Months*?"

"Five, to be exact. We only dated a few weeks."

"What the hell, Patrick? Why haven't you mentioned you're going through a breakup that happened eons ago?"

"You were busy sewing and stuffing your face with gelato. I didn't want to burden you with something insignificant."

"It's not insignificant and it's not a burden. You're my best friend. I want to hear about these things. We don't just share the pretty things with each other." I cross my arms over my chest and glare at him, hoping to get my point across. "I want to see the ugly parts of your life, too. God knows I've shown you mine."

"I guess I was embarrassed. Dating someone for a handful of weeks then breaking up isn't an impressive feat."

"People break up every day. It's nothing to be embarrassed about."

"Yeah. I know."

"Your person is out there," I say. "And until then, stop keeping secrets from me."

"Fine." He holds his hands up in defeat. "No more secrets. You give me your ugly. I'll give you my ugly."

I'm about to ask if he wants to eat his worries away, indulge in another slice of pizza or visit the ice cream shack a half mile up the road, splitting a large sundae to clear his mind, but he moves first. I blink, and he's closer than he was two minutes ago.

We're mere inches apart. Patrick sits upright and his nose almost brushes against mine.

My heart races in my chest.

This close, I can feel the warmth from his muscles. I can count the freckles on his cheeks, spots left behind from a weekend too many outside and a forgotten layer of sunscreen. I see the sun setting behind him. Color bounces off the wall and casts his face in shades of yellows and pinks, a glittering prism. Light spills over his features, the five o'clock shadow on his jaw and the laugh wrinkles around his eyes. I can hear his soft inhales, small puffs of air in a rhythmic pattern.

Patrick is *beautiful.*

Handsome, yes, but also lung-seizingly beautiful in a way I've never found another person before. In a way I've never found *him* before, and now I want to stare at him for hours. I

want to draw him with my charcoal pencils so I can commemo-
rate this discovery with a sketch to show off his beauty.

"Do you know what we should do, Lola?" Patrick asks.

His voice is rough around the edges but velvety soft in the
middle, a seesaw of syllables that scramble my mind. My name
sounds wicked, forbidden, so different from every other way he's
ever spoken to me over the years, and I *love* it.

"What?" I find myself whispering, as if the louder I speak,
the quicker this moment will dissolve, the dream I'm imagining
turning back to reality.

His eyes draw a slow path down my face and catch on the
corner of my mouth, a spot I've never seen him notice before.
They linger there, a fresh flare of heat blazing behind his gaze.

Is he—is he going to ask to *kiss me*?

That's what *feels* like is about to happen, a rush of energy and
charged electricity raising the temperature in the room by at
least ten degrees.

And would I let him?

I swallow and he follows the bob of my throat, the rise and
fall of my chest as breathing becomes difficult, staggered and
labored from his attention.

Yes, a small but mighty voice whispers in my head. *Yes, you
would.*

I've never felt like this, like I want to grab the collar of his
shirt and yank him toward me. Run my fingers through his hair
and pull on the longer stands by his ears to find out what he
likes. To dance with him in the kitchen while his hip nudges
mine and spend the night in his bed with the fourteen pillows
he sleeps with so I can show him what I like, too.

It's possible I'm still tired from traveling and confused by
time zones. Jet lagged and wondering why I'm awake when I
should be asleep. Or maybe, *maybe* I'm a sudden lightweight,

one beer making me experience thoughts I've never previously consider.

Thoughts like Patrick's mouth on mine. The swipe of his tongue and the press of his lips. Whispered words in my ears and large hands roaming up my thighs and under my shirt.

I stare at my best friend as if it's the first time I'm seeing him.

I think it might be.

Does he always sit this close to me, my body practically pinned under his?

When did his fingers fold around my knee, and why are sparks igniting under his palm in the innocent spot he's touched a hundred times before?

How do I get him to stay there and not pull away?

"We should toast to being the perpetually single ones in our group," he says, that velvety softness wrapping around me like luxurious silk. "Who needs a relationship? Maybe I'll start living my life like you do."

Oh *god*.

I'm reading this situation entirely wrong.

The fire in my stomach cools to dying embers. The ache between my thighs dulls. The moment—a brief flash of attraction—sweeps by, caught in an undertow. I panic and reach for our beers on the coffee table.

"Right," I say louder than necessary. I almost shout it at him, hopeful it will snuff out the tension in the room and my stupidity for thinking the man I've known for nearly my entire life suddenly wants to hurdle past the platonic barrier of *just friends* we established years ago. "Sure."

Patrick's fingers touch the inside of my wrist as he takes his bottle from my grasp, and everything gets hazy. I don't know which way is up. I don't know what we were talking about five minutes ago.

I don't know *anything* except I want to kiss my best friend.

I've never wanted to kiss him before, but now I do.

"To failed relationships," I say, lifting my drink in the air.

"And to never being too much," Patrick adds. "Just the perfect amount of enough."

We clink the bottles together and take a sip in tandem, his gaze never breaking away from mine.

It doesn't break when I take a long sip from the bottle.

It doesn't break when we finish eating and he tosses over the remote, making me pick out a movie.

Patrick watches me like he's holding onto another secret, and I desperately want to know what it is.

FIVE

PATRICK

I WAKE TO A BLOOD-CURDLING SCREAM.

Moonbeams filter across my comforter through the half-drawn curtains over the windows, the only source of light in the room. My hand shoots out, fumbling for my phone on the nightstand, bleary-eyed and confused.

"Three in the morning? What the hell?" I groan and toss the device onto the mattress, irritated. It bounces twice and falls to the floor, disappearing under a pile of laundry and a stack of memoirs.

It can stay there.

I rub my eyes, painfully aware of the throbbing in my head. It radiates across my temples and works its way down my cheeks and the length of my neck to the top of my spine. I can sense the makings of a migraine brewing, the pulsing sensation that tells me excruciating discomfort is imminent if I don't get back to sleep or take some medicine.

The scream was probably a drunk idiot on the roof of the apartment complex next door. I've heard them out on the terrace before, entranced by an alcohol-induced stupor propelling them to do something stupid, like jump from one building to the other and think they'll walk away unscathed.

The high-pitched sound could also be coming from my guest room where Lola dragged herself to after we finished two pizzas, a couple more beers, and three candy bars. We put on a sitcom when the night turned late, laughing until our stomachs started to hurt and our eyes started to close.

Her head rested on my shoulder and I sat there motionless, afraid to move, wanting to prolong the moment for as long as possible before I had to nudge her awake and we went our separate ways for the rest of the evening.

I could've stayed like that forever.

I'm on my feet in an instant, kicking the covers away from my legs and nearly ripping the door off the hinges. I skid down the hall and come to a stop outside the spare bedroom. I knock to be courteous, my heart clambering in my chest when I don't get a response. I take a deep breath and push the door open.

I find Lola sitting on the edge of the bed. She's gaping at her phone, and her oversized shirt slips off her left shoulder. I recognize it as one of mine, an old baseball tee from high school with my name on the back and a hole in the arm. Her hair is a tangle of blonde and pink, sitting in a knot on the top of her head.

"Lo?" I ask cautiously. "What's going on?"

She glances up at me with her wide, ocean-blue eyes. Her face is so full of pride and joy, and my breath catches at the sight of her. They're different emotions from earlier when our gazes met on the couch. When we knocked our drinks together, and I watched the bob of her throat with keen interest as she swallowed a sip of beer, licking away the drops of alcohol left behind with a teasing swipe of her tongue.

I shouldn't have liked it as much as I did.

God, I wanted to kiss her.

Here, in a state of delirium, I want to kiss her even more.

"I got an email."

"In the middle of the night?"

"It was from earlier. It went to my junk folder."

"I'm not following."

"I got invited to the Florida Fashion Show. My application was accepted," she says. Her phone tumbles from her hands and lands on the floor. "They want to show my designs, Patrick. My clothes are going to be on a runway for people to see."

It takes a second for it to register. My sleep-fogged brain is slow to sharpen into focus. The tremble in her voice turns to weary excitement. Her shoulders shake and laughter falls out of her, iridescent, full of life, and *fucking beautiful*.

Then it hits me, a freight train knocking me wide awake.

"Lola." I move from the door to the mattress and cover the distance in three strides. I lift her off the bed and into my arms, spinning her around. More laughter spills out of her and now I'm laughing too, my cackle splintering the silence in the room. "Holy shit."

"Maybe I'm dreaming. This can't be real, can it?"

"Of course it's real. You're a damn good designer. You're talented, and you *deserve* this," I say.

"Will you come with me?" she asks. "I know you don't like to travel, but I'd love it if you were there."

"Of course I'll come with you." Her eagerness to include me is a flare behind my solar plexus, a rush of something precious. "When is it?"

"Soon. The second week in June. You'll be out of school. The wedding will be over. I thought about driving down and making it a road trip. You don't have to do that part if you don't want to. I'll rent a car, and you could meet me in—"

"We'll take the Jeep." I set her on her feet and rub my hands up and down her arms. I don't let her finish suggesting an idea where I'm not next to her every step of the way. "A road trip sounds fun."

"Even though we're going to Florida in the middle of summer? You hate summer. It could be the road trip to hell."

"I don't hate summer," I say.

"Patrick." She tilts her head to the side and stares at me. Her mouth quirks, an upward tug of her lips that's infectious and contagious. I find myself grinning back at her, the pressure across my sternum relenting. "You once told me you'd rather spend six hours in a tub of ice water than an hour out in the sun."

"I like summer with you."

"It's so hot, we're going to melt. We might not make it out alive."

"Then we'll be two melted puddles on the ground and I won't care because we'll be celebrating you."

"Two melted puddles. That would be a sight."

"Could be worse. It could be death by mosquitos," I say.

"Or alligators. That would be a shitty way to go. Probably bad for the environment," she says through fractured sarcasm, a witty quip before she bursts into tears.

I reach for her on instinct, my hand finding her hips and pulling her into another hug. My chin rests on the top of her head, her flyaway hairs tickling my nose.

"I am so proud of you," I whisper into her ear. I don't want her to miss hearing the praise and the truth behind it.

Lola sniffs, and I thumb away the tear rolling down her cheek. "Sorry for crying. I don't know why I'm so emotional," she says.

"You're emotional because you did something scary. You chased your dreams, and they're coming true. You're allowed to shed some tears."

"It's better than sobbing over that video of the dog being

reunited with his owner after weeks apart. The one I sent you earlier?"

"You cry. So what? There are worse traits to have. You could be walking around with legs for arms. Or an ass for a face. Imagine the looks you'd get then."

"How do you always know the right thing to say?" Lola tips her chin and looks at me with a runny nose and tear-stained cheeks, a soul-crushing beam and red-rimmed eyes. So pretty, so damn beautiful, even when she's crying. I swear a fists closes around my heart and squeezes with suffocating tightness every time she smiles. "You're too good to me."

Fuck every person who's ever made her feel like she's *a lot* for expressing herself or considered her *too much* and made her shove pieces of herself aside to fit into a mold that's so obviously not her.

This woman is the blueprint, the pinnacle of good.

Of perfection.

Too much?

I'm not sure I can ever get enough.

I've been taking hit after hit of her for two decades, and still, I crave more.

"I'm good to you because it's how you deserve to be treated," I say. "How you *should* be treated. Being proud of you is the bare minimum, Lola, and I'm sorry someone's ever made you feel like you're not worthy of support and encouragement."

I've gotten freer with my touches lately, each graze a little more risky and a little more reckless. Like I'm pushing the boundaries of our friendship and trying to figure out when she'll tell me to knock it off, to stop acting weird.

It isn't now, as I run my fingers down the line of her jaw and capture another rogue tear that almost slips by. It wasn't on the couch earlier either, when I almost leaned in and pressed my lips to hers, caught up in a universe where she was staring at me and I couldn't look away.

"Give me all the details." I grab the green blanket folded in the corner of the room and we settle on the bed, a stack of fuchsia pillows behind our backs. Lola takes the left side and I take the right, stretching my legs out in front of me and letting out a content huff of air.

"It's the middle of the night." Lola crosses her ankles, and I bite back a grin at the socks she's wearing—penguins skiing in beanies. Her favorite pair. Her thigh presses into mine and neither one of us pulls away. "You have an alarm going off in two hours. I can tell you tomorrow."

I pluck her phone off the ground and hand it to her. "It's field day at school, and all I need to do is run the dunk tank. Who needs sleep, anyway? Start talking, Jones. I want to hear everything."

Her grin is wide and her laugh is soft as her shoulders wiggle and she scoots closer. Her head drops to my chest and stays there, as if it's sewn to my skin. A permanent part of me. I wonder if she can hear my heart pounding through the thin cotton of my shirt, giving away just how much I like her being near me.

"The show runs for four days," she says, reading from an email. I try to follow along with the bold words, the lingo that makes me want to go cross-eyed because I have no clue what it means, but the bright light from the screen hurts my head and I have to look away. "I need to—Patrick, are you okay?"

"I'm fine." I rub my forehead and close my eyes. "Just a headache. Keep going."

Lola curses under her breath. The mattress sinks. Her knee knocks against my calf. I hear the drawer on her nightstand open and the rattle of a pill bottle.

"One or two?" she asks.

"One. You keep drugs in your room for me?"

"Of course I do." She drops a capsule into my palm. "I do it for selfish reasons."

"Like what?" I ask, swallowing the pill dry until a glass of water finds its way into my hand.

"You make the best breakfasts. Life would suck if I had to figure out your waffle machine on my own," she says.

"I see. All I'm good for is my cooking."

"And your Jeep. I don't want to carry my groceries for ten blocks."

"You're going to put that in my obituary, aren't you?" I ask.

"Obviously. 'Rest in Peace, Patrick Walker. Thanks for driving a big-ass car,'" Lola jokes with a laugh and then touches my shoulder. I relax under the press of her fingers. "Really though, are you okay?"

"I'm fine. Keep reading. Please," I add, because I know Lola can't say no when I jut out my bottom lip.

She settles against me, her cheek resting on my shoulder. "I need to bring at least ten designs, but I can showcase up to twenty-five in each category. They devote each day of the show to different divisions. Day one is women's wear, day two is men's. The third day is gender-neutral designs, and the last day is signature style, where each designer gets to pick two outfits they haven't previously shown for the final runway walk."

"Which divisions did you decide to enter?" I ask.

Lola also makes suits, wanting to learn how to get inseams and lengths right for the folks who don't wear dresses but still want an outfit with shape and style.

She always asks me to try on the completed outfits so she can snap a photo and upload it to her social media accounts, and I always agree, posing poorly in the artistic positions she puts me in and trying not to grimace at my obvious lack of talent.

Positions with my hand on my hip and my fingers hooked around the belt loop of the slacks she stitched. Me from behind and the coat she sewed slung over my shoulder as I stare at the city below, hoping I look *scholarly* and *refined,* not like a pompous asshole.

I love the way Lola brightens up when I agree to help, the twinkle in her eyes and the dazzling smile she tosses my way. It makes the reluctancy melt away, warmth settling behind my ribs when she murmurs *perfect* under her breath and runs her hands over the lapels of the jacket on my shoulders.

"The men's and the women's," she says. "Plus the signature style. That one is mandatory. I doubt I'll get another opportunity like this, so I might as well go all in and enter everything I'm eligible for."

"And it's judged, right?"

"Mhmm. By industry icons, models, brand-name designers, content creators with a substantial amount of followers. The grand prize is half a million dollars and a feature in eight different magazines. Do you think we'll be able to fit a couple dozen garment bags in the Jeep? We'll also have our luggage. I need to find a suitcase that doesn't take up too much space."

She's talking faster, using her hands to gesture like she does when she's excited and three different plans have started to form in her mind.

"Easily. We have the back row of the Jeep and the trunk, too. How many people are they expecting to attend?"

"Tons. It's open to the public." Realization hits her, and she freezes. The excitement slips out of grasp and disappears into dust as she shakes her head. "That's so many. What if the clothes don't fit the models? What if the colors I pick are more of a winter tone instead of summer? What if a zipper breaks and the entire outfit falls apart? I can't go. They'll think I'm a joke."

I pluck the phone from her hand and set it aside. My palm

laces through hers and I rub my thumb over the ridge of her knuckles, hoping to work out some of the tension in her shoulders and the panic in her voice.

"I think you should table all of these ideas and worries until the morning, love. You're tired and overstimulated. Excited, as you should be, because this is fucking *incredible*. But it's the middle of the night. We'll sit down tomorrow when I get home and make a spreadsheet." Lola blinks at me under dark eyelashes. "What? I know you don't feel as strongly as I do about Microsoft Excel, but I'm telling you, Lo, it's pretty nifty. The shortcuts I can do are—"

"You called me love," she whispers. "You've never called me love before."

It's so quiet, I swear I can hear the blood rushing through my veins, a raging river.

Shit.

"Ah." I scratch behind my ear and wish the ground would swallow me up. "Sorry. I'm—"

"I didn't hate it."

"Oh." Everything in me burns hot at her admission, and I shift on the mattress. "Better than blowhard, right?"

Lola huffs, and we're back to being us, my mistake swept cleanly under the rug. "We should go to sleep. I'm keeping you awake."

"The headache is keeping me awake. Kinda hard to relax when it feels like there's a jackhammer behind your eyes. I don't want to go to sleep yet. I'd rather you read to me," I say, grabbing the book leaning against the lamp next to the bed.

It's become a ritual when we're together.

Lola reads a chapter from the latest romance novel she's enjoying out loud to me. I'll listen and revel in the timbre of her voice. The dip in her tone when she gets to a quote she loves.

How she stops to process her favorite lines, the more profound passages taking her longer to absorb.

"You just like to hear me talk," she says.

"It's better than listening to myself talk. I do that enough at school with the daily announcements and cafeteria chaos."

"Do you ever get tired of sharing the weather over the P.A. system? I think it would be fun."

"No. Sometimes I'll add in something completely out of left field to see who's listening. The first person to come to the office during lunch and tell me what I said gets a lollipop."

"Stop. What do you say?"

"Stupid stuff. It's raining meatballs. Make sure to pack your rulers, a storm is coming. Cloudy with a chance of pie. The kids love it."

"Okay, weatherman," Lola says. "You win."

She opens the book to where we left off last week and tucks the bookmark under her leg. Her fingers trace over the printed words like they're delicate and fragile, important and poignant things she wants to hold close.

I rest my head on the pillow and fold my hands across my stomach. She talks about two best friends, about their vacations of past and present. A small room in Palm Springs without a working air conditioner and a car with a flat tire. It's my favorite book she's ever read to me, a story mirroring our own. People who would do anything for each other. A friendship and love that runs deeper than the center of the Earth.

I smile, close my eyes, and listen.

The last thing I see before I succumb to sleep is Lola's head on my shoulder and my heart in her hands.

SIX

LOLA

"YOU'RE ACTING WEIRD," Emma says, staring at me in the mirror with a piercing gaze.

Her attention makes me fidget and wring my hands together, guilty of a crime I didn't commit as she interrupts our girls' day to interrogate me.

Damn lawyers.

"I am not. That's the last-minute wedding prep talking. Only a few more sleeps until the big day," I answer.

She tilts her head to the side and squints, assessing me through the smudged glass. With her arms crossed over her chest, she hums then snaps, the click of her fingers loud in the room covered in floral arrangements and centerpieces in preparation for her big day.

"That's it. You look different," she says.

"Different how?"

"You look strange."

"A compliment every woman wants to hear," I say.

I turn my back on the conversation and inspect the pair of candlesticks sitting on the dining room table instead of answering her. They're gold and gaudy, on pedestals carved with an intricate design. A gargoyle, maybe?

That can't be right.

I snap a picture and send a message to Patrick.

> Good news. The candlesticks are going strong.

He answers right away.

Is that a gargoyle?

> I was going to ask you the same thing. You're the one who bought them.

Kind of looks like it.

Those things are the best engagement party gag gift ever. Henry and Emma love them. How many years have to pass before I tell the couple I got them for a dollar each at a craft store that was going out of business?

> You can tell them when I tell them the dish towels they use every day were regifted from my mom's linen closet. They said cheap, and I went cheap. I'm a poor and struggling artist, after all.

Weren't you in Rome two weeks ago? Struggling artist, my ass.

> Yes, where I struggled to eat anything but gelato and pasta.

Stop. I'm in a meeting and you're making me laugh.

> What kind of laugh?

> The wheezing kind, where I can't pretend it's a cough.

> That's my favorite laugh of yours.

He sends a blurry selfie in response, his chin in his hands and his eyes half-closed. A smile threatens to overtake his face. I can tell he's trying—and failing—to fight it, the wrinkles on the bridge of his nose and the laugh lines near his mouth giving him away.

I grin.

> The future of education in America, folks. Who let you be an elementary school principal?

> Desperate times call for desperate measures.

> Should I slip the candlesticks into my purse?

> Don't you dare. I'm still paying interest on those heinous things.

> They were a dollar! Fine. I won't steal them.

> Leave me alone, Clepto. I'm trying to learn over here.

> Sorry for bugging you with stupid photos!!!

> You never bug me. I love your stupid photos.

It's silly to feel a swoop low in my belly when I read those words. It's silly to read the message two, three, *four* times in a row before I click my phone closed, yet I do.

I can't help it.

Because Patrick loves my stupid photos. He answers my pointless text messages during important meetings. And two nights ago, my world upended when he called me *love* and fell asleep beside me in bed. Strong arms wrapped around my waist and my head resting on his chest, the beat of his heart a lullaby in my ear.

What the *hell* does it mean?

I was half-conscious when I heard his alarm go off yesterday.

I remember bits and pieces of the morning, disjointed glimpses like I was watching from above. Him, pulling the covers up to my chin and making sure the curtains were closed so I could sleep a little while longer. Me, mumbling something incoherent about birds. Bone-achingly tired and in the middle of a pleasant dream, I'm not sure if the kiss he pressed to my cheek was real or something I made up.

I'm starting to think I'm making the last forty-eight hours up, some figment of my imagination where I've become attracted to the man I've known for two decades without any sort of warning.

I'd like to keep this new discovery to myself and ruminate over it alone without the risk of feeling embarrassed or putting a name to an undefinable thing that has no merit. Opinions from outside sources, though, might be exactly what I need to sort through the contradicting emotions and determine what, exactly, is going on.

"Why are you blushing?" Jo asks.

I sigh and take a seat on the chaise lounge chair in Henry and Emma's living room. I pull a pillow out from behind my back and set it in my lap. My emotional support cushion, I'm dubbing it, as I take a deep breath and quietly admit, "Something happened with Patrick," to my best friends.

The sounds I get in response startle me.

A plate goes flying off the glass table and chocolate chip cookies scatter across the floor. Rebecca claps and Jo lets out a high-pitched squeal so loud, I think I might be hard of hearing for a week.

Emma yelps. She marches across the carpet with bare feet and a dress that swishes against her calves, taking a seat on the sofa beside the other women while her eyes sparkle with glee.

"Spill," she says, and I know I have no choice but to comply.

I grab my glass, the heavy pour of red wine the liquid courage I need to share the rumblings whizzing in my head, a tornado of over-analyzation kicking up every memory from the last two decades and playing them back like a View Master.

"We were on his couch the other night and there was a—*god*, this sounds so stupid to say out loud. It makes me seem like a girl with a playground crush, not a woman entering my mid-thirties with a 401k."

"If you don't tell us," Jo says, "I think I might die."

Their enthusiasm makes me smile, and I feel warm inside knowing they want to hear because they *care,* not because they want to poke fun at my apparent lack of awareness.

"We had a moment," I say. I play with the fringe on the pillow, braiding three strings together to give my hands something to do. "We were talking on the couch, and the next thing I knew, Patrick was leaning in close. He was in my space, staring at me, and I thought... I thought he was going to kiss me. For the first time in my life, I think I *wanted* him to kiss me."

"Have you and Patrick ever kissed before?" Rebecca asks.

"No. No accidental mishaps or drunken hookups. No eyes locking across the room and running for each other. There's never been anything physical between us. We're friends. *Just* friends, and we've never crossed that line. Until two days ago, I never considered it a possibility."

"This might be a dumb question, but why not?" Jo asks. "There's nothing wrong with wanting to kiss someone, even if that someone is your best friend."

"I know. I'm... well, I'm afraid. Fucking terrified, really. You all know I avoid relationships for a reason. Life is easier that way. The less involved I get with someone, the less upset I can be when one of us leaves. I can't imagine going to the next level with Patrick, taking that step only for it to not work out. For it to be weird or awkward or contrived because it's something we think we *have* to do. He's the best thing to ever happen to me, but long term, we want different things. He likes emotional connections, I like physical connections. He wants forever, I want for right now. If we try to fight that, if we go against the innate urge to be who we are, we could ruin our friendship beyond repair. I can't—I can't lose him."

It comes out as a rush of words, a tsunami of gibberish even I have a hard time deciphering.

But what if... what if there was an alternate universe where Patrick *had* kissed me?

A timeline where I didn't read the room wrong and misinterpret his actions.

A timeline where he kissed me and I faced my fears, confronting the dreaded panic head-on.

I close my eyes and sink into a fantasy of us as a couple.

We'd make dinner together. He'd belt out Elton John or Bruce Springsteen songs into a wooden spoon and spin me around. Etta James melodies when he wanted to hold me close and slow dance under twinkling stars and a full moon. I'd laugh at his terrible voice. The spaghetti sauce on the stove would bubble over, and I'd apologize for making a mess. He'd clean up after me with a paper towel and a heart-stopping grin, and it would be so *good*.

It's similar to how we are now, spending time together and laughing until our bellies ache, but the stakes would be much, much higher.

A fight, a breakup, a decision to end our relationship could push him out of my life forever, the experiences we've shared cracking into a million little pieces and fading away with every passing year, eventually withering to nothing, no proof of our friendship ever existing at all.

Patrick is the center of my universe and the most constant beacon of joy in my life. I cannot imagine a world where he's not in it.

There would be a year or two of elation—that honeymoon phase where nothing can go wrong—before things took a turn for the worse. He'd want to stay here in Boston, loving his job and needing his routine. I'd get the itch to travel. He'd go to bed early. I'd stay up late sewing and fall asleep on the couch.

We'd drift apart.

Our communication, the foundation of what makes us *us*, would crumble.

What we're doing *works*—no pressure, no expectations. No need to act a certain way just because we're two single people.

Friendship *works*.

Platonic *works*.

It was working well, until Patrick went and looked at me with fire in his eyes, and now I can't stop thinking about him. The curve of his mouth and how it would feel against the inside of my knee, my hip, the soft skin on my stomach. The flush on his cheeks and his hands under my thighs when he hauled me into his arms that night and held me there. What I want him to do to me, and what I want to do to him.

"He's been in your life for so long, Lo," Emma says. "Nothing would ever force him away, and he's not going to leave willingly. If you took that step with him, you'd have the chance to be happy. Who doesn't want to be happy?"

I fiddle with the friendship bracelet wrapped around my right wrist. It matches the one Patrick still wears, the material faded from blue and purple to tattered gray. The string is turning flimsy and fraying at the ends, but I've kept it on for years. I don't think I'll ever take it off.

I made them at summer camp when we were twelve, sitting out on the old canoe dock during afternoon free time. Patrick was at the boys' camp down the road, and I slipped one into an envelope and mailed it to him for his birthday as a surprise, hoping he didn't get teased if he decided to wear it.

He loved it, proudly showing off the gift to the boys in his cabin and then asking me to teach him how to make one when we got home. We passed the rest of the days leading up to school coming up with new designs and color schemes. Different patterns and ways to tie the knots. It was fun to sit there, our legs dangling out of the treehouse and the heat sticking to our skin, working side by side. Child-like bliss I still hold onto.

"He and I are spending a lot of time together," I explain. "I haven't been home this long in months, so it makes sense I'm feeling attached to him. Observant, too, and aware of him in a way I wasn't before. I notice how close he stands to me. How he hooks his pinky in my belt loop when he reaches over my shoulder to get the coffee filters off the top shelf in my kitchen. The way he watches me when he thinks I'm distracted. I'll look over at him during a movie, and he always has this small smile on his face. One of his dimples pops, and his eyes light up. It's like he's holding onto a secret, and it's infuriating to not know what he's thinking."

"Patrick watching you isn't a new thing," Rebecca says. "He's done that for a while now, and the way he looks at you is beautiful, Lo."

"How does he look at me?" I ask.

My voice trembles as I stare at my friends. The air seems like it's charged, an electric current circling around our conversation. I don't know what they're going to say, but I do know that once they say it, everything will change.

Emma smiles. She reaches over and takes my hands in hers. "Like every second he stares at you is the best second of his life," she says. "Like he never wants to look away, because then it will end. You're his lifeline, Lola, and the only thing keeping him afloat."

SEVEN
LOLA

THE DECLARATION CATCHES me off guard. It makes my heart sputter and spiral and come dangerously close to breaking in two. Emma speaks with so much certainty, so much gusto, like it's a verified fact backed up with evidence and data.

"How can you be so sure?" I whisper.

"It's the same way we all look at our other halves. They're the brightest stars in the sky."

Oh *shit*.

Shit. Shit. *Shit*.

Does my best friend have *feelings* for me?

And do I have feelings for *him*?

How can they pop up after years of knowing each other? Where were they hiding before? And why, *why* have they been dormant for so long, choosing *now* to manifest and show themselves, days before we're about to take a cross-country road trip together in one car with nowhere to hide?

Feelings is a serious word with implications and life-changing consequences behind it. One wrong move, too bold of an assumption or an overstep, and everything we've built could shatter into unrepairable shards.

Patrick is great.

Better than great.

A rare, one-in-seven-billion person, the type that protects your heart. He guides, follows, but never pushes or forcibly leads. It's a balance, a cooperation. The tip of the scales from uneven to steady. He makes me feel special, important, *valued*.

If this is how he treats me as a friend, like I'm precious and adored, how deep would his care go if we were something more?

My body buzzes, feverish at the thought of Patrick's hand in mine. The swing of our arms and a shared bed. Late nights and early mornings wrapped around each other and his fingers anywhere they can reach. A plate of glazed donuts and chocolate chip muffins from my favorite corner bakery for breakfast, a surprise when I wake up to a kiss on my forehead.

Quiet afternoons stretched out on the couch, a mug of tea and a warm quilt. An inside joke. Both our books on the coffee table. Soft kisses and sweet touches that turn sensual, heady, and urgent. His legs on either side of my hips and his teeth pulling at the hem of my shirt, a wicked gleam in his beautiful green eyes.

Maybe it's been Patrick all along, the only one who can calm my racing heart and quiet my restless mind. The person who can put all my broken pieces back together into a completed puzzle and somehow add his own pieces, too.

Maybe I've been too silly to see it.

I shake my head and clear away the daydreams.

"Sorry." I let out a breath and toss the pillow to the ground, bringing my knees to my chest. "I'm so caught off guard. Is it even possible for my feelings for him to switch so quickly? It doesn't make sense."

"Yes," Jo says, and my shoulders relax with the affirmation. "I worked with Jack for years without being attracted to him. The same thing happened to Emma. All it takes is a single moment to see someone in a new light. It doesn't need a lot of build up."

Her logic seems valid.

Is it safe to assume that being put in a situation with Patrick where kissing him was obtainable is what has me in a tizzy? A closeness we've never found ourselves in, and opening the door to a whole new realm of what we could be.

"No matter how I might be feeling, I'm not sure it could ever work. We're too different. He's a relationship guy, and I'm not a relationship girl," I say.

"You might not be a relationship girl, but you acknowledge that Patrick is attractive, right?" Rebecca asks.

I bite back a grin.

The best part about growing up with someone and having them in your life as an adult is knowing how much they've changed since childhood and appreciating the physical features they've been blessed with.

Muscles. Height. Large hands and a kind, gracious heart. Hair I want to run my fingers through and sharp dimples that could bring a woman to her knees. A laugh that warms my soul and brightens the darkest days.

"Patrick is very attractive," I admit. It's the first time I've ever said it out loud, and I like how the newfound discovery sounds. "Hot as hell. The total package."

"You just know he'd do whatever you asked," Emma says, adding a wistful sigh.

"In life," Jo adds. "And in bed. The best of both worlds."

We dissolve into a fit of giggles. I let my mind wander to the idea of Patrick in the bedroom. Would he be nice? Considerate? *Hands here, please. That feels nice. Thank you so much.* Or would he be more aggressive and in control? A new personality unlocked when he's under the sheets and pinning a woman's arms above her head. Bite marks. Scratches from fingernails and hickeys on fair skin.

I blush and I take a sip of my drink to hide the color flooding my cheeks. I'm not sure I can look at my sweet and quiet best friend the same way ever again.

"I have no clue what I want going forward, except when I was on Patrick's couch and he was looking at me, I knew with every fiber of my being I wanted him to kiss me," I say. "There wasn't a doubt in my mind. The moment was there, and he didn't take it. I guess he didn't feel the same."

Silence descends as the women glance at each other. I narrow my eyes and look between them, trying to read their minds.

"What?" I ask.

"It's obvious Patrick wants to kiss you," Jo says.

I blink. I set my drink down and fold my fingers around the edge of the chair, digging into the fabric for support.

"No. It's not like that with us. He treats me like you all do. He's considerate and cooks me dinner. In the morning, he brings me tea. He makes sure I know I'm heard. It's what best friends *do*, and not an indication that he wants to kiss me. Oh my god. Can you imagine? If that were the case, he's wanted to kiss me for years."

I laugh after I say it, the chuckle turning into full-blown hysteria. I shake my head and wipe my eyes, stopping when I see I'm the only one who finds the comment funny.

"Patrick takes friendship to a new level, Lo. That man is head over heels for you. He has been since I met him," Rebecca says. "And that was, what? Six years ago?"

"The first time he mentioned you, I assumed you two were dating," Emma adds.

"*What*? And you never thought to tell me any of this?" I stand up and put my hands on my hips. I pace across the carpet, trying to process the last five minutes of information. "He's never... Nothing he's done has ever made me feel like we've crossed a boundary or done something inappropriate. Am I oblivious? How have I never noticed?"

"You haven't noticed because you never felt that way about him," Emma says. "You weren't looking for a sign that he liked you, and you never gave him a sign that you might like him. I think he's tried to repress those feelings because they haven't been reciprocated."

"We're also not speaking on his behalf," Rebecca says. "He hasn't told us anything, but we do know that you're the most important person in the world to him. He'd do anything for you. Maybe that means he cares about you in a romantic, non-platonic way. Maybe it doesn't mean anything at all. But it's not the same way we treat each other. It's different. And now that you know, I bet you're going to pick up on signs from him you didn't previously see."

"Shit," I curse. "*Shit*. I don't know what's going on in my head. I'm curious about him. About the possibility of... of trying something with him. How can I not be? You have someone in your life for years, and you've never wanted to kiss them, or be physical with them, and now all of a sudden you do? It would be weird if I *wasn't* curious, I think." I sit back down and bury my head in my hands, as if my palms will offer me guidance to these new revelations.

"This trip might be exactly what you need. An opportunity to figure out how you feel about him, and to figure out how he feels about you. You'll see a sign, and there's going to be a moment when you'll just *know*. It'll all make sense eventually. It'll sort itself out," Emma says, peeling my hands away from my face. "Until then, do what you want. Do what feels *right*. You don't need to put a label on it, but if you want to kiss him, Lola, then kiss him."

I nod. "Okay. Yeah."

Easier said than done.

My phone pings and I pick it up, grateful for the distraction.

> A stupid photo for a stupid photo.

> Should I start a food fight?

It's like Patrick knew I was thinking about him, knew I needed to be reassured that we're still *good*. That we're okay. Almost kiss or no almost kiss, maybe feelings or no romantic feelings at all, nothing's changed. We're still Patrick and Lola, friends first, forever and ever.

Then a picture comes through.

Attached is an image of him standing with the lunch ladies at his school. Harriet, Dolores, Margaret, then Patrick, the tallest of the bunch. He's laughing, with a hairnet on his head and an apron looped around his neck. It's bright pink, with dozens of little hearts dotting the front.

He's holding a spoonful of Sloppy Joe's in his left hand, and there's dried mustard on his right cheek. His eyes are wrinkled in the corners. Those little lines keep getting more and more prominent with every passing year. It's funny to think of him as older now, and how I've known him and loved him platonically for over three-quarters of my life.

> Not stupid!!!! It made me smile.

> Lunchlady Land is one of my favorite songs.

> Are there navy beans?

> Obviously.

> I'm glad it made you smile. My job here is done.

Something twists behind my ribs as I read his words, pulling tight and becoming uncomfortable. It's a sensation I've never felt before, and that panic from the other night is back, a gentle rise to the surface.

Strictly platonic, I think with one side of my brain, as I send back a dozen hamburger emojis.

You idiot, I argue with the other side.

The one hundred percent certainty of *never crossing any lines with my best friend* just dropped to ninety-nine percent, because all I can imagine when I close my eyes is his hand running up my leg and how perfectly the curves of his body would fit against mine.

EIGHT

TUESDAY

Don't forget to take your ADHD meds. No, Debra, I haven't printed the files yet.

Whoops. Sorry. Talk to text. Don't forget your medicine.

Ah, thank you! Just popped a pill. Focus time, here I come.

Why haven't you printed the files?

Because, Lola, I only have two hands, believe it or not.

Bummer. Imagine what you could do with three.

———

WEDNESDAY

Busy day at school.

Hey.

Did you remember to eat lunch?

Lo?

Sorry! My phone was in the other room. Nope, I didn't. But I just ordered a sandwich.

How's your afternoon? How are the designs coming?

Finally figured out the neckline of a shirt I'm bringing to the show.

Proud of you.

How are the kiddos? Two and a half more days until summer!

Rambunctious. Excited. Tired. Today the fifth grade girls painted my nails purple.

Thoughts?

Attachment: 1 Image

10/10. They did a great job.

What are you up to tonight?

The guys and I have our final tux fitting. Are the ladies getting together?

Yeah. Emma's making dinner at their place.

What's on the menu?

Tacos, I think.

Delicious. Want to do breakfast at your apartment on Saturday morning and plan out our trip?

I'll bring donuts.

My love language. That sounds groovy. Tell the guys I say hi!

Tell the girls I say hi back.

FYI—The more you say groovy, the more I like it.

It's catchy, isn't it?

Annoyingly so.

———

THURSDAY

Do you ever wish you were ambidextrous?

What in the world? Where did that come from?

I just watched two hours of YouTube videos. Fell straight down the rabbit hole.

Of videos on hand dexterity?

Yup. It's a fascinating world.

Wow, Lo.

To answer your question... No? I'm not emotionally attached to being right-handed, but I don't feel like my life is missing anything because I can't brush my teeth while I write on a piece of paper.

That's a very good point.

You're so logical.

How's the school day?

A kid gave me a drawing of two dinosaurs getting hit by an asteroid. It made me strangely emotional.

Oh, I would've sobbed.

Kids, man. They pull at your heartstrings.

———

FRIDAY MORNING

Would you rather eat hot dogs or hamburgers for the rest of your life?

Hamburgers. Easy question. You?

Hamburgers. For sure.

Speaking of: lunch?

Already ate! On time today too!

Lola. Why is my office floor covered in balloons?

And why are there streamers on the wall?

Is this a cake?

Answer my call, dammit.

Happy last day of school!!!

There's a balloon for every kid.

There are 450 kids at my school. Are there 450 balloons here?

Guess you'll have to count and see.

Open your office door so I can help!!

——————

FRIDAY AFTERNOON

I know I just dropped you off, but I'm bored.

We picked up balloons for three hours and you're bored?

Next year, I'm going to do a ball pit. Way more fun.

What are you doing tonight?

Nothing. Ice cream and a movie probably.

Want to join?

Who's turn is it to pick the movie?

I picked Friday the 13th last week. You're up!

Tough one to follow.

I don't have any food here. I was going to order delivery. Thai food okay?

My favorite. Do it for pick-up. I'll grab it on the way over.

And this is why you're my best friend.

Because I bring food to your door?

That's one reason.

You have others?

Yeah. A few.

NINE
PATRICK

"THIS MAP HAS SEEN BETTER DAYS." Lola wraps her fingers around her mug and taps her nails against the porcelain. "They make phones with navigation systems, you know," she adds, a twinkle in her eye.

The paper in question is crinkled at the corners. Half the west coast is ripped off, rendering California nonexistent. Random cities throughout the country are circled, and a bright yellow line runs from Montana down to Texas. I bought it for a quarter at an estate sale on my walk home from school last week, not caring that it's borderline unreadable.

"Do they?" I take the seat across from her on the wood bench in her kitchen. It's my favorite spot in her apartment, where the sunlight streams in through white, billowy curtains and a breeze drifts through the room. "I like using a map. It's nostalgic. Reminds me of my childhood when we'd drive up to Maine or New Hampshire on the weekends."

"Your family did so many day trips. I'm shocked your mom's old SUV isn't covered in 'This car climbed Mt. Washington' bumper stickers."

"C'mon, Lo. You know Darla isn't a fan of bumper stickers," I say. I fold the map and tuck it under my empty plate. "How are the designs coming?"

"Oh." Lola brightens. She sets down her mug and a slosh of tea runs down the side. "I'm finished. I was hoping some more inspiration would come to me, but creatively, I've felt a bit blocked. There are so many things I *want* to do, I just can't bring myself to do them. I get like this sometimes. I take on too many projects I'm not able to finish."

"That's okay. I'm sure what you have is awesome."

"Yeah. The outfits were good enough to get accepted into the show. With the updates I did, maybe they'll be good enough to win it. I did come up with a handful of new designs I'm proud of last week, and I can't wait to show those off."

"New designs? Like what?"

"A couple of dresses. A matching shirt and shorts set. My signature style creation I'm *so* excited about. It looks like a dress, but it has a jumpsuit underneath. You can take off the train and end up in pants. It even has a cape."

"I've always known you were talented, but I forget how much time and effort you put into your work. It's so innovative. They're going to love it."

She blushes and tucks a lock of hair behind her ear. "It's been done before. Hundreds of times, actually."

"Still. I bet you're putting your own twist on it, and it's going to be amazing. You've done a lot in a short amount of time. Are you sleeping through the night?" I ask. "Eating all your meals and taking your medicine?"

End of the year administrative work has forced me to stay late at school to finish report cards and help teachers pack up their classrooms for the summer. I haven't been able to check in with Lola as frequently as I would have liked, relying on sporadic text messages in the morning and in the evening to make sure she's doing okay.

I take a look at her and see the purple bags under her eyes. Her cheeks are pale, and she tries to hide a yawn with a bite of bacon. It's obvious the answer is *no* to all of my questions, and it makes my skin crawl that she's not taking care of herself.

I pick up my phone and set an alarm to call her tonight so I can hopefully coax her away from her sewing machine and to her bed.

"I'm fine." Lola waves me off and pulls her legs to her chest.

My gaze follows the line of her calf, the slope of her muscles under the plaid pajama shorts that show off inches of skin, up to the bend of her knee before averting my eyes and glancing away.

"I'll let the lie slide," I say. "Okay. Let's talk about logistics for our trip. Do you want to do the drive down to Florida in two days or stretch it out?"

"It would be nice to take our time. We could do some sightseeing. Stop at a rock museum. Find the world's largest rocking chair and catch some fireflies in an open field."

Her gaze tips to mine, and that fists closes tight around my heart.

She's so pretty in the morning, with her face cast in shades of orange and red. It's like the sunshine soaks into her skin and makes her glow from the inside out. Even with a pillow crease on her forehead and sleep caught in the corner of her eye, she's beautiful.

The prettiest girl I've ever seen.

"Definitely," I agree, realizing I need to say something instead of just gawking at her. "How about we make things interesting? I have a proposal for you."

"You haven't been out of the Northeast in years, Patrick. Our trip is already going to be interesting," Lola says. "Wait until you discover Buc-ee's."

"Is that a disease?"

"You're impossible."

"What if we each pick a place to stop for the day? A tourist attraction or spot for dinner? You have my interest with this rocking chair."

"The rocking chair is in Illinois, unfortunately. That would be a hell of a detour. What if I picked an activity I think you would like and you pick a place I would like?"

"Do you think you know me that well, Jones? Enough to find an activity for us to do that won't bore me to tears?"

"You like organizing spreadsheets, Patrick. For *fun*. It can only go up from there."

"Don't tempt me with a good time."

Lola bites her bottom lip and brings her eyes to meet mine again. "I know what makes you happy," she says, barely above a whisper. "I've watched you for years, and I want to surprise you with something special."

Knowing she's watched me while I've been busy watching her lights me up like a Christmas tree in December. I want to reach across the table and pull her into my lap. Kiss the crumbs off her mouth and hug her close, telling her she can surprise me with whatever she wants and I'll think it's the grandest thing in the world.

I want a lot of things I can't have, but that doesn't stop me from wishing for them.

I'm in deep—*way too deep*—with this woman, and I have no escape plan for a chance of survival.

"Okay." I find my voice and nod. I rub my palms on my thighs and sit back on the bench, relaxing against the decorative pillows. The corner of one digs into my spine, and I adjust my position. "Sure. I like that plan. What else do you want to do?"

"Maybe we could go camping one night? In North Carolina?"

"My parents kept that tent we used to pitch in the backyard when we were kids. It was massive then, so it should fit us comfortably now. I'll bring a jar so you can catch your fireflies in the mountains."

When we were younger, we would lay our sleeping bags side by side under the night sky. I could hear the chirp of crickets. The sound of Lola breathing next to me, soft inhales as she drifted off to sleep while I stared at the canvas roof of the tent and wondered why I wanted to hold her hand so damn bad.

Funny.

Twenty-four years later and I still want to hold her hand.

I guess some things never change.

"Perfect," Lola says. "There's also a bookstore outside Orlando I want to visit. It's in this cute small town, and it has a coffee shop inside. A bakery, too, with homemade desserts that look *so* good." She sighs around her bagel, undoubtedly dreaming about an assortment of pastries with whipped cream and chocolate frosting. I like that look of hers, when she's concentrating on something she really, really wants. "They have miniature pies, Patrick. Not just slices of pie, but actual little pies."

"Miniature pies? Forget everything else about this trip. *That* will be the highlight."

"The pies are high on the list, but I'm even more excited about my role model being at the show. I hope I have time to meet her."

"Tell me about her," I say. "Would I recognize her stuff?"

"Vivian Lee. Her work is gorgeous. Do you remember that— oh, there's no way you would."

I lift an eyebrow. "Do I remember what, exactly?"

"The first dress I bought with my babysitting money after watching those horrible twins for weeks."

"Actual spawns of Satan," I agree. "Didn't one of them cut your hair?"

"Yup. The first and only time I ever had bangs."

"What did the dress look like?"

"It was pink with thick straps. Kind of long, and I liked the way it spun out around my legs when I twirled in a circle. I wore it to the freshmen year sock hop with those patent leather shoes and the frilly white socks. Arthur McBride told me I looked like a watermelon. I told him to go to hell and then spent Monday afternoon in detention."

I rack my brain and all the time we've spent together.

Childhood and the treehouse. Lemonade stands and racing down the big hill at the end of the street on our bikes. Building forts in her living room during rainstorms and swimming in the creek behind my house.

Middle school and acne. Homework and baseball games. The first time I realized I had a crush on Lola. She touched my elbow after I helped her with our math homework and smiled really big. I forgot my name and thought I was going to die.

The summer before freshman year when Lola's skin turned from fair to a light bronze after lounging outside every afternoon, a towel laid out on the grass and sunglasses over her eyes. I spent the entire month of July inside pretending I had sun poisoning so I wouldn't have to see her in a bikini.

"You bought it on Newbury Street," I say, thrown back in time and still flipping through memories. Our first cell phones and texting each other from our rooms instead of throwing notes across our yards. Getting dropped off at the dance and when I told her she looked pretty. "We went to the city for your birthday, and you tried on a hundred outfits."

"I doubt it was a hundred."

"It felt like a hundred. It was that day, right? You paid in cash and counted out ones and tens for so long, the sales associate walked away to help someone else."

"You do remember," she says proudly, and I'm rewarded with a bright beam.

Fuck, I'm greedy for her smiles. I'm always scrambling to find a way to make her grin again.

One isn't enough.

I want them all.

"I took the dress home, hung it in my closet, and said to myself, *someday, it's going to be my name on that tag.* I spent years admiring Vivian's designs, so to finally have one of my own? It was surreal. I look at that outfit every day and—it's silly, but it motivates me to want to keep learning. To be a better designer. I know it's just a dress, and what I do is just sew some pieces of fabric together, but when I look at that outfit, I know my purpose. I can see my future laid out in front of me. She's going to be at the show, so it's a full-circle moment."

"We all have things that make us happy," I say. "For you, it's that dress. Never think what brings you joy is silly."

She reaches over and taps my nose. The salt shaker gets knocked sideways and crystals spill on the table. "What brings you joy?"

You, I think.

I'd spend one minute with Lola over a hundred minutes with anyone else and be the happiest person in the world.

"Three weeks off from school," I say instead, giving her the safe answer. It's the answer that won't send her running for the hills in fright and keeps our friendship *safe,* despite how dangerously I've been acting as of late. "The only time of the year I don't have to check my email, answer questions about curriculums and attendance policies, or hear *Mr. Walker* a hundred times a day. I love my job, but I need a break."

"So I shouldn't call you Mr. Walker on our trip?" Lola asks, her voice low and painted with amusement. Her eyebrows wiggle and her teeth sink into her bottom lip before she turns her cheek and *winks.*

A rubber band inside me stretches, close to snapping. My

body heats as fire licks up my spine and spreads across my shoulders.

It sounds obscene when she says it. I don't think I can ever go by my last name again, the word marred with thoughts of her chanting it in my ear as a bead of sweat rolls down her neck and I lick it away with my tongue.

I clear my throat and fumble with my mug. The coffee from twenty minutes ago has turned lukewarm, but it gives my hands something to do. A task to focus on so I don't act like a total fool.

"Patrick is just fine," I say, my throat as dry as sandpaper.

"This is the longest stretch of time you've had off since Christmas. We should celebrate," Lola says.

"How do we celebrate? We're already going on a road trip."

"I don't know. We could get drunk at a bar in Southie and stumble home?"

I raise an eyebrow. "At eight o'clock in the morning?"

"Want to get party hats?"

"It's not my birthday."

"Onesies?"

"I'm hot all the time."

"Mimosas, then." She snaps her fingers and leans forward in her chair, grinning like she's discovered an eighth wonder of the world. "I've got it. *Brunch*."

"*Brunch*?" I stare at her, aghast. "Do you know me at all?"

Lola waves her hands and this time the pepper shaker goes down. "I know, I know... Breakfast should be finished by eight-thirty, and meals shouldn't overlap. It's the Patrick Walker Creed. Come on. What do you want to do? Tell me. This is your day. Whatever it is, we're going to do it."

"Whatever it is?" I repeat.

"Anything," she says.

"Well, I guess I'm spending the day with you. If you want to put on a onesie, we can."

"You're not sick of me yet?"

"Nope. Ask me again tomorrow."

Lola's lips twitch. She hides her quiet laughter with a sip of her tea. "That reminds me," she says. "We need to pick a charity for the wedding next weekend."

"Are we allowed to pick one together?"

"Emma gave us permission. We're the leftovers. The single partygoers. I'm surprised the masses aren't waiting outside for us with pitchforks," she says.

"My grandmother is probably rolling over in her grave right now. Thirty-four and still unwed? She'd think I was sick with the plague."

"Ah." Lola touches her heart and bows her head. "I miss Grams."

"So do I. I even miss her constant badgering about my relationship status."

"I see where you get your romantic side."

"What about Noah? He's single. Is he pairing up with us?" I ask.

"I don't think the rules apply to millionaires. I'm pretty sure he's just going to write a check."

"I knew I should have bought a lottery ticket last night. Bastard gets out of everything."

She smirks and slides her phone across the table to me. I study the website with the pictures of kids in a classroom and pencils in their hands.

"I found a nonprofit that increases literacy in adults and children," Lola says. "They offer resources like tutoring and learning specialists. I thought it was important to raise awareness about the cause for people outside the education sphere. For them to see learning disabilities are real and prevalent and not something to be ashamed of, you know? Hell, even you needed extra time testing in school, and now you've won Teacher of the Year *and* Principal of the Year."

I look up and I blink twice. Lola fidgets under my gaze. She twists her hands together, and a flash of nervousness crosses her face.

"Lola."

"Shoot," she breathes out. "You hate it. I overstepped. I'm sorry."

"No. *No*," I say firmly. "I don't hate it. It's the best thing I've ever heard. Can you look at me? Please." She lifts her chin. Her eyes meet mine, and I smile. Warmth washes over me, a tropical heat wave on my skin. "It's a brilliant idea, and I'm honored you chose a charity with me in mind. You're so wonderful."

"I'm not the one working with kids," she says. "You're the one making a difference day in and day out without taking a lick of credit. That makes *you* wonderful. A selfless person. I only care about myself. The epitome of selfish."

"You are far from selfish, Lola. Just yesterday you let me have the last of the Oreos."

"It's hardly the same thing."

"To me it is. Kind is kind."

I stand and walk around the table. I pull her from her chair and into a hug, smiling when I hear her let out a sigh.

With Lola in my arms, everything is right in the world.

I'm content. Happy, honored, proud.

A million different adjectives and a million different feelings, each as important as the last. They all bubble down to the same five words.

I'm in love with you, I think into the field of hair that tickles my nose. *I'm in love with you,* I think when Lola sighs and relaxes her body into mine. *I'm in love with you,* I think as she buries her face in my shirt, and I wonder if maybe, *maybe,* there's a tiny chance she could love me, too.

TEN
LOLA

THE BOSTON PUBLIC LIBRARY is one of my favorite buildings in the city.

It stretches a full block, the architecture grand with a barrel-vaulted ceiling and large windows. Light from the setting sun streams in and reflects across the main reading room as prisms of color illuminate the interior. It's magical, the perfect place for Henry and Emma's pre-wedding soiree and a spot holding as much history as their relationship.

The happy couple decided against a traditional rehearsal dinner, opting for a celebration a few days before the ceremony with their closest friends and family members instead. Nearly a hundred people are here, the gathering pushing the limits of intimate and cozy to crowded and overwhelming.

I move through the masses of guests after a welcome toast from the groom and bride-to-be. The deeper I get into the room, the more the edges of my smile slip. I'm tired, exhausted from wedding festivities and packing for our trip. Double and triple checking garment bags and wondering if I have space to bring one more dress.

I started it at midnight last night like most of my projects, a random burst of creativity finally coming to me after days of stagnant artistic thinking. It's nearly finished, thrown across my sewing desk in two pieces of fabric, and I'm itching to get home to see if I can work some magic and complete it before we leave in a few days.

I spot the empty open bar at the back of the room and sigh in relief. The bartender glances up from the napkins he's organizing and offers me a dimpled smile.

"Hey." He gestures to the line of stools at the counter. I slide onto one in the middle, the leather cool under my thighs.

"Hi." My head swivels around, and I look back at him. "Either your drinks suck, or you're telling terrible jokes to ward off the crowd."

"A mixture of both," he says.

"So I need to take one for the team and try out your beverages to give you some feedback?"

He shrugs and grabs a clean glass. "Probably for the best. My ego appreciates your kindness. What can I get you?"

"A whiskey and ginger ale if you have it, please."

"For a beautiful woman, I'll track down the ingredients."

I blush at the compliment. "I have to be at least ten years older than you."

"'Stacey's Mom' is one of my favorite songs."

"Are you even old enough to remember when MTV showed actual music videos?" I ask.

"Hey," he says. "Age is just a number. That's Leonardo DiCaprio's philosophy anyway."

"That," I answer, "and the theory I have that he's madly in love with Kate."

"Theory? You mean a proven fact." The bartender leans his elbows on the counter, drawing close to me. "How do you know the couple?"

"Kate and Leo? From watching *Titanic* on VHS years before you were born," I say.

He lets out a laugh. "Funny. I like you."

"If you meant the couple of the hour tonight, my best friend was roommates with Henry, the groom, in college. He added the bride to our group when they started dating a few years ago. What about you?"

"My brother is an attorney. He works with Henry and Emma at their firm. Henry offered a generous amount of cash for three hours of my time and bartending skills." He sets the drink down and scoots it my way. "I'm a senior in college. I can't tell you shit about economics, but I can make a mean drink."

I lift the glass in his direction and take a sip. I cough as the alcohol works its way down my throat. All whiskey, and not a hint of ginger ale. "Holy hell. This is *strong*. I can see why it's empty over here. Everyone's already blackout drunk."

"Means better tips."

"A businessman. You know more about economics than you think."

"I'm Liam."

"Lola. Thanks for the hearty libation. I should find the bride and figure out my responsibilities for the night. It's probably to keep an uncle away from the DJ's microphone, or some other task of similar importance. Can't have any embarrassing stories about botched first kisses or someone's first hangover going around."

"It's for the best. I'd flirt with you if you stayed, then you'd shoot me down because there's a guy heading this way who I'm guessing is your boyfriend."

"Boyfriend? I don't have a boyfriend."

"Are you sure? He looks like he wants to murder me with his bare hands and—" Liam squints, then nods. "Yup. Definitely wants to devour you."

I spin on the stool and almost fall off the seat when my eyes connect with Patrick's.

"That's my best friend," I explain. I throw back the rest of my drink and stand.

"Friend, huh? Could've fooled me."

"Lola," Patrick says, interrupting our conversation.

Goosebumps erupt on my skin as he says my name, an exaltation behind the two syllables. I wonder how it would sound if he whispered it in my ear and told me I was being *good*.

My cheeks turn warm at the vision of his hand trailing up my leg and over my knee, disappearing under my dress as he pressed me against a wall. A dark corner, surrounded by all of our friends who wouldn't have a clue. I clear my throat and awkwardly wave, thankful he can't see my wicked thoughts. "Hey. What's up?"

"You look—" Patrick pauses then mumbles something incoherent under his breath. He runs his hands through his hair and tugs on the dark brown strands. It's curling a little on the sides, just above his ears, where it's still damp from the shower he took earlier in the afternoon before we parted ways to get ready.

"Hot?" Liam supplies, the one to break the silence.

It's laced with mirth, and I wish I could capture the flash of anger on Patrick's face. The way his fingers fold over each other to form a fist and how he shoves his hands into his pockets. He rocks back on his heels and throws a death glare over my shoulder.

"Patrick, this is Liam. Liam, this is my best friend Patrick," I say.

"Can I get you a drink, man?" Liam asks with a grin. "A friend of Lola's is a friend of mine."

"Gin and tonic," Patrick says, adding a grumbled "please" at the end of his order.

I bite my lip to keep from smiling.

Even when he's pissed off, Patrick is infuriatingly kind.

Stops traffic for a family of ducks to cross the road kind.

Heats up a plate in the oven so my eggs stay warm kind.

Handwritten birthday cards to each one of his students kind.

Slipping a ten-dollar tip in the jar on the counter when he thinks I'm not looking kind, because that's the man he is.

One in seven billion.

"Coming right up. Lola, it was great to meet you. When you want another round, you know where to find me." Liam winks, adding fuel to the fire. He makes the fastest gin and tonic I've ever seen, and before I can blink, a full glass is on the counter.

"I don't like that guy," Patrick grumbles. He takes a sip and admits, "But he knows how to make a good drink."

"You don't even know the guy and you don't like him?"

"I can tell he's trouble."

"Some people like trouble."

"Shit, Lo. I didn't mean to interrupt whatever was happening back there."

"What did you think was happening back there?" I ask.

"I don't know. Flirting?"

A laugh bubbles out of me and I pull him by the elbow from the bar to an alcove tucked away from the rest of the party. The secluded spot is quieter, and I can hear the clink of ice against glass as Patrick swirls his drink around four times like he always does. It helps it *marinate,* he explained to me once, apparently a mixologist in a past life.

"Patrick," I say. "I'm pretty sure he's never watched a music video on MTV. He probably wants to name his kids Brayleigh or Huxon. Definitely not my type."

"*Huxon?* There's no way that's a real name."

"There's a fifty-fifty chance it's a character from *The Lord of the Rings.*"

"Stop. I did not make you watch the entire trilogy plus *The*

Hobbit films in twenty-four hours for you to disrespect Tolkien like that. Take it back."

"Fine." I stick out my tongue. "Please accept my heartfelt apology. If you were Frodo and I was Sam, I'd go with you to Mordor."

"Wow. With an iconic line like that, how could I not forgive you? Apology accepted," Patrick says, turning to look at me.

A fog clears from his vision and it's like he's seeing me for the first time tonight. Like the last five minutes never happened. His eyes sweep down my body in a slow perusal, from my hair to the plunging neckline of the black dress that shows off a hint of cleavage. He keeps going to where the material stops halfway up my thigh, the rest of my legs bare.

When he reaches my feet and the pair of red heels pinching my toes, there's a strangled noise, a sound made from the trenches of his chest. He drops his head back and lets out a soft, low groan.

Oh.

That's nice.

I can barely move in this outfit, the stitching tight and the fabric borderline unbreathable, but I'd gladly contort my limbs and put the dress on for a second time if it means seeing *that look* on Patrick's face again.

Tortured, anguished, and undone by the sight of me.

My conversation with the girls has been on repeat in my mind. I've been searching for an inkling, any insight into figuring out how Patrick feels about me. And how I feel about *him*, grappling with the idea that I might be overreacting to a small hint of attraction that's entirely one-sided.

As I watch the bob of his throat, the way his eyes glaze over and how he licks his lips as if staring at me will quench eternal thirst and offer him salvation, I understand I'm not overreacting at all. It's so *obvious* how I've started to feel about him, as

97

certain as the sky being blue and oxygen being necessary to survive.

I see it now.

I like him.

I like him a lot.

In a non-platonic way. In a I want to wake up next to him in the morning kind of way.

I *like* him.

The desire to kiss him is stronger than it's ever been, and with every second he doesn't look away, I'm certain Patrick wants to kiss me too.

"That kid was right," he says. "You do look hot, Lola."

Never in the history of our friendship has he ever called me *hot*.

That's a word reserved for clandestine meetings in the middle of the night. Illicit affairs, not best friends.

The grabbing of shirts and the unbuckling of belts in a cramped coat closet, the hope no one catches you but the thrill that someone might.

I like being the object of Patrick's attention. A hundred people mull around the room, and he's only watching *me*. The building could go up in flames and smoke, and I'm not sure he would notice. I'm not sure I would notice either.

"Thank you," I whisper. Desire blazes through me so strongly, I think I might explode. "You look really nice too, Patrick."

His dark blue suit hugs the slopes of his shoulders, the curve of his muscles. Long arms and a broad chest. The top button of his white shirt is popped open, his neck visible under the crisp collar. I can't drag my eyes away from his throat, the small inch of space under a cluster of freckles and tan skin I'd like to press my lips to and learn what other sounds he makes.

Patrick sets his glass down on the empty table. He hasn't

finished the beverage yet, but he's drawn to something more important. He hooks his finger around my arm and tugs me toward him. "Do you want to dance?"

I swallow, emboldened by the dim of the house lights above us and the band on the stage. By the way my strong drink ignites my blood and gives me an answer I'm not at all surprised by.

"I'd love to dance with you, Patrick," I say.

He offers me his hand and I take it—nearly grab for it—and follow his lead to the dance floor. His left palm settles on my lower back, and we begin to sway to a jazz song. The sway turns into a small circle. A spin here, a twirl there when the tempo picks up. Barely a shuffle when it slows, a gentle rock back and forth like a buoy out in the ocean at low tide. For a moment we don't move at all, standing stationary with our arms wrapped around each other.

One song turns to two, then three and four. Minutes pass. Maybe it's hours. Perhaps it's days. I don't know, I don't keep track. I'm too immersed in the here and now, a sparkling aware-ness of his hand moving an inch lower, down the zipper of my dress. I move a step closer automatically, as if on instinct, a part of me knowing exactly where I want to be.

This is what Emma meant by something feeling *right*. A sign and explanation that isn't based on logic and reason but emotion. This moment with Patrick is the most normal thing in the world. It's like we do this every day, two magnets drawn together by an unbreakable bond.

Destiny.

I rest my cheek on his chest. He runs his fingers down my arm. We're the only people in the world, existing in a secret space. A happy space, a safe space. The treehouse. My couch. The storage room he found me in after my dad's funeral, sitting next to a mop and a broom, broken-hearted, with no direction forward. He sat beside me in his nice tie and shiny shoes, his arm around my shoulder, and let me cry, not saying a word.

Patrick is there in all of those places.

He *is* all of those places.

I recognize the attraction toward him isn't fleeting, the cause of expensive alcohol and finding solace in the arms of a good-looking man.

It's a push and pull that's been brewing and bubbling for decades, always on the edge of *maybe*, now toeing over the line of *we should try*.

He dips me low, the ends of my hair dragging across the floor. I laugh, and the heaviness breaks.

"Where did you learn all these moves?" I ask.

"Henry made us sign up for ballroom dance lessons," he says. "He has this whole thing planned for the reception. The foxtrot. The tango. It's going to look like an episode of *Bridgerton*."

"You guys been going to dance lessons for *weeks*?"

"Secret dance lessons," Patrick says.

"Do you have special shoes? Please tell me you do."

"I will not confirm or deny that I spent over a hundred dollars on a nice pair of ballroom dancing shoes."

"You're a modern day Fred Astaire."

"Yeah right. I'm not entering a competition anytime soon. Do me a favor and keep this between us? Henry really wants it to be a surprise for Emma."

"I will. I promise." I touch the dimple on his cheek. "You're a good friend."

"That's what love is," he says. "Seeing what makes someone happy and wanting to be a part of it. Being excited about what they're excited about, even if you couldn't care less."

"There's Mr. Romantic. Did you all have fun at these lessons?"

"We had a blast. We were the only men in a group with fifteen women, all old enough to be our mothers. They got a kick out of it, and they're all insistent we come to Barbara's retirement party in a couple of months."

"Who's the best dancer in the group? It's Noah, isn't it?"

"Jack, believe it or not. I had to assure the instructor he wasn't angry at her. The frowning is natural for him."

"That doesn't surprise me as much as I thought it would."

The music stops, loud voices and hearty conversation filling the air. We pull apart and step away from each other.

"Need a break?" Patrick asks.

I nod. "And a donut from the dessert wall."

"Greatest party idea ever. Over-under on how many donuts you're going to eat? I'm saying at least eight."

Jo waves at us from a table, and I see the rest of our friends also taking a minute to catch their breath with plates of food and cold drinks.

"I'll take the under," I say as we move off the dance floor. "Only because there are some fried mac and cheese balls I can't wait to get my hands on. Hey. How did you know where I was when you got here? You didn't answer my texts. I searched high and low for you and came up empty—"

I get cut off, slipping on a wet spot on the ground left behind from a spilled beverage. My knees buckle and I almost fall. Before panic about crashing to the floor can set in, Patrick's arm is around my waist to steady me. He looks down at me with a smile on his face. His eyes twinkle, and butterflies take flight in my stomach at the sight.

"You're my favorite girl, Lo," Patrick says. It's a quiet admission, one that almost gets scooped up by the cool summer breeze sneaking in through the open windows. "I always know when you're nearby. I look for you everywhere."

The words are an arrow to the bullseye of my heart. All I can do is nod, grateful for the distraction when we're handed a plate of food and a disposable camera to take a group photo. I spend the rest of the night floating, feeling high above the crowd.

When we split a cinnamon sugar donut and Patrick leans over to brush a crumb away from the corner of my mouth, my throat goes dry. When he brings me a fresh drink, muttering under his breath about *frat bros*, my palms turn sweaty where his fingers brush against mine. And when he looks at me at half past eleven with a sleepy grin that tells me he's utterly exhausted and asks if I'm staying at his apartment, I'm struck by the realization that every minute with him solidifies what I'm learning to be true.

I no longer see my best friend as *just* a friend.

Patrick drives us home, humming along to the tune on the radio. He taps his fingers against the steering wheel, the leather his drum set as he performs a proud concert for one. The noise doesn't bother me at all, because it makes him happy.

The phrase Patrick said earlier in the night echoes in my head, unrelenting.

That's what love is.

I think I might be in a heap of trouble.

ELEVEN

PATRICK

LOLA STANDS at my stove and flips a pancake with a spatula. It sizzles in the butter-coated pan and she lets out a pleased sigh.

She barged into my apartment half an hour ago, the supplies for breakfast in a reusable shopping bag hanging from her arm. *Sustenance*, she told me as she clicked on a burner and the clock chimed six a.m., the nourishment we'll need for a long day of wedding festivities.

"Almost ready?" I ask.

"Yeah. Three more minutes," she answers. "No promises on how they taste. They're not going to be nearly as good as when you make them."

"As long as you don't poison them, we're in good shape."

Her shirt falls down her shoulder as she uses her sleeve to wipe away a clump of batter from her arm. I stare at the freckles on her back, the cluster matching the ones across her nose that haven't faded over the years.

I want to trace them, connect the dots and see what I can draw. Maybe a heart or a square. Maybe I could write *I love you*, and she would never know.

I blink the dream away and dump half a spoonful of sugar

into my coffee.

"Have you packed?" Lola asks. She gives the pancakes a final flip with the flick of her wrist.

"No. It's Saturday, and we leave on Monday. That's what tomorrow is for."

"Do you think you're going to be functional enough to make sure you packed the right clothes come morning?"

"I'm not planning on drinking a handle of vodka at the reception tonight. I'm more concerned about how badly my back is going to hurt after being forced to repeatedly do the Cupid Shuffle. I'm getting too old for such lively dances."

"Don't remind me." Lola groans. "I hate that song. It should go on the Songs to Retire from Weddings list."

"Interesting. What else would you add? Surely the Chicken Dance has to be on there."

"Absolutely. And the Macarena."

"I don't think anyone's done the Macarena since the late nineties," I say.

"I went to a wedding in Texas not that long ago and they did it."

"In this millennium?"

"Mhmm."

"Your first mistake was going to a wedding in Texas."

Lola grins and sets a plate in front of me. I grab the bottle of pure Vermont maple syrup and douse the fluffy, golden pancakes with it.

We picked it up when we went apple picking last fall, just as the leaves were changing from green to red and the temperature dropped from warm to cool. Lola spotted a roadside stand where we purchased eight bottles along with three boxes of maple candy, splitting the snack on our drive back to the city.

"My second mistake was not bringing you," she says. "I know how much you love a themed party."

"What was the theme?"

"One-hit music wonders."

"For a *wedding*?"

"Yup. The couple got divorced two years later."

"No." I pretend to be shocked. "I don't believe you."

"Such a shame. I bought them a nice bowl."

"Should've gotten them ninety-nine red balloons instead," I say, grinning when Lola chokes on a sip of orange juice. "Did you decide where we're staying on the trip?"

"Yeah, and I made the reservations. A hotel in D.C. The campsite in North Carolina. A cute AirBnB in Florida for two nights until we check into the hotel at the convention center for the show. We're all set."

"Are you going to tell me what city my surprise is in?"

"Are you going to tell *me* what city *mine* is in?" she challenges.

"Nope." I spear a bite of pancake and pop it into my mouth, ignoring her puppy dog eyes. "I'm going to make you wait. Patience is a virtue, Lola. You love surprises, and I know you'd be pissed if I caved and spilled the beans. Instant gratification isn't all it's cracked up to be, my friend."

"Fine." She adds a vat of syrup to her plate. "You win."

"I love when that happens."

"Don't let it go to your head. What time are you meeting the guys to get ready?" she asks.

"Around ten. Henry said something about a very expensive whiskey, a very old bottle of wine, and some photos. I don't remember the order though, and I kind of hope the whiskey comes first if I have to pose for pictures. What about you all?"

"Nine. We're doing hair and makeup at their apartment, then jumping in a limo that will take us to the museum to get dressed and do final touch-ups. I had no idea it took so long to get ready for pictures."

"Probably to keep peace and order. Imagine pulling up to the ceremony with only a few minutes to spare. It would be chaos."

"I kind of like chaos," she says.

"I know you do. You thrive on it."

We eat quickly, and when we're finished, Lola stands and takes our plates to the sink. A fork clanks against the stainless steel and rattles the empty glasses. She leans against the counter and folds her arms over her chest.

"We have time before we need to leave. I'm going to get your suitcase and watch you pack some of your clothes. A sock, at the very least. Or a shirt. It doesn't even have to be clean."

"I didn't realize the woman who doesn't unpack for a week when she gets home from a trip would be this committed to filling my suitcase."

"Please, Patrick. It'll help me sleep tonight. You make actual lists about what you want to bring, but you refuse to put the clothes in your bag until the last minute? It makes no sense. Where is the consistency?"

My lips twitch.

I think she's three seconds away from forcing me to shove jeans and underwear in my bag, and I like watching her squirm.

"Fine," I relent. I heave a sigh and stand, my chair scraping over the hardwood floor. "You win."

We walk down the hall to my bedroom and I take a seat on the bed. Lola dives into the closet headfirst, an eager ball of energy. A tie comes flying out from the depths of the walk-in space, followed by a pair of pants I haven't worn since college.

"You have a lot of shit in here," she calls out, a shoe landing near my feet.

"It's not that bad," I say.

Ten minutes later, my barely used suitcase is pushed free. The piece of luggage rolls into the opposite wall and falls to the floor.

"Are you secretly a hoarder?" Lola asks, heading back into the closet for round two. Apparently she's just getting started.

"I like to hold onto things. There's a difference. Remember the time capsule we made in school before Y2K? It's under a shoebox somewhere. The floppy disk inside might be worth millions these days."

"Sounds like the definition of a hoarder to me."

"Says the woman who keeps all of her boarding passes and buys a magnet from every city she visits. You can't even see your fridge anymore."

"Hey! That's different. That's for the memories. Things to look back on to remember my travels."

"And floppy disks aren't kept for the memories?"

A loud thud echoes through the room and rattles the walls. I hear a grunt and something gliding across the floor.

"What—*dammit*—the hell is in this heavy box labeled kitchen supplies? Seems a bit counter-productive to keep your mixers with sweaters. Is it a body? Am I going to be in a documentary?"

"Shit," I curse, realizing too late what she's talking about. "Lola. Don't."

I stand and pull the closet door open. My heart plummets to the ground when I see her weasel out a cardboard box and push it to the middle of the room. She drops to her knees and pulls apart the flaps, her smile twisting into a thin line.

"Why do you have romance books hiding in your closet?" Lola asks.

I glance at the ceiling and scrub a palm over my face. She was never supposed to find that box, a secret I would have liked to keep until my dying days.

"It's a long story."

Lola blinks. Her eyebrows furrow together, wrinkles forming

across her forehead. Her lips droop deeper and deeper, settling into a frown.

"How long?" she presses, a demand I can't ignore behind the question.

"Twenty-four years long."

"I'm not following."

"The first time you read to me, I noticed you paid more attention to certain parts of the story than others. It was subtle, but I could tell. You started to read faster and turned the pages quicker when something excited you. You wrote down lines you liked in your journal, and two weeks later, you pulled those same lines out to read again. As much as you like to write the parts down, you don't like to mark up your books. You never have."

"No," she says slowly. "I don't. And I never will."

"I know. It's easier to focus if you don't because your attention stays on the story, not doodles on the sides of the pages."

The admission flows out of me. Now that I've started, now that she's discovered the only secret I've ever intentionally kept from her out of fear of how she'd react, I want to tell her everything.

She's not running or throwing a paperback at my head like I thought she would. Lola is staring at me with rapt attention, hanging on to my every word.

"So what is all of *this*?" she asks.

"I buy the books you read to me." My voice cracks, and I swallow down the lump rising in my throat. "After we finish a chapter, I tab my copy just in case you want to reread your favorite parts one day down the road. I annotate based on how you react to the quotes and certain scenes. It helps me remember what makes you happy. What makes you smile when we get to the grand gesture and something is incredibly romantic. What makes you blush when something is sexy."

I nearly trip on the word. I imagine Lola using one hand to flip the page, the other to dip under her shorts, eyes closing in ecstasy. It's sinister, wickedly good.

"I've always considered reading our *thing*, so I've kept a collection of your favorite books, just for you," I say, finishing with a big breath.

"And... and if I never asked you for a book? If I never found this box? Then what?" Lola asks, her tone turning soft.

"It wouldn't matter," I say with assurance. "I'm going to keep doing it. I like it too."

Her gaze breaks from my face to the book in her hands.

She opens the pages carefully, like she's handling a precious jewel. She studies the lines I've highlighted with yellow and green and blue, bright bursts of colors against a white backdrop. Circles and squares and underlines, certain words garnering more attention than others.

The annotations and tabs weren't intentional. I meant to pick out a few paragraphs that made her laugh, but it turned into something more. A borderline obsessive hobby that has me staying up way too late on school nights, a rainbow of markers and pens on my nightstand along with sticky notes and a ruler so I get the lines straight.

Annotating made me realize *why* Lola loves love stories so much.

There's a dream infused in the prose, a tangle of belief and a suspension of reality. A guarantee you'll find a happily ever after, even when things seem dark. Evil doesn't exist, and joy is a sure thing. Women are treated well, men are emotional, and you want to kick your feet in the air with how *sickly sweet* the story is.

Cheesy? Yeah. Predictable? Always. But they're also fun as hell.

Why wouldn't I want to be a part of that?

Romance books hold her attention more than anything else

in the world. They put a smile on her face and make her eyes light up. She could talk about them for hours and never get bored.

And me?

I'm the stupid, stupid man who would do anything to make her happy.

Lola brushes away a tear with the back of her hand. She sniffs and looks up, hope etched into her lip-splitting beam.

"This is all for me?" she asks. "You've created a library for me?"

Her fingers trace over the sentences, the paragraphs she's read aloud and the words I know she adores.

"Yes." The affirmation wobbles at the edges, and I rub my hands together. If I don't, I'm going to reach over and pull her to me. Whisper those confessions in her ear and ask what else she wants to hear. "It's for you. It's all for you."

"There must be a hundred books here."

"A hundred and six." The tip of my ears turn pink with how quickly I answer. "I know it's weird, but—"

"It's not weird."

"Oh. That's good."

I nod, burning a hole into the floor with how intensely I'm staring at the gray rug under my dress. Gray, like my life is without her. What a fitting metaphor.

"This might be the nicest thing anyone has ever done for me," Lola says.

I sit on the bed and the mattress squeaks under my weight. The iron bed frame creaks and groans, and I shrug. "It's just some highlighting."

Lola glares at me. She sets the book down and stomps across the room, coming to a stop between my thighs. Her hips fill the space nicely, and for a minute, I pretend that she belongs there.

"Let me rephrase that." She rests her palm on my cheek,

smooth and soft on my skin. "A man willingly listens to me read the books I love. He buys his own copies, remembers the things I liked, doodles around big, impactful words, then keeps the books safe in case I ever want to go back and reread them. Don't you dare try to minimize this, Patrick Walker. It's wonderful and perfect, just like *you* are wonderful and perfect. I'm not sure how I can ever say thank you."

A stick of dynamite explodes behind my lungs, turning into little embers as it sprinkles through my chest like pieces of confetti.

She thinks I'm *perfect*.

My ego grins and gloats, a victorious inner display of glee. I suppress the desire to hoot and holler, choosing to give her a smile instead.

"You don't have to thank me. I do it because I want to. Because seeing you happy makes me happy, Lo."

Her fingernails, the ones painted forest green with flecks of glitter to match the bridesmaid dress she'll be wearing tonight, graze my jaw. It's teasing, taunting, and I inhale, staggered and sharp.

These admissions aren't smart.

They're wildly idiotic, but I'm past being smart with her.

I'm moronic. So far gone for her I'm out of my goddamn mind.

God, it would be so easy to slide my hands up the curves of her body. Settle my palms over the swell of her hips and tug her close until she was in my lap.

It would be easy to flip her onto her back, her hair scattered everywhere like liquid sunshine.

It would be easy to press my lips to her neck, to her cheek, to the top of her chest, right where her shirt dips to show off her flawless skin.

It would be easy to hand over my heart to her.

Who am I kidding?

I already have.

Years ago, on a hot summer day, when she stuck out her hand and introduced herself, Band-Aid on her arm and dirt on her nose. It was cemented then, written in the stars and stitched across galaxies and moons and suns, eons and eons of time all concluding the same observation: it's only ever going to be her for me.

No one else ever stood a chance.

"Patrick," she says. It's barely above a whisper, barely audible over the pounding of my heart. The rush of lust in my vision and the love in my soul. She traces the line of my cheek then drags her thumb across my mouth, my lips parting obediently.

"Yeah?"

Is *this* the moment? Where she leans forward and I finally meet her halfway?

Forget halfway. I'll go all the way for her.

"We need to get ready to leave."

My eyes fly open, her words a bucket of ice water. She's pulling away, stepping back, and I *hate* this. This lack of communication between us. We're *good* at communicating, good at talking about what's on our minds, but she's putting up a wall between us, an invisible barrier I have no clue how to break down.

I think I might have gone too far, done too much or said too much. I should tone it down and reel it in... except... except I *can't* because I watch Lola pick up a book from the box. She clutches it tight to her chest and drops her eyes to my lips, her stare lingering there for a beat too long to be considered friendly. With a smile I can't figure out and a pat to my shoulder, she leaves my room with a lethal swish of her hips.

I groan and bury my face in my pillow.

I am such a damn coward.

TWELVE

PATRICK

"ARE YOU READY TO GET MARRIED?" I ask Henry.

We're in a holding room at the history museum with Jack, Neil, and Noah, waiting patiently until the wedding planner gives us the okay to head to the altar. It's dingy and cramped in here, and I don't think the air conditioning is working.

"I've never been more sure of something in my life," Henry says. He grins and adjusts his tie, and I can't find an ounce of nerves on his face. "I love her so much. I want to go up there and put the ring on her finger already, then take her home and call her my wife every morning when we wake up."

"I'm happy for you, man."

His gaze meets mine in the mirror and his smile dims, burning out around the edges until it slopes into a thin line. "Are we going to talk about why you're so quiet today?"

"I'm not quiet," I answer. I dust off his shoulder, getting rid of an invisible piece of lint to avoid his eye contact.

"I've known you since we were teenagers, Patrick. I saw you puke your brains out after a fraternity party on more than one occasion. You helped me study for the bar exam and gave up three nights of sleep so I wouldn't have to review practice tests alone. Don't bullshit me."

"It's your wedding day. I don't want to make it about me," I say.

I fiddle with the shiny cufflinks on my suit jacket. They're a gift from Henry, distributed in the limo on our way to the museum as he wiped a tear from his eye and thanked us for standing by his side on his big day. He engraved the metal with our initials, and if I had to guess, they probably cost more than my rent.

"As your gift to me, you can tell me what's going on."

"Nice try. You said no gifts."

"Would you look at that? I'm the one paying for this stupidly expensive party, so I think I'm allowed to make the rules," he says smugly. "Spill."

Henry points to a spot on the tweed couch. I sigh and fold my body into the small space, scooting an inch to my left so I'm not sitting in Jack's lap. I close my eyes and take a deep breath, preparing for my confession.

"I'm in love with Lola. So fucking in love with her. I've tried to date other women. I've been happy with other people, even thought I could see a future with them, until I have to end it because my heart keeps pulling me back to Lola. I don't know how to tell her how I feel, especially because we want different things in life. We could never"—my heart cinches tight and I hate how bitter the next words taste on my tongue—"be together."

All four men stare at me. It's so silent I can hear the guests filing into the museum on the other side of the wall. Low conversations, light laughter. There are three hundred chairs set up in the atrium, with bouquets of sunflowers attached to the end of every row.

I wonder how many of those people out there are in love with someone they can't have.

Am I the only idiot in the building?

"Dammit," Jack grumbles, the first to speak. He pulls out his wallet and throws a crumpled twenty-dollar bill on the floor.

Henry snatches it up, grinning wildly as he tucks the money into his shirt pocket. I blink at the exchange of cash and look between the two.

"Did I miss something? Wait a second. Are you all betting on—"

"When you would finally admit to us you're in love with your best friend?" Neil doesn't look up from his phone. "Yup. It's been going on for a while."

"You're not serious."

"Dead serious."

"What the hell is wrong with you? You can't just throw around money when people's happiness is involved," I say, glaring at them. I want to be angry, but curiosity gets the best of me. I sigh and pinch the bridge of my nose. "What were the bets?"

"Henry said before the trip. Noah said never. Neil said three years ago, so he was way off. I was banking for the confession to happen while you two were away and forced to share a bed or something," Jack says. "You couldn't have waited another day?"

"I'm so sorry for not aligning the confession of my feelings with your betting schedule," I drawl. "I wasn't aware—hang on. Why are none of you acting surprised?"

"Oh." Henry looks at the other men and shrugs. "Do you want us to act surprised? Say it again. We'll do better this time."

"It's not exactly shocking news," Noah adds. "We've all known for a while."

"How long is a while?" I ask cautiously.

"For me it was the time she came to visit us at Yale and you threatened to kick my ass if I tried to flirt with her," Henry says. "I've never seen you so pissed off."

"The first night I met you all, and you spent the whole evening grinning at your phone while you were texting her," Jack says. "So... years. You're a moron for not telling her how you feel, by the way. Watching you walk around with your tongue hanging out of your mouth is embarrassing." He pauses, then smirks. "But also hilariously entertaining."

"Fuck." I groan and rub a hand across my chest. "So it's obvious."

"Painfully so. We literally call you Lola Lover. You've *heard* us call you Lola Lover. Is that not a dead giveaway?" Jack asks.

"I thought you all were being facetious assholes. I didn't realize you actually knew I was in love with her."

"We're well aware. The whole world is aware. How she hasn't figured it out is beyond me, because she's a smart girl."

"What made you want to finally tell us?" Noah asks. "Something must have changed."

"Kind of. I don't know. Maybe I'm reading too much into it. Up until this point, everything has always been very one-sided," I say. "Lola's shown no interest in me beyond being best friends. She's set me up with some of my past girlfriends, and she's never flirted with me. Lately, though, there have been a couple moments that have me wondering if maybe her feelings have changed."

"Moments?" Henry takes a seat on the edge of the coffee table, ignoring the ominous creak of the decades-old furniture. He claps his hands together, positively giddy. "What kind of moments?"

"The other night we were on my couch. One minute we were joking around, and the next it felt like I was about to kiss her. I really wanted to kiss her, and I think she wanted me to kiss her too. There was this... this look in her eye."

"Let me guess. There was a look in her eyes and you still didn't kiss her," Jack says without a lick of surprise behind the observation. "Why?"

"Last I checked, randomly kissing your best friend when you've never kissed before kind of changes everything, doesn't it?"

"I think you should tell her," Henry says. He stands up and puts his hands on his hips, pacing around the room with a dopey smile on his face. "Maybe it's because I'm about to marry the love of my life, maybe it's because I just want my friends to be happy, or maybe I'm a little buzzed from the bottle we passed around in the limo."

"Emma is going to kill you," I say. "And she's going to make it hurt."

He waves me off. "We've only got a short amount of time on this earth." Jesus, he *is* buzzed. Introspective Henry is coming out. "I think if it were me, I'd want to take the risk. I'd kiss her. What if it works out? What if it's the best thing you've ever had? The longer you sit here not doing anything about it, the less time you'll get to really, truly be with her. I don't know. I'd jump. Leap of faith, right? Love is... love is like a parachute. Emma is my parachute. Lola is yours. She'll be there to catch you when you fall."

"Lola is already the best thing to happen to me. Imagining her as something more than a friend—" I snap my mouth closed.

How do I finish that sentence?

I could kiss her whenever I want, hold her hand in public, and spend every night by her side. I wouldn't have to leave. I could stay. I'd take care of her the way she deserves. Feed her and make sure she gets enough sleep. Buy a pill container so she never forgets to take her medicine. And every time she smiled, I'd know the beam was for me and me alone.

Henry snaps his fingers and breaks my trance. His giddiness has morphed into euphoria. "There. Right there. That's the look. Did you all see it?"

"What look?" I ask.

"The look that says you just realized risking your friendship for a reward—for her—would be worth it."

"Yeah... So, what? I spill my guts to her and hope she feels the same? That seems like a recipe for disaster."

"Go for it, Patrick. You two are best friends. Either you get the woman you love in the way that you want, or you stay friends. Seems like a win-win to me."

"I don't like you being a relationship guru," I say. "You're freaking me out."

"Sorry. Man in love, remember?" Henry checks his watch and bounces on the balls of his feet. "Can I go marry my girl now?"

"Should be just a few more minutes before—" My phone buzzes in my pocket. I pull it out and see Lola's contact photo: her on a catamaran off the coast of Portugal, holding a slice of pizza and sticking out her tongue, with her sunglasses on upside down and her wild hair whipping in the wind.

Fuck, I love that woman.

She *is* my parachute.

"Hang on. Lo's calling me." I stand up and slide my thumb across the screen. "Lola?"

"Patrick," she whispers. I have to press my finger to my ear to hear her. "Thank god."

"What's wrong?"

"I'm having a situation."

I'm already halfway to the door. "Are you okay?"

"I'm fine. I need help with my dress. I can't walk down the aisle with my zipper halfway undone."

"Tell me where you are," I say, relieved to hear there's nothing seriously wrong.

"Hiding in a room two doors down from the bridal suite. Some creepy taxidermy thing is staring at me. I can't tell if it's a bird or a bear."

"I'll be there in thirty seconds. Stay put." I hang up and turn to the guys. "Lola's having a wardrobe malfunction."

"Go," Henry says. "We'll see you out there."

With a salute, I leave the room, dodging the last-minute stragglers trickling into the ceremony. I make it to the other side of the building and knock softly on the white-paned door I think Lola is behind, heaving a deep breath to prepare for another possible *moment*. "Lo?"

THIRTEEN

PATRICK

"COME IN," she calls out.

I turn the brass knob and slip inside the small space. "Where are you?"

"Sorry. I was hiding." She steps out from behind a statue, letting me see her for the first time since we went our separate ways this morning.

Her hair is in some half-up, half-down style with pieces framing her face. Her lips are bright red and her dress—

Hell.

That *dress.*

It's obscene. Unfair to the rest of the world, because who can compete with her when she looks like *that*, a goddess in a dark green gown like some ethereal vision brought to life?

The silky material dips at her chest and hugs her waist before flaring out over her legs. It subtly shows off her curves, just enough to drive me wild and hint that they're there. The swell of her breasts. The shape of her hips. I want to slide the thin straps down her shoulders and press my lips to her bare skin.

I've seen Lola in a nice outfit before. Half-finished dresses she's workshopping, needing my help to put a pushpin in a place where she can't reach. A rented gown for the gala Henry and Emma invited us to a couple years ago. Prom when we were in high school, agreeing to go to the dance together so we wouldn't have to ask anyone else. She wore a sparkly skirt and stuck a boutonniere to my suit.

This doesn't compare.

Not even close.

There's pressure in my chest, a balloon inflating and filling the space behind my ribs until there's not an inch left to give. The piece of me that's belonged to Lola from the minute I first saw her burns bright as she watches me, lip caught between her teeth and her gaze locked on mine.

"Hey, Pattycakes," she says, using the nickname she called me as a kid.

"Hey, Yoyo," I say, using hers right back.

"Fancy seeing you here."

"Weird, right? You called, and here I am. What's going on?"

"My zipper is stuck. I think it's caught on a thread, and I can't fix it myself. Could you help me? Emma is taking last-minute pictures, and Jo is watching Wyatt so Rebecca can use the bathroom and touch up her makeup. I snuck out when no one was looking. They don't need to be stressed out about something so minor."

"Of course. Whatever you need."

Her grin is bright and blinding, and she gathers the ends of her hair off her neck. "You're a good friend."

She turns around, and I wish she hadn't, because this side of the dress might be even worse.

The useless scraps of fabric show off her whole back. The valley between her shoulder blades, the length of her spine. Smooth, fair skin I so badly want to run my fingers over. So badly want to kiss and taste and bite.

I make my way across the hardwood floor toward her, trying —and failing—to keep my eyes on her shoulders instead of her backside. When I'm within arm's reach, I hesitate.

This is a dangerous line I'm toeing, restraint growing weaker and weaker by the second. I'm holding on by a thin thread that's reaching the end of its spool, about to run out.

I'm a grown man.

A woman in a dress shouldn't affect me this much. Shouldn't make me want to lock the door, barricade it with a chair, and keep her in here forever, but that's what I'm close to doing.

I'm two seconds away from dropping to my knees. Hiking up her gown so I can kiss the top of her leg, drag my teeth down the faint scar on the inside of her thigh, and tell her she's gorgeous. Stunning. Exquisite. Every other damn wonderful adjective there is in the English language. I'll throw the whole thesaurus at her, and then I'll find words in other dialects too.

When she shuffles backward and lines her hips up with mine, zipping her up is the only polite thing on my mind. My thoughts turn wicked. I might go to hell, but Lola Jones is worth the burn.

I imagine her on her knees. Mouth parted, eyes wide as she unbuttons my pants. Smearing her lipstick, wrecking and ruining her so she can't walk straight as she makes her way down the aisle.

So she knows she's mine.

Learning the sounds she makes and doing whatever she wants, again and again, until she has nothing left to give. The taste of her on my lips, better than any dessert I've ever had.

I don't know what I was thinking. This woman will never be *just a friend* to me. She hasn't been in a really long time.

"Going to touch you now, okay?" I murmur.

"Okay," she murmurs back.

I reach for her dress. The zipper is stuck near the bottom, a rogue thread caught in the teeth. I work out the snag and carefully drag it up. It's a slow and painful process that has my breath warm on her shoulders and my knuckles running up her spine.

There's a hitch in her breathing as her head tips to the side and she bares her neck to me, teasing me again as I'd like nothing more than to mark her. To leave a red spot right under her ear so people know she's spoken for. Ask her to give me one too so we can match.

"How'd you get yourself into this mess?" I ask. I haven't pulled away from her yet, too distracted by the length of her throat. The sharp lines of her collarbone. The little sigh she lets out when I give her arm a squeeze to tell her I'm finished.

"There was champagne. Pictures. A hamburger. Patrick, it was the best burger of my life," she says. "Thank god for shapewear or I wouldn't fit into this dress."

"You all got burgers?"

"Fries, too."

"Adding insult to injury. All we got were stale crackers and cheese. I'm sensing some favoritism."

"Do you think you'll survive?" Lola teases.

"I'm going to try. I'm holding out for that five-tiered cake," I say.

She turns to face me and takes a step closer, threading her fingers through my silk tie. Maybe I'm losing my mind, hungry, tired, or caught up in the moment of seeing Lola looking like this, but I swear she tugs me toward her. An inch closer, then another.

"Thank you," she says.

"For what?"

"Helping me."

"You don't have to thank me for doing things I want to do," I say. Beyond the door, music begins to play, a sign to guests that the wedding is about to start, and they need to be seated. A sign to us that we need to be with the group in our positions, but I don't want to leave. "We should probably go. Vows to exchange and all that."

"Yeah," Lola agrees but makes no move to leave. "We should."

"You need to go first, Lo."

"Why?"

"Because..." I rest my forehead against hers. "I don't want to walk away from you. I *can't* walk away from you, especially not when you look like this."

"How do I look?"

"Like a goddamn angel. Perfect. Beautiful. Do you want me to keep going?"

"Maybe," she whispers. It's so soft I have to lean forward to hear her. "Maybe I don't want you to walk away." She presses up on her toes, her lips millimeters away from mine. I can count the freckles on her nose. I can see the little flecks of green in her eyes that only come out in the right lighting and the blush staining the apples of her cheeks. "If it weren't for our friends getting married right now, I'd ask you to stay here with me. We'd be late to the ceremony, and I wouldn't even care."

My heart races under my suit jacket and my hand falls to her hip. I rub my thumb over her backside, and a whimper falls from her mouth. I know what I'm going to be thinking about the next time she's away. When I'm lonely, and missing her like hell.

That sound. On repeat. Forever.

"I'll give you whatever you want, Lola. The moon. The stars. Do you want our entire galaxy and every one beyond? Just say the word and I'll make it yours. I will find a way."

Lola stares at me. She's never looked at me like this before. She's looking at me the way I look at her.

Like she's the most important thing in the world.

Fuck it.

I'm going all in.

I don't care about the consequences.

I want this woman, and I'm going to do something about it.

I lean an inch closer, and so does she. I don't know how there's even a sliver of space left between us, because all I can feel is her. All I can see is her. All I can hear is *her.*

I turn my cheek, ready to whisper another offering in her ear, and she moves at the same time. Quicker than a shooting star, her lips graze against my mouth in the bottom right corner, just above where my smile curves when I'm grinning at something she says.

It's accidental, done without clear intent, but it's enough to send me into near cardiac arrest. Enough to render me useless and confirm what I've known for years, because it's sweet and lovely and the best kind of torture.

Lola Jones has positively ruined me for any other woman.

I yank her to me until her chest is pressed against mine. My hand moves to the base of her neck, and when I add a push of pressure with my thumb, she melts. Her body bows forward, and she holds onto my shoulders for support. Her eyes get a little hazy, glossed over, and she looks dazed. Drunk, almost, on the last thirty seconds.

Me too.

I'm fucking intoxicated by her.

"Sorry," she whispers.

"Don't be," I say. "Remember how you told me you didn't hate when I called you love?"

I watch the bob of her throat as she swallows and lets out a quiet, "Yes."

"I didn't hate what just happened."

Lola rolls her lips together and dips her chin. Just as I'm

about to give her a promise of all the things I would do for her if she asked, the door flies open.

"There you are," the wedding planner says, looking furious. *Shit.* "It's time to go." She snaps her fingers, and we jump into high gear. Lola fans her face. I take four steps back, praying that the armchair in the corner of the room shields how hard I am. "Patrick, I need you up at the altar. *Now.* Lola, you're walking down the aisle first. We're already two minutes behind schedule."

"Sorry." Lola smiles apologetically. That smile could stop wars. Make sinners drop to their knees and beg for forgiveness. Achieve world peace in a matter of seconds. "I had a dress crisis, but we're ready now."

She follows the wedding planner toward the door.

I move after her, feet shuffling on their own accord, and stop her with a touch to her elbow. Something unresolved hangs between us, and I'm not letting her out of my sight until I know she's okay. That *we're* okay.

"Are we good?" I ask.

Her smile twists into something beautiful and secretive. Something happy and serene and mine.

Mine, mine, mine.

My Lola.

She dips her chin and tucks a loose strand of hair behind her ear. She adjusts the front of her dress and nods. "We're better than good," she says. "I'll see you out there, Patrick. You'll save me a dance, right?"

"Yeah," I confirm. "Of course."

"Good." She squeezes my hand and ducks out of the room.

I'm left staring after her.

FOURTEEN

PATRICK

"HOW MUCH DID you pay the DJ to play the Macarena?"

I take a seat in the chair next to Lola at the wedding party table. The dinner plates are empty and drinks get topped off with a fresh pour of wine. The lights have dimmed and the real party is just getting started.

Jack's jacket is in a ball at my feet while Rebecca's shoes are sitting next to her water glass, and Henry lost his tie twenty minutes ago. I can't find my cell phone. It disappeared after I snapped a picture of Lola smiling around a spoonful of mashed potatoes.

"I have no clue what you're talking about," Lola says and takes a bite of her cake.

It's her third slice of the lemon and raspberry dessert. The one she snuck under her dress during Noah's best man speech when she thought no one was looking. I watched her tiptoe around the perimeter of the room, lift the hem of her gown, and hide the plate as best she could.

She didn't do a very good job.

"Talk about ironic timing. We have a conversation about the

worst songs to hear at a wedding, and suddenly, a monstrosity is playing from the speakers," I say.

"Fate," she says and licks her fork. "Okay, I paid enough to make it look like the deviation from a carefully curated playlist was an accident. No one is getting in trouble. Besides, Emma loved it."

"I love accidents."

"Me too."

"Hey." I tap her shoulder and point to the dance floor. "I think Henry told Emma about the dance lessons."

The newlyweds move to a slow tune, the romantic song playing through the speakers—The Righteous Brothers' version of "Unchained Melody." They're both grinning from ear to ear, and Emma is on the verge of tears as Henry whispers in her ear.

"They look happy," Lola says.

"I think that's the point of a wedding, isn't it?" I grab the leg of her chair and pull it closer to me. She's too far away. "True love and all that. Otherwise, it would be a total sham."

"I thought the point of a wedding was presents."

"Also true. One can never have too many blenders."

"Do you want a big wedding?" Lola sets her plate down. She angles her body toward mine. "You do, don't you?"

"I don't know, to be honest. A ceremony would be nice," I say. "Flowers and a cake and the whole nine yards. I'd be fine with the courthouse, too, though. I just want to be with someone who makes me happy. I don't care about the rest."

Lola breaks into a wide grin. "You've always been a romantic, Patrick. Have a wedding."

"What about you, Wanderlust? Would you have a wedding?"

"No way. If I ever got married, I would want it to be just for us. Maybe we'd have a picnic in a field with wildflowers and dandelions. Maybe we'd get caught in a rainstorm after a secret ceremony. Maybe we wouldn't even make it legally binding, just a mutual understanding that neither one of us is ever planning to leave. Just me and them, two souls tied together for eternity. Until we become stardust. We'd wait to tell our friends until they saw our rings and then we'd say, *oh, these old things*? No fuss. No party. And it would be beautiful."

I think of Lola wearing a white dress and holding a home-made bouquet. Saying *I do* to a person who isn't me and finding out about it by seeing the ring someone else gave her.

I *hate* that.

"Sounds nice," I say.

"You look like you just ate a lemon," she says.

"What? I do not."

"Yes." Lola laughs. "You do. Say it again without grimacing."

"I blame the frosting from the cake. It's super tart," I say.

We sit there for a few minutes in silence, watching happiness bleed out in front of us. Everywhere I glance, there's a couple bursting at the seams of infatuation, hopeful looks on their faces as they watch Henry spin Emma out of his hold, then back in, her dress fanning out around her ankles and showing off her white heels.

"Can I tell you a secret?" Lola asks.

Despite that pull of loneliness in my gut, I can't help but smile.

We used to play this game as kids, back when we thought reading under the covers past our bedtime was some dark, confidential admission. We'd lay on the floor of the treehouse and talk for hours until there was nothing left to hide.

Our secrets got deeper as we got older.

Lola's attraction to both guys and girls and how she wasn't sure what she wanted to classify herself as, but it certainly wasn't straight.

My reluctancy about going to medical school, heart tethered to the education field from an early age. I didn't want to follow in the footsteps of my parents and become a surgeon or pediatrician. I wanted to help the kids with bright futures, all the soon-to-be leaders who were just waiting for someone to tell them how *good* they are at things and believe in them.

I wonder what our younger selves would say if they could see us now. Still friends. A constant presence in each other's lives. Healthy and happy. Good jobs. Good friends. Good everything.

"You can tell me anything," I say, exactly like I did all those years ago.

"Promise you won't hate me?"

"I could never hate you, Lola."

"Not even if I ate the last French fry in the bag?"

"We might have to reevaluate things if you did that. That's a capital offense, because everyone knows you can easily split a fry into two. But no. Never hate."

"During the ceremony, I felt angry." Lola's quiet, afraid to share this admission with the world. "Then I was angry with myself for being angry in the first place. How is it possible to be so happy for someone else but feel so fucking lonely at the same time?"

"You're lonely?" I ask. My smile slips into a deep frown, one I can feel in my chest.

I thought I knew Lola better than anyone, but when I look at her, when I *really* look at her, I see the pinched grin. The dimness on her face, like she's been going through life with no one by her side. Tired and exhausted, carrying burdens and fighting demons alone.

"I am. I'm scared to even say it because I'm afraid of losing someone like I lost my dad. For years, I've been adamant about not wanting to be with someone and avoiding relationships, but something in my life isn't right."

"Does it feel like there's a hole in your heart that you can't patch?" I ask.

Her eyes meet mine, sadness behind the blue. "You feel it too."

"Yeah." I nod. "I do."

"I think I'm ready to give relationships another chance. Dip my toes back into the dating pool. That fear of being left is still there. I don't think it will ever fully go away. But that's life, isn't it? Being scared and terrified and doing it anyway. I don't want to have any regrets, and now I'm a little braver. A little more open-minded. I know my worth, and it's so much more substantial than an asshole who breaks up with their girlfriend at their father's funeral."

A burning flare of heat blazes through me, alighting every nerve ending.

I sit up in my chair, a newfound sense of purpose to my movements. She wants to try relationships again?

Talk about timing.

Fate.

"That's a big step for you, Lo." I slip my hand into hers. Squeeze her palm tight and keep our fingers intertwined. "I think that's a great idea."

"It's great until I worry about the possibility of someone not accepting these pieces of me, the shrapnel and broken parts. Is there really a person out there who is patient enough to put up with how I operate? Who doesn't mind that I take a pill to focus and understands I need a little extra time to complete things? Is there someone out there who will accept me, just as I am? Or will they be afraid of what they find and leave?"

"I don't think you need to worry about that," I say, tucking a strand of hair behind her ear and staring into her eyes. The blue sparkles, shimmers, a technicolor rainbow.

"Why not?"

"We have our marriage pact to fall back on. I promise to never break up with you at a funeral, and to always own a bed frame."

A laugh falls from her lips, a delightfully marvelous sound. It's much better than seeing her sad. "You remember the marriage pact?"

"Of course I do. You got glitter all over my GameBoy and the treehouse. It was a mess in there for weeks."

"It wasn't like I dumped a vial of glitter everywhere, Patrick. It was from my dance costume."

"The role of Clara. I remember."

"That tutu was incredible, wasn't it?"

"Yeah." I nod in agreement, thinking about that night. "It sure was."

"Isaac has a girlfriend," I say, "but he doesn't seem to like her very much." I throw a baseball at the ceiling of the treehouse and catch it in my hand.

"Ew." Lola wrinkles her nose and sits on the floor. She's been moving for the last thirty minutes and practicing her dance moves for her upcoming recital, nothing more than a blur of limbs. "I never want a boyfriend."

I stop tossing the ball and prop up on my elbow to look at her. "What about when we're older and supposed to get married to someone?" I ask.

"Then I'll just be alone. People weird me out."

"What about me? Do I weird you out?"

She shakes her head. "No way. You're my favorite person in the world."

"You're my favorite person in the world too."

"More than Jimmy?"

"Jimmy can be mean sometimes. He teases the kids in school who need more time to do their tests."

"Mean people suck."

"What if we made a pinky promise to each other?"

Lola scoots closer. Her knee presses against the Band-Aid on my shin, the bandage covering the cut I got when I fell off my bike last week. "What kind of promise? We already promised to be best friends forever."

"Yeah. But maybe if we both still don't like people when we're older, we can marry each other."

She taps her cheek, deep in thought. "How old is old?"

"Thirty-five?"

Lola sticks out her hand. I wrap my palm around it and give it a shake. "Deal. I don't know if I'll like people then, but if I do, I'll marry you." She giggles and drops onto her back, arms sprawled across the floor. "Lola Walker. That could be my name one day."

"Or I could be Patrick Jones. My uncle took my aunt's last name."

Her head turns so she can look at me, and I take her in as she grins from ear to ear. "I like the sound of that, Pattycakes."

"Are you okay?" Lola of the present comes into focus, the blurry past sharpening into pristine clarity.

"I'm good," I say. "Just reminiscing."

"Would you really marry me?" she asks.

"Of course I would. I hear there's a tax break for married people." She elbows my ribs and I chuckle.

"Even though I get bored with things quickly and have to change the song on the radio after only two seconds because I have to know what else is playing on the other stations?"

"Even then."

"Even though I forget to eat half my meals?"

"That's okay. I set alarms to remind you to eat."

"What?"

"Did you think the message I send you every day at 12:09 in the afternoon is random?" I ask.

"I... I don't know what I thought," Lola whispers. "I always remember to eat after you text me."

"Good. That means I'm doing my job. It sounds like you're trying to give me reasons I—or anyone—wouldn't want to be with you instead of telling me all the reasons we'd be lucky for even a second of your time."

"I'd never push you away, Patrick."

"And I'd never run away from you. It's been twenty-four years, Lo, and I plan to stick around for the rest of our lives. You're never going to get rid of me."

Lola's grip around my hand tightens and she scoots closer. Her eyes bounce to my mouth, the spot she grazed three hours ago.

The kiss might have been accidental, but that look right now certainly isn't.

I'd give anything to know what she's thinking. To ask if she wants to sneak away and find a dark corner, far from the crowd. Just us, so we could talk or laugh or—

"There you are." Jo appears in front of us, red-faced and smiling in a dress that matches Lola's. Jack stands beside her, his tie unknotted and hair a mess. "There's one dance left before Henry and Emma leave. You're coming with me."

"My feet are killing me." Lola groans and slips off her heels. She kicks them under the chair and stands, looking at me. Our hands fall apart, and I'm colder without her touch. "Are you joining us?" she asks me.

I can see that she wants me to say yes, but I'm afraid of what might happen if I do. I don't want us to have a conversation about what a possible future could look like with an attentive audience. It's going to have to wait.

"Nah," I say. "I'll be on shoe duty. You two have fun."

The women depart with a wave and move through the sea of partygoers. Their giggles grow softer as they retreat, finding an open spot on the dance floor. I sigh as I watch Lola spin around.

A glass lands in my hands, and I turn my head to find Jack

studying me. I nod my appreciation and accept the beverage, bringing it to my lips.

"Does it get easier?" I ask after a sip.

"Nope. Hurts like hell, doesn't it?"

"It's certainly not fun. Were you ever scared to tell Jo how you felt?"

"Every day." He leans back in his chair. "The pros of doing the scary thing eventually outweighed the cons of keeping it inside. So, I did it. I think you should too."

"Yeah. I should."

Lola glances over her shoulder and waves at me. She holds up another slice of cake and takes a big bite, victory and triumph written on her face. I smile and lift my glass in her direction.

Three hundred people in the room, and she's only looking at me.

I'm the luckiest guy in the world.

FIFTEEN
LOLA

"IT'S ROAD TRIP DAY." I slide into the kitchen, my socks gliding over the tile floor, and beam at Patrick.

He looks up from the map on the table and returns my smile. "Hey. Have you recovered from your sugar coma?"

"Six slices of cake on Saturday, and I feel great. I also had a donut before you got here."

"That's got to be some kind of record. Your dentist must love you." He pulls a pencil out from behind his ear. It's wooden, the kind that needs sharpening after a few uses. "A guaranteed patient every six months."

"Don't you have our route memorized? You've looked at the map sixty times."

"I do. I'm just double checking. One can never be too sure about the path they plan to take."

"Wow." I grab a glass of orange juice and take a sip. "Isn't it a little early to be getting so philosophical?"

"That's where you're wrong, my friend. It's never too early. How are you feeling?"

"Nervous," I admit. "Excited. I can't believe someone wants me to come and show off my designs in an actual show. I'm waiting for it all to be a joke. I'm not sure it'll feel real until we get to Florida. Until I get my lanyard and see my name on the list of designers."

"I'm going to keep a program and laminate it." Patrick stands and leans against the counter. "Then I'm going to steal another one and blow it up to poster-board size and hang it in my apartment."

"What are you going to do with a giant picture of a program from a fashion show? It's not like it's a van Gogh," I say.

"It's a conversation starter. 'Oh, this? My best friend was in the show. That's her name right there. Look how incredible she is.'"

Hearing Patrick's pride and catching the gleam in his eyes makes me even more proud of myself than I already am. Of seeing this project through, committing to the work and having dozens of products I think are good.

Better than good.

They're *great*.

"You'd really hang it up?" I ask.

"In the foyer, right next to the photo of my family and the shot of us and our friends at Lake Winnipesaukee." He grins. "There's no changing my mind."

"The family picture of you all at the beach? I love that one."

"I had sand in my pants. It was miserable." Patrick folds the map and tucks it in the back pocket of his shorts. "Are you almost ready to go? We've got eight hours on the road, then the adventure begins."

"Isn't there a saying about how it's not the destination that matters, but the journey?"

"The person who came up with that saying didn't have to sit in miles and miles of traffic. Forty-five minutes in a stand-still gridlock on the way to New York might make me lose my mind."

"At least we have snacks." I point to the bag I put together, the canvas packed to the brim with chips and cookies. A veggie tray and crackers with an assortment of cheese. Enough food to last us for days if we got stranded in the middle of nowhere.

"I'd go on a road trip with you any day, Lola Jones."

"High praise from the man who doesn't like to travel," I say. "I'm almost ready. I want to check the garment bags one more time and make sure all the outfits are there."

"You made a list, right?"

"Yeah. I also labeled everything with color-coded stickers and divided them by category."

"Atta girl. I'll do a final check before we leave, too."

Oh hell.

Heat inundates my body. It creeps up from my chest to my neck and face, and I turn my back to him. I grab a dirty bowl sitting in the sink, trying my best to not linger on the way his encouragement—*atta girl*—moves down my spine, reaches around my belly and swoops low, making a dull ache form between my legs.

"You don't have to do that," I say. "There are tons of pieces." A spoon I used for my cereal slips out of my hold and clatters against the stainless steel

"I'm well aware I don't have to do anything," Patrick says. It's sharp and firm, the same voice I've heard him use with his students when he needs someone to listen to him. I knock over a bottle of dish soap and an army of suds erupts in the sink. "When will you learn I do things because I *want* to, Lola, not because I *have* to?"

He's closer than he was a few seconds ago, crowding my space and in my bubble. His chest is against my back and his hands are on either side of the counter, caging me in.

I have nowhere to go, and I think I've stopped breathing.

The memory of his palm on my hip, his face buried in the crook of my neck as we danced at Henry and Emma's party is seared in my mind. He dipped, I twirled, and every time our eyes collided, a wall inside me crumbled. The slow demise of the lines we've meticulously drawn erased and rewritten.

I need him.

I've always needed him, a rock against crashing waves. The lighthouse guiding me to safer water. The anchor keeping me from drifting out to sea. He's persistent, true North.

But now I *need* him.

I didn't mean to kiss him the night of the wedding. I thought I was being bold by pecking his cheek. Then he turned and my mouth found his, as if I had been searching for it all along.

It lasted a second—maybe not even that long—and it wasn't even directly on the lips, and *still*, I felt the planets align. I saw shooting stars and I *yearned* for him, my soul desperate to cling to his.

I wanted to do it again.

I still want to do it again.

I want the curve of his muscles under my palms and the warmth of his skin against mine. To explore every line, every divot, every inch of his body until I have him committed to memory. I want to know him so deeply that I'd be able to recognize him with my eyes closed, relying on steady hands and steady sounds to identify his shape and know that he is there. No barriers, no restraints. Just us.

I dreamed about Patrick after the wedding. He was down the hall in his room, sleeping soundly and unaware of the thoughts coursing through my head. Indecent thoughts about my best friend, ones I've never had before and now can't seem to escape.

Of him lifting me onto the counter and whispering in my ear to show him what makes me feel good. What I like best. His hand under my dress, over my underwear, circling with perfect precision. Unraveling me thread by thread, piece by piece, until I was nothing but a boneless heap of unadulterated pleasure and satisfaction.

"Right," I say. I squeeze my eyes shut and try to get rid of the visions. "I'm still learning."

"It's always going to be the case." Patrick reaches for the bottle sitting on the granite countertop next to the knife block. He turns the top open and drops a capsule in my hand. "Take your medicine."

"Thanks." I pop the pill in my mouth and nudge his stomach with my elbow. "Let's load up before I eat all of this food."

"Except for the raisins in the trail mix. You hate those."

"Another reason I keep you around. So you can eat them for me."

"Get your party pants ready, Jones. The best trip of your life is about to begin."

Patrick walks away and the room grows stagnant. I hear my suitcase rolling across the floor, the rustle of bags and the hum of a tune. Frank Sinatra, if I had to guess. One of his favorites.

I've never told him this, but I don't hate raisins.

I eat them all the time when he's not around.

Back in fifth grade, he asked if I was going to finish the raisins in my plastic bag at lunch and I shook my head no. I handed him the snack and told him he could have the rest. Patrick grinned with delight and popped them in his mouth one by one, happy as a clam. I kept bringing the snack in my lunchbox, and from then on, I gave him all of my raisins, because I liked seeing him light up more than I liked anything else.

———

TRAFFIC STARTS ten minutes into our trip.

Bumper to bumper, with brake lights and car horns, we inch our way down the highway at a snail's pace. Patrick is unbothered, one hand dangling out the window in the summer air, the other tapping the steering wheel. He's wearing his sunglasses, the Aviators covering his eyes and making him look like an old movie star with his plain white shirt and hair blowing in the wind. I pull out my phone and snap a picture of him, wanting to capture every detail of our journey for memory's sake.

"I would have smiled," Patrick says.

"I like it better when it's candid." I pull my legs to my chest, the leather of the seat warm from the sun under my soles of my feet.

"You can try to get all the embarrassing photos of me you want, but nothing beats my album of you falling asleep on different modes of transportation. Trains. Cars. When we took the bus from Boston to New York and back the same day because you wanted to see the Rockefeller Tree."

I groan. "I've never been so car sick in my life."

I wish I didn't remember the brown bag Patrick held open for me, the cold paper towel he pressed to my forehead while he whispered soothing words. The saltine crackers he snagged from another passenger, force feeding me the snack as my face turned green. A ginger ale I swear he produced from thin air, complete with a straw to help me sip. Nothing relieved my aching stomach.

When we finally parked at South Station after hours on the road, I sprinted off the bus and locked myself in the bathroom for forty-five minutes.

Puking your brains out in a public restroom is a humbling—and horrifying—experience.

"The tree was worth it though," he says. "Vomit aside."

"Yeah." I smile. "It was."

I remember the twinkling lights and the snowflakes sticking to his beanie. The hot chocolate we shared to get warm. Huddling together to sing "Jingle Bells" with the rest of the group of tourists, considered ridiculously obnoxious by the locals. We didn't care. It felt like we were in a snow globe, a magical world full of holiday cheer at the best time of year.

"Your surprise is in D.C., by the way," I add, the heat pulling me back to the summer, not winters past.

Patrick glances over at me, curious. "Is it?"

"Yeah. The online forums also say the hotel we're staying in is haunted."

"Wow. Our first night and we're diving right into paranormal activity. Outstanding. Do you believe in ghosts?"

"No." The cars in front of us speed up and we finally gain momentum, the city skyline fading to small specks in the side mirror. "Yes. Maybe. I think it's one of those unexplainable things, like aliens or whatever kind of higher power is out there."

"Aliens are one hundred percent real," Patrick says with conviction.

"What's your proof?"

He shrugs and adjusts the bill of the Red Sox hat he got at a game last summer after complaining endlessly about the sun and heat. "You said it's an unexplainable thing. I think it's on par with love. You can't see it, but you can feel it."

I gape at him. "Did you just quote *A Walk to Remember*?"

"C'mon, Lo. You know it's my favorite early 2000s movie." He grins, and his dimple on his right cheek pops. "Look, all I'm saying is I'd rather be on the believing-in-aliens end. That way, if they turn out to be real and come to take over Earth, I'm already on their good side."

"*E.T.* scared you as a kid. Now you're an alien sympathizer?"

"Getting old has mellowed me out. I liked the aliens in that romance book you read to me. The blue ones."

Romance book.

Like the hundreds he's bought and kept for me, stowed away

in his closet *just in case.*

The painstaking time and energy he's spent highlighting and underlining word after word until thousands of pages were full of colorful notes. The money he's invested in something that's not deeply personal to him, but deeply personal to *me.*

I can't wait to go through the whole box when we get home. To see which lines he picked and if he added anything special in the margins on the pages. A surprise for me to find, maybe.

They don't make people better than Patrick Walker.

"Never in my wildest dreams did I think I'd be sitting next to you on a road trip down to Florida, talking about blue aliens." I drop my head back and laugh.

"I'm also your assistant for the week of the fashion show," he says. "We're checking all the boxes."

"I don't want you to feel obligated to jump in and help. This is a vacation for you."

"So? I'm yours to use for the time we're down there, Lo. To hand over your tape measure. I'll follow you around with a thousand pushpins and hold the hems of dresses so you can make last-minute alterations. Whatever you need."

I wrinkle my nose and frown. "I don't like how that sounds. I never want to use you or make it seem like our friendship has one-sided benefits I'm taking advantage of."

"It's not one-sided. I get to spend the week with my favorite person in the world." He reaches over and wraps his hand around my knee, fingers cool against my skin. "I'm yours, Lola. Plain and simple."

Yours.

Who knew it only took five letters to make my heart skip a beat?

I wonder what Patrick would be like with no rules, no limitations.

Just mine.

SIXTEEN
PATRICK

"I'M STARVING."

"Do you want to check into the hotel then find some food?"

"*Please*," Lola says. "If I eat another Dorito, I swear I'm going to turn into one."

"If you had to pick a Dorito to turn into, which would you pick? Cool Ranch, right?"

"Stop." Lola giggles and holds her side. "I hate that you're making me laugh. I'm so hungry, I think I might wither away."

"We can't have that. Hold on, Nacho Cheese. We're almost there."

I navigate us past the Capitol building and the monuments around the Tidal Basin. We sit in traffic across the George Mason Memorial Bridge and then roll into Arlington—where we're staying for the next two nights—at a quarter past eight.

We find a parking spot in a suspicious-looking garage and load our bags onto a luggage cart with a squeaky back right wheel. Ten minutes later, with Lola's cursive signature on the booking receipt, we're checked in. The guy behind the front desk slides two keys our way and apologizes with a wry smile for any ghost rumblings we might hear during our stay. He directs us to the elevator behind the ice machine, with instructions to head up to the sixth floor and turn left.

I don't miss the way he winks at Lola and blatantly ignores me. I want to grab him by the collar and shove him against the wall, scowling at his pushy assurance that he's here for *anything* she needs and the way his eyes stay glued on her hips as we walk away.

I repeatedly hit the button for six until the elevator doors finally close.

"Are you okay?" Lola asks.

"That guy was a creep."

"How was he a creep?"

"He was looking at you."

Her eyebrows lift. She smiles and touches my arm. "Patrick Walker. Are you jealous?"

"No," I say. I lean against the steel wall and huff. "I was jealous when I saw the bartender talking to you at the party last week. Tonight, I'm just annoyed."

"You were jealous of the bartender? The kid who was so young, he's probably never voted in a presidential election before?"

"Of course I was. You were laughing with him. Smiling. Having a grand ole time."

"I smile at a lot of people. And I laugh at a lot of things."

"I know you do. I didn't like that I wasn't the one making you happy."

There's a moment of silence until the elevator dings and the doors open. We walk down the carpeted hall and I follow behind Lola, tugging the cart with me.

"You don't have to worry about bartenders or hotel receptionists, Patrick. You make me smile the most," she says.

"I do?"

"Yeah." She lowers her chin and stops outside our room. "You do."

Hearing that I make her smile the most inflates my ego to astronomical proportions. A burst of pride explodes inside me. I want to lift her up and spin her around. Find a million new ways to make her happy, then find a million more.

Tell her how you feel, a voice inside my head says.

Soon, I think. *Soon.*

I tap the room key to the door. The lock flashes green and I turn the handle. The barrier doesn't budge, sticking against the frame and refusing to move.

"I think the ghosts might already be messing with us," I say.

It takes some finagling and a strong push from my shoulder that's going to bruise in the morning, but the door finally opens with an unenthusiastic creak. A rush of stale air wafts into the hallway. I stick my head in the foyer and flip on the light switch. The bulb in the entryway flickers twice, then goes out.

"Should we announce ourselves?" Lola whispers. "Offer our kidneys for two nights of good sleep?"

"Probably a good idea. Want me to cut you open first? You won't have to deal with the cleanup."

"Gladly. You know I'm squeamish. Thanks for being so considerate."

As soon as we file inside, Lola unloads the bags from the cart and drops her duffle bag to the carpeted floor. She maneuvers her suitcase to lean against the beige wall and puts her hands on her hips, surveying the space.

The paint is chipping. The curtains over the window look like they've been through a paper shredder. Something smells vaguely like mildew and wet socks. She turns and stares at me before we simultaneously burst out laughing.

"Are you thinking that—"

"We're definitely either going to get sick or die in here?" Lola finishes for me. "Yeah. I am. The smell is—"

"Repulsive," I say. "Maybe we can open the balcony doors and get some fresh air?"

"Fresh, humid air," she says. "Nothing says comfort and tranquility like sweat rolling down your back while you're trying to sleep. I'll take full responsibility for this. The pictures online were a lot nicer than our current situation."

"You mean they didn't have handprints on the wall and a duvet cover from the late eighties as their advertising? I'm shocked."

"We should get out of here, right? Grab our last supper before we're held captive by spirits or die from carbon monoxide poisoning."

"You don't have to ask me twice. I saw a burger joint a block away. We'll eat, then we can see how much time we can spend outside of the room before we're forced to sleep in this hellhole."

"Oh, maybe there are rats!" Lola says, and I tug her out to the hall.

We find Spud's Burger Bar nestled between an indoor cycle studio and a froyo shop. I LUV DEBRA is graffitied with spray paint over wooden beams, and dollar bills are nailed to a post in the middle of the restaurant. It's dark and it's loud, with mismatched barstools and tables without napkin dispensers. In the corner, a Willie Nelson song plays from a jukebox that looks like it's been around since the dawn of time.

It's exactly what we're looking for.

"So," I say when our food comes twenty minutes later. I dip my fry in ketchup and bite off the end. "My surprise. Can you give me a clue?"

Lola swallows a sip of water and grins. "David Bowie. George Clooney. Tom Hanks."

"That's a very eclectic group of people. What else can you tell me?"

"We have to be there early, and you need to wear your sneakers."

"Lola Jones. After all the years I've spent trying to get you to sign up for a 5k, have you finally started running?"

"It's not a 5k, but physical activity is required," she says.

"Consider me intrigued."

"Hey." Lola sets down her burger and dusts off her hands. Sesame seeds fall into the red wicker basket, and I see salt on the tips of her fingers. "I'm not sure if I've said it yet, but thank you for coming with me. It means a lot that you're going to be at the show." She pauses. Her grin settles into a small smile, a brightness in her eyes. "I appreciate you, Patrick. A lot."

"You don't have to thank me, Lo. I'm here because I want to be here."

"I forget to say thank you sometimes. You're a giver. You give so much of yourself to other people. Even when you have nothing left to offer, you still give. I'm a taker. I take and I take and I take, and I'd never want you to think I'm taking advantage of you."

"I don't think that at all," I say. "I know you're glad I'm here. We all show our appreciation in different ways. Speaking of appreciation, is now a good time to tell you I'm only along for this ride because I really want to meet a ghost?"

Lola launches a tater tot at my head and huffs out a laugh. "Worst friend ever."

———

"I DON'T HAVE the energy to shower," Lola mumbles. "Sleep. I want to sleep."

"Five minutes," I tell her. "Then you can get in bed." I shove the door to our hotel room open. Lola staggers inside and kicks off a sandal. The shoe goes flying and hits the balcony door.

"How do you have so much energy? You did all the driving," she says. "Hours and hours of driving. States and cities and so many little towns. There's an entire country out there, Patrick."

"Which one was your favorite? I'm attached to Woonsocket, I think."

"Neversink, New York, obviously."

"You're all about resilience, aren't you?" I ask. "Go shower. I can't be sure the sticky stuff on our table was spilled soda or something more horrific. If I don't hear from you in fifteen minutes, I'm going to make sure you haven't drowned in a bathtub at the Old Virginia Inn."

"And they say chivalry is dead." With a tip of an imaginary hat, Lola saunters to the bathroom and closes the door.

I press the heels of my palms into my eyes as soon as I hear the water turn on.

I don't let my mind wander to those cutoff shorts she's stepping out of. The distracting pair with the long threads of denim I want to wrap around my fingers and tug. The thin straps of her purple tank top I want to pull down her shoulders and toss to the floor.

I do the respectable thing instead. I sit at the desk shoved in the corner, glare at the tattered curtains, and pull out my phone.

My phone is safe.

My phone isn't Lola soaking wet, arching her back and dropping her head against the tiled shower wall.

My phone isn't my hand sliding up her slick thigh, smiling into her neck as she lets out a breathy moan.

Dammit.

Not working.

I click my phone closed and flip through the hotel directory on the desk. The folder is sticky, and I grimace as I turn the page. There's a room service menu, directions to the gym, and a midnight ghost tour offered in the cemetery across the street. I wonder if I can convince Lola to do one tomorrow night.

"We have a problem."

I turn to find her standing with her hands on her hips. Her hair is wet and one of her socks has slipped halfway down her calf, while the other one is on inside out.

"What's up?" I ask, specifically focusing on anything except the spot on her thigh where her sleep shorts end. High up, just under the hem of her tie-dye T-shirt, where her skin turns less tan.

"There's only one bed," she says.

"No, there's not," I say. "There's—" I snap my mouth closed and stare at the bed in the middle of the room. The lone bed I could've sworn was two earlier in the night is now a single mattress, barely larger than a full. "Is it possible someone came in and switched the furniture?"

"Patrick."

"Lola."

"What do we do?"

"I can take the chair."

"The chair," she repeats, walking toward me motioning for me to get up. When I stand, she spins the desk chair in a circle. It squeaks, and we hear a screw pop loose. "This chair?"

"Yup," I say. "Should be fine. Who needs lumbar support, anyway?"

"I don't think I'd be able to sleep knowing you were miserable. We'll share. It's no big deal. Build a barrier if you care so much. It doesn't bother me." Lola grabs a magazine from her suitcase and climbs onto the bed, the side closest to the window. She slips under the sheets and pats the pillows behind her. "You know what? After further review, it's not the worst place I've ever slept."

"I'm not sure I want to know where else you've slept," I say.

I find my sleep shorts and toothbrush and shut the bathroom door behind me. Steam fills the room as I turn on the shower. I shuck off my clothes and kick them aside, stepping into the steady stream of water.

Lola and I have shared a bed before, back when we were eleven and our families took a trip out to the Cape over the summer break. A rented bungalow right on the water, with a wraparound porch and curtains that billowed in the breeze. No air conditioning, just some rickety old fans. We could hear the waves crashing outside and watched the sunrise over the sand dunes.

Our brothers got the bunk beds, leaving Lola and me squashed like sardines in a twin—my legs hanging off the mattress and her stealing the covers.

We stayed up late and whispered about the ocean, the seashells we found, the ice cream we were going to eat the next day. I was clueless about girls, didn't know the first thing about love or relationships or what the hell attraction was. I just I knew I liked being with her.

There, in the quiet of night while everyone else slept, it was only her and me. No responsibilities. No chores or homework. No sports practice or familial obligations. We simply *were*, and no one else mattered.

My days started with Lola's half-awake smile and my days ended with her face six inches away from mine. Her hair smelling like salt and the sea as she curled on her side and told me why today was the best day ever, and how she couldn't wait for tomorrow.

I could never wait for tomorrow either, because it meant another day with her.

When she's in town, we share a couch for movie night, accidentally falling asleep halfway through the film. A dimly lit room. A shared warm blanket, her calf slung over mine. It's never anything intimate, only a few hours of close proximity until I wake up, my muscles cramping and my back stiff. I'll climb off the cushions and carry her to her room, tucking her under the covers and saying good night.

And sure, there was also the other night in the guest room where my eyes got heavy and her voice lulled me to sleep. But it was only for a few hours. Another accident, totally unplanned.

Like that damn kiss at the wedding I can't stop thinking about.

This cramped and tiny hotel room, with a questionable chandelier and a very small mattress, is not the place to share a bed when I can't stop thinking of Lola in less-than-friendly terms. I don't *want* to stop thinking about Lola, and sleeping next to my best friend while I imagine her with her hands against the wall and my face between her legs feels immoral.

I rinse myself clean, my muscles turning languid and pliant under the water pressure, the only impressive feature of the room. I sigh and close my eyes, grateful for a few minutes of solitude after a long day. I don't want to be away from her, and I know Lola would never ask for some time alone, but I understand how she operates. She likes people, loves the socialization and camaraderie of friends, but she also likes time for herself. Time to unwind, time to reflect and catch her breath.

During the day, she's like a hurricane, moving from point to point as quickly as she can. She jumps between projects without a concrete plan because that's how her brain operates—a little different, but no less substantial than anyone else's. In fact, it's better because it's *her*, unique and wonderful and one of a kind.

Lola settles when the stars come out. There's a heavy exhale, a relaxation. She grows quiet, and I love getting to see the side of her so few people know. Peace cloaks her, and it's like she finally allows herself to slow down. She'll tilt her head to the side, beaming at me from across the room with a slow and easy smile, and I can tell she's perfectly content, nowhere else in the world she'd rather be.

The water turns cold, and I shiver at the change of temperature. I turn off the shower and grab the spare towel from the rack, drying my body from head to toe. I slip on my shorts, quietly open the door, and tiptoe back into the room.

Lola is fast asleep, the magazine in her hand close to falling to the floor. I make my way to her side of the bed and pry the reading material from her grip. I set it safely on the bedside table next to her water bottle, the one with a Pride flag sticker and a *read banned books* decal affixed to the metal. The covers are only halfway up her body, and as I pull them to under her chin, I can't resist brushing a lock of hair out of her eyes.

"Love you, Lo," I murmur, pressing a kiss to her forehead.

It takes forever to fall asleep with her so close. I can hear her soft inhales, the sound of the sheets rustling against her legs as she moves, flipping onto her side. I eventually drift off to a dream of Lola in a field wearing a white dress. There's a crown of flowers on her head, and she buries her face in my shirt. She kisses the spot on my chest directly above my heart, and she asks if I'm happy.

I repeat *yes* a thousand times, a million times, because with her, it's impossible to be anything but.

SEVENTEEN
LOLA

"I'M GOING to be honest, Lo. I'm not sure I like you being in charge." Patrick stumbles on an uneven part of the sidewalk and curses under his breath. His hand reaches out and grabs my arm for stability, righting himself before he can fall. "Where the hell are you leading me?"

"Keep your eyes closed for two more minutes," I say. "We're almost there."

We step off the escalator at L'Enfant Station, dodging someone with a violin and a stroller as we head up Seventh toward Independence. It's warm outside, the temperature steadily climbing toward uncomfortable, and I wipe a bead of sweat from my forehead. I can see our destination up ahead, the entrance gleaming under the late morning light.

"Okay." I stop us in front of the building and tap his shoulder. "Spin and open."

Patrick turns in a slow circle. He opens his eyes, squints, and parts his lips as he reads the small words on the top of the glass. "The Air and Space Museum?"

I squeal, unable to contain my excitement. "Surprise!"

"Lola." He looks at me over his shoulder, mouth wide and

jaw slackened. "How did you remember this? It's been on my bucket list since we were kids, but I haven't talked about visiting in ages."

"Not since we were in seventh grade science class and Mr. Parker showed us that video series on planets. You pinched me so hard and whispered about how neat it would be to see the stars. I remember everything you say, Patrick, and today, we're going to see the stars."

He blinks once, twice, then charges toward me, sweeping me off my feet in a tight embrace. My arms loop around his shoulders, drawn to him like a magnet. I laugh into the collar of his shirt—the blue one with melting popsicles on it—and I hear him laughing, too, rumbles of elation vibrating against my chest.

"This is incredible," he whispers in my ear. "You are incredible."

"I wanted to make you happy."

Patrick's smile is crooked and wide as he sets me on the sidewalk. He blinks again, and I think his eyes are glistening with tears. "It doesn't take much to make me happy," he says, stepping close, the toes of his shoes bumping against mine. "You're enough. I don't need anything else."

I snatch the words up and hold them close to my heart. Later, when I'm alone, I'll ruminate over them and weigh every syllable, every swoop of letters. I'll wonder if he knows he's enough to make me happy, and think of ways to prove to him that he is.

I feel warm and fuzzy, like it's the first snow of the year when everything is covered in a fresh blanket of white. When you're curled up on the couch with a mug of hot chocolate and a cozy quilt, watching the snowflakes fall and land on the window, each one different and uniquely beautiful.

It's perfect.

Every experience with Patrick, every memory we've ever

shared stands out, but this moment might be the most important one yet. The elation on his face is just for me. His exuberance is just for me, *because* of me, traversing a depth far greater than friendship.

I see the shift, and I feel it too, the gravitational pull toward a word, a definition, a title far different from the one we've held for two decades. It's slow and steady, a candle burning through the night until nothing but wax remains. Unhurried yet purposeful, the universe guiding us and nudging us along toward the peak of something powerful and remarkable.

My hand finds Patrick's, and he squeezes my palm. I tug him toward the main doors where a bored attendant at the turnstiles scans the tickets on my phone and hands us each a map.

We tumble inside the lobby, grateful for the air conditioning as we join the tour groups lined up against the walls. Children run by and their parents chase after them. An announcement comes over the public address system, reading off showtimes for the short films playing in the theaters. It's loud, it's chaotic, it's overstimulating, but I smile anyway.

How can I not? With the awe on Patrick's face and the reverence in his eyes, nothing in this entire world could ruin my mood. When he's happy, I'm happy, and right now he's full of pure joy.

"Hold on," I say.

I sidestep us out of the flow of traffic and pull my AirPods case from my purse. I hand one to Patrick and he puts it in his ear, laughter bursting out of him as a song plays.

"'Starman?'" he asks.

He's grinning, and it's my favorite face of his.

His Gleeful Face: unbridled bliss, teeth and eye wrinkles and the shake of his shoulders. The dip of his head and his palm against mine. It's beautiful, free, and vivacious, so perfectly *Patrick*. The day is young, and I'm close to exploding with delight. It's barely started, and we still have so much left to do, but I already know it will be cemented as one of the best days of our entire lives.

"Remember when you had your Bowie era? We watched *Labyrinth* every other night."

"My mom wouldn't let me get a lightning bolt tattoo. I was so pissed at her," he says.

"You were twelve, Patrick."

"So? Your mom let you dye your hair when you were twelve."

"With washable dye for Halloween. You know how furious she was when I dyed it for real at sixteen."

"Livid. She was livid," he says, recalling the time I hid in the treehouse until my parents went to sleep so I could avoid being grounded.

Patrick brought me a bowl of popcorn and a bag of M&M's, mixing them together while I asked if the streaks of pink were too dramatic. He shook his head and told me he really liked them. *Badass*, he said as he popped a kernel in his mouth. From that day on, I made the color a permanent fixture in my hair.

"She got over it eventually. Come on. I have a tour booked for us. We're getting special treatment today."

Our guide, Darla, takes us through the museum. She gives us detailed explanations about each exhibit and a behind-the-scenes look at the makings of models and interactive displays. We spend hours in rooms featuring the Wright Brothers and Destination Moon. We study the old Eastern Airlines airplane hanging from the rafters in the atrium, snapping a picture to send to my mom. Later, in the planetarium, Patrick almost falls out of his seat while we watch the film Worlds Beyond Earth, leaning over to whisper, *Aliens, Lola. I told you they were real.*

It's fun. *So much fun.*

I haven't laughed this hard in months, and my cheeks hurt from the sheer joy of it all. *This* is what I miss when I'm away and traveling. The excitement of experiencing something wonderful with someone you love.

We have lunch in the Mars Café, where we share a sandwich and an order of French fries. After, we part ways with Darla, going through the exhibits a second time at a leisurely pace. We read every placard, study every timeline, and take a picture at every photo spot, cheesing into the camera with our cheeks squished together.

It's late afternoon when we step back outside, the sun lower in the sky and the humidity burnt out of the air. Patrick pulls me into another full-body hug and refuses to let me go.

"I can't think of any other way I'd want to spend my day," he says.

"Hold that thought, pal. We're not finished yet," I answer.

"There's more?"

"One more thing, if you're up for it."

"With you, Lola, I'm up for anything."

He kisses the top of my hair, then my forehead and cheek in quick succession. It's far more affection than he normally shows me, slow to pull away and put space between us. I wait to see if it feels weird or uncomfortable, some shudder to run through me, but it never comes. It's the most natural thing in the world, like we should've been acting this way for years.

I like him.

I like him so much.

"I'm not sure how you can top my new favorite museum, but I'm excited to see what else you have up your sleeve." Patrick's voice catches on a laugh as we head away from downtown, out to where the bars are less crowded and the sidewalks are less busy.

His cheeks are fire red from the heat. There's dried sweat on our foreheads from miles of walking, and a fresh sunburn blooms on the back of my neck. We've taken the scenic route to our next destination, stopping for chocolate ice cream cones at the National Mall. Wandering into an independent bookstore and buying the one romance novel on the shelf we haven't read yet. Eating sandwiches from a food truck parked on the sidewalk —a BLT for Patrick and a grilled cheese for me.

"Almost there," I say.

I check my phone for the tenth time and see we're exactly where we need to be: outside a nondescript building. No markings on the door, no sign of what kind of business is on the other side. It looks unoccupied, forgotten in favor of the nicer, newer developments across the street like an apartment complex and health food store.

"Uh, Lo?" Patrick glances up at the facade and frowns. "I'm confused. Are you sure this is the right place?"

"Yup." I push open the door. A bell jingles over our heads, and I smile at the kid behind the counter. "Hey. We're here for a seven o'clock reservation. It should be under Jones."

"Lola," Patrick whispers. His fingers curl around my arm and his eyes dart around the room. There are no couches, no chairs, not even a television hanging in the corner. "Does this involve a cult? A sacrifice? I was kidding about the kidney thing, you know."

"You trust me, right?"

"I do, but that trust is waning slightly."

"Are you two going to do this or not?" The kid stares at us. The smell of pot lingers in the air, and the cell phone sitting on the registration desk lights up, a barrage of text messages flooding the screen.

He clearly wants to be anywhere but here.

"Yes," I say firmly. I drag Patrick to the counter and hand over my credit card.

"Great." There's no enthusiasm behind it. "Sign these waivers."

"*Waivers*?" Patrick repeats. "Lo, I'm sure I can get Henry on the phone and—"

"And interrupt his honeymoon? Yeah, right. Come on, Patrick. They're not asking you to sign in blood."

"We could," the kid says, and this is the first sign of life I've seen behind his eyes since we walked inside. "If that's what you're into."

"A pen is just fine," I say. "What are the rules?"

"You have ninety minutes. No phones allowed. You'll know when you get shot. Ten lives each. If dark and confined spaces aren't for you, I'd leave now. Oh, and watch out for Hank. He shows no mercy, especially not to newcomers."

I nod and put my signature on the paper, not bothering to read the fine print. I sign for Patrick too, because I know he's not going to be willing to scribble on a legally binding document.

Damn the repercussions.

"Any description of Hank?"

"He wears pink. Aim for his left side."

"Got it."

"Head to the next room and pick out your gear. In case of an emergency, break the glass on the wall. Hopefully someone comes to help," the kid says.

"Great. Thanks." I drag Patrick by the arm to the door before he can ask any more questions. The museum was hard to keep secret, but this has been nearly impossible.

"You have twenty seconds to tell me what's going on before I pick you up, throw you over my shoulder, and get us the hell out of here, Lola Jones," Patrick hisses.

"What do you always say you want to do when you retire from education?"

"Open up an escape room or join a laser tag league."

"And what's your favorite movie?"

"*National Treasure*, but I'm not sure how that applies to the situation we've found ourselves in. We're watching out for a guy named Hank in a building I'm suddenly realizing has no windows."

"What if I told you we're about to embark on a once-in-a-lifetime quest?"

"To *death*?"

"Oh, for heaven's sake. It's a *National Treasure* escape room with laser tag."

He blinks once, then twice, dark eyelashes fanning out. His mouth drops open. "You're fucking with me."

"Nope."

"You found a place that combines three of my most favorite things in the world?"

"The only one of its kind."

"*Fuck,* you're amazing." He grabs a vest off the wall and sends four others flying to the floor. He slides it over my head, a glint in his eyes as he attaches the Velcro across my chest, making it nice and snug before humming in approval. "Pretty," he says. His thumb traces down the line of my jaw.

My back arches. I stand on my tiptoes to get closer to him. "What?" I ask. "Me in a laser tag vest?"

"In a laser tag vest. Not in a laser tag vest. You always, Lola." His knuckles brush against my cheek, and I let out a sigh as my heart races in my chest. "Buckle up, buttercup. I'm going to enjoy the hell out of this."

———

"WATCH YOUR RIGHT SIDE," Patrick barks out from behind me. "You only have one life left."

"I see him," I answer.

I roll out of the way of imminent danger, bruising my ribs but successfully avoiding the hit. Hank and his team are *ruthless.*

They're a gang of four middle-aged men who spend their days challenging cocky teenagers to a round of laser tag and mopping the floor with them.

Patrick and I are giving them a run for their money, a crowd allegedly forming on the other side of the two-way mirror. I can hear the cheers when we advance closer to our target—a fake copy of the Declaration of Independence—and the groans when we lose another life. It's been eighty-five minutes of running, jumping and strenuous physical activity, and we're so close to the finish line. To victory.

"Dammit," someone curses from around a corner. "She's too close."

"Go, Lola, go," Patrick bellows.

I forgot how competitive he is. All those years he played baseball in high school and won the state tournament are coming back with a vengeance. I thought he tore his ACL earlier, watching as he gripped his calf after he jumped to safety behind a wall. He shooed me away when I asked if he wanted to tap out, gritted his teeth, and took off again.

"Almost there," I murmur, reaching my hand out to grab the corner of the laminated replica of one of our nation's most important documents. It nearly slips from my grasp but I hold on to it tight, tucking it close to my body.

The house lights kick on, industrial-sized bulbs brightening the space in an instant. I don't have time to react to the sudden change before I'm scooped into Patrick's arms.

"We won. You were *incredible*," he says. "My laser tag superstar."

"Me?" I poke his chest, the shirt damp with sweat and suctioned to his body. "I haven't seen you move that fast since 2003, when an ice cream truck came down our street and you pushed a toddler out of the way for a popsicle."

There's a bruise under his eye where he got elbowed, the

skin already turning a nasty shade of purple, a small gash below his hairline after losing a battle with a door, and a cut on his elbow, just above his funny bone. The wounds don't hold a candle to his megawatt smile, the most dazzling thing I've ever seen.

"We need a time machine so I can go back and do that again and again," Patrick says.

"I think you need to amend your post-retirement plans. If the escape room doesn't have any laser tag or semi-professionals chasing you around every corner, is it even worth it?"

"The barrel roll was impressive, Lo. A game changer."

"Hey, you two." Hank approaches us and unbuckles his pink vest. He's flanked by the other guys in his group, all wearing pink too. An homage to his wife who's recovering from breast cancer, he told us before the game with misty eyes, and I could tell right away that he's one of the good ones. "Congratulations. No one has solved the clues that fast in ages. Our winning streak was close to five hundred matches."

"I have so many questions about how you all are so stealthy," I say.

Hank winks. "If I told you, I'd have to kill you." He looks at Patrick. "You and your girlfriend are a lot of fun. Come back anytime, free of charge. I'll make sure my nephew gets you set up with the gold membership card."

"Are we joining a secret society?" I whisper to Patrick.

"We're going to have to come back every year," he whispers back. "Make it a tradition." He reaches out and shakes Hank's hand, not bothering to correct him on the girlfriend title. I like how it sounds. "We appreciate the hospitality. Drinks and dinner are on me at the bar I saw around the corner if you all feel up for it even though we kicked your ass."

There's a round of rousing laughter. We hang up our vests and rack the guns. The kid from the front desk gives us two VIP cards and we make our way outside. My heart skips a beat as Patrick's hand finds mine and it skips another as he swings our arms back and forth, the rowdy group heading down the sidewalk toward food.

He keeps his hand on my leg at the high-top table after we split a basket of onion rings, his fingers tracing a pattern on my knee. I can't focus on the stories the group of men are sharing about their former Secret Service days.

I'm too distracted by the way Patrick hooks his foot around the leg of my stool. He drags me closer, an emblem of happiness in a warm room with too many people, too much noise, but the perfect amount of *him*.

EIGHTEEN

PATRICK

OUR FIRST STOP when we get back on the road in the morning is Sweet Holes—a Mom and Pop donut shop outside Fredericksburg, Virginia. We order half a dozen before Lola adds a second box, wanting to try one of every flavor.

I moan around the bite of the honey-glazed pastry, ignoring the crumbs that fall on my shorts. The passenger door opens and Lola climbs inside, two large Styrofoam cups settled safely in the crook of her arm.

"Large coffee with one cream and half a packet of sugar." She hands over my drink with a disgusted grimace. "Why don't you just drink a cup of tar?"

"Tar tastes too good." I knock my drink against her cup of tea in a cheers, and we take a sip in tandem. "Hurry and try these donuts. They're fantastic."

"Which flavor do I start with? This is overwhelming."

"The hardest decision you'll have to make today. Do powdered sugar."

Lola glances over at me, her hand halfway to the box, and frowns at the bruise around my eye. "You look like you were in a fight."

"Worth it, though."

"Do you need some ice for your cheek?"

"Nah, I'm fine."

"Any sign of a headache popping up?"

"Nope. We're in the clear."

I shift the Jeep into drive and pull out of the gravel parking lot. It's hard not to yawn as we set off on the highway, sleep-deprived after closing down the bar with Hank and his buddies last night. We listened to their life stories until the early morning, the bartender all but throwing us out on the sidewalk.

Lola fell asleep the second her head hit the hotel pillow, not bothering to take off her sneakers or wash her face. I unlaced her sneakers and collapsed next to her, getting a few hours of shuteye before our alarms went off just after sunrise. It was a struggle to get moving, loading our bags into the back of the car in disorganized disarray. I wouldn't be surprised if I forgot a sock —or half my sanity—in that hotel room.

"These donuts are the best thing I've ever tasted," Lola says around a monstrous bite. "I'm rejuvenated. I need a hundred of them."

"Twelve is all you have. Better ration them out."

She lets out a tiny whine and licks her fingers clean of sugar. I try not to watch her tongue as it darts out of her mouth, but I fail miserably, a lecherous idiot gawking at her from across the car.

"Want to play a game?" she asks, wiping her lips with the back of her hand.

"What kind of game?" I answer, my eyes regretfully darting back to the road.

"It's a question game of things to ask your road trip partner to make sure they aren't a serial killer."

"Oddly specific. Sure. Let's hear one."

"What's your favorite Christmas present?"

"That's going to determine if I'm a serial killer?"

"It might, like if you say a lump of coal or a pair of socks."

"I love getting socks as gifts," I say, and Lola raises her eyebrows. "All right. Favorite Christmas present. That's easy. The autographed baseball cards you got me. Hands down the coolest thing I've ever received."

"David Ortiz and Tony Gwynn. Do you still have them or did you toss them out when they retired?"

"Did I—*Lola*. They're my most prized possession. I'd never get rid of them."

They sit on my desk at school in a tiny frame, right next to the photo of me and Lola on Halloween our sophomore year of high school. We went as Meg and Hades from the *Hercules* movie, winning the costume contest and a fifty-dollar gift card to Olive Garden.

"That's not saying a lot, Patrick. You never get rid of anything."

"Fair." I laugh. "But those are important. What about you? Best Christmas present?"

"The special edition of *Pride and Prejudice* you got me."

I grin. I mowed lawns every weekend for six months straight to save up enough money to buy her the book. She used to check it out from the library regularly to reread, and I thought she ought to have her own copy. I bought myself one too.

"Did you know that was the first book you ever read to me?"

"Really?" she asks.

"Yup. I didn't ask you to. You just did. It was raining and we were sitting in the treehouse with nothing to do. You opened the cover, started reading to me about Pemberley, and you never stopped."

"I talked a lot as a kid."

"I liked it. We balanced each other out."

"Look at us. Hundreds of books later," she says.

"We really branched out with our preferences and tastes. Aliens. Stalkers. Werewolves. Who cares? We'll read it all."

"Don't forget the time my mom found that old regency book hiding under my pillow. The cover with the shirtless guy. *Her Salacious Night with the Insatiable Duke.* God, I was mortified when she sat me down and tried to have *the talk.*"

"You avoided your kitchen table for a week," I say. "My mom didn't know why you were joining us for every meal."

"Ah, the good ole days. Kathy would really panic if she found out what I read now."

"What's next on your question list?" I ask.

"What's your favorite memory?"

"This is a walk down nostalgia lane." I drum my fingers on the steering wheel. "Favorite memory. That's also easy: the day I met you."

"Stop it," Lola says. "Be serious."

"I am being serious."

"Of all the great things you've done in life and all your accomplishments, you're picking that day in July?"

"Given the fact that you've been a catalyst for a lot of those great things, yeah," I say. "I am."

She stares at me. Her fingers play with the ends of her friendship bracelet, spinning the string around and around her wrist.

"I've never told you this, but I wasn't happy before I met you," she says. "I was angry a lot. I felt like I had all this energy inside of me I couldn't let out. I never had someone who wanted to hang out with me, and making friends was hard. I wanted to be liked by other kids, but I was afraid of what they'd see when they got to know me. Deep down, I thought there was something wrong with me. My brain felt wired wrong. My emotions felt wired wrong. Then I met you, and I couldn't stop smiling. I felt different. Lighter. That energy went into our friendship. I felt like I belonged. Like I had a place in this world. You made me feel right. And I've kept feeling right in all the years since."

I reach over and find her hand, squeezing her fingers tightly with my own so she knows how much I mean these next words.

"Your brain is my favorite brain, Lola. You see things others don't, and that's *special*. Before you came along, I was too quiet to make friends and too shy to care that I didn't have anyone to spend time with. Then you walked across your yard and came into my life and... that kind of changed everything, didn't it? I had been so very alone and then suddenly, I wasn't. I haven't been alone since, and I know I never will be again. That's why meeting you is my favorite memory."

I love you, I should add, but I don't. We drive on, my heart dangerously close to falling out of my chest.

———

"NOW THIS IS SOME FRESH AIR." Lola stretches out her arms and ducks under a branch, brushing a clump of bark from her hair. "Look at the trees. Look at the lake. It's so serene."

I kill the ignition of the Jeep and jump out. My feet hit the dirt and I take a deep breath. There's a shift out here in the mountains, buried behind rows of trees and singing songbirds. A steadiness and calmness in the breeze and running creek. The rustle of leaves and the smell of campfires left behind.

"Let's move here," I say. "I'll build us a big log cabin. We could have s'mores and jacket potatoes every night. Our friends would visit, right?"

"They'd visit, but they wouldn't stay. Your snoring would keep them awake for hours."

"Says the woman I had to shake away this morning when our alarms went off. Didn't seem to bother you too much."

I purposely leave out how we've woken up the past two days

—with her leg thrown over my hip, my hand under her knee, her head on my chest, and my arms wrapped firmly around her waist.

The pillow barrier I built to separate our sides lasted all of three seconds. I don't know who moved first, her or me—me, probably, if I'm being honest with myself—but we gravitated toward each other in the night, moths to a flame.

I feel calm with Lola in my arms. Like I have a purpose, a reason to break from my regimented routine. I haven't worked out since we left Boston because leaving her alone in bed sounded a lot less enjoyable than staying under the covers and savoring the warmth. Relishing the press of her body to mine. Her soft inhales and exhales and how she clutched my shirt in her unconscious state.

I could've watched her sleep for hours. I was scared to move, afraid I'd wake her and destroy the dream world we were existing in, one where I could hold her close and protect her from all the daunting parts of life.

There's nothing special about a shitty hotel room in Arlington, Virginia at four in the morning.

With her?

With her, it was fucking magic.

I ignore that yank in my chest as I watch her pick flowers from a patch of weeds, the sputter of my heart when she tucks one behind her ear. It's hard to look away and unload the camping supplies, but I do it anyway. The tent, two sleeping bags, some food we bought at the Walmart Supercenter ten miles down the road where our cell phone service went out. A head lamp, a lantern, supplies for s'mores.

We search for a spot to set up for the night, landing on an area near the water, at the top of the slope, behind a line of bushes with flat ground and a handful of sticks and piles of rocks. Secluded, quiet, and perfect.

Lola grabs a bag from me and pulls the tent out. She scrunches her nose and flips it upside down, then right side up.

"You know how to put this together, right?" she asks.

"I do, but it's time to show off your mountaineering skills."

"I spent all my time at camp in the arts and crafts room. Friendship bracelets were the priority, not learning how to survive in the wilderness."

I hold up my arm and the bracelet she made for me all those years ago slides down my wrist. It matches hers, the same color and style. A birthday present, she wrote in her note with hearts over the i's, telling me she would understand if I didn't want to wear it and risk being teased by my cabin mates.

I put it on the minute I tore open the envelope.

I forgot about it at first, leaving it on in the swimming pool and during baseball games. For high school graduation, then college graduation too. We've altered the jewelry over the years, extending the string and cutting off the frayed pieces. It's become a part of me, a physical representation of my friendship with Lola.

Two people tied together, lasting as long as the twine. I don't think I'll ever take it off. Maybe I'll be buried with it. Long after my heart stops beating, she'll still be a part of me.

"We should make new ones," I say. "This one definitely has mold on it."

"Adds to the character," she says. "What do you tell people who ask about it?"

"The truth." I shrug and set the lantern and sleeping bags on the ground. A patch of dirt kicks up on my shins, and I crouch down to search for the tent stakes. "That you made it for me."

"Do the women you date care?"

"About the bracelet?"

"Yeah."

I remember the night Jessica asked if she could cut off the

jewelry, and how I curled my fingers around my wrist, protecting the pieces of string. She didn't understand the sentiment behind it or why I wanted to hold on to something from when I was a kid.

Because Lola made it for me, I shouted. A rare burst of anger slipped out at the thought of severing the symbolic representation of my friendship I had worn for years.

Because you're in love with her, she shouted back.

We never talked about the bracelet again.

Jessica withdrew and I withdrew, until finally, us not being together made a lot more sense than trying to salvage a relationship that neither one of us wanted to save. We broke up four days later.

The breakup was a moment of clarity. An awakening that told me unless I was with Lola, I would never truly be happy.

I had played off my attraction to her for years, assuming it was a crush from childhood carrying over to adulthood because she was always around. We spent all our time together, and she gave me attention. She touched me and when she tossed a smile my way, my insides turned to mush.

It'll fade over time, I told myself in my twenties, and again at the start of my thirties. *When you meet someone new.*

I've met plenty of someone's. I've had numbers slipped into my pocket and first dates. Tons of maybes, but no yeses.

Because none of them are her.

I've tried so hard to fight it. I've tried to prevent myself from falling for my best friend, but I'm weak. I'm weak and I failed and I couldn't help myself. She's too wonderful, too goddamn perfect to ignore.

I do love Lola.

I love her with everything I have, and I think I've always loved her. I love her more than anything else in this world, and I know I'll never date another woman ever again. I can't give anyone else a piece of my heart. Not when Lola owns the whole damn thing. It wouldn't be fair.

If that means ending up alone and existing in the state of best friends forever, then so be it.

I'm going to tell her. I *need* to tell her. Keeping a secret from her is the last thing I ever want to do, but I want her to figure out her feelings on her own. Unaided, without pressure from how I might be thinking. She has to be the one to decide what's going to make her the happiest, even if it hurts me in the process.

"Some of them have cared, yes," I say after seconds of silence. There's no point in lying to her. "But I don't want to be with someone who doesn't respect our friendship and the history we have."

"Oh," Lola says. A frown seeps through the word, harsh and brittle. I shield my eyes and glance up at her. The late afternoon sun frames her face like a halo, and she's biting her lip, deep in thought. "Did you know I was mad at you when you introduced us to Jessica?"

"What? Why?"

"You lied to me. You were keeping your new relationship a big secret, and then when you finally shared what was going on in your life, you told everyone else at the same time you told me. It made me feel like you were hiding it, like you didn't want me to know." She waves her hands and crouches beside me. "It's in the past. No big deal."

"Hey. No. I'm sorry I ever made you feel that way. That was shitty. I was afraid to tell you about her. It meant we would spend less time together. You always pull back when I'm dating someone. We hang out less, talk less. It was selfish of me to want to hold on to you a little while longer."

"I pull back because I don't want the woman you're dating to get the wrong idea or think I'm going to swoop in and try to steal you from them. Men and women can be friends with no romantic undertones to their relationship," Lola says, sounding frustrated.

"Of course they can. But what happens when there are romantic undertones?" I ask.

"I don't... I don't know." Lola wipes her hands on her overalls, a handprint of dirt staining the denim. She's puzzled by my question. "That changes things. Can you still be friends with someone after you've been with them in a non-friendly way?"

"We kissed—almost kissed, I guess, if we're being honest— and we're doing okay. That was far past friendly."

She jerks her chin up and stares at me. "You don't consider that a kiss?"

"No."

"Was it bad?"

"What? No, it wasn't bad."

"Then why don't you consider it a kiss?"

"Because if I kissed you for real, Lola, it would be intentional. It would mean something. It wouldn't be a half-second, accidental graze in some cramped room because we were both turning different ways. It would be special. Carefully planned and Hollywood-level. A display of sickening affection, so the whole damn world knows you're mine. It would last long enough to figure out what you like and what you don't like." I lean forward, eliminating the free space between us until the air grows thick and heavy. "And then I'd do it again because I *could,* because I wanted to."

Her eyes bounce to my mouth and linger there for a half second before darting away. "Well," she says. Her voice squeaks and she drops a stake to the ground. The metal rolls away, down a small ravine toward the water. "That's good to know."

"Very good to know."

"It's better than fine," she answers, and I snort out a laugh.

I've flustered her by laying it all out there, by showing her my hand and putting the ball in her court. She knows what I want. It's time for her to decide what *she* wants, and *fuck*, I hope it's me.

I grab the mallet by my thighs. "Can you hold the stakes steady? We should get everything up before nightfall."

"What? Oh. Sure. No problem." She sits up on her knees and grabs another pole. "Like this?"

"Atta girl," I say, and she flushes deep scarlet, pretty shades of pink on her neck.

"Promise not to hurt me?" she asks.

Her eyes meet mine. She has dirt on her forehead and fresh freckles span over the bridge of her nose. Here we are, surrounded by incredible nature, incredible scenery, incredible displays of how big and vast the world is, and I can't look at the trees. I can't look at the water or the birds flying overhead.

I can only look at her, and I've never seen anything so fucking beautiful in my entire life. I could search for a thousand years, and I still wouldn't find anything as breathtaking as Lola Jones.

There's a meaning behind her question, fear clear in her tone. She's not talking about the stakes or the mallet. Neither am I when I whisper, "Never," so softly it gets snatched up by the breeze.

NINETEEN
LOLA

"PATRICK WALKER, if you throw me in that water, our friendship is over," I bellow, putting my hands on my hips. "Do you hear me? *Over.*"

He grins at me from the other side of the picnic table, his palms splayed out on the wood. I'm cornered, nowhere to go as I try to move left, then right, frantically searching for an escape.

Jumping into a lake with icy mountain water seemed like a good idea thirty minutes ago. That was when we were busy wrestling with a tent that didn't want to cooperate and sweating under the late afternoon sun.

Now I'm tired and hungry, ready to make the soft tacos we bought ingredients for back in town. I want a shower and a campfire. A sleeping bag where I can rest my head for a few hours before we get up early and hit the road again tomorrow.

Patrick ran and jumped off a long fishing dock without a care in the world as soon as we got our site set up. I've never heard someone holler as loud as he did when he plunged under the water, coming up for a breath with drenched hair and a deep laugh.

"Really, Lola? Twenty-four years of friendship gone because

of a little water?" He shakes his head and droplets fling from the end of his hair, landing on my arms. "Seems a little dramatic."

"It's not a little water, you nut. It's the whole damn lake, and it's freezing cold."

"It's ninety degrees outside. It'll feel good."

"Is that why you screamed? Because it felt *good*?"

"It invigorated me. I'm soaking up the greatness of life. One of those you-only-live-once moments."

"No. We're not bringing back that phrase. It's staying in—"

I don't get a chance to finish my sentence.

Patrick moves like a viper, darting around the table and grabbing me by the waist. He hauls me over his shoulder and jogs toward the water.

"Oops," he says without a hint of remorse, and I can hear the grin in his voice.

"Put me down," I squeal. I swat at his back with half-assed effort, giving up after two taps to his broad shoulders. "You're going to hurt yourself carrying me, and I don't know how to drive a stick shift."

"Fuck that," Patrick says. It sounds like a growl from the back of his throat, his voice turning deep. His hand tightens around my leg and slides farther up my skin. His touch is no longer in a safe zone near my knees but moving steadily closer to my hips, a spot that treads toward intimate. "You're light as shit. And if you don't stop talking so poorly about yourself, we're going to have a problem."

"Yeah?" I challenge, wanting to play with fire. "What kind of problem?"

"I've forgotten how much of a smart ass you can be," he says.

"You've never hated it before."

He moves his fingers up, up, up, until *oh.*

They press into the curve of my ass, the bare skin not

covered by the fabric of my swimsuit, a spot he's never come close to touching in the past.

Heat races through me, and I think I might be burning alive. Patrick's fingers stay there for a fraction of a second, gauging my reaction.

I like it, I want to scream.

Do it again, I want to add.

I'd like for him to drag his thumb across my stomach. Over my ribs and across my breasts. I want him to pull the straps of my bathing suit down and kiss my shoulder and my throat.

"I still don't hate it. I'm thinking about all the things I could do to that mouth of yours if you don't drop the self-deprecation. Don't test me," he says in warning.

A second later we're airborne, soaring off the dock and into the water.

It's frigid, and it feels like tiny little needles are stabbing my limbs. The air leaves my lungs and a shriek tries to escape from my mouth. I'm disoriented, unsure of my surroundings, and my vision blurs. I jerk my chin up and see the light above us growing brighter and brighter until we finally break free to the surface.

"Shit," Patrick curses. He slides me down the front of his body until I can wrap my legs around his middle. "Are you okay? I didn't mean for you to go in upside down. I'm sorry, Lo. I wasn't thinking."

Water sluices down his arms. He pushes the hair matted to my forehead off my face and touches my cheek, reverence and care embedded in the press of his fingertips. He moves to the pulse point on my neck, watching the rise and fall of my chest. I open my mouth, take a breath, and burst out laughing.

"Oh my god," I wheeze. "You are such an asshole, but that was so much fun."

"Did you hit your head?"

"Stop." I laugh and put a hand on his chest, the skin dusted with fine hair already warming under the glow of the sun. His heart races under my palm. "You held onto me the entire time. I wasn't worried."

"Are you sure you're okay? Did you scratch your hands on any rocks?"

"I'm fine, Patrick. Really. You were right, it is invigorating."

"I was worried," he says.

"That's karma for acting like an idiot. A fun idiot, but still an idiot. I like road trip Patrick. He's daring."

"Daring and stupid."

"You can't win 'em all. You look like a drowned rat."

"You look like a drowned raccoon," he answers. He walks us toward the shore, the water becoming shallower and receding from our bodies. "Want me to set you down?"

"You made such a big deal about carrying me. We might as well keep the chivalry going. Can I stay here?"

"For as long as you'd like," he says.

I let out a content sigh and close my eyes. I hold my arms out to the side and bask in the heat on my face. "This is nice."

"What are you thinking about? You look pensive."

"Pensive," I repeat. "That's a good principal word."

"Part of the training for the job is reading the dictionary every night," he says.

"I can't tell if you're kidding or not."

"I'm being serious, Lola. Very serious."

I blink my eyes open and glance at his handsome face, only to find him looking right back at me. Drops of water hang on the tip of his nose and he's smiling.

Of course he's smiling; Patrick is *always* smiling.

His Happy Face.

I shift my gaze to the sky, the open water, and the tall trees.

The sun dipping behind the peaks of the slate-gray mountains and the smoke rising from the fires started by other campers.

"I'm thinking about how lucky we are," I say, matching his smile. "Of all the places on Earth we could be, all the thousands and thousands of miles of land and paths our lives could have taken, we've somehow ended up right here, right now. Happy and healthy, having the time of our lives. Together." I laugh and tilt my head back, the ends of my hair skimming the top of the water. "What a gift."

When I'm with Patrick, nothing else matters. I think I can take on the world, no fears, no hesitations. I can soar and spread my wings, be anything I want and know that he'd support me, no matter what dream I wanted to chase.

We should talk about that accidental kiss during the wedding and how he laid out in great detail how he would kiss me *for real*. I should ask what he wants to do to my mouth. Or I could play it safe and talk about our plans for tomorrow and when to put on another coat of sunscreen.

Should, should, should. So many things we *should* talk about, but I don't want to.

Speaking, having any of those conversations, will pull us out of this moment. This precious moment of being in a place so grand and so beautiful, with the person I care about more than anything in the world.

I want to enjoy it a little while longer.

Forever, if I can.

———

"WHAT ABOUT THAT ONE?" I ask, pointing up to the night sky.

"Ursa Major," Patrick says. He takes my hand and guides me through the shape of the constellation. "There's the Big Dipper."

"I've never seen so many stars before. Where do they all hide?"

"Away from the city. They're much easier to see with no light pollution." He moves my hand up, his thumb caressing over my knuckles. "That's Polaris, the North Star."

"It's beautiful," I whisper.

"Yeah," he says. "It is."

I turn my head and find Patrick looking at me, his face painted in silvers and grays from the full moon. Hooded eyes traverse over my face, from my forehead down to my chin, and his smile grows wider and wider the longer he stares at me.

He's not talking about the stars.

I'm not sure I am either at this point because he burns brighter and hotter than any of the celestial bodies, thousands of little lights twinkling and flickering above us.

I make a wish on one, a hope and a prayer that we can stay like this forever, a perfect moment suspended in time. Just us, side by side, like we've always been. Patrick and Lola, the best of friends, both ready to take that step to something *more*, something as beautiful and vast as the constellations above.

"Did you have a good day?" I ask him.

"The best day." He flexes his palm over the back of my hand and loops his fingers around mine. "The s'mores were the icing on the cake."

"You and your burnt marshmallows." I stick out my tongue. "Disgusting."

"You're the heathen who eats them uncooked. What's the point?"

"The point is texture, Patrick." I prop up on my elbow and look down at him. "Can I ask you a question? I've been thinking about it for the last week or so."

"This wide-open space might as well be our own truth or

truth game." He drops our hands and puts his arms behind his head, staring at the heavens above. "Ask away."

"It's personal. I know we share everything with each other, but this might be something you want to keep to yourself."

"Doesn't change my answer. You know I'll tell you anything."

"You and Jessica looked happy together. She was perfect for you. I know you only dated for a few weeks, but did you love her?"

"I loved her as a person, but I knew right away I could never be in love with her. There's a big difference between the two when it comes to relationships. She could tell I wasn't all in. It wasn't intentional or mean, I just wasn't present. Not in the way a partner should be."

"You could never be mean," I say.

"That's one of my flaws. I'm too nice. I'm afraid to let people down or hurt someone, and I dragged out my time with Jessica for weeks too long. I should've let her go earlier. I should've never asked her out in the first place. It would've made her happier instead of giving her false hope."

"I didn't think there was a difference between loving someone and being in love with someone until my last relationship. That's when I learned you could care for someone deeply without being out of your mind for them."

"That was Simon, right? The fucker whose nose I broke?"

"His name was Steven, but close."

"It's been eleven years. Cut me some slack."

"I was going through the motions with him. Even before the breakup, I could tell he wasn't who I was going to spend forever with. My heart didn't skip a beat when he looked at me. I didn't miss him when he was gone. When he broke up with me, I didn't have any room in my heart to be angry. I didn't care. I was too busy being sad about my dad. It made it easier to see that if I wasn't angry over someone hurting me, they weren't the kind worth fighting for."

"The ones worth fighting for will never make you angry in the first place," Patrick says. "Mad, yeah. Irritated and annoyed as hell? Of course. But never angry. Anger isn't love."

Silence settles around us. It's the comfortable kind, where you don't feel you have to say anything else or stretch a conversation past its end point. You can exist with another person, content to just *be*.

Quiet usually puts me on edge, my mind working in overdrive as it thinks about all the things I need to accomplish. The need to get up and move, the inability to sit still. With Patrick, I welcome the quiet and the calm. It's a change. A *good* change.

There's another question on the tip of my tongue, but I'm hesitant to learn the answer. If my thoughts on dating can change, so can Patrick's. His dreams might have dimmed. He might feel like he's been burned too many times, leaving him jaded and ready to throw in the towel.

I draw my legs to my chest and drop my chin to my knees. "I have something else I want to ask," I say tentatively, nerves clawing at my back.

"I know you do. You're so easy to read, Lola."

"Do you still think your person is out there? You haven't given up on finding love, have you?"

His lips pull into a smile, and he sits up. "Can I tell you a secret?"

"You can tell me anything, Patrick."

"She's out there. I have hope."

"What's that phrase you and the guys use? It's the hope that kills you?"

"You're hitting these sports metaphors out of the park. The phrase is right, but I don't like it for this scenario. What's the point of doing anything—chasing a dream or going after something you want—if you don't believe in it? So I had a failed relationship. Big deal. People break up every day. My person—nah. Fuck that. Person is too insignificant of a word to describe her. My *soulmate* is out there. She's the other half of my heart, made specifically for me. *Just* for me. Custom ordered. It's why it hasn't worked out with anyone else. And I don't care how long it takes for her to realize it and for us to be together. This year, next year, two decades from now. Hell, when we're seventy-five. I'm a patient man. One day, it's going to happen. She's worth the wait."

I hear the certainty and conviction in his words.

I see that small smile tugging at his lips—the same one he gives me when he thinks I'm not paying attention. The softness behind his eyes and the way he looks at me is not like I'm one in a million, not even like I'm one in a billion, but like I'm the *only one* in the entire world.

"That's good, Patrick. Lovely to hear," I say. "I'm so happy for you."

At least, I think I say it.

I can't be sure, because he's staring at me so rapturously, so blindingly, I have to glance away. He's the sun and I'm Icarus, flying far too close and at risk of getting burned.

I might burst into a thousand tiny pieces the longer he stares, and I *want to*. I want to split myself in two, so one part of me is always with him, and he's always with me too.

Soulmate.

He has a *soulmate*, a certified fact, and *god*, I've never wanted to be something so bad to someone in my life. Forget the fear, forget the numbness of being left behind. *I want that*, the all-encompassing love and a foreverness of *good* and *hope*.

I want it with *him*.

With him, I wouldn't be afraid.

"Hey." Patrick's voice pulls me to the present. Concern laces his tone, and he touches my shoulder. "Where'd you go?"

I shake my head. I stare at the trees past his shoulder, the edge of a deep, dark forest. "Nowhere."

His eyebrows wrinkle together, and his smile slips into a frown. He can tell I'm lying but he lets me have my secret, just like he has his.

"Can I ask you a question now?"

"Seems only fair," I say.

"The accidental kiss at the wedding."

My cheeks flush. I pick up a stick and break off a twig. "What about it?"

"Would you do it again? Purposely this time?"

I drag my gaze back to him. I see the vulnerability in asking. My answer will change the dynamics of our relationship, and Patrick's letting me be the one to decide how this plays out.

Friends? Or something more.

I inhale a breath of courage and nod, a single bob of my head. "Yes," I whisper.

"Would you do it with me?"

"I would."

"Ah." Patrick nods. He runs his hand through his hair, ash from our campfire falling from the brown strands. "That's good to know."

"Yeah." I smile and tip my head back to the sky, a weight lifting off my shoulders with the admission. "It is good to know."

TWENTY

LOLA

I SHIVER in my sleeping bag, cursing myself for not grabbing my sweatshirt out of the Jeep before we went to bed.

The inside of the tent is freezing, cool mountain air sneaking in through the half-open zipper. I miss the afternoon sunshine and the campfire, desperately wishing I had put on an extra layer of clothing. I need something more substantial than the thin T-shirt I'm wearing and the pair of socks with holes in the heels on my feet.

The Jeep is only a few yards away. I wonder if I could slip out without waking Patrick up. I could pull on my shoes and—

There's movement behind me, the shift of nylon and polyester, and then a hand folds over my shoulder.

"What's wrong?" Patrick asks. His voice is rough, a man half-dead to the world and woken up by his obnoxious tent mate who can't sit still.

"Sorry," I say. "I'm just cold."

"C'mere," he mumbles. It's slightly slurred, a delirious invitation to move closer as he unzips his sleeping bag and gently tugs the ends of my hair.

"And do what?" I ask. "Share?"

"Yeah." His hand dances down my arm and rests on my hip. He presses into the exposed sliver of skin under the hem of my shirt, and I hear him inhale sharply. "Sweetheart. You're freezing."

Sweetheart.

The endearment makes my head spin. It's a precious word I tuck alongside the time he called me *love*, another middle-of-the-night meeting with lowered inhibitions that left me starry-eyed. I like this collection of affection I'm gathering from him, and I wonder what else I could add.

"I'm fine," I say. "Go back to sleep. We have a long day tomorrow with lots of driving."

I turn to face him. Even in the shadows of the night, I can make out his sharp features vividly. The dimples on his cheeks and the spot on his lips where his smile likes to sit. Dark eyebrows and tan skin.

"Get in here, Lola, or I'm going to make you."

It's the same way he spoke to me earlier in the lake, and a twist of heat settles between my legs with the fierce tone. It's a departure from the way he usually talks, kindness gone and replaced with a demand behind the words. I've never heard him so pushy, so determined to get his point across. There's no teasing or joking, and I understand this is an argument I cannot win.

I kick off my sleeping bag and shimmy across the ground until my chest connects with his. He's shirtless, bare skin and a human furnace I want to nestle into and stay for a while. His chest is sturdy, a study of masculinity. Like a great Renaissance sculptor carved him out of fine marble, a chisel to create his perfect form.

"Spin," Patrick says, the sharpness abating and ebbing toward the compassionate side of him I know so well. "Back to front."

"Bossy," I mumble.

"With you and your well-being, I'm always going to be bossy, Lola."

Well *shit*, that's hot as hell.

I turn and shift and bend until I find a comfortable position on my side. One foot crossed over the other, knees to my chest. My cheek is against the small cushion in the sleeping bag that tries to call itself a pillow, and I do my best not to squirm as Patrick's arm snakes around my waist. His palm splays out across my stomach, pinky running along the waistband of my pajama shorts.

He's been more open with his touches on this trip. Purposely physical, with subtle grazes of his body against mine that have me close to panting. It's nothing downright scandalous, just enough to drive me wild and put ideas in my head. Imagining his hand sliding further up. My hand sliding down. Wondering how well we would fit together and knowing it would *work*.

"Here's where all the warmth was hiding," I joke.

"You should've woken me up."

"You were sleeping soundly. I think I heard you mumble something about a parrot."

"Don't care." His words ghost over the shell of my ear and he pulls me closer. I can feel every inch of him, his body aligned perfectly with mine. "I always want you to wake me up when you can't sleep. Because you're cold. Or I'm snoring too loudly."

"Let's pretend I didn't wake you up. You woke *me* up with your sawing logs."

"Whatever you have to tell yourself. Are you more comfortable?"

"Yes." I sigh. "I'm perfect. Thank you for coming to my rescue. I'm learning you do that a lot."

"Not rescuing," he mumbles. "Helping. There's a difference."

"And what's that?"

"Rescuing implies you're incapable, which isn't true. You're very capable. You just need someone by your side now and then. A sidekick, if you will."

"We could go on tour. Start a comedy club or fight some crime," I say.

"Knock 'em out with laughs or a sucker punch. They'll never know what hit them."

"Oh, boy. Here come the dad jokes."

"My best content comes in the middle of the night," he teases.

"I have a habit of keeping you awake, don't I?"

"Don't care. Don't mind. That's what friends do."

"Keep each other awake?" I ask.

"And stay awake to listen," he says.

"Then you're my very best friend. I need a few minutes, then I promise I'll be asleep. It takes my brain a while to shut off." I pause and reach for his hand, wrapping our fingers together and measuring the length of his palm, so large around mine. "Tell me a secret?"

His smile curves against my shoulder and his lips brush against my skin.

"You're going to win the fashion show," he says immediately, without an ounce of hesitation.

"That's not a secret." I turn so I can stare up at him. "That's an opinion."

"Which makes it a secret."

"I'm going in with no expectations, but..." I trail off and bite my bottom lip, afraid to say it out loud.

"But it would be really fucking cool if you won?" he finishes for me, reading my mind.

"Yeah. Really fucking cool."

I picture it. How my life would change and the dreams I could accomplish. A life a little more rooted, grounded, settling into consistency and stability. The store I've envisioned, with bright lights and large dressing rooms. Outfits on display in the windows, high-quality and cute designs without costing a fortune. My name on the outside with a little logo next to it.

"Are those wheels still turning?"

"Less now," I say.

"Sleep, sweetheart. I've got you."

Like everything else Patrick says, I believe him.

My eyes close, and I drift toward unconsciousness. All the while, his grip around me never wanes. There's a lucid moment between sleeping and dreaming, fantasy and reality. A tiny window of time where I'm aware enough to know that this position, the two of us woven together, feels more like home than my any room in my apartment.

It's a place I never want to leave.

———

I WAKE several times throughout the night, once to an owl hooting, another to a bird chirping in the distance. Patrick's face is buried in my hair, a long leg wrapped around my calf, and a palm resting on my thigh.

I pry my eyes open after the bird's second song. I see hints of light sneaking through the top of the tent zipper. Sunbeams chase each other across the ground. Tires crunch over gravel in the parking lot as other campers hit the road before breakfast to make it to their next destination on time.

It must be morning.

I shift from my back to my side, and a rush of heat follows me. It encompasses me from my neck to my feet, pleasantly warm. The kind I snuggle into, exhaling a content sigh. The warmth intensifies and grows as a hand rests on my belly. Long fingers stretch out over my skin, trying to touch every space on my body they can find. A thumb traces over my ribs, counting each one to make sure they're all there.

Nice.

That feels nice.

"Morning, Lo," Patrick says.

His voice is raspy and low. I'm used to hearing his greetings over a cup of coffee in my kitchen or after a post-run shower when he's wide awake and using a towel to dry off his hair. He sounds wicked so early in the day, a side not everyone gets to know.

The *real* Patrick Walker. A little rumpled, a little disheveled and unbelievably sexy.

How the *hell* did I never notice it before?

"Morning," I say. "How'd you sleep?"

"Like I was dead to the world. Did you warm up?"

"I did. Thanks for being my personal heated blanket."

"Anytime."

I scoot back half an inch, and a hardness presses right into the curve of my ass. He inhales as I let out a small, startled gasp. The sounds mix, and there's a moment where we both freeze, wondering who will move first.

Half a second later, Patrick rolls his hips forward.

I've never heard such silence before.

The rational side of my brain says I can't grind into my best friend's lap and expect us to eat breakfast across from each other without any awkwardness. To carry on with our road trip like we haven't found ourselves in an intimate position: me, halfway on his dick, and him, dangerously close to groping me.

Then there's the other side of my brain. The ninety-nine percent certainty of not crossing any physical lines with him steadily plummets closer and closer to zero, leaving me unsure.

Time stands still, waiting for me to decide how we proceed. How does this end? How do I *want* this to end?

Naked under my best friend, it seems.

That's the side that eggs me on.

Do it, it says.

So I do.

I put a trembling hand on his thigh and run my nails up his leg to his gray athletic shorts. I dance my fingers across his arm and urge his palm up my shirt, just beneath the band of my sports bra.

There's no logic, no thought, just ravenous want.

Need.

"Lola."

I love how Patrick says my name.

It's strangled, wobbling and cracking around the edges. Both an ask and a plea, seeking my approval. He touches me like he's at war with his mind. Convincing himself he *shouldn't* be doing this when I think—no, I *know*—he really, really wants to.

There's another tilt of his hips before his knee wedges between my legs and nudges them apart. I don't know *what* we're doing, only that I know we can't stop.

I can't stop.

I shift back into him until our limbs are molded together. He could slide into me so easily. Two pieces of fabric is all that separates us. He blows out a long, stuttered breath, gasping for air.

"Please," I whisper, and his grip tightens.

"Okay," Patrick answers. His lips brush over the spot where my shoulder and neck meet. "Okay," he says again, and this time, I believe him.

His hand moves from under my shirt to my shoulder. He turns me so we're front to front, eyes colliding, chests rising and falling at the same tempo. His cheeks are flushed, and the pink works its way down his chest.

I touch a lock of hair that falls over his eyes and brush it away. "What are we doing?" I ask.

"I don't know," he admits, and I like his honesty. "I just know that I want to. I've always wanted to. Badly."

Want, want, want.

"I want to too," I say.

"Is this a dream?" he asks. "Or for real?"

There's so much hope behind the question, it makes it easy to whisper, "Real. Totally for real."

"Fuck," Patrick exhales. "Yes."

My reassurance ignites him.

I might regret this in an hour or maybe even in the next ten minutes, but right now, I want to make him feel as good as he's making me feel. Searching for the edge, so ready to topple willingly over. It would be easy with him. A free fall of lust into a hazy burst of pleasure.

I hitch my leg over his hip and bring my lips to the line of his jaw. I kiss the stubble on his cheeks, below his chin, the hollow of his throat. His shoulder, warm under my mouth. My teeth sink into his skin, the gentlest of bites, and he lets out a low hiss. His hips buck forward once, twice.

He runs his thumb along the underside of my breast and settles his hand on my stomach. I arch my back, asking for *more*.

I can see how badly he wants me, the outline of his length long and thick through his gym shorts. It spurs me on to know that I'm desired. The object of someone's affection. I lift my chin and my eyes settle on his lips, showing my intent.

"What else do you want?" he asks.

The hand on my stomach shifts lower, stretching the waistband of my sleep shorts and dipping below the elastic.

"A million things," I say.

"Tell me. List them all."

"I want—"

A sharp sound blares through the tent, and the spell breaks.

"Shit," Patrick says. "That's my alarm. Let me turn it off."

"That's okay," I answer, crashing back to reality. "We should probably—I should... I'll be right back." I wiggle myself free from the sleeping bag and scoot toward the tent flaps.

"Lola. Please don't run. Not from me."

"I'm not... I'm not running. I promise. I just need a second. A minute."

My feet land on the grass and I take off at a sprint toward the bathhouse. I lock the door behind me and turn the sink on as cold as it will go. I lift my shirt and stare at my reflection in the mirror.

There might not be a physical mark where Patrick touched me, but I know.

I've been burned. Torched and branded in the spots he caressed.

Above my belly button. Below my ribs. Under the swell of my breasts and over my heart. For as long as I live, if anyone else ever touches there, I'll think, *Patrick touched me there first.*

Nothing will ever be the same.

"Breathe," I say to myself, splashing a handful of water on my face and curling my fingers around the porcelain basin. "So you almost got off with your best friend? It's no big deal. Everything is fine."

We need to talk before we get physical. Use our words, not our hands, to find out what the other wants. Long-term. Short-term. Any term between. We—*I*—have to be sure, because if—*when*—he finally kisses me, I know we can't take it back.

I wash my face until you can no longer tell if the red on my cheeks is from the memory of him behind me, his knee nudging my legs open, or the thorough scrub I'm giving myself.

Still worked up and not anywhere close to being satisfied, I exit the bathroom and hope I'm not shaking like a leaf. I spot Patrick climbing out of the tent. He's pulled a shirt over his head and he's scanning the camping area. When he finds me, his shoulders relax. He tilts his head to the side, a silent question in place.

Are we good? he asks.

We're grand, I say back. *Just grand.*

Moisture clings to my shins and calves as I make my way back to our site. A mosquito buzzes near my nose, and I swat it away. Patrick's eyes brighten as I approach.

"I thought you might have gotten eaten by a bear," he says, his voice back to normal. Calm, cool and collected.

Awesome.

I guess we're just going to ignore that whole *I saw my best friend's erection* part of the morning.

"Nope. Still here."

"Everything okay?"

"Yeah." I nod and give him a thumbs up, cringing internally at how lame I must look. "All good."

"Okay," he says. "That's good."

"Are you good?"

If I blinked, I would've missed his eyes dipping to my chest and how quickly they drag away. "I'm great."

"That's great."

"Super great."

"Stop being weird," I say, knocking his shoulder with mine.

"You first. You practically sprinted from the tent."

"I had to pee."

"Mhmm. Whatever you say. We should pack up. We have a lot on the agenda today."

"Shower before we hit the road, then pack up. Then food. I'm starving."

"There's an all-you-can-eat pancake house back in Hendersonville."

"Are you challenging me to a short-stack eat off, Patrick Walker?"

CHELSEA CURTO

"I am, Lola Jones. Want to play?"

"Yeah. I do. Game on, Walker."

I brush past him to grab a fresh pair of clothes. I definitely don't touch the inside of his wrist as I pass, and I definitely don't grin from ear to ear when I hear him mumble my name either.

TWENTY-ONE

PATRICK

WE DON'T TALK about what happened in the tent on our drive
to Florida, trading conversation for a playlist that takes me back
to when we were teenagers as we cross state lines.

Lola told me she isn't running, and I'm going to believe her.
The last twelve hours have given us a lot to think about. We
confessed we'd be open to kissing each other—for real this time
—and I all but told her I'm waiting for her. Add in her grinding
on me this morning and my hand practically down her shorts
and it's enough to want to turn our minds off for a few hours, an
important discussion looming on the horizon.

"This place is massive." I pull off my sunglasses and look up
at the Orange County Convention Center, the building where
Lola's fashion show is taking place.

"Yeah." Lola stands beside me and pulls her hair into a ponytail. "They host tons of events here at the same time. It's wild."

"Make sure we read the signs carefully," I say. "We wouldn't
want to walk into the regional quarterfinals of the figure skating
competition happening on the north side of the building," I say.
"You might get confused."

"That's ironic, isn't it? A state with a temperature hotter than the sun is the one hosting a sport where ice is involved."

"With Florida, Lola, it's best to just let it be."

We unload her garment bags from the back of the Jeep, dozens of metal hangers hooked around my fingers. We climb the stairs to the long line of glass doors, a wave of air conditioning greeting us when we step inside.

"Looks like we need to go left," I say, nodding toward the sign with **Florida Fashion Show** written on it in big, bold letters.

"Right looks fun, too. The Postal Workers of America training session."

"Maybe next time. We need to keep our day moving along."

"We do?"

"Yup. There's a strict schedule to adhere to, so fewer inquiries about stamps and more pep in your step to get your name tag, please."

We take the escalator to the second floor and walk down a long, carpeted hall. After a wrong turn that leads us to a service elevator that smells like rotten eggs, we finally find the room where we need to be.

The space is massive, larger than two football fields, with hundreds of booths set up around the perimeter. Music plays from speakers, and a long runway is being constructed on the opposite end of the room.

"Holy shit," Lola whispers, her hand finding my free one. "We're here."

"Deep breaths," I murmur. "Let's check you in, then we can make a lap and see everything, okay?"

Lola gets her name tag and welcome packet. I hand off the garment bags to an assistant, checking to make sure they're labeled correctly with Lola's name visible and easy to read. After, we weave our way through throngs of people. Almost everyone waves hello, a mutual level of respect in the room despite not knowing faces and names. A few stop us outright, recognizing Lola and giving her a hug.

Friends from social media, she explains. She introduces me as her best friend. Her road trip companion and reason for staying sane, and *hell,* I like when she leans into me for support. I rest my hand on her lower back, around her shoulder, at the base of her neck. Anywhere I can reach so I can convey a sense of calm to her.

"This is so cool," she says as we circle the large room. "Some people here will be the next big things in the fashion industry. The ones I'll read about in magazines for years to come. We're going to watch history be made."

"Or you're going to make it yourself. Hang on." I tug on her arm and stop in front of a long banner displaying all the designers taking part in this year's show. I scan the long list of names, tapping the canvas when I spot hers. "There you are. Look at you."

"That's me," Lola whispers excitedly. "Holy *shit,* Patrick."

"Stand in front of it. I want to get your picture to send to the group."

"Oh, they don't care about a banner. It's no big deal."

"No big deal? This is your big break, Lola, and our friends instructed me to document our trip extensively. Emma told me they were buying Wi-Fi at their villa in Santorini just so they could download the photos I would be sending. Get your ass over there, please, so I can show you off."

Lola blushes and lets out a huff. She hands me the folder with the welcome information and her purse, draping the strap over my shoulder. "Fine," she says. "But only because you said please."

I snap a couple shots of her grinning. One of her pointing to her name and acting silly. I catch one of her mid-laugh, nose scrunched and head thrown back after I tell her the copy of the program I want to print out is going to be even bigger than this. Twice the size, I declare, and she rolls her eyes, a sparkle behind the blue. She pulls me to her side and I take a picture of us, cheeks smushed together and all our teeth on display.

I attach them to a message in our group chat.

> All good here in Florida. First up, Lola's name on a banner. Next, her name in lights.

My phone pings right away, Jo, Rebecca, and Jack chiming in and answering in quick bursts.

> Holy crap!!!!! I'm so proud.

> Lo, you look so happy. Remember us when you're famous!!!

> Cool.

Lola's blush deepens as she reads over my shoulder. "Jack has the right idea. It's a banner, Patrick," she says. She dips her chin to hide the tears springing in her eyes, but I catch her before she turns away.

"No." I cup her chin with my hand. "No way. It's hours and hours of hard work. Of trying and failing and trying again. That banner? That banner is what you've dreamed about since before I met you: creating designs that look high-fashion, but come at a price anyone can afford. Wouldn't that little girl be *proud* of how far she's come?"

That starts the waterfall of tears that roll down her cheeks and fall to the floor. Her shoulders shake and she buries her face in my shirt. "Sometimes," she says, voice muffled, "I think I'm living in a dream. A dream I hope I never wake up from, because how is this all real? How are *you* real? Even with help from all the galaxies, all the planets and stars in the sky, bits and pieces of every realm and every timeline where you exist, the universe couldn't have made you more perfect if it tried. You are my favorite soul."

That's what love is.

Striving to be the best you can be for the person who makes you feel complete.

"There's no me without you. You're my favorite soul too, Lola," I say. I use my thumb to wipe away a tear, to clear the smeared mascara from under her eyes. "In all of those timelines, I hope I have you by my side,"

"Every single one," she says. She pulls back and stares at me. "And if I wasn't, I would find you."

"That's my girl," I murmur and trace the line of her jaw. Her fingers twist in my shirt, and her eyes drop to my mouth. It's the same look she had on her face this morning in the tent, and I know exactly what she wants to ask. "Do you—"

"Is that Lola Jones?"

We spin and find a gorgeous woman walking toward us. Dark skin, cropped hair, shiny bangles adorning her arms. She looks official, with a walkie talkie and set of keys dangling from her neck.

"Vivian Lee?" Lola asks. She lets go of my shirt and steps back.

"That's me." The woman stretches out her hand, and Lola shakes it with enthusiasm. "I've been looking forward to meeting you. When I saw they checked you in, I thought I'd try to hunt you down."

"You've been wanting to meet *me*?" I hear the incredulity in Lola's voice, and I wrap my arm around her shoulder. "Me, specifically?"

Vivian laughs. "Yes. Since the moment I saw your application and spent two hours one night watching your sewing series, Learn with Lola. It's fantastic."

"Wow. It's such an honor to meet you. You've been my role

model and inspiration since I was a young girl. Thank you so much for the kind words."

"They're all true. I've been dying to ask what sparked your idea to start creating videos."

"My friend told me she loved my clothes but didn't know where to start to make her own. I figured I could film a couple of designs so people could learn the basic foundations of sewing and stitching. Sewing isn't a secret, and making clothing isn't a competition. Accessibility is important to me, and doing step-by-step videos so anyone, regardless of their skill set, could learn how to create their own pieces seemed like a good place to start. I didn't think they would gain any traction, but after two videos went viral, that kind of changed."

"I love that mindset." Vivian nods in agreement. "There's a place for everyone in this industry if they want it." Her eyes dart to me and she smiles. "I'm so sorry. I'm being rude. I'm Vivian."

"I'm the one being rude," Lola says. "This is my best friend, Patrick. Excuse his bruises. They're souvenirs from a rowdy round of laser tag."

"Patrick, it's lovely to meet you."

"You too, Vivian. We were just snapping some photos of Lola and the banner with her name on it," I say, gesturing behind us.

"Is this your first show?" Vivian asks, and Lola nods. "Don't let it overwhelm you. There's a lot going on, but try to just focus on yourself and your designs."

"Do you have any other advice?"

"Have fun. If you're not having fun, it's not worth it. The show is a celebration of everything you've accomplished. The minute it feels like work is the minute when you need to take a step back and remember why you wanted to get to this point in the first place, which I assume is for no other reason than because you love fashion."

"Lola adores fashion. I was with her the day she bought her first designer dress," I tell Vivian. "It was one of yours."

"What?" Her mouth drops open, a caricature of surprise. "When was this?"

"Back in 2004. She bought it in Boston, where we live."

"Which one was it?"

"Your spring line," Lola says. "The bright pink one with—"

"The thick straps and the boat-neck neckline," Vivian finishes. "It's one of my favorite pieces."

"It's what made me want to stay with this dream of mine. It's still in my closet. If my apartment was on fire and I only had ten seconds to grab something to take with me, I'm taking that dress." Lola shakes her head and smiles softly. "I'm sure you hear that kind of praise all the time."

"Would you believe me if I told you that line didn't sell well? People thought the colors were too loud, especially for spring. 'Better for late summer,' they tried to tell me. 'I don't care,' I told them. I loved that set of designs."

"Maybe that's why it resonated with me so deeply." Lola bites her lip and she sniffs. I move my hand from her shoulder down her back, rubbing small, comforting circles as I go. "I saw a part of myself in it."

"Making money is nice," Vivian says. "Seeing your name in lights never loses its thrill, even years later. But I've always said that I don't care how many pieces I sell. If only one person likes it, if only one person resonates with what I'm trying to share, then I've done my job. That's all it takes to make me happy."

"That's so important," Lola says. "And such a lovely sentiment."

A phone rings, and Vivian sighs. "Speaking of work, I told them I was here to kick back and relax, not run a dozen errands."

"Don't let us keep you," Lola says. "Thank you so much for saying hi."

"Come find me after the show. I loved the sketches you submitted, and I can't wait to see what you put down the runway," Vivian says.

"I absolutely will."

Lola and I wave goodbye to Vivian, and then Lola turns to me with stars in her eyes.

"That... Holy *crap* was that cool," she all but squeals. "She liked my application."

"Of course she did." I pull her into a hug and rest my chin on her head. "How could she not? You're so talented, Lo, and I'm so glad you finally get a stage to show off all of that talent."

"I couldn't have done this without you. No." She holds up her hand to stop me from interrupting. "Besides my parents, you are the only person who has never told me to pick a different career. Even when I was working shitty hours in retail to make enough money to afford fabric, you said everyone has to start somewhere. You encouraged me to apply to the show. You drove down here during your time off from work to cheer me on. You've believed in me even when I didn't believe in myself, and you've been there every step of the way, Patrick. Without you, none of this would have ever happened."

I swallow down those words. *I love you.*

I do it because I love her. I'm so stupidly in love with her. If she told me her dreams were to jump off a cliff at the end of the world, I'd be right next to her, ready to jump too. I'd do anything to support her. Anything to help her get what she wants, no matter the cost. Anything she asks really, because that's how far gone I am for this woman.

Maybe we'll work better as friends. Maybe we'll kiss for the first time and it'll be *fine*, not *great*, but I have to at least try. What we have is special. *She* is special, and you don't let special go.

"I've told you this before, but you're my favorite girl, Lola." I tuck a piece of hair behind her ear. "Watching you put in the work, watching you succeed, that's just a nice bonus. I'm always going to be here for you, okay?"

"You promise?"

"With everything I have." My phone buzzes in my pocket, the alarm I set to keep track of time going off. "I don't want to rush you, but if we could start working our way back to the car, that would be great."

"Are you hiding something from me?" She pokes my chest and I capture her hand with mine. I press a kiss to each of her fingertips, my eyes never leaving hers.

"Only one way to find out."

TWENTY-TWO
LOLA

"YOUR SURPRISE IS HERE IN FLORIDA," Patrick says. He spins the baseball hat on his head, and my mouth goes dry.

What is it about a man in a backwards hat that makes me weak in the knees?

"Is it?" I manage to say.

The words taste like dust. I'm remembering that hand on my thigh, up under my shirt, tracing my breasts with the faintest of touches. His lips on my shoulder and the sound of his sigh echoing in my ear.

"Surprises," he says as we pull out of the convention center parking lot. The right side of his mouth lifts as he glances over at me. "Two of them."

"What do you mean, two?"

"More than one. Less than three. C'mon, Lo. You're a smart girl."

I narrow my eyes and cross my arms over my chest. "We agreed on one."

"We agreed on nothing. You got me two. The museum and the escape room."

"That was one and a half, if we're being generous. You don't need to stretch yourself thin on my behalf."

"Sometimes you do more for me, and sometimes I do more for you," Patrick says. "That's how friendship works. Are you keeping a scorecard I don't know about?"

"Of course not."

"I'm not either. Let me do this for you, yeah?"

I nod and play with my bracelet. "Okay."

Admitting defeat isn't easy, but I'm too tired to argue, my limbs heavy and my eyelids beginning to droop.

"When it comes to you and making sure you have a good time, Lola, I don't give a flying fuck how much effort it takes or how much money it costs," Patrick says.

Holy shit.

That wakes me up.

I blink at him and stare into his eyes, watching the vibrant green shift to dark emerald. His knuckles flex around the steering wheel, and I inhale at the sight of his corded forearms, veins running up to his elbows.

My cheeks heat. I wiggle in my seat, blood rushing to the surface of my skin the longer our gazes hold, a prickly sense of awareness of how *attractive* this man is.

Kind and generous and gentle, yes.

Handsome and gorgeous too, with sharp lines and devastating features. He's so captivating, so entrancing, I can't look away.

I'm still waiting for it to feel wrong that I'm gaping at him, gawking and leering in a way I've never done before, but the wrongness never comes.

"Right." My voice squeaks with the word, and I clear my throat. "Do I get a hint?"

"All I'm going to say is there's something in the car that would give away one surprise if you found it."

"Will you at least tell me when the surprises are?"

"Tonight," he says. "And all day tomorrow."

"Tonight?" Exhaustion melts to giddiness, adrenaline crashing over me. "It's almost seven."

"That's why we're on a tight schedule."

"No wonder you wanted to get out of the convention center so quickly."

"I have my reasons. Can you remind me of the plans for the rest of our time down here? I want to make sure I know exactly what's going on and when."

"You don't have detailed notes on your phone?"

"Of course I do. I just want to hear it from you."

"Tomorrow is the second surprise. The next day is the hotel check-in with a mixer in the evening. The day after is a networking event. Then the show will start."

"So many things to look forward to."

"I'd like to check out that bookshop if we can before we head out to the hotel. They entered a holiday decorating competition a few years back, and their store turned out so cute."

"How did you find out about them? They're thousands of miles away from home."

"They posted something about reading banned books a while back that went viral. Do you know what that means?"

"I know what going viral means." Patrick rolls his eyes. "I'm six months older than you, not sixty."

"Says the man who bought a newspaper at the last rest stop just to cut out the crossword puzzle. I've never asked.... is there a reason you love to do puzzles so much?"

"Yeah." He smiles, transported back to a different time in his life. "Grams. She did one every single day. In her lounger in the living room, feet kicked up with a paper folded in quarters. She wanted to keep her brain sharp, and she got me hooked on doing them."

I hear the longing in his voice, how much he misses her and

the memories they had. It's how I talk about my dad. A mix of sadness and joy, competing emotions at opposite ends of the spectrum.

I love to tell stories about him. The fun times we had together, like when he bought a monster water slide and laid it out in our street so all the neighborhood kids could play. When he wrote to me every single day I was away at summer camp, even if it was one sentence that said *miss you*. At the Cape, where we built sandcastles until the sun set.

Then the stories stop, I remember there won't be any new ones, and sadness washes over me like the pull of the tide.

"I loved her," I say. I rest my elbow on the console between us and reach over, my palm settling on his forearm. "I love that she taught us how to play bridge. We were the only twelve-year-olds who even knew what that card game was."

"Yeah." He chuckles, but there's pain laced around the edges. "She was a wonderful lady."

"The best lady. Who I aspire to be, honestly. Ice cream every night after dinner? A collection of friends at ninety-one? What more could you want?"

"She loved you. She would always tell me—" Patrick stops short of finishing his sentence, chuckles again, and shakes his head. "Never mind. It's not important."

"Excuse me." I flick his ear. "Everything that woman had to say was important, buddy. Don't hold out on me."

"She would always tell me you were a special girl." His voice grows soft and tender. "And I would always tell her she was right."

I stare at his profile. The curve of his jaw. The twist of his mouth like he's about to add something else, but is choosing to stay quiet instead. The years of life showing themselves around his eyes. So many of those years spent together, fond memories and pictures in a scrapbook.

"Grams asked me something once," I find myself saying, propelled forward by an invisible force. My hand moves down his arm to the matching friendship bracelet. I play with the frayed edges, the string we've had to cut and add to and stitch together to hold up over the years. I find solace in the twine, and it makes me want to share this story with him.

"Something philosophical, I take it?" Patrick asks.

"Yeah. It was right after I dropped out of college. That semester of being away from home was jarring. My course load was heavy. I missed my parents. I missed *you*. I missed the easy life we had as kids and I just... I gave up, I guess. Grams and I were drinking tea in your parents' living room, and I was in a bad place. Confused about the future. About what I wanted to do and how to make fashion my full-time job. She looked at me over the rim of that teacup she loved to use—"

"The one with the flowers on it," Patrick says. I nod and smile, the afternoon as clear as day in my mind.

"That one. She asked, 'When are you the happiest?' And I didn't have to think very hard about the answer. I immediately said, 'When I'm with Patrick.' She leaned over, patted my hand with those four rings she wore across her fingers and said, 'Then you have nothing to worry about. It'll all work out.'"

"Are you?" he asks. "Still happiest when you're with me?"

"When I'm with you, Patrick, I'm the happiest person in the world. I feel like I can fly."

He nods and wraps his palm around mine, intertwining our fingers and squeezing once. Our joined hands drop to his thigh. "I'm happiest when I'm around you too, Lola," he says. "When I'm with you, I'm invincible. I'm the luckiest guy in the world."

It's not an outright *I love you*, but it's close because it's *Patrick*, and those words are worth more than any weight of gold.

———

"I NEED you to close your eyes," Patrick says.

He taps his hand on the steering wheel to the beat of a song, a nervous energy thumping through the cab of the Jeep. He keeps checking the clock and the watch on his wrist, or his phone at a stoplight, as if the time is going to be different between them.

"Okay." I close my eyes tight. "Whatever it is, I'm already excited."

I hear the turn signal click on. We make a left, then a right, and then a left again. The car slows to a gentle roll, then shifts to park.

"Stay there," he says.

"Couldn't go anywhere if I tried," I answer. As tempted as I am to cheat and look at my surroundings, I follow his instructions and wait until my door opens.

"One step down." He guides me to the sidewalk. "There you go. We have a short walk, then you can look."

"A short walk? Plenty of time for a question from the *is your travel partner a serial killer?* list. If you could live anywhere in the world, where would it be?" I ask. "You'd stay in Boston, right?"

"I don't know. Lately I've been thinking I might want to branch out a little. See the world," Patrick says.

"Like Rhode Island and Connecticut? New Hampshire would be cheaper. No state tax."

"No." He laughs and maneuvers me around a bump on the pavement. "I'm talking about a trip. Maybe next time you go somewhere abroad, I could tag along for a few days if it were okay with you."

Never in the fourteen years that I've been traveling has Patrick ever come with me on a vacation out of the country.

We made vague plans once in our mid-twenties. The year after my dad passed, I needed a distraction and to get away.

We decided on England since it was close, a short six-hour

flight from Boston. We'd take the train to Brighton. Eat fish and chips. Visit Buckingham Palace and Camden Market. Stop by Daunt Books and the Waterstones that's five stories tall.

The closer we got to our departure date, the less enthusiastic Patrick was, so I wasn't surprised when he asked if we could raincheck. Seven days away from home is a long time for someone who craves the familiarity of consistency and order.

He had to get ready for the school year, he told me. A first-time assistant principal with a laundry list of to-do items. Bulletin boards. Safety protocols. Updating the filing system from paper folders to digital copies.

We never rescheduled.

"You want to take a trip?" I ask, almost opening my eyes in surprise.

"I do," he says.

"I would love that. Of course you're welcome on my trips. Whenever you want."

"Okay." He squeezes my hand. "We'll plan something. I'd like to visit Japan. I know you've already been, so I don't expect you to—"

"I'd go again," I say right away. "With you. It would be more fun with you."

"Yeah?"

"Yeah." I nod, then grin. I can't see him, but I know he's grinning right back. "Let's go to Japan."

"We have a few things to do before we cross the ocean on a fourteen-hour flight." Patrick whooshes out a laugh. "You have a fashion show to win. I think my passport is expired."

"Soon," I say. "We'll go soon."

"Speaking of soon, you can open your eyes."

I hadn't realized we'd stopped walking. "We're here?"

"We're here."

I blink and see a store with a huge bay window. There's a

loveseat inside, with square pillows adorning the dark velvet. Rows of bookshelves are lined up against the walls, and round tables are set up in front of a marble countertop toward the back of the building. It's busy, people milling about everywhere and lines of chairs filling up the center of the room.

"What is this place?" I ask. Patrick tugs me back a step, and I read the words attached to the facade. "A Likely Story. This is the bookstore I wanted to visit!"

"It is. But that's not all," he says, and then he points to a chalkboard on the sidewalk, fancy calligraphy announcing an author signing.

Tonight.

Hosted by my favorite romance writer.

"We're seeing Mia Dunn?" I almost screech. "Are you *kidding* me?"

"Nope." He grins. "I called the store to ask about their hours—"

"You know they're posted online, right?" I say.

"I got to chatting with Bridget, the owner," Patrick continues, ignoring me. "She told me about the signing and set aside five of Mia's books for you. That's why we had to hustle through today, so we didn't miss the signing event."

For the second time today, I burst into tears.

Somewhere between passing the evergreens of northern Georgia and the orange groves at the Florida state line, every wall between us has been torn down. Every platonic line erased. Every fear of mine eliminated. It's a certainty I feel with every fiber of my being. Every bone in my body, every beat of my heart.

I'm falling in love with Patrick.

I want to spend every waking second with him. I've always wanted that, but now I want to kiss him and hold him close. Lie in bed with him and watch him fall asleep. I want to be there when he wakes up and start every day together. I want him in every way he'll have me, and then I'll still want him some more, because I don't think I'll ever get enough of him.

I want to tether my soul to his and carry his heart around in a glass jar, protecting it with steadfast loyalty until the end of our days. I will never leave him. I will never not walk by his side, willing and ready to give all of myself to him until we're nothing but little particles floating through time and space. And even then, I will follow him into the unknown, the only one to make me whole.

Patrick may want a mortgage and I may want to see the world, but I know we could make it work. We would find a balance, a happy medium, a way for us both to get what we want without ever having to compromise.

How could I *not* be falling in love with him, the selfless and gentle man who knows me better than I know myself? Who anticipates my needs and wants, who lifts my dreams on a pedestal and gives all that he has to help me achieve them?

The person who, above anyone else in this world, accepts me and cherishes me like I am his and he is mine.

Mine.

Why did it take me so long to see it?

I'm head over heels for my best friend, the one who's been there all along.

Fate has a funny way of showing itself.

I'm fucking *terrified* of what could happen to us if we try to be more than friends and it doesn't work out, but I can't stop it now. I don't *want* to stop it. I want to exist in this dizzying place of happiness for the rest of my life with Patrick Walker—my very best friend—by my side.

He pulls me close, his arms around my shoulders. Chin on my head. Fingers brushing up and down my spine. His Welcome Home hug. The I Missed You hug.

"What's wrong?" he asks, voice soothing and calm.

I don't care that he's sweating and I'm sweating and it feels like we jumped into a pool with our clothes on. Our skin sticks together, and I still don't care.

I want him, and I'd give up everything to have him.

I don't want him just as a best friend. Not as a physical release of pent-up frustration, only keeping him around for a night.

No.

I want his body, his brilliant mind, his gracious heart.

I want his dreams and his nightmares.

I want his bright Saturdays and every Monday after. The dreary days. The middle-of-the-road Wednesdays way down in the middle of November when there's nothing to look forward to. I want them all.

"Nothing is wrong. Everything is perfect," I say. "Thank you, Patrick. This is—" I close my eyes, at a loss for words. How do you convey the depth of your gratitude when someone does something so incredible for you that *thank you* isn't nearly sufficient enough? "You're my favorite person in the world."

"Out of all of them?" he asks.

"Every single one."

He laughs. He presses a kiss to my forehead, to my cheek, to the tip of my nose. I want to tilt my chin up and capture his mouth with mine.

"You're my favorite person in the world too, Lola. No one else stands a chance."

I'm falling in love with you.

I'm falling in love with you.

I hope you're falling in love with me too, because I don't think I can bear it if you're not.

I have to tell him.

TWENTY-THREE

PATRICK

LOLA IS JITTERY.

She's rearranged the books in her arms eight different ways.

Alphabetical order first, then a rainbow pattern. Shortest page count to longest was next before finally deciding to put her favorite novel—the one with a purple cover and yellow writing—on top with an exhilarated grin.

Her head is on a swivel, looking left then right. She laughed—loudly and vivaciously—during Mia's talk. Teared up when she listened to how the love stories were crafted and created, a little bit of reality and a little bit of fantasy behind the prose and plot ideas. Jumped to her feet and cheered during the standing ovation at the conclusion of the panel.

Me? I'm just happy she's happy.

There are a handful of other men here. Partners of some of the audience members doing their best to look enthusiastic. A dad with a teenage girl at the back of the room, leaning against a wooden post with his arms crossed over his chest. A couple in front of us, with matching heart tattoos on their wrists and holding hands while they wait in line to get their books signed.

"It's almost our turn," Lola whispers. "What should I say to her?"

"What would you want someone to say if they came up to you and talked about your designs?" I ask.

"I think it would be similar to my conversation with Vivian. I'd want to know that they enjoyed what I created. That they saw a part of themselves and related to it, even if it was just some fabric stitched together. I'd like to know it meant something to them."

"Then that's exactly what you should say to Mia." I move my hand to her lower back and give her a gentle nudge forward. The couple in front of us steps away, letting out dual squeals of excitement as they fawn over the signatures and notes written in the interior of their books. "Ready?"

"Ready." Lola perks up and stretches out her hand to the redhead behind the table. "Hi, Mia. It's so nice to meet you."

"Hi there," Mia says. She smiles and shakes Lola's hand. "What's your name?"

"I'm Lola." She sets her stack of books down and glances up at me. "And this is Patrick."

Mia stands and grins from ear to ear. She flips her hair over her shoulder. "You're the one Bridget told me about." She looks back at Lola. "He's been working very hard to pull off this surprise. He's definitely a keeper."

"Ah." I fix the bill of my hat to give my hands something to do. I don't like all of this attention, the tips of my ears turning pink with bashfulness. It didn't seem like I was going above and beyond when I came up with the idea. I knew it was something Lola would like, so I just did it. "I didn't do anything special," I say. "I just wanted to see if this was possible."

"Still a keeper." Mia winks and pulls out a black Sharpie, poised to sign. "Any special personalization?"

The women talk for a few minutes, exchanging stories as

Mia pens her name on the title pages of each book. Lola asks what it's like living in the even-smaller town up the road where everyone knows everyone's business. Mia asks if Uber-EATS really delivers at one in the morning, and they joke about swapping lives for a week. I snap a picture of the two while Lola tilts her head back, her laugh echoing through the shop.

"Thank you," Lola says as she closes the cover of the last book. "I hope you have a great rest of your night."

"You too. Thanks for coming by," Mia says.

"Thank you so much for having us," Lola says. "It's been a dream come true."

Mia points at Lola's shirt, the green crop top she stitched a couple summers back when it rained for a week straight. We were confined to our apartments and Lola went on a sewing rampage, creating a whole new wardrobe for herself—and me—in the span of a few days.

The top shows off half her stomach and her shoulders, so much distracting skin. Every piece of Lola's clothing has become public enemy #1 on this trip.

"Where'd you get your top?" Mia asks. "It's so cute."

"I made it," Lola answers.

"She's a designer who's going to be in the Florida Fashion Show," I add, because I'm too damn proud of her to let the accomplishment slip under the rug.

"No *way*. That's incredible. Do you do commissions? Is that your full-time job?" Mia asks.

"Yeah. I travel and do some brand partnerships, and I also make YouTube videos. My biggest passion is helping people bring their clothing visions to life."

"I'm starting a book tour next spring, I'd love your contact info for it. I've been wanting a few new dresses," Mia says.

They swap social media handles and phone numbers. Lola

drags me into a picture with the two of them, her arms around my waist and her head on my chest as we smile for the camera.

After a final parting hug, we step off to the side of the shop so the next reader can have our spot.

"Mia was so nice. And she liked my shirt." Lola opens a book and taps the page with her pointer finger. "She signed my name. Do you see this? I've never had a signed book before. *My name.*"

"Yes." I laugh, caught up in her excitement. "I was there."

She sets the books down on a nearby table and throws her arms around my neck. "Thank you," she says softly. "Thank you so much. This is the best day of my life."

"My goal is to make sure you keep saying that for at least the next week."

"I don't care about mosquitos or alligators. Bury me here in the land of orange trees and sunshine. I'm going to die happy."

"Are you ready for the next thing that's going to make you want to buy some Florida license plates and eat dinner at four in the afternoon?"

"There's *more*?"

"There's always more," I say. "And this time, it's miniature pies."

"God." Lola sighs. "I love it here."

———

"STOP STEALING MY FOOD." I nudge Lola's arm away and cover my chocolate pie with a protective hand. "Eat your own."

"I can't help it. I want them all."

"I bought us one of everything and you're still not full?"

The blonde woman behind the bakery counter didn't raise an eyebrow when she wrapped up the twenty-five treats, handing them to me in a large pink box tied together with a white string. Lola and I found a table by the window where we're currently sitting, digging into the pies while we watch people pass on the sidewalk.

"The chocolate pie is just so good." Lola evades my defense, cutting off a piece from my plate and scooping it away.

I don't try to stop her.

"If you could only eat one flavor of pie for the rest of your life," I ask, "what would it be?"

"Are you taking questions from my serial killer list?"

"I have to be sure about you, Jones. Twenty-four years isn't enough time to get to know a person."

"Pumpkin. Definitely pumpkin." She pauses and considers her answer. "Or cherry."

"Cherry pie? Wouldn't the crust get soggy?"

"Not when you have some vanilla ice cream with it. Then it's perfect."

"It's a shame I don't keep vanilla ice cream in my pocket."

"Lots of missed opportunities for a joke about cartons or if you're just happy to see me."

"Never a carton, Lola. Think of the mess."

"Fine." Her lips twitch. "If you say so."

"Excuse me. I'm sorry to interrupt, but are you Patrick and Lola?"

I look up and find a woman smiling at us. There's a man standing behind her—the same one I saw earlier with the teenage girl.

"Yeah. Hey." I stand and try to wipe my hands clean with a napkin. The chocolate on the tips of my fingers refuses to come off. "That's us."

"I thought so. I know everyone in this town, but I didn't recognize y'all. I'm Bridget Boylston, and this," she gestures to the man who watches her with a faint smile, "is my fiancé, Theo. We're the owners of the place, and we wanted to introduce ourselves in person instead of over email."

"It's so great to meet you. Thank you for being so helpful and accommodating with the books and letting me know about the signing. It means a lot," I say.

"It's my pleasure." She points to Lola's books on the table. The stack of five we started the evening with has turned into twelve, an unsteady tower that could fall over at any second. "Mia Dunn fan?"

"If I could get her quotes tattooed on my face, I would," Lola says. She pushes her chair back and stands beside me. "Her writing is—"

"Poetic, right?"

"*So* poetic. I swear there's magic in her words. What's your favorite book by her?"

"How do I pick? I guess Midnight Hour, but I also love Summer Book and Before the Storm."

I look at Theo, and he lifts a dark eyebrow.

"Expensive hobby," I say.

He hums. "You're telling me."

"Do you work at the bookstore?"

"No." He hooks his thumb over his shoulder to the other side of the building. The walls are full of hammers and boxes of nails. A rickety metal ladder leans against a corner space in the front of the room, and twenty-foot extension cords sit piled high on a table. "Hardware store."

"Cool," I say. "That's handy."

His eyebrow lifts higher. "Mhmm."

Theo clearly isn't all that talkative. He and and Jack could have a competition to see who could say the least amount of words. Our conversation ends, neither side having anything else to add.

"If you have any other free time while you're down here, please come back," Bridget says. She and Lola exchange a brief hug, then she looks at me. "Let me know if there's anything else I can help with."

"Thanks, Bridget."

"My pleasure." She waves goodbye and tugs Theo by his elbow toward the front of the store. His shoulders relax as they walk away and he slips an arm around her waist.

"He didn't like my joke about how handy it is to work in a hardware store," I say. "Bummer."

"You didn't nail it, did you?" Lola answers.

"Nope. Came up a yardstick or two short."

"Stop." She giggles and shakes her head. "Your jokes are abysmal."

"You're laughing, aren't you?"

"Only out of pity."

"You're a good friend, Lola."

"I can't believe we just met my favorite author. How long have you been planning this?"

"Since the day after you found out about the show. Bridget did most of the work. She ordered the extra books so they'd be ready when we got down here. Made sure the signing started at seven-thirty instead of seven so we wouldn't be late."

"So many secrets. This kicks laser tag's ass."

"Nah. They're both pretty awesome."

"Imagine laser tag in a bookstore," she says, plopping down in her wrought iron chair and taking another bite of pie. "Now *that* has some marketing potential."

Thirty minutes later, we're outside in the sticky humid air. The sky has turned dark, and a gentle breeze kicks up Lola's hair and blows it across her face. A canvas tote bag with the signed books rests on my right shoulder, and Lola's cheek rests on my left.

"Are you hungry?" I ask. "For dinner, not for a second round of pies. I'm cutting you off."

"No. I'm stuffed."

I open the door of the Jeep and help her inside. I set the bag on her lap and slide into the driver's seat. "You look tired."

"I'm just happy." Lola smiles at me, exhaustion on the brink of delirium. Heavy eyes, the droop of her head against the leather seat, and a content sigh. The moon is bright tonight, shining on her face and making her almost glow. "You know that happiness where it feels like you're going to burst? Your cheeks hurt from smiling so much and you want to sleep for ten hours, but you also want to stay awake because you don't want the best day ever to end? That's how I feel right now."

"So it was a good surprise then," I say, turning the key in the ignition.

"Patrick." She yawns and closes her eyes, her smile staying in place. "It was the best surprise."

———

LOLA FALLS asleep on the drive to the AirBnB.

Her legs are up near her chest. Her arms are around her shins, and her head lolls to the side, blonde hair curtaining half her face. There's dried drool just below the left corner of her mouth, and at a red light, I lean over and wipe it away.

Beautiful, I think when I park us in front of the house.

Beautiful, I think as I lift her into my arms and kick the passenger door closed with my foot.

Beautiful, I think as she nestles in my hold and lets out a content sigh. She mumbles something about pie, then something else about squirrels, and I smile.

I can't help but smile when I look at her.

I walk up the small stone path to the porch and punch in the door code Lola told me earlier. I find the living room and set her on a couch, grabbing a blanket to cover her legs. She doesn't budge when I head back to the car and bring in our bags. I haul them to the bedroom and prop them against the wall.

The bathroom is next on my agenda. It's large, with white floors, a walk-in shower, and a clawfoot tub. There's a towel warmer and a fuzzy rug in front of a vanity.

Perfect.

I turn the faucet on, warm water filling the basin and steam rising from the porcelain. When I walk back to the living room, I find Lola curled on her side, her eyes half open.

"Is it morning?" she asks.

"Still nighttime," I say.

"Oh." She blinks and stretches her arms above her head. "I guess I was more tired than I thought."

"I grabbed the suitcases. They're in the bedroom. I also started the bathtub for you. Figured you could use some decompressing after a long day."

"A bath? That sounds like heaven."

"I'll shower when you're finished. I'm going to crash on the couch tonight so you can get some decent sleep. We need to be up early in the morning."

"The couch?" Lola frowns and sits up. "Why?"

"There's only one bed, and it's fairly small. I figured you'd be more comfortable alone."

"Why don't we just share? We did the other night in the hotel. And in your guest room."

"Because the only other spot in that hellhole was a rickety desk chair. This couch can at least fit my legs."

"And last night? In the sleeping bags?"

"You were cold."

"Right." Lola nods and her eyes meet mine. We both know that's not why we shared a sleeping bag. "If I asked you to stay in the bed with me, what would you say?"

I swallow and lean against the wall. I cross my arms over my chest and stare right back at her. "I'd say yes."

"Okay." She nods again. "I'm going to take a bath. You're going to take a shower. Then we're going to get in bed. Together."

"That's what you want?"

"Yes, Patrick. That's what I want."

"Then that's what we'll do."

TWENTY-FOUR
PATRICK

"HEY," I say.

Lola looks up from her book and slips the receipt she's using as a bookmark between the pages. It's one of her new Mia Dunn ones she got tonight, and I made sure to write down each title so I can buy my own copies when we get home.

Her hair is wet from her bath, clinging to her shoulders and soaking her shirt. She can barely keep her eyes open, drowsiness threatening to overtake her. Still, she smiles at me with a beam that's a shock to my heart. I wonder if there will ever be a day where it doesn't feel like I'm seeing stars when she glances my way.

I doubt it.

"Hey," Lola answers, setting the book down on the bedside table. "How was your shower?" She leans back against a stack of white pillows, her legs stretching out in front of her.

"Amazing. What about your bath?"

"I could've stayed in there all night. Thank you for doing that for me."

"You're welcome. It's probably for the best you got out when you did. After a few hours, you'd turn into a prune."

"Would you still like me if I were a prune?" she asks, her smile wry and teasing.

"I'd like you even if you were a shriveled up grape." I climb onto the bed next to her, the mattress sinking under my weight. "Do you want to keep reading? Head to bed? Watch a movie?"

"None of the above. I was hoping we could talk."

"Sure." I prop myself up on my elbow and stare down at her. "What do you want to talk about?"

Lola plays with her bracelet, turning it around and around on her wrist. It's one of her habits, constantly needing something. "I want to talk about us."

"What about us? Our schedules when we get home or something?"

"No. About what's been going on the last few days."

I blow out a breath. "Thank god. It's been weird not talking about it, right?"

"*So* weird. We're good at communicating, but it feels like we're skirting around this."

"You did run from the tent this morning," I point out.

Lola bites her bottom lip and smooths her hands over the comforter. "What we're doing... what we've done... that hasn't been weird, has it?"

"No," I answer quickly. "Not at all."

"I don't think so either. Maybe we can keep doing what we're doing?" she asks softly, nerves hedged around the question.

I reach out to her and wrap our fingers together. I run my thumb over her knuckles and she sighs.

"You're too far away. Can I come closer?" I ask.

Lola's smile is soft and certain as she blinks at me under a thick fan of dark eyelashes. "Yeah," she whispers, a word I want to tattoo across my chest. "Come as close as you'd like."

It takes all the diminishing power in me to not launch myself at her. To not scoop her in my arms and rock her back and forth, telling her that her and me? We're inevitable.

I decide on the subtle route. I scoot leisurely across the mattress, taking my time. Unhurried. Calm. Understanding that you don't rush perfection. And this woman? She's the definition of perfection.

Lola turns on her side and faces me. I pull her to my chest and her hair tickles my neck. She sighs again and brings our joined hands to her mouth, pressing a kiss to the back of my palm.

"Okay?" I ask.

"Better than okay," she answers.

"Tell me what's going on in your head. You want to keep doing what we're doing—which is what exactly? Humping each other in tents and running away when the alarm goes off?"

Lola blushes a furious shade of pink. She gives my shoulder a gentle shove and buries her face in my shirt. "I'm not great at talking about my feelings," she says, voice muffled by my sleeve. "That's your area of expertise."

"I'm hardly an expert, and you're doing fine. I'm just giving you a hard time." I run my finger down her jaw and play with the ends of her hair. "Do you want me to keep touching you?"

I didn't think it was possible for her skin to turn an even darker shade of crimson, but at the tail end of my question, it does. Like the sky at sunset, the color seeps into her skin and makes her glow in the darkened room. A beacon of light and beauty and *hell*. It hurts to look at her.

"I want... I want us to..." She huffs, frustrated, and takes a second to regroup. To sort through her thoughts until she settles on the one she likes best. "I like when you touch me. I know that's not something friends do, so I think I want to try being... not friends with you."

I frown. Regret grabs at me, shaking me and scratching at my throat. My muscles go stiff. "You want us to stop being friends?" I ask slowly.

"No. *No.* I want us to still be friends. We're always going to be friends. I want us to be more affectionate with each other," she says through a rush of words, her face still hidden. "I want to hold your hand and I'd like to kiss you too."

This changes everything.

No more secret pining or wistful looks when she's not paying attention. I could touch her when I want. Invite her to spend the night in my bed and cook her breakfast every morning. Wash her hair and help her keep chasing after her dreams in whatever way I can.

And I could *kiss* her, like I've dreamed about doing for years. Unabashedly and repeatedly. Not on accident, but with intent and purpose.

"Can I tell you a secret?" I start. My thumb and finger tilt Lola's chin to look up at me and she nods. "I've been out of my mind mental about you for years."

She frowns, sits up, and stares at me with so much intensity, I think I've said something wrong.

"Years?" she repeats, drawing out the word. "How long?"

"Since we were thirteen, give or take a couple months."

"And you never—we never—*years*?"

I can't help but chuckle at her surprise. I guess I wasn't as obvious as the guys thought.

"No, I never. And no, we never. You never showed any interest in me romantically, so I tucked the crush away and dated other people. I chalked it up to something that would fade over time when we drifted apart... Except we didn't drift apart, we only got closer. It threw a wrench in my plan. Then your dad passed, and relationships became a no-go for you. There were some days I was afraid of losing you as a friend because you were so sad, and I didn't dare make it known I thought about what more than friends might be like.

"But we had established a line, and I wasn't going to cross it. Not with flirting or an attempted one-night stand. I hid it from you, and as much as I've tried to play off how I feel as just being a crush, I've realized in the last six months it's much, much deeper than that."

"I didn't... I didn't realize," she says softly. "Clearly I didn't realize. I'm not sure I would have reciprocated anything a year or two ago, but that's changed on my end. I... I *do* have a romantic interest in you, Patrick."

"It's okay that you didn't realize. I wasn't exactly standing outside your window with a big sign that said KISS ME, LOLA on it."

"I was with the girls a couple of weeks ago and I told them about the night at your place when we were eating pizza on the couch. I thought you were going to kiss me then, and they told me it was obvious how you felt... See? This is why I'm hesitant to date. I'm already messing up."

"No, no, no. You're not messing up. This is on me, Lola. I didn't want to jeopardize our friendship over something that was one-sided. It's probably a good thing you didn't realize. I'd never want to make you feel uncomfortable or like you were forced to have feelings for me."

"But now? Something's also changed on your end," she says. "I can tell something's changed. You're acting different. More... more determined."

"Because now when I look at you, I see you looking at me, *seeing* me. So I decided to go all in and try to show you without saying it outright. I think about you, and lately I can see that you're thinking about me, too."

"I do think about you. I think about you a lot, Patrick. I've expected these feelings and emotions to feel wrong or... or funny and out of place because it's *you* touching me, but they haven't. What I feel for you is real and it's strong and it's *right*. I might be shit at it, but I want us to do life together. To try, as more than friends. As two people who care deeply about each other, like we always have, but with the added physical components too."

"Look at you with the relationship talk. You're a pro, Lola Jones." I lean forward and kiss her forehead, letting my lips linger on her warm skin because I *can,* and then I do it again. "We should get some sleep. Tomorrow is another long day, then the events with the fashion show kicks off. You need your rest."

"Why did you and Jessica break up?" Lola's question is deafening in the quiet room. My gaze meets hers. She knows the answer without me having to verbalize it, but she deserves to hear the truth.

"Because she isn't you. None of the women I've dated are you, and I realized that letting someone else make me happy was a Band-Aid, a temporary distraction from the fact I've lived with for over half my life: you've always had a piece of me, Lola, and no one else will ever be able to compare. It wasn't fair to keep dating Jessica—or anyone—when in the back of my mind, I'd always wonder what it would be like if you were mine. You were my end game."

She wrings her hands together and leans back against the pillows. "Thank you for telling me."

"I've known how I feel about you for a while now, but I also know this is new for you. I want us to take this slow. You're not playing catch-up, and there's no rush to get to where I am, okay? We're taking this one day at a time."

"And... and on the off chance something goes wrong? What happens then?"

"We're friends first. Always. No matter what, I'm going to be by your side. If we try to be in a relationship and it fails, I'm not

CHELSEA CURTO

going to walk away from you. I promise. We'll figure out a way to navigate friendship on the other side."

Lola's bottom lip trembles. She nods and touches my cheek. "Okay. I trust you, Patrick. Friends first, always. But I want to give this a chance. I think what we have could be great."

"I think so too." I kiss her forehead again, her cheek, her chin. She grabs the collar of my shirt and pulls me close. I can smell her toothpaste, and there's a tiny crumb of chocolate pie left behind in the corner of her mouth.

"Then why haven't you kissed me yet?" she asks.

"Remember what I told you, Lo? Hollywood-level. Having patience is all part of the plan."

"The plan?"

"The plan," I say.

She huffs. "Fine. I can be patient."

"Good." I bring her to my chest, our bodies flush together. She draws her legs up, socked feet against my calves. "Sleep, sweetheart. There's only a few hours until morning, and it's going to be another long day."

"I can't wait to see what you have planned." Lola yawns and closes her eyes. "I don't care if it's watching paint dry. Every day with you is my new favorite day."

I hold those words close to my heart, alongside all the other things she's told me. How when she's with me, she thinks she can fly. How happy I make her. She's handing over the keys to her heart, and I intend to protect it. Fight for it. Make her see that she's worthy of a forever, and I have no plans to leave her behind.

Lola's breathing turns soft and steady. Her hand stays in mine, grip slackening ever so slightly but never letting go.

I lie there for hours, knowing it wasn't a shitty hotel room that made this moment feel like magic.

It was *her*.

She's the magic, the brightest star in every sky and the reason I don't want to go to sleep. Because sleep means a second away from her, and I don't want to waste any time.

And as the sun starts to creep in through the curtains and my eyes get heavy, I whisper "I love you" into her ear, because I've never been more sure about anything—*anything*—in my entire life.

TWENTY-FIVE
LOLA

PATRICK TIED a scarf around my head when we left the house this morning on our way to my surprise. I can't see where we're going, but I know we've been in the Jeep for close to forty-five mintes. I'm fidgety and hovering near the edge of my seat, not used to sitting stationary for so long without any stimulation. He said we were close, and I'm growing restless with every mile we drive in the car.

I tap my foot. I braid my hair and fiddle with my bracelet, turning it clockwise then counterclockwise. I count to a thousand then I count backwards, wondering how much longer it's going to be.

"Almost there," Patrick says. It's soothing and calm, a breath of fresh out. I relax with his voice and he reaches over, squeezing my knee. "I'm sorry this is taking so long. I didn't anticipate us sitting in traffic."

"That's okay," I answer. "Good things are worth the wait."

The car slows, nearing a crawl. A window rolls down and a rush of heat kisses my skin. Warm air, music playing. There's a low conversation, and a laugh I know belongs to Patrick.

I'd know his laugh in the dead of night. It's one of my favorite sounds in the world.

"Are we spending time outside?" I ask when the car moves again. I figured as much, when he told me I could wear shorts and a tank top but no jeans.

"And inside."

"Is it a museum? What museums do they have in Florida? Ones with fossilized mosquitoes?"

"Or a reptile one, featuring the world's most terrifying creatures. As fascinating as that would be, it's not a museum. It's better, I hope."

The engine shuts off, taking the air conditioning and radio with it. I sit up in my seat and turn my head from side to side despite not being able to see anything.

"Are we here?" I ask

"We are, but I need you to pop in your AirPods. It's going to amplify the surprise," he says.

"Earphones and an eye mask? People are going to think I'm being held against my will," I say.

Patrick unbuckles my seatbelt and the polyester moves across my chest. I feel his hand linger on my hip and his fingers flex against my thigh, the space where the denim ends and bare skin begins. Every place he touches me is a zap of electricity, a lightning bolt of awareness.

My senses are heightened without sight, hyper-aware of the small space we're in. The rising temperatures from seconds in the sun and the lack of noise, no sounds except for our breathing.

I remember how it felt when he slipped his palm under my shirt. Ran it up my stomach and over my ribs. Fanned his fingers out and outlined my breasts with his thumb, mumbling in my ear when I rocked back into him and arched my spine.

I want to do it again.

"I'll help you out," he says after a stretch of silence, and the heat extinguishes between us.

I fumble with my purse and slip my AirPods into my ears. I still have the Bowie playlist queued from the other day and I hum along. My door opens and I'm guided to solid ground. We walk a short distance, then we're sitting on something warm. Metal, I think. A train or trolley? We lurch forward and the vehicle moves onward.

There are a few steps, then more walking. Patrick keeps his hand in mine, a strong and sturdy grip he doesn't ease up on.

It's like how we woke up this morning, our legs intertwined and our palms pressed together. The cuddling was on purpose, an alarm not pulling us apart. I opened my eyes and saw him smiling at me. He tucked a piece of hair behind my ear as he kissed my cheek, and I can't wait for us to be in a place where I can show off our relationship. Shout to the world, *Hey! Look at us! We're together and happy as shit. Aren't you jealous?*

The right AirPod gets plucked out of my ear, the chorus from "All The Young Dudes" replaced with Patrick murmuring, "Hey." He's close, his chest against my back.

"Hi," I say.

"How are you doing?"

"I'm okay. I see why you didn't like having your eyes closed when we were in D.C. It's disorienting."

"You've done so well," he says, his knuckles running down my jaw.

"And do I get something for doing so well?" I ask.

"I already told you, Lola. You can have whatever you want." He takes the AirPod out of my left ear. I can hear people passing and whimsical music, loud laughter and shrieks of young children. He works on the scarf knotted at the back of my head, the silk falling away. "Anything," he reiterates, a whisper in my ear that sends a shiver down my spine, so many implications behind the word.

I feel dizzy.

"Noted," I whisper back. "Can I open my eyes?"

Patrick loops his arm around my front, across my clavicle. His chin rests on the top of my head and he nods. "Yeah, sweetheart. Go ahead."

I slide my sunglasses over my eyes to help with the glare and squint into the sunshine, finally able to read what's in front of me.

"Magic Kingdom?" I ask. I whip around and stare at him. "We're going to Disney World?"

"Yeah." He grins. "All day. I've planned out everything minute by minute."

"No." I shake my head and take a step back. "No. Patrick—this must have cost a lot of money. We'll be outside, and I know you hate the heat. I can't... I can't ask you to do any of this for me."

Patrick reaches out and offers me his hand. I bite my lip and take it, letting him tug me back toward him. "I'm not asking. I'm doing. Because I want to, remember? And I'm going to tell you a secret."

"A secret?"

"Yeah. I didn't pay for anything. Henry and Emma did."

"What? How? Why?"

"Your charity choice had the most donations at their wedding. Over fifty thousand dollars, they said. The organization has never received a monetary payment that large before, and they were beyond appreciative. When Henry and Emma found out I had a plan to bring you here, they gave us their Club 33 access. I guess it means exclusive benefits and not having to wait in line? I'm not totally familiar with it, but Henry made a call and told us we were all set. Free tickets. A special restaurant just for club members. Front of the line access at all the attractions. You talked about me deserving nice things, but you deserve them too. So, you're going to let me spoil the shit out of you while we're here, and you can be mad at me when we get back to the car." His lips tug into a smile. "Deal?"

A laugh comes out of my mouth the same time I start to cry. A whirlwind of emotion that I don't know how to prioritize. Soon I'm cackling hysterically as tears stream down my face and I hug Patrick in a tight embrace. "I could never be mad at you."

"Never?"

"Never," I repeat.

"Good." He uses his thumb to wipe away the smudged mascara under my eyes. "Because we have ten minutes until we need to be walking into the park, and we still have to ride the monorail."

"I know how much you love strict schedules and a plan. Lead the way, Patrick."

We go through the long security line, waiting among big families with exhausted parents and eager kids, over-packed strollers, and umbrellas for sun protection. Ralph, the nice man who asks us how our vacation is going, checks our bags and sends us on our way.

There's a quick ride on the monorail to the park entrance, and soon we're walking down Main Street hand in hand. I glance up at Patrick and that damn backwards hat. He's scrolling through his phone with his free hand, reciting the timeframes he picked for each of the attractions. I notice he's timed the indoor rides to line up with mid-afternoon, when the sun is highest in the sky and the heat is sweltering.

We've only been here for a few minutes, barely enough time for him to grab a coffee and guide me to our first stop—the Pirates of the Caribbean ride—but I already know I couldn't dream up a better day if I tried.

———

"YOU DID NOT *BEAT* ME, Lola. My laser stopped working," Patrick argues. "There's a difference." He lets out an huff and crosses his arms over his chest, glaring at the building behind me. I've never seen him look so irritated. "It betrayed me."

"We could always try again, if you're so sure it wasn't a user error," I suggest, shrugging one shoulder. "Best two out of three?"

"No. I'm not giving you the satisfaction of being right." He glances at his watch. "Besides, we have to move on to the next thing. How does The Haunted Mansion then dinner sound, honey?" he asks, twirling my ponytail through his fingers.

I'm still not used to him calling me something other than my name, and it catches me off guard. I misstep and lose my footing on the train tracks in the center of the road. "What? Oh. Sure. Sounds good to me. I'm starving," I say when I catch my breath.

I derail his carefully laid plans as we head toward the other side of the park, making it five minutes before we stop for an ice cream sandwich. We split the dessert, chocolate on our hands and crumbs clinging to our lips. I apologize for the diversion, knowing how he's allotted specific minutes to our entire day, but he doesn't seem to care. Patrick gives my arm a squeeze and kisses my forehead, letting out a jovial *fuck the plans* as he tugs us into the VIP entrance at The Haunted Mansion.

People crane their necks, glancing curiously as we pass, assessing us and wondering if we're important or famous. Like maybe one of us is a B-list celebrity or a former child actor.

Nope, I want to say. *Just a guy and a woman who's falling in love with him.*

He helps me into the moving ride vehicle and we take off into a dimly lit room.

"How's the day so far?" Patrick asks softly, his arm curling around my shoulders.

"Everything I hoped it would be and more. I don't think I can say thank you enough times to convey how appreciative I really and truly am. This must have taken hours to set up."

"I know you're appreciative." He pulls me across the bench, his shoulder pressing into mine.

I rest my head in the crook of his neck, under his chin. "I'm still going to say it."

"Worth me not answering your questions?" he asks, and I roll my eyes in the dark.

"Yeah, yeah yeah," I say. I squeal when he pokes my ribs and tickles my stomach. "Hands to yourself, buddy. You're going to make me laugh, and I'd hate to ruin the ride experience for all the children who think the ghosts are going to follow them home."

"If we've learned anything on this trip, we know ghosts can and will definitely follow us home," he says, dropping his hand to my knee, a safe zone. "But fine. I'll stop."

I feel bold, fueled by the dark lighting and the heat from both our bodies. My hand covers his and I drag it up my leg. "I like when you touch me," I whisper.

Patrick blows out a breath, a rush of air I feel against my cheek. His fingers press into the top of my thigh and he rubs his thumb over the silver button keeping my shorts in place.

"Where do you want me to touch you?" he asks in a husky voice. He drags his fingers along the waistband of the denim cutoffs and dips just under the top of my underwear. "Here?"

My legs widen without thought, opening for him willingly. Forget being in a public place. This is what I *need*.

"Yes," I say. "There."

"I'll add it to the pile of evidence I'm collecting."

"Evidence?"

"To see what you like. What you don't like. Maybe..." He runs his knuckle down my zipper, adding a push of pressure against the stitched seam. I bite my lip to keep from moaning and giving us away, and my back arches forward. "Ah. Definitely there. Listen to the sounds you make. Fucking sexy," he murmurs.

"Patrick," I whine.

"You can't say my name like that, Lola, or we're going to get kicked out of this theme park for the things I'm going to do to you," he says, low and deep in my ear. "And I haven't gotten to feed you like I want to. I haven't gotten to buy you a souvenir. I haven't gotten to spoil you in all the ways that I want, so you need to behave."

His hand falls away and I wiggle in the seat, craving the friction his touch could give me. "That's not fair." I drop my head back and close my eyes. "I'm all worked up."

"That's how I've felt around you for years." Our ride vehicle pulls back into the station, and I'm off-balance as I step onto the moving walkway toward the exit. "Out of my goddamn mind."

———

"WHY DID you get the pizza tattoo?" I ask Patrick. I toss a caramel popcorn kernel into the air and catch it in my mouth.

It's late and we're sprawled out on the grass in front of the castle, waiting for the fireworks show to begin. I glanced over his shoulder at dinner and saw the next half hour written in bold with capital letters on his phone. Being here is clearly important to him, the perfect end to the perfect day, and I'm not going to argue.

I want to be here too.

He looks indecent propped up on his elbow, his hair mussed and messy from wearing a hat all day and his white T-shirt making his skin look tan from hours outside. My body is still buzzing, itching to get his hands back on me. He knows it too, continuing to touch me but only with limited contact and brief grazes. He's teasing me and I want to hate it, but I don't.

I love the build of something new, of something we've yet to share. It's there, close within reach, and I know it's only a matter of time before it's ours.

"What do you mean?" Patrick answers. His long legs stretch out in front of him, right ankle crossed over his left, and he glances at me from under the light of a dozen streetlamps.

I lean forward and lift his sleeve. My thumb traces the outline on his arm. "The slice of pizza. It was a stupid idea, and the most spontaneous decision you've ever made in your life. Why did you go along with it?"

"Dunno," he says around a yawn. We've walked close to forty-thousand steps today, reaching every corner of the theme park in the thirteen hours we've been here, and I know he's spent. "Because you suggested it."

"You could have done anything. Like a dragon."

"A dragon tattoo? That's just absurd. I'm not cool enough to pull that off."

"Okay, fine. Not a dragon, but something better than a slice of freaking pizza."

"You like pizza," he says, and the three worlds hold so much weight. "And I like you. Seems like pretty simple math to me."

Time slows as understanding dawns. "It's not about the pizza," I say.

"No, Lola," Patrick says gently. "It was never about the pizza. You could've thrown out any idea and I would've been glad to get it inked on my body. Everything has always been about you, and nothing has ever been accidental."

I let out a breath, the weight of decades of fears lifting off my shoulders. This man is never going to leave me. I knew that then, when I met him for the first time and he tossed a paper airplane across our side yards and into my room. It had a smiley face on it and his messy handwriting scribbling out *thanks for being my friend*.

I know that now, years later as he sits outside in the temperature cresting over ninety degrees even with the sun down because we're doing something I've always wanted to do. No matter what might have happened to me in the past, no matter who I might have lost or how much my heart ached, there won't be another day of my life where Patrick isn't by my side.

"I want to be with you," I say. The surrounding lights dim and music begins to play, an orchestra with harps and violins. I scoot closer to Patrick, and he sits up.

"What does that mean?" he asks.

"It means I want to do this for real. Not as a vacation thing. Not as a two-week thing. A real relationship with real feelings. The messy ones. The happy ones. Good days, bad days, and every day in between. I'm scared. I don't think I'll ever stop being scared, but I want to be scared with you."

"Lola." Patrick tips his head and rubs his nose against mine. "Everything with you has always been real. I want your messy parts. The ugly parts. I want all of you, sweetheart. Do you want me too?"

"Yes," I whisper, having never been so sure of anything in my life.

It's there, under a million fireworks in the night sky, where Patrick presses his lips to the corner of my mouth, then right on my lips, finally kissing me once and for all.

Hollywood-level, I think, and the whole world can see that I'm his.

TWENTY-SIX

LOLA

I'VE NEVER HAD a kiss like this.

It's soft. Searching and experimental. Finding what the other person likes and cataloging it away to try again later in a place without an audience. A place where I'll be able to hear Patrick's every reaction and every breath. Every glide of fabric between our bodies and every beat of his heart.

It feels like we've been waiting for this for days. Hours and hours of torture while we teeter on the precipice of something remarkable. Looking and watching. Not touching but itching to, unsure of how to go forward and afraid to make the wrong move.

Now though, we both know. A confirmation behind the teeth sinking into my bottom lip. The sound of approval from the back of his throat and the moan from deep within mine. The hands running up my arms and holding me steady, a metaphor for how Patrick has held me steady for years.

It's the easiest, most seamless kiss of my life. Our first time, and we know exactly which way to turn our bodies, which angle to tilt our heads to avoid knocking teeth. It's like we've done this a hundred times already. A thousand times, familiarity in our movements and one step ahead, anticipating what the other wants before they ask for it.

Maybe in his mind, we *have* done this a thousand times. A thousand daydreams coming true and culminating to this moment, a kaleidoscope of color and feelings and waiting and bursts of magic splintering into confetti pieces of perfection.

Patrick pulls away and an immense wave of frigid cold washes over me with his absence. I'm empty, incomplete. I blink, bringing the blur of lights and people back into focus.

He tucks a piece of hair behind my ear and rubs his thumb across my cheek. "Hey," he whispers with a smile that rivals the sun. A secret hello just for me.

"Hey," I say, suddenly aware we're in public and I'm nearly straddling him, a half second away from climbing into his lap.

I have his shirt in my hands, holding on to the material clinging to the slope of his shoulders. His palm is on my neck, stroking up and down the length of my throat and over the clasp of the necklace hanging against my chest. I let out an indistinguishable sound as he caresses me, an embarrassing noise of approval for him to keep moving, to keep doing whatever it is he's doing, and a solar flare of heat flashes behind his eyes.

My skin turns hot and I move away from him, putting unwanted but necessary distance between us. Being so close to him makes my mind turn to ash, obliterated shards of sanity and rationality crumbling to the ground and scattering with the wind.

I touch my mouth and run the tips of my fingers over my swollen lips, the reminder of how Patrick kisses like he does everything else in life: with every ounce of himself. Dying moments on Earth and I'm his sole source of survival, breathing life into him with every movement. It's hot and it's sweet and it's both light and heavy, so much conveyed through such a simple action.

I kissed my best friend, and it was amazing.

I break out into a slow grin, my teeth showing and my nose wrinkling. A laugh sits on the tip of my tongue, not because it's funny but because it's so *right*.

"We should do that again," I say.

Patrick's eyebrows lift. I didn't think it was possible for a smile to stretch so wide, but his does. "Yeah?"

"Yeah. Yes. Immediately. Right now."

"If you insist. This *is* the place where dreams come true."

He cups my cheek and tilts my head back until all I can see are the stars in the sky and the fireworks above. This kiss is just as good as the first one, with care and consideration and *lust* behind it. His smile curves against mine, twin displays of glittering and gleaming elation.

"Do we have to stay until the end of the fireworks show?" I ask.

I run my hand through his hair and tug on the caramel strands against his neck. He makes a noise from the caverns of his chest, deep and low and so unholy.

I *knew* he would like that.

"We can leave whenever you want," he says. His voice is a little breathy, his words a little slurred around the edges, restraint chiseling away. "Are you ready to go?"

"Yeah." I dance my fingers down his jaw, the makings of a beard pricking my skin. "Take me home, Patrick."

It's not our home—we'll have to wait for that—but it's still a place where I feel safe and secure with him. A place where we can learn and explore and be ourselves.

He stands and helps me to my feet. His hand laces through mine, grip tight and bracing as we work our way through the crowd. We pass masses of people who have no idea that a life-changing kiss just took place on a small patch of grass thirty feet from here. Everything I've ever known forever upended and turned on its head.

We're the lone tourists heading to the parking lot while the rest of the world watch the entertainment. If they asked how I could leave in the middle of something so beautiful, I'd say I have something even more beautiful waiting for me on the other side. A man who adores me, a man who *wants* me, a heart more dazzling than any pyrotechnic show.

The ride to the house is quiet, the songs on the radio the only noise in the Jeep. An incendiary energy builds between us, cackling to a crescendo with every mile we drive. Patrick's hand never leaves mine, our fingers welded together as strong and sturdy as metal and iron.

When we park in the driveway, Patrick turns off the ignition. He jumps out of the car and hustles to my side, hauling me into his arms with a firm hold on the underside of my thighs.

"My bag," I say as he walks us up the path toward the front door, past the clay pots and the rocking chairs on the porch.

"Fuck the bag," he answers with gusto. "I'll get it in the morning."

I laugh into the crook of his neck, his determination and urgency astounding. He punches in the door code and walks us inside, kicking it closed with his back of his heel. I think his sneaker leaves a scuff mark on the white paint.

Instead of heading straight to the bedroom like I thought we would—*hell*, I'd even take the couch—he sets me down in the foyer and takes two steps back.

His chest is rising and falling, eyes locked on mine. He licks his lips and his hands tighten into fists hanging by his sides.

"Why are we stopping?" I ask.

"Because I just realized we've been at a theme park in the Florida sun for hours. We need to shower."

"Okay." I push the strap of my tank top up my shoulder and Patrick's eyes follow the piece of clothing with excruciating intensity and interest. "Do you want to shower together?"

"In the grand scheme of things? Yes, Lola, I want to shower with you. But not tonight. Not like this. I want..." He rolls his lips together and moves toward me. He spins us so I'm pressed against the living room wall, his hands bracketing my head. The plaster is rough behind my shoulder blades, and I arch my back.

"Want what?" I ask, prompting him to keep talking.

"I want to go slow," he says with a kiss to my throat. "Take my time." A kiss to my collarbone. His teeth bite the strap I just pushed up my arm and bring it back down slowly, methodically, with so much precision you'd think he did it every day. "Savor this. Savor you, honey."

I've never heard something so sexy, so *earnest* before. The desire to be kind and gentle snaps. I want him unrestrained, and I want to be the one to bring him to his knees. I crush my mouth against his. It's rough and it's wild, with more want and need behind the press of our lips. He runs his fingers across my shirt and over my chest, and I roll my hips into his.

Patrick breaks our contact to bend his neck and lower his chin, mouth working its way down my body before closing around my breast. His tongue sneaks out and circles my nipple. Over the cotton, wetting the material until it's practically translucent with saliva as he gently bites. I see stars and fragmented self-control crumbling away behind my eyes.

"Patrick."

I say his name desperately, close to begging and shamelessly needy. I've never felt like this before, like I might die without someone's touch, twisting and bending and finding any way to ask for more.

He hums against me, and the vibrations pulse to my toes.

Unrelenting, he moves his mouth to my other breast, tormenting me with renewed vigor and mind-numbing pleasure.

"You like that," he says with breathless wonder. It's not a question but a fact because he can tell. He *knows*, able to read me better than anyone else. "I like it too. You'd beg for my fingers, wouldn't you?"

Yes, I want to scream.

I'd do anything he asked.

The same man who once bought me three boxes of tampons because he didn't know the difference between brands is the same one plucking me apart, string by string, with just his words and his sinful mouth.

I fumble with the hem of his T-shirt, trying to pull it over his head without forcing him away.

"Please," I say.

I don't know what I'm asking for. Him? Everything? The stars and the moon? I can't tell, can barely remember my own name, but I know that whatever it is, *I want it.*

"Okay," Patrick says.

He folds his hands over mine and lifts his shirt over his head, throwing it into a crumpled heap on the floor. I rest my palms against his bare chest and run my fingers over his muscles. My nails drag down his stomach, a faint pink line blooming in their wake.

"Okay," I repeat.

"Let's"—he drops his forehead to mine and squeezes his eyes shut—"shower. You shower. First."

"You want to stop?"

"Stopping is the absolute last thing I want to do. I just—I need a minute."

"A minute?"

"Yeah. I haven't gotten to touch you the way that I want." His eyes open and he presses his thumb into the space just above my collarbone. "Fuck. *Fuck.* I want to make you feel good and I don't want to—you're the priority, Lola. If you keep looking at me like *that* and touching me like *this,* I can't make you the priority. Let me put you first. Please."

His honesty pulls at my heart, warms my insides, and makes me press my thighs together because it's so sincere. It's so *him,* and it's the most attractive I've ever found another person. We're slowing down instead of speeding up, enjoying every second, not just wanting to reach the finish line. My legs quake and I drop my head against the wall. "Fine. Shower first."

"Come here."

Patrick pulls me to him, both large hands cupping my cheeks. I feel small but important in his hold, not just a person but *his* person, relishing in calculated touches as he threads his fingers through my hair and works out a knotted strand then pushes the pad of his thumb into my neck.

I melt, body bowing and heart racing. Everything in me pulls tight, liquid heat pouring over my body, bucket after bucket.

"I'm going to walk away," I say against his lips, reluctant to put even a millimeter of space between us. "If I don't, nothing about this will be slow, and I'll ruin your plan."

Patrick laughs and nods. "You're trouble. Go. I'll come find you in the bedroom soon."

"Promise?"

He takes my hand, kissing my knuckles and placing it over his heart. "Promise."

Walking away is difficult, almost impossible, but I know there's a promise of better things soon. New beginnings and so much more to learn. It's a temporary parting, a pause, a couple of minutes of separation before I see him again.

The shower is the fastest of my life. I wash my hair and scrub my body clean, rub lotion on my face and arms. I wrap a towel around my body and slip into the empty bedroom, trying to decide what to wear.

I overanalyze everything in my suitcase, settling on an oversized T-shirt—one of Patrick's I stole years ago that's faded and soft—and pajama shorts. I take a seat on the edge of the mattress before standing, tidying the sheets and pillows.

Counterproductive, probably, but I can't sit still, nervous and eager and excited about what's coming next.

It feels like forever passes before the door finally opens and Patrick is there in clean shorts and a white shirt, with damp hair and red skin.

God, he's so handsome. A boy I've watched turn into a *man*, his body changing into one that's perfectly crafted and beautifully sculpted. Broad shoulders. Muscular. Masculine, without being overly fit or bulky. The kindest heart and the warmest smile.

And now he's *mine*.

"Hey," I say.

"Hey." He leans against the wall and crosses his arms over his chest. "Can I join you?"

I sit on the bed and swing my legs on top of the comforter, patting the pillows next to me. "Please."

He moves across the room and sits on the mattress. He looks down at me and brushes a piece of hair out of my face, his touch lingering on my cheek. "Pretty," he whispers. "So pretty."

I swallow and grab the collar of his shirt, yanking him toward me. "You're pretty too. I like looking at you."

"Lo." He trails his fingers down my neck. "I know we kissed, but that doesn't mean we have to do anything else." His eyes bounce to my throat and across my chest. "We can turn out the lights and go to sleep."

"We could," I agree. I push up on my knees so we're near the same height. I lean forward and brush my mouth over his. "We could also leave the lights on."

"Okay." He rests his hands on my thighs, fingers curling around my skin. "Whatever you want."

"I want you, Patrick. But I have to tell you something first."

TWENTY-SEVEN

PATRICK

MY HEART STOPS BEATING.

There's an edge to Lola's voice. A secret she's afraid to share. One she's probably had buried for years, finally being pulled out of its hiding place and brought to life.

"What is it?" I ask.

"It's embarrassing." She averts her gaze, staring at the wall past my shoulder instead of at me. "It might make you change your mind."

"Change my mind?" I repeat. "What do you mean?"

"I overthink in the bedroom. A lot. It could be my medicine messing with my head, or maybe it's just me. No one has ever made me—I can't—"

"Lola." I take her chin in my hands, utterly confused. She's not making any sense, and I desperately want to understand her. "Will you look at me, please?" Her lips tremble and her blue eyes meet mine. "Hey."

"Hi." She sniffs and wipes her nose. "I'm sorry."

"I want you to know something right off the bat, honey. With us, there are zero expectations. You don't owe me an explanation of anything happening in your life. If you want to talk to me about something that's important to you, I hope you know I'll gladly listen. But if you want to keep things to yourself, that's also okay."

"I want to tell you. I don't want us to have any secrets."

"Then I'm all ears."

"No one has ever made me come."

I blink. My eyebrows wrinkle and I stare at the spot on her neck I'm learning I really, really like. Just above her collarbone, the sliver of skin I want to drag my tongue across. "What?"

"No one has ever made me come," she says again. It's louder this time, with more confidence.

"No one?"

"No."

"Ever?"

"Nope."

"Can you—you *can* come, yeah?"

"Yeah. On my own. With toys and my hand. I just get in my head when I'm with someone else. I'm worried I'm taking too long or they're not enjoying themselves. Then I think about all the other things I could be doing, but I'm not, and it takes me out of the moment."

My mind wanders to Lola in her room. One hand under her shirt, the other beneath her shorts, teasing and testing. Learning and finding the exact spot that drives her wild. Slick fingers, a parted mouth, and soft moans. It's wicked. It's sexy. It's *so fucking hot*.

Does she keep a toy at my place when she stays over? In the drawer by her bed, next to my headache medicine? Does she use it when I'm home, holding back a gasp so I don't hear her down the hall?

Christ.

I can never look at her nightstand again.

I clear my throat. The room is warmer than it was five

minutes ago and I'm going to need to set the thermostat down a couple degrees. Twenty, maybe, if Lola keeps talking like this.

"So," I say. "To summarize: you've gotten yourself off, but another person hasn't been able to make you come. Is that right?"

"That's right."

I think I'm going to have an aneurysm trying to process all this information. I'm tugged between nineteen different emotions. Irritated that people have given up on her in bed so easily, making her experiences lackluster and forgettable. Ecstatic that I might be the first one to help her to the finish line. Contemplative as I consider how the *hell* I'll get her there and what she might like best.

It's hard to focus on anything rational when Lola is watching me, her cheeks bright red and her bottom lip between her teeth. I haven't even touched her yet, not really, and she's already driving me wild.

"Thank you for telling me," I say.

"I've never admitted that to anyone. Not the girls. Not past partners. I feel safe with you, Patrick, and I wanted to tell you."

"You are safe with me," I say, reassuring her. "Even if you haven't been able to come, does it still feel good?"

"What?"

"Does it still feel good? If I do this..." I graze my thumb over her nipple and her eyes flutter closed. I remember that it's the same reaction she had when I licked her over her shirt in the living room. My stomach swoops low and a white-hot sensation pulses up my spine as I watch her. "Ah. It *does* feel good."

"Yes," she whispers, twisting her body and grabbing the sheets, the cotton an anchor under her fingers. "I always get close, but I can never tip over the edge. I don't want you to think it's you. It's me. It's definitely me."

"It's not you, Lola. You want to know why?"

"Why?"

"Because someone who cared about you wouldn't give up that easily. They'd like the challenge. They'd put in the effort. It might not happen the first time, but they'd keep trying to find what makes you feel good. What you like best. And I'd like to try, if it's okay with you."

"What happens if I can't finish?"

I move my body and straddle her legs, then lean forward and graze my teeth down the slope of her neck. "Did you bring any toys with you?"

"No. I didn't think this was ever a possibility, especially before the trip. I wasn't planning on using a vibrator while you slept four feet away from me."

"That's a shame. It sounds hot." I nip at her ear. "If you can't finish, I'll still get to spend time with my head between your legs, and you're never going to hear me complain about that. Arms up, Lola. I want to take off this shirt so I can see more of you."

She sits up, our mouths inches apart. Her arms lift and I bring the large T-shirt over her head, tossing it into a forgotten corner of the room. My eyes stay locked on hers, waiting until she lowers her chin in silent approval before I look at her the way I *want* to look at her. The way I've dreamed about looking at her.

Permission granted, I drop my gaze to her throat and watch her play with the silver pendant on her necklace. It's a bumble-bee, the piece of jewelry a gift from her dad on her eighteenth birthday.

There's a second or two where I forget to breathe, where my face turns blue because of the lack of oxygen getting to my lungs. I inhale sharply when I get to her chest, nearly choking on air.

Nothing—not a goddamn thing—in life prepared me for

seeing the woman I've loved for months practically naked under me. Writhing and wiggling, her pupils wide. Chest rising and falling, as if she's been sprinting for miles, and cheeks impossibly red. She releases the sheets from her grasp, her fingers moving to my hair and pulling hard.

It's like she's trying to control herself. Trying to hold back and not go too fast, too soon. I know I told her I want to savor her, but seeing how perfect she is makes it really difficult to remember *why*.

"Patrick," she whispers.

I've never heard my name sound so beautiful. I want to record the two syllables so I can play it on a continuous loop every day. It's just on the edge of begging, and I've never seen Lola—independent, fierce, determined Lola—so needy for something before.

It ignites me. It makes me tilt my hips into hers so she can feel how hard I am and how badly I want her. When she arches her body into mine, it's encouragement, adding fuel to the fire.

"Can I try?" I ask again.

I cup her bare breast and run my thumb over her nipple. Relish in her quiet sigh and how touching her is even better without any clothes. Her skin is smooth and warm, with tan lines and freckles. I smell the faint trace of sunscreen and a hint of flowers.

I decide right this very second that if a day comes when I know I only have two minutes left in this world, I'll ask to be right here, touching her. It's heaven.

She nods her assent and kisses me. "I'll do my best," she murmurs against my lips.

"You're perfect. Lie back for me."

Lola rests her head against the pillows. Her hair really does look like liquid sunshine, blonde strands scattered across the silk. I hover over her, my elbows on either side of her shoulders.

"Are you going to tell me what you like?" I whisper in her ear. I pull at the waistband of her shorts and snap the elastic against her hips. Her moan is low and long, a sound of pleasure from the back of her throat. "Or do I get to spend all night figuring it out for myself?"

"I like a lot of things," Lola says. She rests her hand on her stomach, fingers drumming against her skin.

"You don't sound too sure."

"Because you're making it impossible to think straight."

Good.

I don't care how long it takes. I'm going to be the first—and last—person to make her come. Whether that happens tonight, tomorrow, or in a month, I don't care. I'm going to wear the damn badge with pride, knowing she's wholly and completely mine.

My lips move to the top of her chest, then farther down. I take her breast in my mouth, tasting her, and her moan is louder than before. It echoes off the walls and rings in my ears.

I need to learn what else I can do to hear that sound.

"Found the first thing you like," I say. My teeth bite down on the soft flesh around her hard nipple. I'm awarded a string of muttered words, my favorites being *fuck* and *yes* and *again*. "Let me guess. No one has bothered to pay attention to you before. Learned the little things and worshiped you like you deserve."

"I guess not," she says, gritty and rough. Her hands move to grip my shoulders then my arms, sharp nails leaving pink marks on my skin from where she's trying to hold on. "More. I need more."

I enjoy watching her come apart, and I like knowing she needs me. I think she's always relied on me a little, and this is another moment where she's trusting me, needing me, and I plan to deliver.

"What else do you need? What else do you like? Maybe if I

put my hand here?" I place my palm on her thigh, my thumb playing with the hem of her pajama shorts. I thought they were cute before, but now I want to rip them off her body. "Do you like that?"

"I like that a lot."

My fingers move up her leg to the front of her shorts and I press the heel of my palm against her. I can feel how wet she is through the thin scarp of cotton. Telling me just how much she wants this, and how much she wants *me*.

I look down at where we're touching as I slide my hand under the only barrier separating me from nirvana. I nudge her chin with my nose, silently telling her she can watch too, and she blows out a breath. I'm greeted with bare skin and nothing stopping me from sinking my fingers into her. Stretching her wide and seeing how much she can take at one time.

Patience, I tell myself.

I hate that damn word.

"Fuck," I whisper. I'm so hard, I use my free hand to palm myself. "*Fuck*, Lola."

"Take them off," she says. "Please."

My mind spins into overdrive as I wrap the tiny drawstrings around my finger and give a little tug. She lifts her hips and I gently yank the shorts, watching as they fall down her thighs to her knees and over her shins before I cast them aside.

She's naked in front of me, her body like a goddess made of curves and divots and stretch marks on the sides of her thighs. Something you'd find in a painting—perfect proportions, perfect size, perfect everything. I could get lost in her, the skin around her hips and the tone of her legs. I've never seen a more wondrous sight.

"Patrick. Look at me."

I raise my chin and meet Lola's eyes. A bead of sweat rolls down my cheek and she wipes it away with her thumb. I'm

CHELSEA CURTO

trying to be good. I'm trying so fucking hard to do this *right*, but when her eyes are hooded and she's asking me to look at her, it makes me want to say *fuck it* and sink into her with a single thrust.

"You're beautiful," I say, my voice hoarse, my throat dry. My vision is hazy, her figure blurring around the edges the longer I stare. "So beautiful."

"Talk to me. What are you thinking about?"

"Selfish things. Greedy things. How I would have you and what I think you'd like."

"I want you to be selfish and greedy, because I'm giving you all that I have," she says, the intention thick with desire.

"Fucking *finally*," I say around a long exhale. "Spread your legs, honey. Let me see how wet you are for me."

Her knees part and drop open slightly. I wrap my hands around her thighs and spread them farther apart, wide enough to accommodate me. I move down the mattress, my stomach against the bed, ready for more.

"Last time you were with someone?" I ask.

"Five months ago," she pants, the end of the sentence going up an octave when I kiss her hip. "Tested recently."

"Me too. I want you to communicate with me, okay? You're going to tell me if you like something so I can make this good for you. And if you don't like something, you're going to tell me that too."

"Always so selfless. You're such a giver," she says through a strained breath, and I can hear her smile.

"I am a giver. But tonight, I'm going to take what's mine. What's *only* mine. For good."

It's the only warning I give her before my thumb finds her clit and I stroke her twice.

TWENTY-EIGHT
LOLA

I CAN TELL the moment Patrick's restraint breaks. The exact second his control shatters into a million fragmented pieces of wonderment and want.

He turns less polite and becomes more in control, touching me with deft precision and the one to set the pace. The flick of his wrist against my thigh and the circle of his thumb between my legs. Finding the places where I'm most sensitive and humming in approval when I arch my back off the mattress and chant *Please*.

He adjusts each time he decides I'm not giving him enough affirmation of my enjoyment, changing his rhythm or his position to get a better angle. He figures me out in a heartbeat, nodding and smiling against the inside of my knee when I make a particularly grateful noise like he's *proud* of me.

My spine pulls tight as he touches my clit, and warmth builds in my stomach. My toes curl against the sheets. It's difficult to see, my eyes starting to close as I chase a high, but I fight it, wanting to see *him*.

It's unreal to watch him like this, the man with an affinity for spreadsheets and calendar reminders with his head between my legs and his gaze locked on mine. His cheeks are flushed and the tips of his ears are pink. There's a determined look in his eye, tenderness in the way he's studying me as I lie here, bare and open for him, not an ounce of boredom or indifference on his face.

When he finally slides a finger inside of me, the sound he makes is obscene. My moan matches his, satisfaction on the tips of our tongues.

"Good?" he asks. It's like he's drunk, slurred words and reluctant movements, wanting to drag out the moment to last forever.

"God, yes," I answer.

It's loud and it's needy and it's depraved, but I don't care. I do need him.

This is different from any other intimate experience I've ever had. Those encounters were hurried. Quick and fleeting. A rub here, a jerk there. No one has ever paid this much attention to me, realizing I prefer slow circles instead of fast. Discovering I like my hair pulled, wrapped around a wrist and yanked with a gentle tug. And when Patrick presses a kiss between my legs, his tongue following the same path he created with his finger, I almost obliterate into smithereens.

I'd be happy to go.

"You like that too," he says with pride.

He's close to gleeful at being able to discover parts of me no one else has ever found. When I don't give him a response, he pinches my clit and my back bows forward.

"Yes," I say around a panting breath. "I like it all."

I'm close to being embarrassed by my enthusiasm, but Patrick doesn't give me time to dwell on my eagerness, adding a second finger and making me see stars. He stretches me, whispering all the things he wants to try, telling me I'm doing *good* and he *loves to watch*.

Two minutes pass, then three, then four. It's fantastic. Exceptional. Out of this world. I like hearing how it sounds when Patricks slides his fingers out of me then back in. Slick with moisture dripping down to coat the inside of my thighs. It's a tease, a game to see how long it takes me to ask for more.

Is he enjoying himself? I wonder.

He seems to be, with his quiet words and the smile he's giving me. Should I be touching him? *Yes, yes I should.* I thread my fingers through his hair and massage his scalp. Patrick lets out a soft groan, and I'm going to assume he likes that a lot.

Should I offer to switch positions so he's on the bed and I'm over him? Maybe I'm taking too long and he's losing interest. Maybe I should've skipped my medication this morning. That might have made my reaction time better. We could be moving on to the next thing by now, the main act, but I'm slowing us down. Maybe I shouldn't have skipped my medicine, because then I'd be thinking about the clothes hanging in the closest and the last minute changes I want to do before the show. No one can possibly like foreplay this much, can they?

Shit.

The pleasure dissipates. The warmth cools. I fall from the cliff and back to the ground, so far from the high I was close to reaching.

My legs tense and I close them tight around his head as shame works its way up my body. I cover my face with my hands, my cheeks burning with mortification.

"What's wrong?" Patrick asks, and I hear the concern in his question.

"I'm not going to finish," I say. "I'm sorry."

Here I am with the most wonderful man in the world, the most patient person who sees me exactly for who I am, and I *still* can't shut off my brain. I'm ninety-eight percent there. Maybe even ninety-nine percent there. But wherever I am, it's not one hundred percent, and disappointment claws at my elation, turning it to shredded defeat.

"That's okay. That's all right," he says.

The mattress shifts and sinks. Patrick pulls me into his lap and kisses my cheek. My forehead and my neck. He kisses anywhere his mouth can reach, marking my body in every way he can.

"I liked it so much. I just—" I start.

"Remember what I said? You never have to explain yourself, Lola. We'll take a break and try again later."

"You want to try again?" I ask, moving my hands away and glancing up at him.

"Of course I do." He leans forward and kisses my lips. I can taste myself on his tongue, sinfully delicious. "See how good you taste? You'd want to keep trying too."

I feel so *wanted* by Patrick. Wanted and adored. I try to convey that I feel the same way about him without using words. By sliding my hands under his shirt, my palms splaying out over the taut muscles I've been dreaming of touching. His body lurches forward and his shaky exhale is a phantom caress against my ear.

"I want to make you feel good," I whisper. "I want to touch you for a while. Can I do that?" My hand moves to the front of his shorts and I stroke up his length. "That would help me, I think."

"Lola, you can do anything you want," he says, a raspy gasp.

He eases me out of his lap and stands on shaky legs. He pulls his shirt over his head and I see the firm lines of his chest. The result of the hours he spends running before school, honing his body to peak physical shape. The dark hair that trails down his stomach and the tattoo on his arm.

He hooks his fingers in the waistband of his shorts and tugs them down, stepping out of them and kicking them aside. I blink, nearly overwhelmed at seeing him naked for the first time. His jutted hip bones and his cock, thick and heavy between his legs.

I reach out to touch him but my eyes snag on something at the top of his thigh. Three somethings, each the size of a postage stamp.

"What are those?" I push onto my knees and crawl across the mattress.

They were hidden under his clothes, and now that he's naked, I can see them as clear as day. I've never noticed them before.

"Ah." Patrick runs a hand over his face and blows out a breath. "They're tattoos."

"Since when do you have more tattoos?" I stare, getting close enough to try to decipher them. Maybe they're another drunken mistake. Something he got in college and never bothered to get rid of but was too embarrassed to tell me or let me see. "It's—" My head jerks up. "No."

His smile is sheepish and shy. He reaches out and takes my hand, guiding it to his body and letting me trace the outlines with the tips of my fingers. "Like I said, Lola. With you, nothing is accidental."

There, in a secret space no one would ever see, is a stack of books. A needle with a spool of thread. And a treehouse, complete with a ladder and two tiny windows, an exact replica of the one we spent so much time in together as kids.

My lips tremble as I lean forward, kissing the first one then the second and the third. I run my finger over them again and again, learning their shape and colors and the angles of their lines. I'm afraid that the more I touch them, the more likely it is they'll disappear, erased forever.

They're never going to disappear.

They're a permanent fixture on him. Reminders of our friendship, always with him wherever he goes.

Reminders of *me*.

"When?" I ask.

"The summer we left for college," he says, tapping the tree-house. "When you sold your first commission," he continues, tapping the needle.

"And the books?"

"A couple of weeks ago. Right before you got home from Italy."

"You've had these for years? While you've dated other women? And you've kept them hidden them from me?"

"Yes," Patrick answers. He doesn't deny it.

"Why?" I ask, more than a couple of words difficult to find.

"I miss you when you leave," he says. He cups my cheek and his thumb wipes away a tear I didn't realize had fallen. "I miss you so fucking much. I feel empty when you're not around. It's like a piece of my soul is missing. A piece of my heart is carved out when I can't see your smile or hear your laugh. I turned to tattoos as a way to always have you around. Even when you aren't here, you're still *here*. You've ruined me, Lola, for anyone else. I'm utterly destroyed and totally wrecked. I have been for a while now. Only you can put me back together."

The words pierce my soul. Of all the books we've read together with their romantic declarations and grand gestures, his confession is the most prolific and poignant one. It's real and it's raw and it's *perfect*.

I'm ruined too.

Every single part of me belongs to Patrick.

I think I've always belonged to him, some subconscious lock placed around my heart years ago. Guarding it until I was strong enough to realize the reason I've been so terrified of trying with anyone else, the reason I've been hesitant to let anyone have my imperfect parts and allow them to see all of me, is because they weren't *him*. I didn't trust them or believe they wouldn't leave. Not like I trust Patrick.

I think I've belonged to him for twenty-four years, and every moment that passes where he stares at me and I stare back, I know exactly what these feelings mean.

I love him.

Of course I love him. I've always loved him.

I'm *in love* with him.

Hopelessly, irrevocably, completely, and totally in love with him.

It wasn't fast, infatuation at first sight or a hot and heavy rendezvous. It's been a slow and steady kind of love that's taken time and patience and restraint. Mistakes and fears and hesitations. A love worth waiting for.

I love him, and I never want to love anyone else.

Our eyes meet and we lunge at the same time, a flurry of limbs and hands and touching. Patrick tackles me just as I reach out for him, our bodies landing in a tangled heap on the mattress.

"Patrick." I kiss him and run my hands down his chest. "I miss you so much when I'm gone. I play your voice memos a hundred times a day. I look at your pictures and wonder what you're doing."

"The next time you go somewhere," he whispers in my ear, "I'm going with you."

"I can spend more time at home so neither one of us is lonely again."

"Compromise," he says. "Look at us."

"I want you," I say, and it comes out like a plea.

He flips us, my legs on either side of his hips and his back flat on the bed. "Sit on my face."

I choke on a sputtered breath, the mood shifting at the drop of a hat. Desperation and wildness replacing reflective and sweet. "What?"

"We're going to try again just like I said, and this time, I want you to sit on my face."

"You'll get tired. I don't want to keep you down there for an hour."

"I don't give a shit if it takes one hour or five. Sit on my face, Lola, and let me eat you out."

"Okay. *Okay.*"

I can't deny the man who literally inked his skin because of me. The man I adore more than anything in the world. Who's willing to try and try and *try*, determined to make me feel good. I climb up his body, my thighs bracketing his head. I look down and see a wicked glint to his smile. His dimples pop and he licks his lips, his fingers digging into my thighs.

It looks like he's about to feast.

God, he's hot. I love so many parts of him, all the kindness and gentleness of his heart and mind, but I can't deny how damn attractive he is, especially like *this*.

"I know you don't like to squat, honey. Fucking sit, and let me take care of you how you deserve. Let me show you how much those tattoos mean to me. How much *you* mean to me." His words put me in a trance and I lower myself onto his face as he pushes my legs farther apart. "There you go. That's my girl," he says. And then he licks me without abandon.

It's messy. Loud and unhinged. I grind into his mouth. He uses his tongue, his thumb, his free hand. As he squeezes the curve of my ass, I decide I need to get my own tattoo of his fingerprints on my skin in the places I'm learning he likes the most. The sensations come in stronger this time, starting at my toes and working their way up to where we're joined.

Patrick groans and his grip tightens. I hope he leaves a bruise so I never have to forget how wonderful and pleasant this feels.

My skin burns and I drop my head back, my hands tugging at his hair.

"You're so hot, Lola," he mumbles, and I know he's enjoying this too.

"Close," I say. "Patrick."

His name is both a prayer and an ask. Before I can blink, I'm on my back. Lifted off of him in a motion so quick I don't even register it happening. He shoves my thighs apart and pushes two fingers inside of me. "I want to see you when you come, Lola. Open your pretty eyes."

I do as he says, tiptoeing on the ledge and inching toward the fall I crave. We stare at each other, gazes locked, and nothing else in the world matters.

"Don't stop," I whisper. "Please."

"I'm never going to stop," he answers, a myriad of meanings behind the words as he licks me again, the most incredible feeling following the path of his tongue.

It's a tsunami, a volcanic eruption I feel everywhere. My hands, my back, my chest. I've ascended to the stars, out of the room and high above, to the most magical place I never want to come down from. Wave after wave of pleasure knocks into me, unrelenting, and I ride it to the shore.

I'm shaking on the sheets as the orgasm starts to subside. My limbs are heavy, weights attached to my arms and legs. It's nearly impossible to open my eyes until the euphoria abates, relinquishing its grip on me as I settle into mindlessness.

There's a hand on my face brushing the hair out of my eyes. Rubbing my shoulders. I hear whispered words soothing me, and I blink, the room around me coming into focus. Four walls, a ceiling fan, dim lighting and *Patrick*. The one responsible for my elation.

"There she is," he says, kneeling above me.

I reach for him and he kisses my palm. "Hi."

"Doing okay?"

"That was…" I trail off and break into a grin. "You made me come."

"Yeah." His ears turn red and he dips his chin. My shy and respectful best friend is back. "I did."

"And it didn't feel weird."

"No," he answers, his mouth pulling up in the corner. "It was anything but weird."

I sit up and look between his legs. He's still hard, and I wrap my hand around his cock, giving him a gentle stroke.

"I like knowing you're hard for me," I say. I circle his head and drag my fingers through the pre-cum I find there. "I like knowing I affect you."

"Lola. I'm out of my mind for you. Affect doesn't even scratch the surface."

He thrusts his hips and my hand works up and down his length. Just like our first kiss, it makes *sense,* and the rhythm of finding what he likes is easy to learn. My palm runs from the base to the tip, back and forth in quick movements.

"I can't wait until you're inside me. I can't wait until you fuck me. Until you make me yours," I say, adding a twist of my hand. I bend from my hips and lick his shaft, mouth closing around his head, and that's when Patrick snaps.

He pulses in my grip and lets out a long groan. His shoulders roll forward and his arm shoots out, using the wall to stabilize himself so he doesn't topple over. I pull off his cock just before he finishes, and Patrick covers my hand and my stomach with his release as he groans again.

"Jesus," he mumbles, gasping for air. "Fucking hell."

I bring my fingers to my mouth and lick away the mess he left behind, swallowing the remnants. His eyes turn molten, following the swipe of my tongue with ragged interest. "Delicious," I say.

"You're trouble."

"You like it."

"Lola, that's the fastest I've come since I was in high school. Of course I liked it."

"We should've been doing that for years," I say.

"We never would have left the apartment," he answers. "You're too distracting."

Patrick drags me to the shower, where he proceeds to scrub my my arms and my legs with a bar of soap. He crouches to his knees and kisses my thighs and my hips, telling me my body is beautiful and a thousand other affirmations I vow to hold close to my heart forever.

When we climb into bed and shut off the lights, we don't sleep, staying awake until the morning hours as the sun rises outside the windows. We talk. We laugh. We hold each other close because we finally *can*, and I know then that I am never going to let this man go.

TWENTY-NINE
PATRICK

"GOOD MORNING," I whisper, dropping a kiss to Lola's forehead.

She looks like an angel in the white sheets, her cheek in her hand and her eyes blinking open.

"Morning," she answers, exhaustion around the edges of her greeting. "What time is it?"

"Earlier than you like to be up."

"Why the heck are you awake?"

"I guess I'm just excited to be next to you." I brush a lock of hair away from her face and laugh when she scrunches her nose.

"Cheesy, but that line worked," Lola says. "You made my heart all fluttery."

"Fluttery. There's an adjective I haven't heard before. I'm taking it as a good thing."

"A very good thing. Maybe you'll see it in a crossword puzzle one day."

She sits up and stretches her arms above her head. We didn't bother to put clothes on last night and the covers fall away from her naked body, pooling around her waist.

Lola is always beautiful, but Lola in the morning light is exquisite. I want to take a picture of her and capture the way the sunrise looks on her skin. Reds and yellows and oranges, like a work of fine art that deserves to be immortalized in a portrait gallery. Her messy hair and swollen lips. The bite mark on her chest, just above her breast.

"Want me to make some breakfast?" I ask, my gaze slipping away from her hips to her face. Her stomach grumbles, an answer to my question.

"Is there any food here?"

"Besides the rest of the miniature pies? No. I can run to the store and get some eggs and bacon, though. I'll make toast with lots of butter, just the way you like it."

Her smile is soft. She cups my cheek and stares into my eyes. The windows to her soul, letting me see so much of her. Hope and joy. Love, too.

"I'm not over how right this feels with you, Patrick," she says. "I don't think I'll ever get over how much I like being in your arms and how wonderful you are. I think I expected to wake up this morning and feel like we did something wrong, but I know we haven't. We're exactly where we need to be, and I wouldn't want to be here with anyone else."

I'm glad to hear her say that, a confirmation that everything we've done up to this point has been okay. I know her fears. I know what she's afraid of, and I plan to spend every day proving to her that I'm not going to leave. Until the end of time, I'm going to be by her side.

I'm weak. I know I'm weak, a complete and total pushover when it comes to her—I always have been—but I don't care. When you love someone, when you want to show them all the *good* parts of life, why wouldn't you give them anything they ask? Why wouldn't you compromise and give a little to take a little so both of you could be happy?

There's going to come a time—soon, probably, if I had to guess—where we'll have to figure out how to make our differences work. Sleep schedules, work schedules. Travel preferences and routines. But I'm not worried. I know we'll figure it out. People who love each other *always* figure it out, and I undoubtedly love Lola Jones.

We're going to be okay.

"Was that a yes to breakfast?" I ask.

"Yes." She laughs, wrapping her arms around my neck. "Yes to breakfast. Yes to everything."

Yes to loving you, I think, pulling the sheets off of her legs and kissing her senseless.

———

"YOU KNOW I'm not a guy who needs fancy things, but this is much nicer than the room in Virginia," I say, walking around our suite at the convention center hotel later that morning.

It's three times the size as the shoebox we slept in the other night, with a separate living room and a bathroom that could rival a small apartment.

"You don't miss the ghosts?" Lola asks, putting her clothes in the dresser under one of the three televisions in the room. "It added to the charm."

She started to unpack the minute we got the keys and stepped inside the room. It's not something she would normally do, usually living out of her suitcase. I know she's doing it for me, wanting to get the bags out of the way so I'm not on edge with clutter all around us for the next few days. Her consideration makes me all tingly.

"Charm? The ceiling leaked on us the second night."

"It was antique," she answers. She giggles when I pull her

into my arms and spin her around, my hands sliding into the back pocket of her shorts.

"We made it. We're here. You're one step closer to your dreams. Have I told you today how proud I am of you?"

"You told me you liked my ass when I bent over to pick something up, but I haven't heard about how proud you are."

"I'm so proud of you, Lola Jones," I say. "I cannot wait to watch your clothes come down the runway in a few days."

"Thank you for being here with me."

"There's nowhere else I'd rather be." I kiss her cheek and notice her eyes bounce over my shoulder to the desk where she set up her sewing machine. "What's wrong?"

"Nothing's wrong. I think an idea just came to me," she says cautiously. Her head tilts to the side, wheels turning.

"It did?"

"Yeah. A different top to go under one of the blazers I'm showing for women's day. I'm not sure if I should try it. It's a little different from my normal style."

"Do it," I say. "Why not? You're here to test yourself and do things you've never done before, right? Could you get it finished in time?"

Lola nods, and I can tell her fingers are itching to grab the patterned fabric leaning against the wall. She brought extra yards for this very reason, in case inspiration hit her while we were on the road.

"I could have it finished in a few hours," she says.

"Have at it, sweetheart."

"No. Wait, no. I don't want to make you sit around while I work."

I take her by the hand and guide her to the desk chair. I set the bag with all her supplies—scissors, tailor's tape, needles, and threads—in front of her and kiss the top of her head.

"I'm going to the gym. Do your thing, Lola. I can entertain myself. Maybe I'll see an alligator."

"At the gym?"

"We're in Florida. This place is unpredictable. Never say never."

She reaches up and grabs my collar. "Thank you," she murmurs. "You'll have all my attention later. I promise."

"I'm going to take my phone so you can call me if you need anything."

"Okay." She turns to the machine with determination in her eyes, and I know our conversation is over.

Lola's been like this since we were kids, carrying a sketch-book in her backpack and dissolving into silence when an idea pops into her brilliant mind. She's quick to tune things out like she's doing with me right now, focusing solely on the idea in front of her. She might only have an hour or two before that attention wavers, so I kiss her cheek and grab my gym clothes from my bag, leaving her to work without my interruptions.

I slip in my AirPods and send a message to the guys in our group chat as I walk down the hall.

Hey. Anyone free for a FaceTime call?

My phone rings a second later, and I laugh as Henry's name pops up.

"Are you sure you should be calling me on your honeymoon?" I ask, punching the down button on the elevator. "Your wife is more important than me."

"I know she is." I hear a muffled voice, then his face appears on my screen. He's wearing sunglasses over his eyes and a hat is on his head, bright sunshine and blue ocean water in the background behind him. "She's the one who told me to call you."

"Hey, Em." I wave. "How's Greece?"

"Sitting by the ocean all day is *horrible*," she says, her wedding ring catching in the light.

"I'm so sorry to hear about your struggles."

"We're having a great time. How was Disney?"

"Incredible. Thank you for making that happen. It's amazing what exuberant wealth can buy, like not having to wait in any lines at the world's busiest theme park," I say.

I smile, remembering the massive pretzel Lola and I split. Riding Big Thunder Mountain in an afternoon rainstorm, our clothes soaked to our bones and how quickly they dried when the sun came out. The photo of us on Space Mountain, Lola grinning at me over her shoulder and me reaching for her hands.

And that *kiss*, forever seared into my brain.

"Hang on. Why are you smiling like that?" Henry shoves his sunglasses up his nose and into his dark hair. He squints at me through the lens. "Did you and Lola get together? *Holy shit*. We've got to bring the other guys in for this."

"It's only nine in the morning. No one wants to be bothered—"

"Did they kiss?" Jo pushes Jack's shoulder out of the way as they join the call, diving in front of the camera. "Please tell me they kissed."

"Why the hell are you two awake?" I ask. "Henry and Emma, I can understand. They're halfway around the world."

I step into the lobby and head through the glass doors at the back of the hotel, bypassing the gym for the outside running path. I find a spot under an oak tree and take a seat on the grass.

"Because I've been waiting for this moment for *years*," Jo says.

I recall what Lola said to me at the wedding. How if she got married, she'd wait to tell her friends. It's like right now, I think. She's not beside me to break the news, and talking about her without having her by my side feels wrong. Like we're gossiping about someone else and not the love of my life.

A white lie for a few days won't hurt anyone. Lola will understand.

"Sorry. Nothing new to report. Still in just best friend territory over here. We made it to the hotel where the show is, and the contest kicks off the day after tomorrow," I say, leaning back against the trunk of the tree.

"How's Lola? Where is she?" Emma asks.

"In the room. She's working. I think she's doing okay. Not on edge, but super excited."

"Tell her we're proud of her," Jo says. "And we wish we could be there."

"I will, I promise. We'll call you all later to check in."

"We know you're lying," Jack says, his eyes narrowed.

"Lying about what?" I ask, picking up a blade of grass and running it between my fingers.

"You and Lola. Something happened. And it's fine if you want to keep it to yourself, but it's so obvious. I haven't ever seen you smile this much."

"Normal people smile, Jack," I say.

I look at my reflection in the camera and bite back a laugh. I *am* smiling, with puffy cheeks and wrinkles around my eyes. I look sleep-deprived, missing hours of slumber to indulge in Lola before we crawled under the covers far too late last night.

They don't know I'm thinking about what she looks like when she comes, her head thrown back and her hands in my hair. The shape of her hips and the sounds she makes. How if I press my thumb into her and *then* circle, she reacts with a guttural moan, heels pressing into my lower back and wordlessly asking for more.

"No idea what you mean." I stand and dust off my shorts. "I'm off for a run."

"Liar," Jack says, and I wave goodbye, clicking the screen closed.

The sun is warm and the temperature is oppressive, but I pound the pavement anyway, knowing the faster I run, the faster I can get back to see my girl.

———

"YOU LOOK GORGEOUS," I say.

I'm staring at Lola in her thigh-length dress and sky-high heels. My tongue is probably hanging out of my mouth and my heart is thumping in my chest, erratic and out of control as I watch her get ready for the welcome mixer tonight.

She's leaning over the bathroom counter, a tube of mascara in her hand as she finishes her eye makeup. I'd like to stay up here for the rest of the night. Bend her over and run my hand up the back of her leg and under her dress. Order room service and lock ourselves away, feeding her an ice cream sundae in nothing but a bathrobe.

She promised some of the other designers we would stop by though, so instead of keeping her to myself, I know I have to share.

At least I can show her off.

"It's not too much?" she asks about the bright purple outfit, the fabric clinging to her body and showing off every one of her curves.

"Depends on what you're going for." I lean against the bathroom wall. "Want to send me into cardiac arrest? Already done. Trying to look hot and showing off something you made? Mission accomplished." I move and step behind her, my hand dipping down the front of the outfit and pulling her right nipple. Her eyes flutter closed, the makeup brush falling to the countertop. "Might be a little extreme for a walk in the park, but I wouldn't complain."

"We're going to be late," she says, resting her head against my neck.

"Then open your legs and let me make you come really quick so we can head downstairs and meet all your friends," I whisper in her ear.

Now that I've gotten a taste of Lola, I don't think I'll ever get enough. How did we go so long without touching each other? I'm insatiable for her.

Her feet wiggle apart and her thighs press against mine. I kiss her cheek then her neck, one hand still down the front of her dress and the other carefully bunching the material up around her waist.

"You're going to watch how well you take my fingers, honey," I say. "One leg on the counter."

Lola whimpers and lifts her right leg. I can see all of her in the glass, magnified and multiplied. There are two of her and *fuck*, that's a beautiful sight.

"What are you thinking about?" she whispers. "You just got hard."

"Nothing," I murmur, using two fingers to circle her.

"Liar." Her left arm reaches around my neck, pulling on my hair as she grinds her ass into me.

I groan, my eyes closing at the same time I slip a finger inside of her. She's tight and wet, ready for me, and I'm daydreaming about how she's going to feel when I fuck her for the first time.

"I thought about there being two of you," I admit, setting the rhythm she likes.

Her back bows, a weight dropping against my chest, and I force my eyes open to watch her. She's busy watching me, mouth parted and cheeks flushed, following the movements of my hand.

"Who knew my sweet best friend was so wicked?" she breathes out. "It's always the nice ones."

"Do you not want me to be nice?"

"I want you to be whatever you want with me, Patrick. Do whatever you want with me. I'm yours."

Some side of me I've never tapped into before wants to growl in response. Lay her down and bite her neck, her chest, the insides of her thighs. Show her off to all the people who look at her, spreading her legs so they could see I got there first.

I'm possessed, claiming her in a way I've never wanted to with another person before.

"Keep your leg up," I say, voice gruff as I drop to my knees.

I grip her dress and ass with one hand and bend my head so I can lick her. Taste her again. Make her push up on her toes and grind against my face. My tongue teases her clit and my fingers fuck her like how I can't wait to fuck her for real. Hard. Demanding. Taking and taking and taking.

"*Patrick.*"

"There you go," I say, holding her open. My fingers and mouth are coated in her arousal, and I've never seen something so hot in my life. "That's my girl. You're doing so well, Lola. When you're ready, can you come for me, honey? I want to make you feel good again."

She tightens around my fingers, and her moan is long and low. Her leg drops to the floor and her thighs shake, telling me she's close just before she leaps off the edge. I stand and catch her before she falls, my thumb rubbing over her sensitive clit until the moment passes, kissing her neck as she comes down from her high.

"How"—she swallows and fans her face, cheeks red and a bead of sweat on her forehead—"are you so good at that?"

"Because I know you, Lo. Better than anyone else. If you know what to look for, you're incredibly easy to read."

"I don't want to move. I want to stay here," Lola says, letting out a sleepy yawn and leaning her body against mine.

"We should go see your friends. Just for a little," I say. "Then we'll come back and get some sleep." I pull her dress down and run my hands up her thighs.

"I'm going to clean up," she mumbles. "Ten minutes, and I'll be ready."

"Okay." I kiss her cheek and grab the migraine pill bottle on the counter, opening the top and throwing a capsule back.

"Do you have a headache?" she asks, her eyes meeting mine in the mirror.

"Just some tension. It's probably from running in the sun and not drinking enough water. It was hot out there today."

"We can stay in if you aren't feeling up to it."

"I'm fine." I kiss her other cheek and give her backside a tap. "C'mon. Let's get this week of celebrating you started, sweetheart."

THIRTY
LOLA

WE STAYED out too late last night, socializing over food and music until the early morning in the hotel's swanky lounge. There's an excitement building in the air as we get closer to the start of the show, now only twenty-hour away. I got to meet people I had only talked to through social media for the first time, falling into easy conversation as if we were lifelong friends catching up.

The best part of the night was Patrick, his hand threaded through mine and his laughter ringing in my ear. I introduced him as my boyfriend and he grinned like a maniac, full of glee.

It was our first time out in public as something more than friends. We're pulling back the curtain of our relationship and revealing this new title to the world. Touching him freely and showing affection is exhilarating. Getting to kiss his cheek when he sat by my side and listening to him answer questions made my heart full, knowing there's a space for him in *my* space, that my two worlds are able to coexist without any strife or strain.

It was easy, a reassurance that we can be two different people with two different lives but still come together and celebrate the each other's accomplishments.

We made our way back to the room around two, stomachs full from the buffet and cheeks sore from laughing so much. I fell asleep after Patrick helped unzip my dress, dozing peacefully until my alarm sounded ten minutes ago.

I rub my eyes and roll over in bed, grinning when I see Patrick. He's still asleep, one arm above his head and the other holding onto my hip in a vice-like grip. Now that he's allowed to touch me, I've learned he doesn't want to stop. He finds any way for us to have physical contact, even if it's our pinkies interlocking as he hands me the tube of toothpaste in the bathroom, brushing our teeth side by side.

That made me smile.

I kiss his cheek and slip out from under the sheets. I know he he can't function without caffeine or food immediately after waking up, so coffee and a breakfast sandwich from the shop downstairs sound like a good idea. It's the fuel we'll need for our busy day.

I throw on his T-shirt and a pair of jean shorts, leaving the room as quietly as I can. Patrick doesn't stir when I close the door, his eyes still closed and his chest rising and falling with uneven breaths.

The line for food is long, and I get sidetracked talking to a couple I met last night. They created a label together, she tells me, but she's the real visionary, he adds. I wish them good luck with the show, and by the time the two egg and cheese croissants and drinks come out, I've been gone for almost an hour.

I balance the cups in the crook of my arm and hold the bag of food in my teeth. I check my phone, surprised to not find any missed texts or calls from Patrick. A flicker of worry lights up inside of me as I hustle back to the room because he never sleeps this late. I tap the key against the lock and open the door, standing in the entryway.

"I'm back and I have breakfast," I call out through the living room.

I don't get a response.

I was expecting to find him sprawled across the couch in his boxers, a pencil behind his ear and the crossword puzzle in his hands, but he's nowhere to be found. The curtains are still drawn and it's dark, making it difficult to see.

"Patrick?" I try again, the worry increasing to panic.

There's a groan from the bed, a sound coming from under the pile of covers on the bed that echoes through the room. I drop the food and drinks on the glass table and hurry across the floor. I find his head peeking out from under the fluffy white comforter I had wrapped around my body a short while ago.

"Hey," he whispers, his voice cracking.

"What's wrong?" I ask. "Are you sick?"

I sit next to him and touch his forehead, checking for a fever. He didn't sound like this last night when we fell asleep wrapped around each other. My legs were like vines, clinging to his body anywhere I could find space.

"Migraine," he answers. It sounds like there's a patch of dust clogging his throat. "A bad one."

"What do you need?" I ask, ready to jump into action.

Patrick shakes his head and throws his arm over his eyes. "Everything hurts so bad. It's never been like this. My vision is blurry. I'm nauseous. The pain—*fuck*. It's awful. It's like a hammer to my skull."

His excruciating pain is probably because he's deviated from his regimented routine: eight hours of sleep in his own bed every night. Five servings of fruits and vegetables a day. A half a gallon of water before lunchtime, and another half in the afternoon.

He never stays out until two in the morning, consuming

pounds of fried food and a couple beers. I've thrown a wrench in his day-to-day life, and I feel immense guilt at the realization.

"Where are your pills?" I ask.

"Already took two. I'm okay. You need to get ready for the show."

"The show is tomorrow," I say, keeping my voice soft as I brush a piece of hair away from his forehead. "I have nowhere else to be."

"What about the networking event? You have a poster with your name on it. A booth and designs you get to show off."

I was looking forward to today, a chance to tease some of my outfits in a less-formal environment before things officially kick off tomorrow. The board of directors thought free admission for the public would drive interest in the show, and from what I've heard, they're expecting thousands of people to stop by throughout the week.

As much as I want to be on the convention center floor, talking with fellow designers and meeting the judges who will be critiquing my work, I need to be here with Patrick. He'd stay back for me, and I *want* to stay with him, making sure he's okay.

"It doesn't matter. I'll see all of them tomorrow. You're my priority," I say honestly. "Tell me what you need."

"A shower, but I'm afraid to stand up. I tried before you got back and I felt dizzy."

"What about a bath?"

"I haven't taken a bath since I was six."

"It's been that long? You strike me as a bath guy."

"Mhmm. The idea of swimming in my filth is disgusting."

"I'll make it nice. It's dark in there. And quiet."

"Okay," Patrick agrees. "I'll give it a go."

"Stay here. I'll be back in a few minutes. So help me god if you try to get out of this bed on your own, I will kick your ass."

"Your threats are useless, Jones," he mumbles.

I kiss his cheek and head to the bathroom. I keep the lights off, using my phone's flashlight to guide me as I turn on the faucet and test the water temperature. It's warm enough to relax his muscles but not scalding where he'll be uncomfortable or overheat.

When the water fills to the brim of the basin, I make my way back to the bedroom. I squeeze Patrick's hand so he knows I'm there.

"I'm going to help you up now, okay?"

"This is embarrassing," he says through gritted teeth. "I'm sorry you have to see me like this."

"Like a human being with a chronic health condition? The horror," I say. "Use my shoulders to hoist yourself up."

Patrick slings his arm around me, and I help lift him from his hips. There's a moment where I think we're both going to topple back onto the mattress, but I keep us steady, evening out our center of gravity. He lets out another groan as we shuffle across the carpet.

"Can you give me a minute? I need to use the bathroom."

"I'm not leaving you alone. I'll turn my back and cover my ears if it bothers you that I'm here. You could fall and crack your skull open. There would be blood everywhere. Imagine the cleanup," I say.

Patrick huffs. "Your imagery is vivid. It's like I'm in the middle of a crime scene."

"Well you could be if you don't let me stay in here with you."

"You don't care about hearing me pee?"

"I care about *you,* Patrick. Not bodily functions."

"You're so good to me."

"Because you're good to me. That's what people who really, really like each other do. They look out for one another and lend a hand when the other is in need."

"I do like you, Lola. I like you a whole fucking lot."

After he uses the bathroom and washes his hands, I pull off his shirt and start a pile of dirty clothes. I hook my fingers in the waistband of his boxers and tug them down his thighs, over his tattoos, the little markings I never knew existed.

Now that I know they're there, I want to study them every day so I can memorize every detail. The exact size and shape and the way they're shaded so I could write a dissertation on them if asked.

"How's the temperature?" I ask when he's settled in the tube after some careful maneuvering and a slew of curse words.

"Perfect," he says.

I lather a washcloth with soap and rub it across his chest and down his arms until his skin is pink and clean. He closes his eyes, his head lolling back and a sigh escaping from his lips. There's nothing sexual about my actions as I move the terrycloth to his stomach. It's tender and caring and *loving*, seeing someone at their lowest low and doing whatever you can to help them back to their feet.

My heart aches to know Patrick is in pain and I can't do anything more except wring out the washcloth and kiss the slope of his jaw. To whisper soothing words in the quiet room, telling him it's okay.

I've never seen him so vulnerable. The man is usually so put together, and now I'm watching as he comes apart, his neck resting against the rim of the porcelain and his fists curling into balls.

"I'm sorry," he says. "I'm ruining your day."

"Honey," I whisper, trying the endearment out for size. I like how it feels on my tongue, slipping out without any thought. "It's okay to not be okay around me. Our relationship has always been showing parts of ourselves that aren't perfectly put together. That doesn't change now that I've seen you naked. In fact, I want to see even more. Tell me how I can help you. *Let* me help you."

"Can you get in here with me? I always feel better when you're nearby, and you're too far away."

"Of course." I take off my shirt and slip out of my shorts and underwear, adding them to the pile of clothes. I set my phone on the vanity with the flashlight angled down, making sure it's pointed away from Patrick's face.

I've done research on migraines, wanting to be prepared if I'm ever with him when one strikes. Light sensitivity and loud noises are a big culprit of prolonged pain, and I want to do everything I can to mitigate any further ailments.

I lower myself into the tub, water sloshing over the sides and making a puddle on the tile floor. I'll worry about the mess later. Patrick opens one eye, and for the first time since last night— when the moon cast his face in shades of silver and gray and he gave me a sleepy laugh after one of my half-delirious jokes—I see him smile.

"Hi, sweetheart." He reaches out and takes my hand. His lips graze over my knuckles, kissing each of them. "I didn't think the first time we shared a bathtub would be when I was in pain and nearly out of commission. I had so many other ideas. Candles. Music. Flower petals. You riding me."

"Don't worry. There are many more baths in our future," I say, laughing at his vision.

His hum is soft and low, and even in the darkened room I see his smile pull wider around the edges of his mouth. "Why don't you head downstairs? You have plenty of time to make the event. I promise I won't drown."

I know he's trying to prove to me that he's fine. That he doesn't need my care and attention, but I don't believe him.

"Because I'm not going." I glide through the water until I'm in front of him. I spin so my back is against his chest, and I rest my head in the crook of his neck. "Is this okay?"

I can feel every inch of him—the bend of his knee, his arms as they settle around my front, the broad shoulders almost caging me in. I like his body behind mine, a sturdy rock and a puzzle piece that fits me perfectly.

"It's perfect. Lo, this is your career we're talking about. I'll be fine by myself for a few hours. Honestly."

"I'm sure you will be, except I'm not going anywhere. I'd think about you the whole time I was gone. What if you needed me? It would take me forever to get back up here. The walk from the elevator alone is nearly a mile."

"I think it's more like a few feet," he mumbles, a laugh in the words.

"Math has never been my strong suit."

"Fine. I'm warning you, though. If I start to feel better, I'm kicking you out."

"I'd like to see you try."

Water runs down his elbows and across my chest. We're so close, and even though I don't think it's possible to be any closer without sewing myself to him, I wish there was a way.

We stay like that for a while, our limbs intertwined and our hearts beating in unison, synced up in a tempo only lovers get to experience, until the water turns tepid and still. The steam dissipates and I know I need to get Patrick back in bed before he starts to get cold.

I climb out of the tub first, wrapping a towel around my body and offering him a hand. He steps over the ledge carefully, and I drop to my knees to dry off his legs and feet. Patrick cups my cheek, and his fingers twirl in my hair.

"You're not feeling well. Now is not the time, Walker," I say.

"I'm weak, Jones. I can't help it. You're so pretty on your knees."

"And you're as white as a ghost. Come on, we're going to bed."

"I've dreamed about hearing you say that."

"Back to *sleep*," I amend, leading him to the sitting area of the room. "Wait here. I'm going to change the sheets."

I deposit him in an armchair and get to work. I strip the bed and find the spare set of sheets on the top shelf of the closet. I switch the pillows around, arranging them so he has the more comfortable ones on his side to keep his neck supported. I put a glass of water on his bedside table, and when I finish, I find Patrick asleep in the chair.

I take his momentary state of unconsciousness to put on a big T-shirt and a pair of his boxers, hustling down the hall to fill up a bag with ice. When I slip back into the room five minutes later, Patrick is still sleeping.

"Hey," I whisper, gently waking him. "Let's get you into bed."

"Don't want to move," he grumbles.

"I know you don't, but the bed will be much better. You can stretch out. I'm going to bring you an icepack and you can relax."

"An ice pack? You have one?"

"I have a Ziplock bag that has makeup powder in it and ice from down the hall. I'm improvising, but I think it'll do."

"You're so smart, Lola. Such a smart and pretty girl."

Patrick winces as he stands, and when we make it to the bed, he drops his towel to the floor and crawls under the covers. I grab the cold bag and set it on his forehead.

"How's that?" I ask.

"Better. I just need a little more sleep. Maybe another hour or two. Will you stay with me?"

"I'm not going anywhere, Patrick," I say again, climbing into bed behind him and wrapping my arms around his waist. Taking care of the person I love is the only thing on my mind.

I kiss his shoulders. His neck and his arms. I kiss everywhere

I can to convey I'm never going to leave him. Not now, in his weakest moments. Not when he's strong and proud. Not ever.

I don't know how long we lie there. His breathing turns into soft snores and his muscles turn limber against my body. My own eyes grow heavy as the sun hangs higher in the sky, the day slipping away.

"I love you," I murmur against his skin as I fade into unconsciousness. I want to release the words before I fall asleep, set them free so I don't have to hold on to them alone anymore.

"I love you too," I think I hear Patrick murmur back, but maybe it's just a dream.

THIRTY-ONE
LOLA

"LOLA. You're number twenty-eight on the runway today. You'll have access to the backstage area a half hour before your call time to get your models ready, which should be in ten minutes. There will be coordinators keeping track of time. Utilize them. They are your team for the next few days. If you have any preferences for organization or order lineup, convey that to them." Janet Ross, the Florida Fashion Show director, looks up from her clipboard and gives me a frazzled smile, clearly winded from talking a mile a minute. I've barely been able to keep up. "Do you have any questions?"

Only about a million and one.

I return her smile and shake my head, knowing there's no way she can answer everything whirling around in my brain. I haven't had a second to think since I came downstairs an hour ago and was taken directly to have my credentials checked, my garments verified, and a photo snapped for the show's website. It's been running from point A to B to C, and the chaos hasn't allowed me any time to panic.

I might be stressed as hell, but at least I'm not totally freaking out.

Yet.

Small victories.

"No," I say. "You covered everything."

"You'll see people walking around with both cameras and their phones. They're doing PR for the show. If they ask you a question, feel free to answer, but keep it brief. It gives you a better chance of actually ending up on their social media accounts. Marjorie is the head makeup artist and Karl is in charge behind the curtain. Any issues or problems, you let them know and they'll handle it. Sound good?"

"Yeah." I nod and swallow, a fine sheen of sweat forming on my forehead. I brush it away with the back of my hand and hope my smile doesn't look like a grimace. "Sounds great."

Janet reaches out and gives my shoulder a squeeze. "Good luck, Lola. We're excited to have you here."

I blink and she's gone, off to give the same spiel to the next fifty designers. Seventy-five are entered in the women's division alone today, with dozens more slated for the remaining three days. I've never seen an event of this magnitude, a broad scope of talent and varying styles. Winning the show would be a dream, but I'll also be happy just hearing my name called as an honorable mention among people who have been doing this for years.

I take a deep breath and head to grab my purse, ready to make my way backstage when I run into a firm body and almost tumble to the ground.

"Whoa, hey. Easy, Lo," Patrick says, his hands settling on my arms. "There you are."

"Hi," I answer, taking another deep breath and wrapping him in a hug. "You're here."

"Of course I'm here. Where else would I be?" He pulls out of my embrace and smiles down at me. "Did you remember to eat breakfast and take your medicine?"

"Yeah. I met up with some friends and got plenty of nutrients. Eggs and oatmeal." I gesture to my bag off to the side of the room and the two cups next to it. "I also brought you a coffee. I wasn't sure when you'd be downstairs or if you'd have time to get one for yourself."

"You're a lifesaver." Patrick kisses my forehead. "How's everything going so far this morning? How're you feeling?"

"Fine." I nod and play with my bracelet. "I just got a ton of information thrown at me and I'm replaying it over and over to make sure I understand it all."

"What can I do to help?" he asks. "Where do you need me?"

"Out in the audience. I really appreciate you coming to say hi but only staff, models, assistants, and designers are allowed behind the curtain," I tell him. "Why didn't I think of hiring someone to give me an extra set of hands backstage? Such a rookie mistake on my part. I read articles that all said to make sure I had a helper. A person who can follow directions well and is familiar with how I like to organize my area. *Shoot.* I got caught up in a hundred other things and forgot. I guess it's too late it find a stand-in now."

"I can fix that." Patrick reaches into the back pocket of his jeans, pulling out a long lanyard with his name attached to a plastic holder. "I randomly met someone in the buffet line and when I mentioned you, he said he was a big fan of your work. I asked if there was any way he could get me a backstage pass."

"A *backstage pass*? Patrick, this isn't an Aerosmith concert, you groupie."

He grins, both dimples popping under the harsh artificial lighting. "It would be pretty fun if it was, right? The guy told me the only way I could get access is if I was an assistant to a designer. I might have fibbed a little bit and said I was your apprentice, not the guy you're sleeping with. A perfectly logical explanation as to why I'd want to be by your side."

CHELSEA CURTO

"You did that for me?"

"I'd do more detrimental things to society than giving a small lie about being your assistant if it means helping you, Lola."

I touch his forehead. His migraine finally relented late last night. We stayed in bed all day, enjoying the quiet and eating room service for dinner.

I can tell he's feeling better. The color is back in his cheeks and his eyes are sparkling again, mischief and glee behind the green, but being backstage at a fashion show is a lot of work. It's loud and there are strobe effects, coupled with tons of people moving every which way. I don't want to compromise his health again.

"Any lingering symptoms?" I ask softly. I massage his temples and his eyes close with the press of my fingers into his skin. I add a hint of pressure, just enough for his head to drop back and a soft moan to escape from his lips. "Did you take *your* medicine this morning?"

"I did. Two pills. I feel as good as new."

"It's going to be noisy back there with a lot of sounds. It might exacerbate your pain."

"The pain is gone." Patrick turns his cheek and kisses my palm. "I wouldn't have come down if I didn't feel up for jumping in."

"Do you promise you'll tap out if you start to feel tired or a headache coming on?" I ask. He grins and I run my thumb over his dimple.

"I know the only way you'll let me stay is if I agree, so sure. I promise I'll communicate with you," he says, and I have a feeling he's crossing his fingers behind his back.

"The second I see you wince, I'm banishing you to the audience, Patrick Walker."

BACKSTAGE AT A FASHION show is pure pandemonium.

I've scoured hundreds of blog posts, watched dozens of behind-the-scenes videos, and nothing prepared me for the scope of insanity I would find in the minutes leading up to walk down the runway.

There are people everywhere. Assistants hold up the train of a dress. Models run by with skirts half-zipped. Hair stylists try to add last-minute volume to someone's ponytail. It's hot and it's loud and I'm in *love*, ready to enter every show possible so I can come back and do it all over again.

I'm in awe of the production level and efficiency it takes to run a successful operation. I like that there are so many things happening at once, my head on a swivel instead of fixating on one specific situation.

I like hearing my name shouted from fifteen directions and someone giving me a warning that I have eight minutes until it's my turn on the runway.

I'm giddy when I crouch down and cut a rogue thread from the hemline of the green slacks I'm obsessed with, the pants paired with a yellow blazer and a black crop top. I'm grinning from ear to ear as I ask the girl to hold still while I make a last-minute adjustment, smoothing over the pleats and working out a wrinkle with a steamer.

I love watching the last model in my line gush over the sundress she's wearing, doing spin after spin and laughing at how the skirt fans out around her waist. I'm in my element and I never want to leave.

I feel like I *belong*.

"I'm going to jump into the audience," Patrick says, a tape measure around his neck and a spool of thread tucked into the front pocket of his frayed Levi's. There's a magnetic pincushion attached to his wrist, which I unhook from his arm. "I want to watch your clothes come down the runway."

"Are you sure? Someone is probably going to film it. We can watch it online later."

"Yes, Lola, I'm sure. I want to take my own video and send it to our friends."

He smiles and cups my cheeks with his palms, kissing me in front of hundreds of people. The world stops spinning when he presses his mouth against mine, and for a second, I forget where we are.

Fashion show, I think. *The biggest event of your life.*

It amazes me how easily Patrick can get me out of my head. One touch from him and I relax, not a single worry left inside.

"Will you let me know how everything looks? Pay attention to what I might need to fix before the men's division tomorrow?"

"Everything is going to be perfect, but I'll let you know if something seems out of place," Patrick says.

"Okay." I nod and kiss him one more time, not wanting to let go. "Thank you."

"You're going to knock 'em dead," he says, disappearing to the right of the large black curtain and out into the crowd.

I let out a sigh and release the tension in my shoulders, double checking my watch and the call sheet with the model order. I've spent years working for this. Spent countless sleepless nights and frustrating mornings where I feel like I'm close to a breakthrough, close to finding my voice in a saturated market, just on the brink of something big.

I think of all the tears I've cried over ideas that have grown stale, ideas I can't find a way to bring to life, sketchbook after sketchbook of charcoal drawings and chicken-scratch doodles shelved away to try again another day.

All the money, all the time, all the classes I've taken to better my skills and learn from the best of the best... It all comes down to this.

My future hinges on the next five minutes, and at this point, everything is out of my control. It's up to the judges to see my creative vision and the story I'm trying to convey: fashion for *all*. A line that doesn't care about your finances or the other brand names you have in your closet. A line whose soul focus is wanting to be affordable for anyone while still looking high-quality.

"First show?"

I look up at the model in front of me.

She's giving me a kind smile. Her legs are long and her hips are curvy, breaking from the traditional mold of women the industry salivated over fifteen years ago. She looks stunning in my favorite outfit of the day, the dress covered in stitched flowers and bright colors.

"What gave it away? The sweat stains on my shirt?" I ask.

She laughs. "No. I can tell you're a natural."

"I'm Lola."

"I know who you are. I saw your initial application and was hoping I'd get paired with you. I'm Brielle."

I blush, the flattery catching me off guard. "Really? I didn't know you all saw the designers ahead of time."

"We see portfolios, but to keep it fair, we don't get to pick who we wear. So, I manifested the hell out of hearing my name called under your set of models. It's obvious when someone puts their heart and soul into their work, and it's even more obvious when they're mass-producing clothes for monetary gain, not caring who ends up buying them. You love what you do, Lola, and it shows. It makes wearing the outfits you create even more special."

I put my hand over my heart, touched by her words. "Thank you. That's incredibly kind of you say. I just love designing clothes. I've always loved designing clothes. The only time I feel like my brain truly shuts off is when I'm in front of my sewing machine. It's when I'm the happiest."

"I feel the same way about the runway," Brielle says. "I step out there and the lights disappear, the people disappear and it's just me and the stage." She takes my hand in hers. "It's an honor to wear your name today."

"You're going to make me cry. Thank you. That means a lot."

"It's my pleasure." She glances over her shoulder. "Looks like it's almost time. Are you ready?"

"Yeah." I nod and fix one of the buttons on the front of her dress. "Let's do this."

"Lola Jones," Brielle says. "You're going to make the internet lose its mind."

A coordinator comes over and directs the line of women to the steps at the back of the stage. They all smile at me as they pass, giving me nods of encouragement. I wish Patrick were here to experience this moment with me, but I know he'll be back once my outfits have been paraded down the runway. I already can't wait to see him again.

The music shifts, the beat picking up speed to a quicker tempo. It's electric, the thump of the bass vibrating in my blood, and I grin. The woman with the headset nods to Brielle leading the line, and just like that, they're off. The picture of pure professionals, they march up the stairs and onto the runway, their elegance, grace and confidence shining through in their high-heeled shoes and leather boots.

As they disappear one by one, I wring my hands together, trying not to place too much emphasis on the way the crowd cheers. The crescendo of applause, the whistles, the catcalls. It sounds like they like the lineup, but it's also possible someone fell and got back on their feet quick enough to garner some pity claps.

The judges of the show hold the primary votes for the winners of each division, plus the overall Best Of winner, stopping backstage at the conclusion of each day to look at stitching, needlework, and overall cleanliness of the designs. The audience also votes though, their opinions contributing a small percentage of the outcome. An enthusiastic response is a good thing.

I bite on my fingernails as I wait, time crawling by before I turn my head and find the models returning. They're laughing and beaming and pulling out hair accessories. Coordinators start unzipping their skirts and tops and dresses. Hangers are shoved into sleeves, and that's it.

It's all over.

"Lola." I hear my name shouted across the room and I turn to see Patrick standing there, a grin on his face and his cheeks bright red. He moves through the masses of people, offering an apology to a poor intern holding a tray of sandwiches who he nearly runs over. "Holy shit, baby, they looked so good. The colors popped. The fabric moved like it had a shape of its own. Those dresses were *hot*." He scoops me into his arms, spinning me around, and I promptly burst into tears. "No. No, no. Don't cry. Hang on." He sets me down and my shoulders shake, a sob racking through my entire body.

"Did you see the whole thing?" I ask.

"Every second." He pulls out his phone and taps his screen. "Watch."

I know these are my designs. I've stared at them every day for weeks. I've fallen asleep dreaming about these hemlines, wondering if I should make them shorter or longer. I know the exact shades of blues and purples, the shape of the busts and the flares of the skirts.

Seeing them on real people as they strut with their model

posture and hips swaying is... an out-of-body experience to say the least. It doesn't seem real because they look *so good*.

"Oh my god," I whisper. I bring the phone closer to my face, my nose almost pressed against the screen. "This is—"

"Unbelievable," Patrick finishes for me. "Look at your clothes. You're a fucking superstar. The crowd loved it. The dress the first girl was wearing? With the silver buttons and the half sleeves? They went ballistic when they saw the back, honey. *Ballistic*."

"For me," I say. My lip quivers and I almost drop his phone, my hands shaking too much to get a good grip on it. "That's all for me?"

"Yeah," he murmurs, his arms around my shoulders and his face buried in my hair. "For you."

I'm attacked by a swell of emotions. Mainly happiness and joy, followed by anxiety, and then the intense desire to want to work on something new right this very second.

"I can't believe I made it to this point. I can't believe I did it and I did it well. I'm so proud of myself." I pause and blush, embarrassed by the admission. "Does that make me conceited?"

"Hell no it doesn't," Patrick says. "It makes you an incredible artist whose work is finally being recognized on the stage and scale it deserves. This is just the beginning, sweetheart. I have a feeling everything in your life is about to change."

"Except you." I settle my cheek against his chest and listen to the beat of his heart. "I don't want you to change."

"I'm not going anywhere, Lo. You're stuck with me until the end of time."

THIRTY-TWO
PATRICK

"WHAT DO you want to do tonight?" I ask Lola as I clear away our empty dinner plates.

We ordered room service again instead of accepting an invitation to go out with her group of friends, exhausted after a long day of being at the show and socializing. Food takes over the entire spare queen bed on the other side of the room, one of everything off the menu spread out on the comforter because she couldn't pick what she was in the mood for. Soup, salad, pasta, and burgers for entrees. A stack of French fries and a massive bowl of tater tots as sides.

"I want to stay in," she answers, dusting off her hands and stretching her arms above her head. Her robe falls off her shoulder with the movement, sliding down and bunching up around the crook of her elbow. "We could put on a movie and relax. Or take another bath and pretend we're at a spa."

"It would be rude to not use the seventy-inch television in the living room," I agree. "Want to go pick something to watch? I'll try to fit our leftovers in the fridge and meet you out there in a minute. We can take a bath after the movie. I'm sure you could use some decompressing. It was a busy day, and tomorrow won't be any slower."

"Sure." Lola pushes up on her knees and wraps her arms around my neck. "Thank you for today. It means so much to me you were there."

"Anything for you, Lola Jones."

"Anything?" she asks, taking my hand in hers.

She trails our joined palms down the front of her robe to the thick ties holding the Egyptian Cotton in place. I've been glaring at those pieces of fabric all night, wishing I could pull them open and make the entire thing disappear.

I swallow, my thoughts becoming less coherent as she drags my fingers underneath the opening against her chest. I find warm, bare skin and I almost groan the realization that she's been naked and two feet away from me all night.

"Yes," I say shakily. I swallow again and try to find my voice, but words are difficult. "Anything."

Lola hums and tilts her head back, her long blonde hair bright against the mahogany headboard. She pulls on the belt around her waist and lets the knot free. The robe falls away in slow motion, and with it, so does my restraint. I feel like I'm watching a private show. An intimate moment no one else will ever see.

I want to touch her. I want to kiss her and taste her and have her in every way she'll let me. And this... this seems like an invitation to do just that. An offering that barrels past slow and steamrolls into frenzied and frantic and desperate.

"I want you to fuck me," she says in a tone so low and seductive, I think my eyes roll to the back of my head.

She lies on the bed, her knees bent and one hand on the inside of her thigh, gorgeous body on display. I love every inch of her. Every stretch mark, every freckle, every mole. The sexy skin on her stomach and her thighs, a place for me to hold onto later when she's riding me.

"I can do that," I say through a strained breath. I pull my own robe off and toss it to the floor. "But I want to make you come first."

"You don't have to, Patrick. I—"

"How many times do I have to tell you that I do things because I want to, not because I have to?" I fold my hands around her thighs and spread her legs. "Hold on to the head-board, honey, and don't think about letting go."

Her whimper echoes through the room and her hands fumble up the wooden backdrop behind her, fingers curling over the edge.

I want to be inside her more than I want almost anything else in this world, but I don't want her to feel any pressure while she's on top of me. I want her to enjoy and let go, uninhibited and free, and that will be easier for her if we start with what we both know works between us.

"I liked what you did the other night," Lola says. "With your fingers and tongue. Together."

"Yeah?" I move down the bed until I'm between her parted legs. A bead of sweat rolls down her calf and I lick it away. "What else did you like?"

"I liked when you're inside me."

I run my hand up her thigh and stroke her clit with my thumb. She's already wet, just my words turning her on. "That's good to know. Let's play a game. Each thing you tell me that you enjoy in bed is another finger inside of you, Lola. You took two so well. Do you think you could take three?"

"I like when you're in control," Lola almost shouts. Her chest rises and falls. I prop up on my elbow to look at her and *fuck* she's decadent like this. Spread out and *begging* for it.

"Atta girl. That wasn't so hard, was it?" I ask, slipping my pointer finger inside her. I have to bite my lip to keep from moaning at how tight she is. I pull my finger all the way out before pushing inside her again. "What else do you want to tell me?"

"I like..." She stops to take a breath. "I like when you talk to me. Like right now. I don't..." She stops again and squeezes her eyes shut. "I don't want a full narration, but I want to know how I feel. How it makes you feel. If I'm doing good."

"You want me to tell you how wet you are? How your pussy makes me hard just by looking at you? Should I say how hot I think it is when you get needy?" I add a second finger and her moan is music to my ears. Her legs open wider. She lifts her hips, fucking my finger instead of letting my finger fuck her. "There you go, Lola. Taking me like such a good girl."

"Patrick. *Please.*"

"Please what? Give me one more, honey, so I can add a third finger and make sure you're ready for my cock."

"I like when you aren't nice," she blurts out. I move my free hand to her stomach, rubbing circles over her belly button as I kiss her hip bone. "When you're wild. It's hot to know I make you that way."

"Ah, Lo. You make me dizzy out of my mind. Deep breath, love. *Fuck yes,* just like that." I bend forward, my tongue tasting her as I add a third finger.

The room around me spins. I've never tasted something so delicious. She's soft and warm and I want to sink into her and stay there forever.

I feel her tighten around me. Her ankles hook around my shoulders, driving me deeper into her.

She's close.

"Greedy," I murmur against her, my tongue lapping up every drop she's willing to give me. I'm desperate, determined to watch her finish and willing to do whatever it takes to get her there.

"I'm going to come," she whispers. "Patrick."

"I've got you, Lola. You can let go," I whisper back, and that's when she reaches the peak, an orgasm racking her body and turning her into an exhausted pile of limbs on the mattress as she moans and whimpers a collection of sounds I keep for myself.

I work her through the high, my tongue easing up and my fingers slowing down until all I hear is her huffing uneven breaths of air as she tries to calm down. I kiss her knee. Her thigh. Her hips and her stomach. I work up her body and kiss her chest and that spot on her neck I love. I reach her mouth and kiss her lips, smiling and pulling back when she lets out a content sigh.

"That was... Yeah." Lola nods and keeps her eyes closed, humming softly. "You're a miracle worker."

"No. I pay attention," I say, tucking a piece of sweaty hair behind her ear. The room feels stifling, the best kind of warmth. "I listen and I take mental notes."

"Thorough notes," she says, her left hand sliding down the headboard.

"I don't hear you complaining."

"No." She laughs and pulls me closer. Her eyes open and she grins. "And you won't."

"Good." I wipe my lips with the back of my hand and Lola watches me, riveted. "What? Why are you staring at me like that?"

"I'm thinking about what you said at the lake in North Carolina."

"What did I say?"

"You told me all the things you'd do to my smart mouth. I'm wondering if that was all talk or if you're going to deliver."

I raise an eyebrow and sit back on my heels. "Wow. One orgasm brought out the smart ass in you, didn't it?"

She shrugs and props herself up on her elbows, her mouth inches away from mine. "I think you like it."

"I definitely like it."

I also like the way we can communicate and understand each other in the bedroom through sounds and touches, the words only an added bonus. It's never felt so *easy* before, a naturalness to our movements. Knowing exactly where she wants my hands and grinning when she touches me in all the places I like. A lightness to our conversation, even in a heated moment.

"How do you want me, Patrick?" Lola asks, kissing my neck.

She trails her mouth down my chest to the top of my stomach. Her teeth sink into my skin, and I almost fall forward and crush her.

I wrap my hand in her hair and give a firm pull, her neck elongating with a wicked smile in place.

"I'm going to stand up. You're going to move your ass to the edge of the bed and you're going to suck my cock. Then I'm going to fuck you, Lola, like you asked me to. Because you're always going to get what you want." I run my thumb over her mouth and pull her bottom lip down. "How's that for talking?"

Her eyes twinkle and her hands settle on my hips, nudging me backward until I'm at the edge of the bed. I chuckle at her urgency, standing up and planting my feet on the hotel carpet.

"It's good," she says, moving into the position I asked her to take. "So good."

"Open up. If you're going to talk a big game, you need to be able to back it up," I say, my fingers curling around her chin. Lola parts her lips and I nod. "There you go. Good. Two taps on my leg means stop. Got it?"

She nods, and I use my free hand to guide my erection to her mouth.

It's probably silly to feel a rush of love as she looks up at me, my dick halfway to her lips, but I do. Because she trusts *me*. She wants to do this with *me*, eager and excited as her mouth closes around my cock. She hums and she sucks and she does something with her tongue I've never experienced before, and it becomes my new favorite thing.

"Fuck, Lola," I exhale. Ever since I touched her for the first time, those two words have skyrocketed to the top of my vocabulary, and I'm not mad about it. My grip on her hair tightens. Her eyes start to water and her fingers dig into my legs as I thrust an inch deeper, almost hitting the back of her throat. "Do you want me to stop?" I ask.

The shake of her head is erratic, an insistent *no* conveyed with a quick jerk of her neck.

"I didn't think so. When has my girl ever been a quitter? You can take all of it, honey. I know you can."

Her mouth relaxes around me at the encouragement and I use the second she's distracted to thrust again, groaning when her fingers move from my thighs to my ass, asking for more. She hums her approval, the vibration making my toes curl and my head drop back.

Saliva coats my length and a drop of drool hangs from the corner of her lips. Lola brings her right hand to my shaft, popping me out of her mouth and stroking me up and down, adding a twist of her wrist.

Oh *fuck*.

I like that move.

She can tell I like it because she does it again, twisting the other way as her fingers run through the pre-cum on the head of my cock.

Lola's making this feel too good. I'm trying to last, trying to make sure she gets what she wants, but it's really fucking hard to concentrate on that goal when she reaches between her legs and starts to touch herself. I can *hear* how wet she is, the slick glide of her fingers a roar in my ears.

"Do we have any condoms?" she asks, craning her neck to run her tongue up my shaft from base to tip.

"Yes," I grit out. "I bought some this morning."

"Dreaming big?"

"One can never be too prepared," I say. Lola taps my leg twice and I stop immediately, jerking my chin down to stare at her. "What's wrong?"

"Nothing's wrong." Her hands run up my thighs. "I just want you inside me."

"I *am* inside you."

She laughs and kisses my stomach. "You know what I mean."

"Go wait on the pillows," I tell her, taking a step back and taking a deep breath, a lungful of air I'm going to need to survive.

I find the condoms in my suitcase, an impulse purchase when I stopped by the hotel convenience store earlier in the afternoon for a Gatorade. The kid behind the cash register stared at me, probably assuming I'm going to be participating in an all-night sex fest with my hydration and protection needs.

I rip the box open, causing half the packets to go flying across the room. Lola giggles from the bed, and I turn to find her fingers dancing across the inside of her thigh, her eyes on me. She touches herself between her legs and the other half of the packets drop to the floor.

"Watching you is torture," I say.

"Then stop watching and come join me," she says.

I scoop up the latex and open the wrapper. I work the condom down my length and make my way back to the bed, kneeling on the mattress.

"Okay," I say. "But I want you on top."

THIRTY-THREE
LOLA

MY JOKES STOP when Patrick says he wants to watch me.

There's reverence infused in the words, the sizzling electric heat extinguished and replaced with care and tender compassion.

I nod and let him take the spot against the pillows, waiting for him to get settled before I straddle him, one leg on either side of his hips.

"Promise me nothing changes," I whisper into the silent room as I hover above him.

An inch.

That's all we are apart, mere centimeters away from becoming one. My knees quake and my thighs burn from holding myself up, but I can't go this final step until I hear him say it.

An inch.

That's all that separates us from never being able to go back to how we were before.

As I look down at Patrick, his brown hair dark against the white pillowcase and his gaze on me, I know with absolute certainty I don't ever *want* to go back to the life we had before. A world where we didn't touch and we didn't kiss and we didn't show each other how much we care.

I want to sprint past whatever final boundary we're about to cross, barrel toward the finish line, and solidify him as mine forever.

"Lola," Patrick says softly. "You have my heart. You have my soul. I promise this doesn't change anything. Tomorrow I'm going to wake up and still feel the exact same about you. Obsessed, if you haven't been able to tell. I'm never going to leave you, and I also promise to prove that to you every single day."

He runs his fingers through my hair and rubs my neck, right at the top of my spine, where I feel the pressure melting away with his touch. I think there might be stars in his eyes as he looks at me.

I've never had anyone look at me like this before, like I'm the single most important thing in the world. It's overwhelming and intoxicating in the best ways. I want to get lost in his stare, get stuck in the expanse of green, and never return home.

I know Patrick's being honest, nothing but truth behind every syllable. He'd tattoo them on his arm or forehead if he could. Maybe he will one day, another addition to his stash of designs dedicated to me.

I'm never going anywhere, he'd write on his skin, the first thing I see when I open my eyes and the last thing I read before I fall asleep, drifting off to dreams of us and the future we could have.

I love you, I think he'd also write.

He hasn't said it yet, not in a way that's real and not sleep-deprived, a figment of my imagination, but it's imminent. I know it is. I can feel it the way you can feel a storm rolling in. Hyper-awareness of your surroundings. Nerves alight with anticipation. Those three words hover between us, just barely out of reach and waiting for the perfect moment to release themselves into our world.

I'll be ready when they do. I'll welcome them with open arms and an open heart, giving them back to him freely and wholeheartedly.

I nod, pulled back to the present with a gradual swell of emotion behind the bob of my head. I rest my hands on his chest and I can feel his heart beating under my palms, a staccato melody I've memorized from the times we've been in bed, hearing nothing except the sounds of our breaths as we drifted toward unconsciousness, at peace and utterly content in the arms of the other.

"Fuck me, Patrick," I whisper into his ear. "Make me yours."

It's the most intimate thing I've ever said to someone.

I hear his shaky exhale as he runs his hands up my backside. He squeezes around the curve of my ass and the shape of my hips, fingers digging into my skin. I hope he leaves a mark so I can remember tonight, fondly looking back on it tomorrow and the day after.

I want to see the handprints left behind by the man I love, caught up in the throes of passion where he loses all semblance of control simply because I drive him wild. The man made of careful calculations and restraint is withering away in front of me, and I've never felt so powerful.

"Lola," he mumbles, his voice thick with need. "I want you so bad."

"So have me," I say.

Patrick's grip on me tightens, a possessive hold on my body I never want to break free from. His nose brushes against my chin and I lift my neck to find him watching me rapturously, eyes wide and cheeks flushed a pink that matches my favorite time of day: sunset, when the heat cools and the clouds break.

There's adoration in his gaze, desire and heat, longing and so much patience, years of waiting and waiting and *waiting* culminating to this exact moment.

He kisses my jaw and the inch of skin below my ear. He reaches his hand between us and rubs his thumb over my clit, enough of a tease for me to arch my back and squeeze my eyes shut, already chasing that wonderful high for the second time tonight. My body awakens under his touch, a million stars in the night sky.

"No," Patrick says softly, his hand falling to the inside of my thigh. He pinches the skin there and my eyes fly open with the fleeting burst of pain. He rubs over the spot right away, soothing me. "I want to see you when I sink into you for the first time, Lola. I want to see every second of you coming apart for me."

I flush hot at his words knowing how many times he's already made me come in the span of a few short days. He's an expert on me now, saying and doing the exact right things that tip me over the edge every single time. It's what I've always wanted with someone between the sheets.

It boils down to compatibility, the piece of the puzzle I've always been lacking with a partner. I might have had to fake a few orgasms, but it's never been *bad*. Just... okay. Not ripping-off-clothes intensity or being comfortable enough to say what I like. What I want. Letting myself express pleasure vocally and proudly.

I feel *safe* with Patrick, allowed to move without embarrassment and react without expectations. I can take my time and ease into it, having a second chance if I need it. That's how I know I have the right person underneath me right now, because he loves me for exactly who I am.

Our gazes lock as I lower myself onto his length. We hiss in unison, sounds of pleasure filling the room and the small sliver of space between our bodies.

"More," I say, the word catching in the back of my throat. I think I might be dying, too much stimulation all at once. "More, Patrick. All of it."

He lifts his hips—maybe I lower mine, I'm not entirely sure who initiates what—and pushes another inch inside of me. He groans into my shoulder, teeth gently biting around the tendons at the base of my neck. I see bursts of color and sparks of light as he thrusts inside me until I'm fully seated on him, taking a second to breathe and get used to the feel of him stretching me and consuming me.

"God," I whisper, feeling drunk and high with lust. "That feels so good."

"It's never been this good," Patrick says. "Never." His nails sink into my skin, heightening the heat and intensity of the moment to a deadly inferno. "Fuck, Lola. You're incredible."

I relax, getting used to the sensation of being so full. Of being ravenous for him, a void of unsated hunger only he can fill. My thighs open wider and I push up, nearly sliding his length out of me before lowering myself again. I get deeper this time and our moans sync, long and low and echoing off the walls.

"What do you like?" I ask. I lean forward, canting my body weight toward him and brushing my lips against his forehead. "What makes you feel good? Fast? Slow? What makes Patrick Walker out of his mind?"

"You," Patrick pants. "You, Lola."

He looks possessed and tortured, a bead of sweat rolling down his cheek and his head dropping back against the stack of pillows. I watch his gaze track over my body, staring at my chest then dropping to where we're joined, one hand sliding away from my legs to pinch my nipple.

It's sweet and sexy at the same time. Hot and heavy while being carefree and light. Patrick thrusts. I roll my hips. He pulls my hair and I bite his earlobe, earning me a noise I've only dreamed about.

There are whispered words and quiet chuckles. Exploration and learning with soft kisses and fingernail scratches. I'm convinced the center of the universe can be pinpointed to our room, two people showing their love for each other with hands and mouths and soft encouragement

When I get too eager and slide off of him entirely, instead of drawing attention to my mistake, Patrick takes the opportunity to flip us, my back on the mattress and him towering above me.

He holds his cock in his hand and teases along my entrance. He licks his lips and nudges my knees apart. "Pretty," he murmurs, reaching out and resting his palm against my throat, testing me. "I want to hear you beg for it."

I squirm on the once-cool sheets, kicking off the blanket as heat rises up my chest. "Please," I whisper.

"You can do better than that," he says. His fingers lightly squeeze around my neck, the faintest bit of pressure, and when I nod my assent, they tighten further. "Beg for me, Lola."

"Please fuck me, Patrick. Ruin me. Destroy me. I want you to own me. I want you so bad."

"That's my girl," he says, his free hand running up my thigh and fanning out across my ribcage. "You know I'll give you whatever you want."

I take a breath and he slams into me, my body jolting and my hands flying out to find something to grasp on to. His shoulders, his arms, anything with purchase. He brings his fingers to my clit and circles, a torturous pattern I might perish from.

It truly hasn't ever felt this good. Sweat-soaked limbs. Loving caresses and singing praise. Patrick tells me I can *take it*. He's *proud* and he loves to see me *spread open* for him. I answer with nails running down his back. My mouth on his chest, kissing any space of skin I can find. I whisper that he's my *one and only*, the *best yet*, the *only one to treat me right*.

His tempo is perfect, his angle is perfect, *he* is perfect. And when he grabs under my legs and yanks me to him, pressing my thighs against my chest and nearly folding me in two, I think I leave my body. I feel that satisfaction building up my spine. That wave of wonder spans across my stomach and toward my neck. It's delightful, a cocoon of pleasure and bliss I never want to live without.

Until Patrick stops, pressing a kiss to my knee as that delicious nirvana washes away.

"What?" I pant. "No. No, no, *no*. I was so close."

"I know you were," Patrick says. He kisses my other knee, his movements slowing to gentle and steady.

"Did—did you come?" I ask hesitantly.

"I almost did. That's why I had to stop." He looks sheepish as he says it, bashful as he dips his chin and looks away. "I'm sorry. I want to make this last for you."

"I don't care about lasting," I say, my palm resting on his cheek. "I don't care if you finish in five minutes or fifty. I like knowing I'm the one who gets you there. I want you to come, Patrick. I want to watch you while you do. Will you come for me? Show me how good I feel?"

"Fuck, Lola," Patrick groans. "Your pussy is the best thing of my life. You're so tight and so wet. Wet for *me*."

"For you," I answer. "Just for you."

"Just for me," he repeats with awe and wonder. He takes both of my hands in one of his and brings my arms above my head. He keeps his fingers clasped around my wrists, locking me in place, and his movements resume. I'm entirely at his mercy. He's *using* me to get off, and it's the hottest thing of my life.

How can a man be both sweet as sugar and sexy as hell, performing two sides so well? None of it is fake or an attempt to be something he's not. This is Patrick Walker—the man who cooks me breakfast with a smile on his face can also rail me into oblivion.

How is he *real*?

"Deeper, Patrick," I say. "Put my legs on your shoulders."

He follows my lead, his free hand lifting my left leg then my right before settling them around his neck. "Holy *shit*," he breathes out. "You feel so good, baby. You take me so well. Look at you."

This angle is the best one yet. We're so connected, so wrapped around each other I can't tell which are my limbs and which are his. Patrick kisses my calf and runs his tongue up my knee. I'm so immersed in him I don't even realize I'm falling over the edge until it's too late, the orgasm surprising me when he bites my nipple and tugs on my hair. Tears spring in my eyes and I whimper as my legs tighten around his neck, probably close to suffocating him.

"Come inside me, Patrick," I say through staggered breaths, my heart racing and my vision blurry. "Please."

Patrick lets out a groan and drops his head forward, finding his own ecstasy. His body convulses until I finally feel him relax, his thrusts ceasing. He's panting, his shoulders rising and falling rapidly. I ease my wrists out of his grip and lower my legs. I run my hands up his sides, soothing him and calming him down.

"I think I'm dead," he says, pulling out of me. I immediately miss the closeness we shared and I shiver at the loss of contact. "You've killed me, Lola Jones."

He settles on his back and pulls me into an embrace, my head resting on his chest and my eyes fluttering closed. I hum and nod in agreement.

"You killed me too," I say.

"That was—"

"The best sex of my life."

"Without a doubt."

"You told me to *beg*, Patrick."

"Did that go too far?" he asks, tucking a lock of hair behind my ear. "Maybe we should have talked about boundaries and preferences before we dove headfirst into the deep end."

"It didn't go too far," I say quickly. "I told you I'd let you know when I liked or disliked something. I really, really, *really* liked *that*."

"Okay." I hear his smile as he kisses my forehead. "I really, really, *really* liked it too."

"Why are things so easy with you? It's starting to scare me."

"Because we're soulmates, Lola," Patrick answers without a moment of thought. He's getting tired, his voice waning at the end of his sentences. His breathing has become steady, leveling out to soft puffs of air. "When you're with the person who's your perfect match, it's effortless."

He *is* my soulmate. The missing piece I've been searching for, and all the while, he's been right in front of me. Patiently waiting. Caring for me as if I was already his. Loving me in my darkest, most vulnerable state and never running away. Imagining a life without him even decades down the road already fills me with remorse and dread.

I plan to live every second with him like it's my last. Appreciate every small moment, even the mundane and boring ones, because with him, life is never dull.

I love him. I love him, I love him, I *love him,* like I've never loved anyone else before. Like I'll never love anyone else ever again. All the people in the world, and he's mine. *Mine, mine, mine.*

It's my favorite word.

THIRTY-FOUR
PATRICK

"MORNING." I stifle a yawn and wrap my arm around Lola's waist, glancing around the busy room. "Ready for day two?"

"Yeah." She pushes up on her toes and brushes her lips against mine. "I brought you another coffee."

"An angel in the form of morning beverages," I say as she hands me the large styrofoam cup. I can smell the caffeine through the plastic top and eagerly take a sip. "Ah. I'm revitalized."

"That quick, huh?"

"I'm a simple man, Lola."

"Sorry for leaving you in bed alone," she says. "I hope you didn't think I was bolting from you after last night. I was just excited to get down here and get started."

Last night when we had the best sex of my life.

Three times.

In the bed. On the bathroom counter. Against the wall after our shower. I can't get enough of Lola. I'm consumed by thoughts of her, if the pillows scattered around the room and the bottom sheet pulled off the corners of the mattress are any indication. I had to put the Do Not Disturb sign on our door when I left ten minutes ago, too embarrassed to have housekeeping come in and see the mess we've made of the place.

"I didn't think that. I figured you wanted to get an early start today," I say.

"I did. You also looked exhausted and I wanted to let you sleep as long as possible." Lola touches my chest and runs her fingers over the stitching of my shirt. "Are you sure you don't have any lingering symptoms from your migraine?"

"Honey, I think you fucked all the lingering symptoms away when you were riding me last night," I say in a low voice, and she swats at my arm, a shade of red creeping up her neck. "I feel better than yesterday, Lo, and yesterday I felt great."

"The second you start to feel crummy, I hope you'll tell me," she says.

"I promise. Do you need me to run back up to the room and grab you anything before the show starts or—"

"Thank god. There you are," Janet, the show director, interrupts us. She puts the walkie talkie she's holding in her pocket and looks down at her clipboard, rifling through the stack of papers. An assistant approaches behind her, holding one of Lola's garment bags. Dread claws at the base of my spine as I take in their harried expressions. "We have a situation."

"What's going on?" I ask.

"We're missing one of Lola's models."

Lola frowns. "What do you mean missing?"

"He's not here."

"Is he just late? There's still ten minutes until the first designer walks."

"Nope." Janet shakes her head. I think she's close to pulling her hair out or breaking her clipboard over her knee. I don't think the poor wood would stand a chance. "Definitely not late. He's not coming. Called and said he's too hungover."

"Fuck," I curse. Then, remembering I'm in front of the

woman who could determine the future of Lola's career, I wince at my choice of words. "Sorry, ladies. I apologize for the vulgarity."

"Don't worry. I said a whole lot worse than that when I found out about the crisis five minutes ago," Janet admits.

"Is there an extra model?" I ask. "Someone else who can fill in? I've seen three hundred people walk through those doors this morning. Can't any of them do it?"

"No. We've allotted the exact number of models to pieces on the runway," the assistant explains.

"Plus, I'm not sure we'll find someone who fits in the clothes in time. Something to add in for next year," Janet adds, making a note on the top sheet of paper and circling it six times. The tip of her pencil breaks and she lets out a frustrated sigh.

"I could do one less design," Lola says. She bites her bottom lip and her eyes flick down to the floor, disappointment flooding her features. "I won't be penalized, will I?"

"Absolutely not," Janet answers quickly, seemingly elated we've found a solution. "I'll mention what's going on to the judges and—"

"No. Fuck that," I bark out, apologies for my language forgotten, and all three heads turn to stare at me. "You're not changing your lineup because someone can't handle their liquor and didn't show up on time, Lola."

"What do you propose I do?" Lola snaps back, her voice rising in steady increments with every syllable. "I can't make a model appear out of thin air, Patrick." Her hands shake and a single tear rolls down her cheek "Sorry. I'm sorry. I didn't mean to yell. I'm taking this out on you when it's not your fault."

"It's okay, honey. I know you're frustrated," I say, keeping my tone soft. I rub my hands up her arms, getting rid of the goosebumps and pulling her close. I glance over at Janet. "How much time until you absolutely need someone in line to walk the runway in Lola's clothes?"

"Twenty-five minutes." Janet checks her watch and blanches, her face turning pale. "No. Twenty minutes."

"Okay. Here's what's going to happen. I'm going to do it," I blurt out before I can talk myself out of a plan I'm making up as I go. A plan I'm not sure will even work.

Lola's chin jerks up and she stares at me. The woman holding the garment bag lets go of the hangers, the canvas gathering in a heap next to the wooden clipboard that slips from Janet's grasp.

"What? Patrick, you're not a model," Lola says.

"My Hanes briefs don't scream couture to you?" I joke, and none of the women laugh. It's a feeble attempt, a desperate Hail Mary I'm throwing at the end of the game with no time on the clock, trying to do something, *anything* to wipe the devastated frown off Lola's face and clear the tears from her eyes. "I've worn the suits before. Dozens of times. You used my measurements to make them."

"To pose for pictures, not walk in front of a thousand people. Even if the clothes do fit, you won't know the marks to hit."

"I saw some of the women's show yesterday. At the very least I know to go to the end of the stage, pause, then come back. All those years of watching *America's Next Top Model* with you taught me something, Lo. I'm not totally clueless. I can do it."

"Patrick," she whispers, and I hear the fear behind my name. Years of her hard work is threatening to come undone, all because of someone else's mistake. "I don't know if it will work."

I step toward her and wipe away her tears with my thumbs. I cup her cheeks and give her a gentle kiss. She tastes like syrup and powdered sugar from donuts, lingering spearmint, and the bright Florida sunshine.

"It might not, but I want to try. I know you can do things by yourself," I say. "You've been doing them effortlessly for thirty-four years. But I'm here, sweetheart. I'm willing. Let me help. I want to help. Those people deserve to see the beauty of your art. *All* of your art."

Her nod starts off weak, growing more resolute as she ponders the idea and becomes more onward with the plan. Lola's a pragmatic woman, taking her time to see the big picture and not make an impulsive decision based on emotion.

"Okay," she says. "Okay. Yes. *Yes.* That would... Patrick, are you sure?"

"I've never been more sure of anything in my life."

"You'll have to wear makeup."

"Sounds like the time you used my cheeks to learn how to contour."

"Your picture will be in magazines," Lola says. "People will find your social media accounts. I know you like your privacy. I never even show your face in my photos because I know how much you value your privacy. Who knows what the people on the internet will say?"

"Fuck 'em," I answer. I drop my hands to her shoulders and give her arms a gentle squeeze. "I don't care what they'll say. I'll be wearing your clothes, and that's all that matters. Do you know how cool that is? You've come a long way from that shirt you sewed me for my thirteenth birthday."

A laugh slips out of her, and the tension in her shoulders begins to loosen. "The front and back were two different lengths," she says, sniffing and wiping her nose.

"And look how far you've come," I say. "I want to do this for you."

There's a moment of tense silence while I wait for Lola to make her decision. I don't think Janet is breathing and the assistant scoops up the suit from the floor, her hands trembling.

"Okay," Lola whispers. "Let's do it."

"Yeah?" I ask, my lips stretching into a grin.

"Yeah," she says firmly, meeting my beam with one of her own. "Hell yeah. Why not? This is the trip of firsts. Let's keep it going."

I scoop her into my arms and spin her around. "Let's keep it going," I agree.

"Do you promise to tell me if you feel uncomfortable?"

It's cute how much she's worrying, as if I wouldn't go to the ends of the earth to make her happy, no questions asked.

I kiss her forehead and say, "I promise."

I love you.

I love you. I love you. I love you.

I want to scream it so every model, every volunteer, every person out in the audience can hear the declaration, but it's not the time.

Not yet.

First, I've got to get the clothes created by the woman of my dreams down the runway for everyone to see. Then I can pour my heart out to her.

One step at a time.

———

I THOUGHT HELPING Lola backstage yesterday was chaotic, but today is even more of a whirlwind. There's a laundry list of tasks and not enough time to accomplish even half of them.

Racks of clothes are pulled from one end of the room to the other. Mirrors and vanities are set up with makeup I can't pronounce and products I don't know the purpose of. I get pulled in a dozen different directions as my hair gets combed with a thick brush. My cheeks get coated in something sticky. A hanger is thrust my way as someone takes off my shirt.

I'm about to slip the dark slacks on over my briefs when I see a safety pin secret through the loophole, a handwritten note attached to it.

Pattycakes,

Thank you will never be sufficient. You are my knight in shining armor and the most wonderful man. I'm lucky to be yours and I'm thankful every day you're mine.

Xoxo,

L

I grin and tuck the paper in my pocket like a winning lottery ticket. It's worth more than a million bucks.

"Patrick," Janet calls out. I turn to look at her as I slide the blazer over my shoulders. I remember this design, with the navy-blue color and gold buttons. It fits me like a glove, hugging my body like it was made for me. Maybe Lola designed it specifically with me in mind. "How are you doing?"

"Good." I make my way over to her, dodging a line of men heading for the runway. They glance at me, confused, and I nod in greeting. Glad to know I look ridiculously out of place.

"I'm glad you made the trip down with Lola. Not because you're saving our butts by walking in the show, but because a supportive partner is important in this business," she says as we head toward the cluster of models I'm joining. "She's extremely talented."

"I'd cheer for her no matter what job she wanted to do," I say earnestly.

"I can tell." Janet winks as we arrive at the tall black curtain hanging from steel metal rods. A thick piece of fabric is all that separates me from the thousands of people in the audience. I was out there yesterday and it was madness, with cheering and applause and whistling. I don't imagine today will be any different, and I take a deep breath. "Ready?"

I nod, lifting my chin with as much determination as I can muster. I'm sweating buckets underneath my shirt, nervous about messing anything up for Lola. The guy in front of me turns around and says something about tape and tempo and keeping my distance so I don't run anyone over or throw off the pace. I nod again, halfway confident I understand what he was saying, and rub my palms over my thighs.

"Yeah," I say, hoping there's conviction behind the word. It's too late to back out now. I'm committed to seeing this all the way through, even if that means potentially falling on my face and becoming some video the kids at school will see.

I glance around, trying to spot Lola, but she's nowhere to be seen. She disappeared ten minutes ago after she kissed my cheek and fixed a tie for the man at the back of our line. I wish she were here to tell me I'm going to be fine, but I'll have to settle for reassurances from people I've never met before.

"You got this, man," the guy behind me says.

"Thanks," I say weakly.

Someone with a headset holds up their hand, counting down from five. When they reach one they point to the guy up at the front of the line, motioning for him to start moving. We shuffle forward one by one, four men disappearing to the other side then five. Then it's my turn, lucky number seven, and I throw up a prayer to whatever higher power is out there watching this all unfold that I can get through the next two minutes unscathed.

The music is loud as I walk onto the runway, and it takes a second for my brain to remember I need to *keep* walking down the long stage. I take a deep breath and start my trek, one foot in front of the other, again and again, hoping I don't look like a douchebag or Neanderthal.

The guys are definitely going to give me shit for this.

I keep my chin up and my eyes ahead, just like I've seen the other models do. My walking is clunky, out of sync with the beat of the music and hardly professional, but I don't care. The further down the runway I get, the more I feel myself relax, sinking into the motions and the glide of linen against my skin.

I can fucking *do* this.

There are a million lights flashing in my vision with the spotlights marking the path of the runway and the click of large cameras and smartphones. Through the haze of the fog machine and over the heads of the crowd, the only thing I can see with clarity is Lola grinning from ear to ear, the most perfect smile plastered on her face. Our eyes meet and my body heats. Not from worry or fear or anxiousness, but from *love*.

It's here, as I pause at the end of the catwalk so the audience can soak in the clothes and throw a wink at her, I realize my heart has *always* belonged to her. Ever since that first day she tumbled out of her family's minivan and steamrolled into my life knocking away mundane and average and replacing the grays of the world with color and light and so much good.

This hasn't been a few-months thing.

It's been an all-my-fucking-life thing.

I love her so much.

Just the sight of her happy and elated makes my chest ache. I want to keel over. I want to jump off the elevated platform and charge toward her, sweep her in my arms, and whisper how much I adore her. How much I want to give her, from now until forever. I may not have a lot, but everything I do have is hers for the taking.

She twirls her finger, reminding me I need to spin and walk away. I didn't even notice I was at the end of the long stage. I'm too distracted by her beauty, a tape measure around her neck and a white ribbon in her hair, to remember how to move.

Keeping my eyes on her, I tap my chest three times, right over my heart, hoping she understands the meaning.

I love you.

I almost burst when she answers with the same three taps back, the smile on her face nearly sending me to space. I retreat down the runway giddily, a pep to my step and a blush on my cheeks.

A grown man blushing because of the attention from a woman?

I'm a fucking goner.

I've never had such a strong surge of happiness before, the kind that makes me want to pause this moment and not let it pass. It makes me want to dance. It makes me want to yell. It makes me want to do a lot of things, and at the root of them all is Lola.

There are seven billion people in this world. How lucky am I that the universe brought me her?

When I make it backstage, I'm met with handshakes and clasps on my shoulders. My blazer is tugged off my arms and someone starts to wipe the makeup from my face.

There's a flood of activity, a rush of people and questions. I look over my shoulder and see *her*. Blue eyes. Blonde hair. The most beautiful woman and the sole owner of my heart. She's grinning wildly, pulling her phone out to take a picture and squishing our cheeks together for a selfie.

"You were amazing," Lola says. "I'm pretty sure you're trending on Twitter under: Hot Guy Who Jumps In To Save Fashion Show."

"I have no clue what trending means," I answer. "It's a good thing, right?"

"A very good thing. Will you come with me to do an interview?" she asks.

I nod and follow her over to talk to a journalist from an independent magazine. I listen to her talk about the show and the immense gratitude she has for being invited to participate. When the woman tells her she looks happy, Lola's gaze meets mine.

"I am happy," Lola answers. "I'm so happy I think I could die."

THIRTY-FIVE

PATRICK

I'M BEING HELD hostage in our hotel room bathroom, a chair in front of the mirror and an army of makeup remover products lined up on the marble counter.

"This eyeliner is a pain to get off," Lola says. She laughs as she wipes under my eyes with a warm washcloth. The water drips down my cheek and onto my neck, pooling in the hollow of my throat and soaking the collar of my shirt.

"I thought about leaving it on for the rest of the night," I say. "Thoughts?"

"It's sexy. You pull it off well. You looked so great out there today, Patrick. If I didn't know you were an elementary school principal, I would have assumed you were one of the models from the get-go."

"You're trying to be nice. I stomped down that runway like a linebacker. I'm pretty sure I rattled the metal with every step I took."

"Stop." Lola laughs again and swats at my shoulder with the damp rag. I grab it from her and drop it in the sink, pulling her into my lap. Her legs settle around my waist and my hands loop around her lower back. "I'm serious. The audience loved you.

CHELSEA CURTO

The two girls in front of me were flipping through the program trying to find your name."

"They're going to be disappointed to learn my social media is *not* me posing in my underwear. What do they call them? Thirst traps? All I have on my page are leadership tactics for teachers to use to implement classroom management."

"You also have the photo of a stack of your ties where you polled your eighty-seven followers to see which one you should wear for Tie Tuesday."

"And three people responded, thank you very much."

"Classroom management sounds sexy," Lola murmurs against my mouth, nipping at my bottom lip. "Tell me more."

"Now you're lying to me." I thread my fingers through her hair. I smell her shampoo, the bottle she keeps in my bathroom when she goes a day or two without showering, too fixated on her work or not wanting to leave the couch before she remembers she needs to clean herself. She brought it with her on our trip, and I get a whiff of lilacs and roses. "You don't care about the Encourage Initiative or keys to offering praise. Are you an expert in model behavior?"

"That's not true. I love praise."

I dip my head to kiss her neck, trailing down the line of her throat that's been teasing me all day under the strings of her black halter top. I drag my teeth over the expanse of her fair skin, sucking on the spot right above her collarbone and earning a heavy exhale and a tug on my shirt.

"Then why don't you be good and open your legs, Lola? I want to taste you," I say.

She hums and closes her eyes, rolling her hips in a circle against my shorts. I'm already hard, and I don't bother to hide the effect she has on me.

"I love when you say that."

"Which part?" I ask.

"All of it."

I lift her from my lap and set her in the chair. I'd build her a throne if I could, but for now, the squeaky wood will have to do. I nudge her thighs apart and kneel between her legs like she's a queen and I've come to ask for repentance. I reach up and slip my hand under her leather skirt, running my palms up to the elastic of her underwear. I snap the waistband against her hips and she lets out a hiss.

"You're so sexy, Lola," I say, pushing her skirt up to her stomach. I drag my nails down her legs and grin when I find her panting, her head dropping back and her hands clutching the arms of the chair.

Next time we're together, I'll be patient and really take my time. I'll be gentle and sweet, making love to her with wandering touches and slow thrusts.

Now, as I look up at her her blonde hair spilling over her shoulders and her hard nipples, I want to take and claim and make her mine in every damn way known to man.

I'm about to slide her underwear off when Lola's phone rings. I glance over my shoulder and see Jo's name on the screen. I reach over and hand it to her.

"Answer it," I say.

"We're kind of in the middle of something," she says with irritation.

"I never said I was going to stop." Her eyes widen in understanding and she sits up, fumbling with the device. She nearly drops it, catching it by the corners at the last possible second before she shatters the glass screen. I press a kiss to the inside of her knee. "Answer it, Lola."

She swipes across the incoming call. "Hello?" she answers, her knuckles turning white as she grips the wood with one hand and her phone with the other. "Hey, Jo."

I don't bother taking her underwear off. I leave it on, my

mouth working over the white lace. I've always liked a challenge, and getting Lola to come while she's on the phone with a friend is going to be a challenge.

"Don't be obvious," I murmur.

My tongue runs over her clit, finding the spot she likes. I've gotten a head start, but I'm going to memorize every inch of her when we get home. Lay her out on my bed and study her like I study the books she likes to read. I'm determined to know everything about her. What else makes her toes curl? What else gets her nipples hard? How can I get her to bite her lip and let out the soft moan that I love?

Lola's hand shoots out and grips my shoulder. I chuckle into her leg and kiss her knee, rubbing my cheek against her thigh and smiling as her hold on me tightens.

"Yeah. Everything's good here. What? No, nothing's wrong," she says. I snap the elastic against her skin again, a pink mark blossoming just below her hip bone. She'd look sexy with a tattoo there, a drawing only I'd be able to see. "I promise I'm not being abducted in my hotel room."

I lick over her underwear again before dragging the small piece of fabric down with my teeth. I tuck them in my back pocket and Lola mouths *fuck*, drawing out the word. Her legs spread wider as she scoots her ass down the chair, cheeks hanging off the edge.

"How's Boston?" Lola asks into the phone. "Good. Yeah. Everything is great down here. Patrick modeled in the show today. Yup. I'll send some pictures later. I'm busy right now."

I push two fingers inside of her, smiling when she bites the inside of her cheek to keep quiet. The smile stretches to a grin as she puts the phone down at her side and takes a deep breath, wiping a bead of sweat from her forehead.

I'm distracting her. I think she's going to have a slew of harsh words to say to me when she hangs up, but for now, I'm in control and going to enjoy this.

"So pretty," I whisper, adding a third finger. "So ready for me. I could fuck you right now and Jo would have no idea I was sinking into you. She wouldn't know how many times you've screamed my name the last few days. Do you want me to talk to her? Tell her how wet you are? How sexy my best friend's pussy is? I could feast on you forever."

"Jo? I'm going to have to call you back. Something just came up."

Without waiting for a response, Lola hangs up and tosses the phone onto the tile floor. She grabs me by the scruff of my hair and pulls me to her, crashing her lips against mine. It's hot and bruising and hurried. I untie her shirt, sliding it over her waist along with her skirt. I don't care if I stretch them out. I'll buy her new ones.

She fumbles with the button on my jeans and I'm already shoving them off, my left foot getting stuck in the pant leg.

"Want you," she says against my mouth. "Now."

"Impatient," I say back. I shove my boxers down my thighs and kick them aside. I lift Lola from the chair and hold her in my arms as her legs wrap around my lower back. "Need to get a condom first."

"I'm not very good at being patient." Lola puts her forehead in the crook of my neck, her hand running across my chest. I walk us out of the bathroom and to my suitcase, keeping her in my hold as I squat to rummage through my bag.

"Hang on," I grumble. I toss a running shoe out of the way and my favorite baseball hat goes flying after it. A belt falls to the floor and I kick it away.

"How are you this disorganized? You can't stand things not being in their place. Every single container in your kitchen is labeled."

"I've been distracted," I say. I grab three condoms from the box and stand, heading us to the bed. Overzealous, probably, but I don't care.

"Oh? What's been distracting you? Anything in particular?"

"This hot blonde I can't seem to get out of my head."

"She sounds great."

"She is," I agree. "She's smart and she's kind and she's beautiful. Funny too, sometimes."

"Only sometimes?"

"Sometimes she's a smart ass." I drop Lola on the mattress. She bounces twice and giggles, shimmying up the sheets. "Which way do you like best?" I ask, climbing on the bed and crawling toward her.

"I like you on top," she answers. "I like watching you." Her fingers wrap around my cock and she strokes twice.

"Then that's what we'll do," I say.

I roll the condom down my length and let out a sigh. It's like my last breath of sanity. When we're like this, naked and nothing between us, I lose all rationale. I don't know which way is up, and it feels like I'm walking dangerously close to a fire.

I want to burn.

Lola reaches out to me, hands roaming up my forearms and drawing me closer. I line up with her entrance and before I have a second to breathe again, she's lifting her hips, guiding me inside her.

I give her a minute to get adjusted to me, her legs relaxing as I rock forward, planting my palms on either side of her head. I look down at her and find a twist of pleasure in her smile. There's satisfaction brimming in her eyes as she breathes out, "That feels good, Patrick," and plays with her breasts.

I never know where to look when I'm with her. Her chest, watching as she pinches her nipples and draws them to pointed peaks? Between her legs, seeing myself sink into her, each thrust loosening my grip on reality? Her mouth, following along as she says dirty things, filthy things, telling me exactly what she wants to try and how I fuck her like no one else has ever fucked her? Her heart, racing as fast as mine, showing just how much we love each other without actually saying the words?

Lola lifts up and kisses me, her tongue finding mine with a hum against my mouth. She hitches her leg up on my hip and I get deeper, deeper, *deeper*, finding new areas of her body I've yet to discover.

"Yes," she whispers. "Right there. That's perfect."

"Perfect," I repeat, my eyes squeezing closed.

"No," she says. She pinches my hip and I glance down to find her wearing a smirk and throwing my words back at me. "I want you to watch when you come inside me. I want to watch you fall apart. Eyes on me, Patrick."

My orgasm claws at my back from her demand. It starts at the base of my spine, working its way up to my shoulders then back down my chest until I'm filling the condom, a few words from her enough to catapult me off the edge of *fuck* and *yes*. I grunt and bury my face in her hair as I jerk forward, my hips lining up with hers until we're flush together.

My movements slow and I release a breath, lowering myself onto my elbows above her and thrusting one more time, emptied and utterly spent.

"Incredible," I mumble. "I think you're a sex goddess."

Lola blushes, her chest and cheeks turning red. She smiles and kisses me again, softer this time. "We work well together. I think that's why it's so good between us."

"Did you come?" I ask, noticing her steady breathing. "You didn't, did you?"

"No, but it's—"

I pull out of her and peel the condom off, tying it in a knot and dropping it on the floor.

"Don't finish that sentence," I say. "Of course it's okay that you didn't come, but that doesn't mean you don't deserve to keep trying. This isn't a one-sided physical relationship, Lo. I understand sometimes we might not be able to get you there, but it doesn't mean we just give up after five minutes. Do you want to keep going?"

"Yes," she says softly, like she's afraid to admit it. "It's easier for me when you use your fingers. You can touch more places."

"When we get home," I say, kissing her neck and running my hand up her leg, teasing her until she's raising her hips and grinding into the heel of my palm, "I'd like to watch you with your toys. I want to learn."

"I want to show you," she says, and I spend the next hour helping her tip over the edge.

Twice.

THIRTY-SIX

LOLA

I PACE from one end of the hotel living room to the other. The carpet is going to be nonexistent when we check out later this afternoon, a section rubbed off from the path I'm walking.

It's our last day in Florida and I've been up since dawn, crawling out of bed and moving to the couch so I didn't interrupt Patrick's sleep. The nervousness I've managed to avoid over this past week has slowly creeped up this morning, gnawing at me with every minute that passes on the clock. In a few short hours, the winner of the fashion show will be announced. In a few short hours, my life could change.

There's also a good possibility it *doesn't* change, staying entirely the same. I'm prepared for that, expecting the realistic outcome while clinging to a lofty dream with cautious optimism. Last night I watched a playback of yesterday's signature style while hiding in the bathroom after I tossed and turned for an hour, unable to turn off my mind or think of anything else.

I'm blown away by the sheer talent of the designers here. It's been four days of nothing but creative artistic flair, perfectly cut fabric with not a single thread out of place and enthusiastic crowd support. It's impossible to distinguish a real fan favorite or any insight into what the judges might be thinking.

I knew the show would be competitive, a selective process that whittled thousands of applicants down to a select few hundred deemed good enough to chase the grand prize. Seeing that talent up close, though, passing by it in the hall and watching models contort their bodies to highlight the sharp cuts and fine lines of impeccably sewn clothing, only amplifies how *incredible* the people are.

Each day on the runway was full of surprises. There were outfits that pushed gender stereotypes and defied gravity. Some outfits that looked like there wasn't an outfit at all, the material translucent until the model hit the exact spot on the stage where the spotlights shone on their shimmering gowns.

I heard gasps of surprise and rounds of applause. I saw standing ovations and the audience shocked into silence. They seemed to like my final signature style piece, fond of the dress with a cape that turns into a jumpsuit. Brielle modeled it, detaching the black adornment from her neck and letting it billow behind her like it was caught in a gust of wind.

The crowd went wild, but it's hard to be sure.

They've gone wild over a design from almost everyone, their untrained eyes appreciating the jaw-dropping outfits with plunging necklines and short shorts. They aren't critiquing on finesse or skillsets. They care about the *wow* factor, something I think I might have.

Everyone else might have it too though, and that's where things go up in the air.

"Lo?"

I look up, pausing my forty-fifth lap around the room to find Patrick leaning against the door frame. He crosses his arms over his bare chest and his lips bow into a thin line. His hair is sticking up on the sides and there's a pillow crease on his cheek.

"Hey," I say. "Did I wake you up?"

"By walking around the living room? No. Reaching over in the bed and finding it empty woke me up. Are you okay?"

"Yeah." I nod twice then turn the bob of my head into a shake. My toes curl into the floor and I rock back on my heels. "I don't know."

Patrick steps into the room and pulls me into a hug. I sigh into his skin and run my hand across his back. He's still warm from bed, the secret cave we created with pillows and sheets and the comforter.

"Talk to me," he says and we stand there, arms wrapped around each other, dissolving into a serious conversation at half past six in the morning because he cares about my feelings and wants to know how he can help.

"I'm nervous. What happens if I don't win? I've come all this way. It would be a lie to say I wouldn't be disappointed. I'd be heartbroken."

"If you don't win, it's not the end of the world. It'd sting for a few weeks, but we'd go home and you'll keep doing what you've been doing. You generally like how things have gone up until to this point in your life, right?" Patrick asks.

"Right. I do. I really do. I feel thankful every day that *this* is my life. I love traveling. I love making outfits for other people. I love creating what I want when I want."

"So if you don't win, you'll still love your life. And that's important."

"What if I *do* win? Hypothetically."

"If you win, you get to do the things money might have prevented you from doing before. What are your dreams, honey? What do you think about late at night when your mind starts to settle and you're sorting through the thoughts in your head?"

"I want to open a store," I say. It's the first time I've ever shared this with anyone besides the journal entries I've scribbled down over the last few years, an idea and vision I'd love to see come to light.

"Tell me about this store," Patrick says, tugging me toward the couch and sitting us down. "I want to hear about it."

I love how much genuine care Patrick has for the things in my life. He's not asking to hear because he wants to appease me, a check in the box as he fulfills his duty as my partner. It's because he *wants* to know, and it makes my heart go all fluttery and turn to mush.

"I'd love a spot on Newbury Street," I start, relaxing into the plush cushions of the sofa and keeping my hand in his. "It doesn't need to be very big, just a place where I can have racks for my clothes and a couple of couches. Big windows, so natural light can flood in. I hate artificial lighting. It makes people self-conscious, and the last thing I want when someone comes into my store is for them to feel bad about themselves."

"That's why you always make us take the long way home when we walk back to your place after dinner at a restaurant. You're scoping out retail spaces," Patrick says, connecting the dots without me having to explain. "I get it now. I thought you just really liked waiting three minutes at every traffic light."

"I can envision the inside so clearly in my mind," I say. "I close my eyes and I'm there. Vintage pictures hanging on the walls. Jeans that don't cost as much as a mortgage payment. Dresses for sweet sixteens and homecomings, rehearsal dinners and family photos. My name on the outside with a couple of hearts next to it."

"What would you call it?"

"Lola Jones Designs. It's simple and not catchy at all, but it's *me*. I'm a designer. It's taken me a long time to believe that even though I don't own a brick and mortar location yet, I'm no less valuable than the designers who do."

"You're damn right you're not less valuable," Patrick agrees. "Everyone's journey is different. You took a little longer to get to the big stage and that's *fine*. You're here now, with so many incredible ideas I know people will love. Whether that's in a physical place people can stop by and visit or online where they can browse through your portfolio, it doesn't matter. Just like it doesn't matter if you don't win the grand prize, Lo. You're already a winner in my eyes. You're chasing your goals, you're working hard, and that's more than a lot of other people can say."

"I do everything else in life so sporadically, but this... this has been a labor of love. It's carefully thought out. I know color schemes and the way I would arrange the clothes. Where I would put the dressing rooms and how big of a rug I want on the floor. Knowing I *could* open a store with the winnings makes me want it even more. There's no way I'll ever be able to do it without financial assistance."

"I'll help you run overhead costs when we get home. I'll do some research on property taxes and square footage. You'll need a warehouse and an industrial-sized order of materials. A handful of employees and someone who handles your social media accounts, because I have a feeling you'll be too busy to manage them yourself. I can figure out a break-even point for you based on how many sales you've done just through commissions in the last year."

"You'd do all that for me?" I ask and Patrick nods. He looks at me like I'm out of my mind, like there isn't a world out there where he *wouldn't* do it all for me.

"Yeah," he says. "Whatever you need. I might not be great with industry lingo, but I am proficient with spreadsheets and data. We'll do this together, Lola."

"God." I groan and bury my face in his shoulder. "Not the damn spreadsheets and data. It's too early for that."

"You like data and experimenting. Trying things for research purposes."

"I certainly do *not* like research purposes."

"Sure you do. You like when I learn that when I do this"—his thumb traces over the front of my shirt, drawing a circle around my nipple—"you do *that*."

I let out a breathy moan, the panic from moments earlier abating the longer he touches me. He spins me so we're back to front, and he slides his hand under my pajama bottoms.

Soon I forget what I was worried about altogether, the only thing I can think about is *Patrick* and the mind-numbing bliss he brings me.

———

"IT'S PACKED IN HERE," Patrick says later that morning after a shower and breakfast.

We work our way through the group of people to the section of the room roped off for designers. The runway has been broken down, a small stage is set up in its place in front of hundreds of chairs. Some of the general public stuck around for the announcement of the winners. Some of the people congregating and chatting eagerly are friends and family, waiting with bated breath for the final results.

We find two seats toward the front of the room at the end of the row. Patrick lets me take the chair on the outside, correctly assuming I may want to run from the room and hide. His hand settles on my thigh and I rest my head on his shoulder, taking a second to breath before the announcements gets underway.

Janet climbs onto the stage first, followed by Vivian, and a roaring round of applause bursts through the crowd while the distinguished designer waves, mouthing *thank you.*

What a life to be recognized everywhere you go.

"Good morning," Janet says into the microphone, pausing momentarily to let the sound techs fix the staticky feedback. They switch out a cord and give her the thumbs up to continue. "We're so excited to see so many of you here to watch as we unveil the winners from the 2023 Florida Fashion Show."

There's another round of applause and Patrick leans into me.

"How many winners are there?" he asks in a low voice.

"One from each day, then Best Of," I answer. "The winners from each day get a smaller cash prize, and the Best Of winner takes home the grand prize."

"You've got this, honey."

I smile at his enthusiasm, the positivity radiating off of him as he taps his knee up and down, clearly just as nervous as I am.

"First up is the winner from the women's division," Janet starts, reading off a card from an envelope. "This year's top designer is... Matilda Paige!"

Cheers ring out around the room. I see Matilda jump up, her blonde curls bouncing as she hugs the people around her. I remember her designs because she walked three spots in front of me. Vibrant colors, bold patterns, and the kind of whimsical clothes you'd find at the mall in the eighties. I liked her style and she's a nice human, stopping to wish me good luck this morning in the hallway, so I'm glad to see her win.

We watch her walk across the stage and shake hands with Janet and Vivian, collecting a check and a bouquet of flowers.

"She's peppy," Patrick says, and I giggle into his shirt.

"Shh. I'm trying to listen."

Three other names get announced for the remaining divisions. My heart sinks further into my chest each time I hear someone else get called, my dream slipping out of grasp.

"Best Of," Patrick whispers. "This is the most important one."

"Yeah," I say. "We'll see."

I know he's trying to make me feel better but it's hard to watch something you worked so hard for go to someone else. *They're just as deserving as you,* I tell myself. *Stop being bitter.*

I shove the selfish thoughts away.

"Before we move on to the Best Of winner, we have a slight amendment to the program," Janet says. "When we first set out to do the show this year, we knew we'd have the highest number of participants than ever before. Thanks to the hard work of our designers and our judges, we surpassed our initial fundraising and sponsor goal. Because of this, we're able to award another winner in an additional category: Best Up-And-Coming Designer. This winner will win an additional $500,000 and a photo shoot, as well as an exclusive mentorship with Vivian Lee."

"Holy shit," Patrick whispers. "Lola."

"There were sixty-five first-time designers," I say. "It could be anyone."

"It could also be *you.*"

I swallow down the lump of excitement in my throat and fidget in my seat. My heart is racing and I think I've forgotten how to breathe. There are murmured voices around me and I can hardly hear when Janet announces, "Our first ever Best Up-And-Coming designer is... Lola Jones."

I blink, staring at the stage in pure disbelief. I turn my head to ask Patrick what she said but he's hauling me into his arms before I have the chance, kissing my cheek, my nose, my forehead.

"You did it," he whispers in my ear. His shoulders shake and I realize through his jubilation what's happening.

I won.

I *won.*

Me.

A winner at the Florida Fashion Show.

"Oh my god. Is this real? Did she actually say my name?" I ask.

"Yeah." Patrick sets me down on my feet and squeezes my shoulders. "She did."

He's crying and I realize I'm crying too, tears streaming down my face as people reach out to congratulate me. People I've never met offer their praise and then gesture for me to go to the stage, so I do, balloons raining from the ceiling and my vision blurring from my tears.

I miss a step and almost trip, righting myself at the last minute as Vivian reaches out to me, pulling me into a hug.

"I'm sorry. I'm probably getting mascara on your shirt," I say.

"That's okay," she says. "It's allowed under these circumstances. Your designs blew us away, Lola. Your creativity, your attention to detail, your overall love for fashion. It was impressive. You're going to do big things, and I can't wait to help you get there."

"This is... I don't know what to say. I wasn't expecting this at all."

"You don't have to say anything. You can take the check and flowers and walk away."

I burst out laughing. "That seems so rude. Am I supposed to smile for a camera? I see flashes going off."

"Turn to your left," Vivian says, giving me the patience and grace I'm not sure I deserve given that I'm a blubbering mess. "Smile. There you go."

"Do I have clumps of makeup under my eyes?" I ask.

Vivian drapes her arm over my shoulder and squeezes. "Yes, but you look happy. That's all that matters."

Spots form in my vision from all the bright lights, but I can still see Patrick in the crowd. He's standing on a chair, his fingers in his mouth as he lets out a loud whistle. I laugh again, burying my face in my hands.

I'm overwhelmed, just a little embarrassed, and so, so elated. Everything I never thought would come true just *did,* and I don't know what to do besides smile and wave, probably looking like a damn fool but at least I'm a *happy* fool. A fool who tried and succeeded. There's nothing else I'd rather be.

THIRTY-SEVEN
LOLA

PATRICK and I are sprawled out in the grass, a full sheet cake sitting between us. Two forks balance precariously on the paper plates we bought at the grocery store, and cheap champagne bubbles up in the plastic glasses sitting by our knees.

The afternoon and early evening have passed in a blur, leaving me struggling to remember the last few hours. We Face-Timed my mom when we got back to the room after the announcement of the winners, only hanging up with her to call our friends. We spent an hour giving them details about the show and the wait to hear my name, laughing over the video Patrick captured of me on stage, my mess of tears probably already making embarrassing rounds on the internet.

After the celebrations died down, we slipped out of the hotel to find food, deciding on pizza and a box of tacos for dinner. I kissed Patrick's tattoo as he ordered the large pepperoni and he smiled down at me, big and wide.

I've thought every day with him on this trip was been the best day of my life, but I was naive. This one, today, is really and truly the best one. I haven't smiled this much in years. I alternate between laughing and crying, my emotions a pendulum as I process everything that's happened and everything that's *going* to happen with a new future ahead of us.

I left my cell phone up in our room, wanting some peace and quiet before we start our journey home in the morning. The screen kept lighting up, hundreds of comments and likes flooding my social media as my follower count increased by the second. Patrick could tell I needed some fresh air, some time with just *us*, and he led me past the pool brimming with tourists to a small garden off the main walking path.

He bought the cake at the hotel coffee shop, an eight-inch wide dessert covered in chocolate and whipped cream. *A celebration,* he'd said, sticking a candle on top and putting a party hat on my head.

My stomach already hurts, full from dinner and the first two slices of cake, but I forge on, picking up my fork to take another bite and wiping the crumbs from my mouth with the back of my hand.

"What time do we need to get on the road tomorrow?" I ask. I shove my plate away and give Patrick a warning look. "Please don't say anything before eight in the morning. I will revolt."

He grins, pieces of chocolate cake covering his lips and his dimples popping under the night sky. I lean over and kiss away the crumbs, using my tongue to help clean up the mess. He hums against my mouth and I laugh lightly, shoving his chest so he'll let me go.

"I was planning on a six a.m. departure," he says. "Does that not work with your schedule?"

"I really, really hope you're joking. We might have to reevaluate this relationship."

"Do you know how beautiful the world is before the sun rises, Lola? You can hear the crickets chirping. You get to see the sky light up for the first time. We're literally in this massive rock floating though space, around and around again. How cool—"

I cut him off by pushing my fingers into his ribs, right above the spot where he's the most ticklish. He head-butted me the last time I tried this, and left me with a bruised chin. Tonight I'm awarded a high-pitched squeal as he swats at my hand like I'm an obnoxious fly that won't leave him alone, and I burst out laughing.

"Nothing before nine," I say. I push him to the ground and keep my elbow over his upper chest. He could break free from me if he wanted to, but he doesn't.

"Nine is midday," he argues, his hand reaching behind me. "I'll settle for seven-thirty."

"Seven-thirty? Absolutely not. Eight. That's my final—"

Patrick smashes a piece of cake into my face.

Buttercream frosting hangs from my nose and whipped cream covers my forehead. A drop of chocolate syrup rolls down my cheek and I stare at him, flabbergasted.

"You are a menace," I say. "And out of your damn mind." I reach for the decimated cake, grabbing a handful and smearing it across his chin and cheeks. "Payback is a bitch."

He laughs, a deep sound I feel behind my ribs and in my chest. He runs his knuckles up my spine and pulls me close, our noses brushing against each other. "God, I love you."

I freeze. My body goes stiff and rigid in his hold, and a clump of whipped cream falls to the grass. I blink and tilt my head to the side, my world wobbling on its axis with his four words.

"What did you say?" I ask.

I'm waiting for him to take it back. For him to yell out a *just kidding* or pretend it didn't happen. A heat-of-the-moment declaration with lowered inhibitions and mistaken confessions. Instead, I see Patrick smile, his face alight with glee.

His Exuberant Face.

I've seen this one many times before. More frequently, as of late. It's the same one I get when he glances at me from across the room, making butterflies flutter in my stomach. I can see his teeth. His eyes wrinkle in the corner and his nose scrunches, little lines forming between his eyebrows because he's so *happy*.

"I said I love you, Lola," he repeats. There's no reluctancy, no hesitation. He speaks it with his lungs, from his heart and from his soul.

"You love me?"

"I do."

"You do?"

"Quite a lot, actually."

"How—" I swallow and take a deep breath. "How much?"

"More than I love anything else in the world. I've felt like this for so long and I can't keep it inside anymore. Not when I want to tell you every single day. It's been torture to not say it, eating me alive because you deserve to hear it, so I'm finally doing it. I love you, Lola Jones. And I know you might not be in the same place as me yet, and that's okay. I'm not going to rush you. I just want you to know how incredible I think you are and—"

"I love you too," I blurt out.

I say it from every part of me that belongs to him. All the pieces that have repaired themselves over the years, fractured fragments stitched back together, healed from Patrick's friendship and his unwavering love.

Maybe I've always unknowingly been a little bit in love with him, the boy who shook my hand all those years ago. The one who grew into the kind of man who puts a heating pad on my stomach when my cramps get too intense and talks with me on the phone until I fall asleep when I'm five thousand miles away from home.

The one who's been by my side from the very beginning. A single hello, a silly little handshake forever altering our history. He's the one who's encouraged me, who's believed in me, who's supported me well before I was ever truly, fully his. He's been my one constant, the weight on the scales that tips me back to steady from unbalanced.

He's the reason no one else has ever measured up. The reason I've shut others out so quickly, because maybe, *maybe* I've been subconsciously comparing them to him. To know Patrick is to know that no one, not a single person in this world, could ever come close to how wonderful he is. As a friend, as a partner, as a lover, as a human being. He is the best of the best. The blueprint for what everyone should strive to be. And he's the one who loves me, *all of me*, flaws and all.

He welcomes those imperfections with open arms. What others have teased me about, what others have drawn attention to and called shortcomings, he considers rarities, blessings, precious jewels only found buried in a treasure chest. Not something to hide but something to embrace. Something to hold close because they're special and they're important, far from blemishes on my personality.

I love him. I love him. I love him. *I love him.*

And he loves me, two people head over heels for each other and a destiny of forever ahead. Uncharted waters, undiscovered paths of life now all ones we'll travel together, side by side, until the end of time. I'm going to find a way to attach his soul to mine. To stitch our hearts together so there's never a day when I don't have him with me.

"You love me?" Patrick asks.

He sounds uncertain, like he wasn't expecting me to ever say it back. A far-off daydream he's only thought about while alone, convincing himself he'd never hear those words from my mouth. It hurts my heart to think there might have been a time when he didn't know I feel the same about him, and I'm going to do everything in my power to prove to him how certain he should be.

"Yes, I love you. I love you a whole lot, Patrick Walker. And

I'm not just saying it because you said it. I've spent this whole trip becoming more and more sure of how much I love you and hoping you feel the same. How could I *not* love you? You are the most wonderful thing to ever happen to me."

"I think I might be hallucinating," he says.

I wipe the frosting away from my face and see the stars reflected in his eyes, the twinkle of elation and the joy in his smile. *My* smile. "This is real. As real as it'll ever be."

"Real," he repeats. "Really real. I've been waiting for this for a long time. I never thought—I hoped it would happen but— Lola. You. Love. Me."

"I do." I laugh and lean forward, kissing his forehead and the tip of his nose. "I love you."

"I love you too. I don't think I'm ever going to stop saying it."

"Please don't. Say it again and again and again."

"When did you know?" Patrick asks. "When did you realize?"

"I realized I wanted to kiss you that night we ate pizza on your couch. I realized I was falling in love with you outside the bookstore. I realized I was totally head-over-heels in love with you when I saw your tattoos. How I feel right now though... I've felt like this with you for years. Warm and fuzzy. Like everything has fallen into place. I'm finally a completed version of me. Saying the words might have taken me years, but I think that pull to you, that emotional connection has always been there." I take a breath. "When did you realize you loved me?"

"The first day I met you I thought you were the prettiest girl I had ever seen. I told you I had a crush on you for years. It was harmless, I thought. You were always right there. Always making me laugh and smile. When I started dating other women, I noticed I enjoyed spending time with them, but it was like my heart was only halfway in it. Jessica and I got in a fight over the friendship bracelet, and that's when I really knew."

"A fight?" I ask, tracing the line of his jaw with my finger. "I don't remember you telling me about a fight."

"We broke up not too long after, and it didn't feel worth rehashing. I told her I didn't want to take off the bracelet, and she told me it was because I was in love with you. I denied it at first, but once she said the words out loud, it was all I could see. That was when I knew I *was* in love with you, but I've been yours since the very beginning. I've never told another woman that I love her. I haven't wanted to. There was always something holding me back from saying the three words and sealing the deal, and now I know that something was you."

"Jesus," I whisper, my heart growing three sizes. "Talk about a grand gesture and a sweeping declaration."

"Do you think they'll write a book about us?" he asks, tucking a strand of hair behind my ear.

"Maybe. We deserve it."

"I'm so glad you moved in next door and became my neighbor."

"I'm so glad you were outside playing basketball when we pulled into the driveway. Who knows how long it would've taken us to meet and become friends if I hadn't seen you that first day? What if I had found another friend?"

"It was fate," Patrick says and I nod.

"Fate," I agree.

"The guys know."

"What do you mean the guys know?"

"They know I love you. I shouted it at them the day of the wedding after you found the box of books."

"And they haven't teased you?"

"Oh, they've teased me mercilessly. They had a bet on when I would admit that I had feelings for you, Lola. They've apparently been talking about this for years."

"The girls told me the same thing," I say. "There was a detailed conversation about how you look at me."

"How do I look at you?" Patrick asks. I think he already knows and just wants to hear me say it.

"Like I'm you're lifeline," I whisper.

"You are my lifeline," he says. "Without you, I'd be lost at sea. That's how I feel when you're away."

"I love you, Patrick. You're my lifeline too. My little dingy lifeboat amidst crashing waves."

"That's it? We've got to upgrade to a yacht. Buy me one with your winnings."

"Sure. Okay. Anything else on the list?" I ask. "Might as well get out all of your demands."

"Your heart," he says. "Your mind. Your body and soul. You. That's my list, Lola. That's all my list is ever going to be."

I don't know why I'm crying when he's saying something so nice, so romantic, so special and uplifting, but I am. Because it's me and because it's him. We were tied to each other long ago, drifting through the years until we finally, *finally* found each other.

I can't believe this man is mine. He's always going to be mine, the kindest, most gentle soul and fiercest protector of my heart. I know we're going to have hurdles to face when we get back to reality, readjusting to our lives at home and our different priorities.

School for him. Traveling and opening a business for me.

It doesn't matter. Those differences between us that once seemed like a roadblock are now an opportunity. A chance to learn and grow and be together. To listen and communicate, ask and answer. To help and give. To love and love and *love* with so much of it I think I'm going to be sick.

I've always wondered what it would be like to be out of your mind with infatuation for someone. To be embarrassing and loud and boastful about it. Kissing in public on the middle of the sidewalk on a busy Monday morning. Pinkies linked together. Silly, stupid, obsessive gazes across the table, itching to touch even though you've hardly stopped.

I wasn't sure if I'd be lucky enough to get to experience that level of love in all its beautiful, heartbreaking, ugly, and devastating glory, fear almost keeping me from the greatest gift I've ever been given.

And now that I have it? Now that it's mine, I know it's the best feeling in the world. I understand why my friends flaunt their relationships. I want to flaunt mine too. I'm going to show Patrick off, my best friend and my soulmate, owner of everything I have.

"Would it be stupid to say I love you again?" I ask. Patrick reaches up, his thumb wiping away my tears.

"No, honey." He smiles, and it's the one specifically for me. His I Love You smile. "You can say it as much as you'd like."

"I love you," I say again, and I really, truly do.

THIRTY-EIGHT
PATRICK

IT'S BEEN a week and a half since we got home from Florida, and Lola and I have fallen into an easy routine. I spend my mornings at school. There's planning, interviews for the open fourth grade teacher position, a deep clean of the cafeteria's stove, and a hundred other tasks I'm trying to accomplish before the kids start classes up late next month.

Lola's been just as busy, working on logistics for her store and handling the administrative side of owning a business. She's planning to hire two full-time employees and three part-time employees. She's also looked at eight different properties and gotten approved for a loan. The winnings from the fashion show don't cover the total cost of owning her own space, but they put a nice dent in her estimated monthly payments to make a space affordable.

Despite working opposite hours—I leave the apartment by eight, she sleeps until ten and stays up sketching until past midnight—our new normal has been easy. There are no arguments about me waking with the sun or her slipping into bed when I'm deep into a REM cycle, my hands finding her even in a dream. We're making it work.

We stayed up late on Friday night, watching a movie on the couch and sharing a bowl of popcorn. We went to a breakfast diner on Sunday morning, splitting a stack of pancakes and a chocolate milkshake. In the afternoon, I did the crossword puzzle while she flipped through a magazine, smiling at each other from across her coffee table.

We've found our rhythm, the pieces of our lives slotting into the others without disturbing or hindering. I wake up to coffee loaded in the machine and a sticky note with a heart over the power button. Lola runs interview questions with me over dinner, pretending to be a teacher fresh out of college who's eager for a classroom of their own.

While I've loved the bubble we've created between our apartments—some nights we stay at my place, other nights we're at hers—tonight I want to take her out for real. Our first official date.

I'm nervous as hell.

"What do you have planned?" Lola asks.

She angles her body in the passenger seat so she's facing me. Her yellow sundress rides up her thighs as she crosses her right leg over her left, impossibly distracting tan skin on display.

I hum and turn down the radio, the rock and roll song we were bopping along to fading out through the speakers. "A few things."

"You're taking me to a fraternity house, aren't you?" Her eyebrow arches, and I can't help but laugh.

"That's one of the stops, yes. I know how much you love a college rager."

"Hopefully we're going to buy a bedframe after. I've been in the market for a new one."

I glance over and find her smiling at me. Her beam is bright and her eyes sparkle in the light of the setting sun. She's been smiling nonstop these days, a constant turn to her lips and a lightness in her step. Whenever I ask why she's grinning, what's bringing on that glee, she shrugs and says, "I'm just happy."

Happy.

That might be my new favorite word.

I like to know I'm the one making her that way.

"IKEA is our second stop after we get wasted on Natty Ice," I say.

"Okay, now you're definitely lying. I know IKEA is your idea of hell. One way in, one way out," Lola says.

"What happens if you only want to look at dining room furniture? You're forced to see bunkbeds, couches, desk chairs and office filing cabinets. It's cruel to make someone walk that far for a table."

"If you won't tell me where we're going, will you at least confirm that food is included?" she says. "I'm starving, and I need to know if I should dip into my contingency snacks."

"What do you have hiding in your purse, Jones? A seafood buffet?"

"Gross. No. I hate lobster. I prefer to stick to the more refined meal choices of pretzels and a peanut butter sandwich." There's a mischievous curve to her mouth as she adds, "And a sleeve of Oreos."

"A whole ass sandwich? That's commitment. For what it's worth, I would never plan an excursion with you that didn't include food. I know you better than that," I say. I switch lanes as our exit off the highway approaches in the distance, the green sign directing us to our final destination, Topsfield Fairgrounds, thirty miles outside the city.

"Sometimes I think you know me better than I know myself," Lola says. She reaches over and rests her hand on my forearm, her palm warm and soft on my skin.

"That's what happens when you're around someone for

years. You learn everything about them. All their nuances and inner workings. I know you're the same way with me," I say.

"Yeah." She grins. "Like how you can only sleep with the top sheet on your side of the bed. You have to eat your breakfast before you have your coffee. You hate Brussel sprouts but love broccoli. You'd live in those frayed Levi's of yours if you could. Wow. I do know you. Think of all the time we've lost, not telling each other how we feel."

"I wanted to keep it to myself so I didn't scare you away. I couldn't bear the thought of losing your friendship, and Lola Jones is not a relationship woman. Imagine if I had barged into your apartment and shouted that I loved you before our trip."

"I might have thought you'd lost your mind."

Lola laughs, the sound filling the cab of my Jeep. I want to hold onto the noise forever and find a way to get her to do that every day. I wasn't lying when I said her laugh is one of my favorite things about her. It sinks into my skin, a song that makes me feel alive. Like I have a purpose and I'm loved.

"Instead of thinking about time we've lost, think about all the time we have to look forward to," I counter, slowing as we approach a red light. I rest my arm over the back of her seat and play with the ends of her hair. She's wearing it down today, the pink streaks almost entirely faded from the blonde strands. Pieces frame her face and I tuck them away behind her ear so I can lean over and kiss her cheek. "I'd rather look forward to the future than regret the past."

She sighs wistfully and inches her fingers down my arm, her palm settling against mine. "You've always been so insightful. Wise beyond your years."

"It's better than being a blowhard, right?"

"Infinitely better than being a blowhard."

We settle into comfortable silence as we turn left then right, driving closer and closer to the fairgrounds. A rush of nerves floods my veins when I pull up to our first stop of the night, suddenly worried I've massively fucked this up. Gone overboard with our first outing on our home turf, back in reality and away from the blissful bubble of vacation.

I put the car in park and set the emergency brake. Lola sits up, her interest piqued, and glances around. There's a massive screen in front of us, and other cars lined up in rows. People are spreading out blankets, and the smell of popcorn hangs in the air.

"Patrick. Are we at a drive-in movie theater?" she asks, awe and wonder behind the question.

"We are. I wanted to take you on a real first date," I say.

"We've already slept together." Lola laughs again. "We've also already said I love you, and we've been home for over a week. I feel like we're doing everything out of order."

"Maybe we are, but I wanted you to have some fun outside our apartments. You've been working so hard on finding a building for your shop and catching up on the commissions you've gotten since the show. I'm proud of you, honey. You need a night off though, so that's what we're doing."

"How did you know I've always wanted to go to a drive-in theater?"

"I have a confession to make." I turn and face her across the center console, taking her other hand in mine and staring into her eyes. "I created that list about your bad dates for selfish reasons. It was a way for me to keep track of all the things you didn't like, because if I was somehow lucky enough to ever get the courage to ask you on a date, I wanted it to be perfect. I know you like to be somewhere outside so you don't feel constricted. You want to do an activity so if the conversation turns awkward or stale, you have something else to focus on. Food has to be involved, obviously, and a showing of your favorite film doesn't hurt either."

Lola launches herself at me, her arms looping around my neck and her lips pressing a kiss to my jaw. "Thank you," she says. "Best first date ever."

"Worth the wait?" I ask.

"Definitely worth the wait."

THIRTY-NINE

PATRICK

WE SHARE A PIZZA, grease on our fingers and a pile of napkins at our feet. I folded the back seats down and took the roof off the Jeep so we could have an unobstructed view of both the screen and the stars in the sky. It's cooled down, the heat from the day now tolerable as a light breeze billows through the air. Pillows and blankets surround us in the trunk, a pile of comfy and cozy as the credits for *Jurassic Park* start to roll.

"It's oddly unsettling to watch a dinosaur chase a Jeep when you're sitting in a Jeep," Lola says. "It's kind of like *Inception*." She props up on her elbow and looks at me from across the car.

"I don't know how the girl whose first nightmare involved a T-Rex chasing her around a balcony ended up loving a film series centered around a T-Rex chasing people."

"I think the love started with *The Land Before Time*," she says.

"A cinematic classic. Are you ready for our next stop?"

"There's more?"

"Of course there's more. You didn't think I'd end our night here, did you?"

"No, but it's getting late and you have school tomorrow."

"It's just paperwork," I say, arranging the pillows into a neat stack and then folding the blankets. I brought the fuzzy purple one I keep on my couch that Lola loves. "It doesn't require a lot of my brain power. Besides, it's only ten."

"Since when have you ever stayed out past ten by *choice?*" she asks, jumping out of the back and onto the ground. She dusts off the front of her dress, leftover crumbs from the pizza scattering to the ground.

"I'd stay out until sunrise with you," I say, shutting the trunk.

"You're as cheesy as that pizza we just ate," Lola says. "But I love it. Where to next?"

"Somewhere we haven't been in a while. Somewhere I think we need to revisit."

"What are you up to, Patrick Walker?"

"Wait and see, Lola Jones. Wait and see."

I'm even more nervous as we head to stop number two, my hand drumming against the steering wheel and my left foot tapping on the floorboard.

The roads we pass are familiar, memories of our childhood embedded between the rows of homes and tall, tall trees. The corner to our left is where I fell off my skateboard and Lola dusted off my knee before helping me to my feet.

The curb on the right is where the two of us sat when her girlfriend broke up with her three weeks before we left for college, citing a desire to explore herself and not be tied down.

The yellow mailbox we drive by is the one we ran into when Lola stood on the back of my bike, her arms outstretched as I miscalculated the speed of the downhill and sent us tumbling to the grass. We took the mailbox out with us.

"We're going to visit our parents?" Lola asks as I park the Jeep in the road outside her mom's house.

"No. Well, we can if you want, but that's not the planned stop."

"You have my attention," she says.

I jump out of the car and hustle to her side, opening the door and guiding her to the ground. If I look close enough, I think I can see the silly string still clinging to the tar under my tires from a prank war gone wrong all those years ago.

Me and Lola versus our older brothers. We owned them.

"I want to show you something. Something I've been working on for the week we've been back. It's not totally done, but I think it'll still get the point across," I say.

We walk quietly toward the tree between our houses, making sure to duck low so we don't turn on the motion-activated security light attached to the left side of my parents' garage. When we get to the treehouse, Lola climbs up first. I give her backside a lift as she starts to ascend the ladder made of rope. I think my heart lurches out of my chest when she misses a step and I refuse to let her go the rest of the way.

She disappears inside and I follow behind, hoisting myself up over the ledge and onto the floor of the space we used to spend all of our childhood nights.

"Wow," Lola whispers. She tilt her head back and looks at the fairy lights hanging from the ceiling. "What is all of this?"

"It's my way of showing you I'm all in, Lola I've always been all in. Ever since that first day in July. Come here."

I take her hand and lead her to the center of the room. We duck our heads and take a seat on the bean bag chairs I set up. They match the pair we had decades ago, larger now to accommodate our adult-sized bodies.

"It's pictures," she says. She reaches up and detaches a Polaroid from a clothespin hanging from the long piece of twine attached on either end of the room. "Oh my god. Look how little we are!"

"We're practically infants," I agree. I rest my chin on her shoulder and smile at the image.

We can't be older than twelve, both of us with elbow pads on our arms and helmets on our heads. It was the summer we tried to learn how to rollerblade and failed epically. I busted a lip and Lola knocked a tooth out. Our moms were *pissed*.

This picture is before any injuries, our limbs scratch-free. She's looking at the camera, a hand over her face to shield her eyes from the sun. I'm looking at her, smiling wide and laughing at something she's saying. I've forgotten what it was over the years, I just remember it was funny.

"Oh! Our junior year homecoming," Lola exclaims, pulling down another photo. I'm in a tux that's three sizes too big and Lola has a fake tan. She's putting up bunny ears behind my head and my chin is turned toward her, a gleam in my eyes. "You got food poisoning and had to be escorted out in a wheelchair."

"Yeah, and the principal didn't believe me when I said it wasn't alcohol."

"Is this one from the beach? Which time?" she asks, pointing to another picture.

"The summer after our freshman year of college."

"I was so sad after not seeing you for three months," she says.

She touches the glossy picture and outlines our silhouettes. It's from behind, me with my arm around her waist and her leaning into my side. Waves crash in front of us but I'm looking at her with wistful expression on my face.

My heart knew long before my brain did.

We spend the next forty-five minutes looking at the photos one by one until they're piled in a stack on the floor.

"I asked our friends and family for some help," I admit. "What's the same in all the pictures?"

Lola frowns and sifts through the images a second time. It takes her a minute to realize, and when she does, she inhales sharply. "You're looking at me in all of them," she whispers.

"Even when we were kids, well before I knew what love was,

my heart and soul knew they loved you. I've been yours for years, Lo."

She drops the pictures and touches my cheeks. "Can I tell you a secret, Patrick?"

"You can tell me anything."

"I'm scared. I'm so scared," she says. Her voice turns soft and unsteady, and I fold my fingers over hers as her hands tremble.

"Scared?" I repeat. "Of what?"

"Of being with you. I've never loved someone as much as I love you. I love you so much it hurts. I've never experienced a love like this, and it's terrifying to realize how much you mean to me. How much is at stake and how much I have to lose."

"We can be scared together." I laugh and pull her into my lap. I drop my forehead against hers. "I'm so fucking petrified that something could happen to you. When you're away, my heart hurts. It physically *aches*. I've learned what it means to be lovesick, to miss someone so much when they're gone that you don't feel like you can go on. But I want you to know something. You're it for me, Lola. My life started the moment I met you."

"I've never told you this, but my mom almost didn't pick Boston as her base," Lola says. "Our bags were packed for Salt Lake City until my dad woke up one night and told her something was telling him we had to go to Massachusetts. In a way, I like to think he knew I would find you. He knew we were both out there existing, waiting for each other." She sniffs, and I wipe away a tear. "And I think he'd be very happy to know we're together."

"He knew I cared about you," I say.

Lola pulls back. "What?"

"Yeah." I nod. "You went downstairs to the hospital cafeteria for lunch one day, and I said I'd spend some time with him while you took a break. We were chatting and shooting the shit. He was complaining about the Celtics' losing streak."

"God, he hated when they lost."

"'Nobody on the team plays any defense,'" we say in unison, and Lola bursts out laughing.

"That," she says, "was the best impression I've heard."

"I asked him if he was scared about dying and the unknown of what comes next. He said he wasn't scared, just so incredibly sad he had to leave you, your mom, and your brother behind. He told me to take care of you and to keep an eye on his little girl. I don't know what possessed me to say it, but I told him I cared about you a lot. I said maybe one day down the road, you and I would have a life together. A house, some kids, no kids. Whatever we wanted. I was basically crying my eyes out and he *laughed*. He said, 'I might be dying, but I'm not an idiot. You love her.'"

"He said that to you? He knew?"

"Yeah. He gave me his blessing. He said whenever I got my shit together and asked you out, it better be for real and it better be for life, because that's what you deserve."

"Fate," she whispers.

"Fate," I agree, kissing her forehead then her cheek. "I know your fear of being left isn't going to go away overnight. I know you're going to have moments of doubt, but I hope you never, ever doubt my love for you. In every lifetime, in every realm, in every universe out there, I find you, and you're it for me. My one and only. The day I leave you won't be by choice, Lola. They'll have to pry my hands from yours because I'm not going to go willingly. And then I'll find you again. You're my soulmate."

"How do you know?" she asks. "What if it's not enough? You can't see the future. You can't predict what's going to happen five or ten years down the road."

"You're right. I can't see the future, but I know how I feel about you in this moment. Right here, right now. Because you and me? We're inevitable. A sure thing. The grass is green, the

369

sky is blue, and I love you. People search their whole lives for a fraction of what we have, and our lives are just beginning. Our love—my love for you—transcends well out of this world. Our souls are tied together, and my heart belongs to you. I've tried to love other people, and I can't, Lola. I can't and I never will be able to because they aren't you. And that's enough for me."

Tears stream down her face, a waterfall of the pent-up emotions she's been keeping inside. I might have scared her, saying too much too soon, but I don't care. Even if she pushes me away, I'll stick around, loving her long after she stops loving me.

"I've never been so scared or excited about something in my life," Lola whispers. "It's going to take some learning on my end, remembering to share my feelings instead of holding them in and thinking I can tackle everything by myself, but I want to try. You're the only person I'd ever want to try with."

"We'll try together. I'm a pushover sometimes. I'm going to work on that. I give in to things too easily. I need to learn to stand my ground," I say.

"I'm going to travel less," Lola says. "With opening a store and my commissions through the roof, I want to be home more. Home with you. If you want to buy a house or stay in the city, I don't care. Where you go, I go."

"We'll figure it out. We're always going to figure it out. I promise you, Lola."

"A sure thing, right?" she whispers and I nod, grinning at her like I've won the lottery.

"The most sure thing," I say, then I kiss her. Then I kiss her again and again because I can, and that's the most important thing that's ever happened to me.

She laughs against my lips. "It's funny."

"What's funny? Kissing me?"

"We drove all the way to Florida, but I don't think it was for the fashion show. I think that was a road trip to forever. A journey to find each other and our future. Without the show, we might have gone years without saying anything about how we feel."

"My next tattoo might have to be a car," I say. "In commemoration of a trip we'll remember for a lifetime."

"Where would you put it?" she asks.

"Over my heart. The spot that's yours."

"Maybe I'll get one too. We could match."

"Matching tattoos? That's a serious commitment."

"I'm not scared." Lola lifts her chin. "Are you?"

"No. With you, Lola, I'm never scared."

FORTY

PATRICK

"WHY AM I SO NERVOUS?" Lola bounces on the balls of her feet and twirls her hair around her fingers. "This isn't a big deal. People do this all the time."

"It's very obvious you don't do this all the time," I say.

She's been on edge since I picked her up fifteen minutes ago, adjusting her ponytail eight different ways and tapping her hand against her thigh. Riding the elevator up to Henry and Emma's apartment is amplifying her anxious energy, a current circulating through the small space. I don't know if she's about to charge into their place like a bat out of hell or go back to the ground floor and wait patiently in the car.

I'm following her lead.

"Says the guy who never panics about anything," she grumbles, folding her arms over her chest. "A hurricane could come through and I don't think you'd be stressed out."

"That's not true. I panic about plenty of things. I sweat through my shirt the first day of the fashion show because I was so nervous for you," I admit, watching the numbers above the doors climb higher and higher. "Someone asked if I was ill and needed a doctor."

"You didn't tell me that."

"Because it's embarrassing. These are our friends, Lo. They're going to be happy for us. And if you want to wait another week to tell them, we can. We can hold them off a little while longer."

"I know they're going to be happy for us, but they're also going to be weird as hell. I wouldn't be shocked if there's confetti and pre-made save the dates for the wedding we haven't planned," she says. "I don't want to wait to tell them. I'm so bad at keeping secrets, the girls would get me to fold right away."

"You are terrible at keeping secrets. You ruined my sweet sixteen because you let it slip I needed to buy a Hawaiian shirt for an important surprise party that coincidentally fell on my birthday."

"I wanted to prepare you," Lola exclaims. "You hate themed parties."

"True. I think my mom believed my shocked face."

"She definitely did. Darla was so proud she pulled off such an epic party. I just wish we could make our friends sweat a little, you know? I kind of want to piss them off while they try and figure out what's going on between us."

I arch an eyebrow, a plan forming. "What if we're weird first and beat them at their own game?"

Lola pushes off the wall and stands on her toes, her lips near mine. "Do you have something in mind?"

"They all assume something happened on the trip. Henry won't stop texting me a dozen question marks."

"The girls are the same. I think Jo keeps FaceTiming me in hopes she'll catch your naked ass hiding in the bathroom."

"Dammit. That's what we should have done."

"Next time we hide our relationship, we'll go the accidental-nudity-on-camera route," she says.

"What if we start off the night by acting like we normally do

—as friends? Halfway through dinner, you could walk over and sit in my lap or kiss my cheek. We'll catch them off guard and be the ones to dictate how the night goes."

Lola blinks. She breaks out into a grin and slowly nods her head, clasping her hands together like she's an evil villain planning to wreak havoc on society.

"That's genius. It's better than genius. It's the smartest thing I've heard in my entire life," she says.

"Let's not get carried away. Can you keep your hands to yourself?" I ask.

"Someone thinks highly of themselves." She kisses my cheek and rests her head against my chest. I feel her sigh, and I think this might be the first time all evening that she's settled down.

"I do think highly of myself, considering I made you come twice before we left your apartment," I say, laughing as she swats my arm. "And because I make you smile."

"Nice save there, buddy," she says. The doors open to a long hallway and Lola moves away from me, creating unwanted distance. "For the record, I love the idea, but I hate pretending you're not mine."

"Want me to take off my shorts and show you my tattoos again?" I ask. "Those really prove that I'm yours."

"Eh, that would probably would give away our plan too quickly," she answers, stepping out of the elevator toward our friends' apartment.

"If the girls don't pull you to the side and ask to see a ring right away, I'll be shocked," I mumble as she knocks, transferring the bottle of chardonnay she's holding to her other arm as we wait on the doormat. We picked it up on the way over, not wanting to show empty-handed to taco night.

"I didn't realize a ring was on the table," Lola says, hiding her grin by biting her bottom lip.

"With you, Lola, everything is on the table."

The door flies open and we're greeted with six expectant faces, all staring at us like we're the main act of a circus show. I roll my eyes and put my hand on the small of Lola's back, ushering her inside and flipping off Henry who wiggles his eyebrows in greeting.

Sure enough, Lola is whisked away, the women bowing their heads and whispering under their breath. She glances back at me over her shoulder, a soft smile on her lips that tells me she's happy. Well and truly happy.

"Hey," I say, grabbing a beer from the cooler in the kitchen. "What's up?" I ask my four best friends.

"What's *up*? You have a lot of nerve walking into my apartment with a smug grin on your face and not telling us what's going on," Henry says. He knocks his bottle against mine and we take a sip in tandem.

"Will you keep your voice down? Lola doesn't know how I feel, and I'd appreciate it if we kept it that way," I say, pretending to check that she's not eavesdropping.

"Wait." Neil frowns. "You two aren't a thing? I thought you were going to talk to her on your trip?"

I shrug nonchalantly. "We were there for her and career. I didn't want to ruin her special moment by talking about *feelings*." I wrinkle my nose like the word disgusts me, not like I'm close to bursting at the seams with giddiness, and take a sip of my drink.

"Damn. Sorry, man. I know how much you were looking forward to making things official with her," Noah says, clasping me on my shoulder.

I almost feel guilty for lying and keeping this secret from our friend group, until I remember they literally threw cash around on my behalf and didn't tell me until after the fact.

Assholes.

I shrug again. "It is what it is. Can we help you get dinner ready, Henry? I'm starving."

———

AN HOUR and a plate of tacos later, I lean back in my chair at the dining room table and set my napkin next to my water glasses, stuffed.

"I can't eat another bite," Jo says, staring down her last taco like it's a hurdle she has to jump. Her eyes narrow and she snatches it up, teeth sinking into the crunchy shell and cheese going everywhere.

"Josephine. Stop," Jack says, using her full name and shaking his head as he pries the food from her hand. He pushes her plate out of the way and folds his palms over hers. "You're going to be sick, sweetheart."

He's lucky I don't make fun of him for the way he acts with Jo, like some infatuated idiot who sprinted into the living room earlier when she said *ow* after stubbing her toe on the leg of the couch. He acted like she had torn a ligament, carrying her to an empty chair to inspect the bruise.

I glance at Lola across the table. "How was your dinner, Lo?"

"You know I'm a pizza gal, but Henry makes a mean fresh salsa." She smiles and wipes her lips with her napkin. "How was yours?"

"Delicious. The salsa is the only reason why I'm still friends with him, to be honest," I say, laughing as a tortilla chip gets launched at my head.

It feels so good to be surrounded by our friends, where everyone knows exactly who we are and exactly what we mean to each other. The guys know I love her, the girls know Lola's been thinking about me, and it's refreshing to know that when we *do* tell them we're together, they're going to be nothing but supportive.

And maybe give us a little bit of shit.

"Who wants dessert?" Lola asks, standing up and scooting her chair back. "I'll bring out the ice cream."

"Me, please," Jo says, ignoring Jack's sigh.

"Me too," Rebecca says. "I'm starving."

"Maybe you're pregnant again," Emma says, and Neil's fork clatters against his plate.

Lola's eyes meet mine as she disappears around the corner toward the kitchen with a knowing tilt of her head.

Kids.

It's a topic we haven't discussed, but one I think we're on the same page about. I get to spend my days with over four hundred elementary students for two-thirds of the year, which is enough rambunctiousness for me. I'd be open to adopting or fostering though, making space in our home for a child who needs love. Lola has so much love in her heart to give. She'd be a wonderful mother if it were something we wanted down the road, but I think for the foreseeable future, it's just going to be us.

"Here you go," Lola says, carrying out a tray of desserts. She distributes the bowls one by one before walking around the table and standing by my side. "Ice cream?"

"I'd love some," I say.

She hums and scoops out a spoonful, bringing it to my lips. I raise an eyebrow and she grins, one of our silent conversations passing between us.

Trust me, she says, adding a wink.

Always, I say back, opening my mouth.

The metal is cold against my tongue and I barely have time to swallow the bite down before Lola's lips are against mine, fused together by the sticky dessert. I pull her into my lap, my hands on her waist and the smell of vanilla bean in the air. She sighs, a sound I keep for myself, reveling in the way her body goes pliant and relaxes into mine.

A yelp breaks our private interlude and we pull apart, grinning at each other. I tuck a lock of hair behind her ear and kiss the tip of her nose.

"I love you," I say, soft enough so only she can hear it.

"I love you too," she answers, that lip-splitting, ear-to-ear grin back on her face.

"Oh my *god.*"

I look over to find Henry standing on his chair, feet dancing across the upholstery in some obnoxious jig. He raises his arms above his head, a victorious gleam in his eye as he points to Lola and me and says, "It's about time, you damn liars."

"Yeah, yeah, yeah," I say. "I've watched you all be disgusting with your other halves for years. Prepare to be sick of us and our PDA."

"It's probably going to be right on par with how you've stared at each other for years," Jack says, not an ounce of surprise on his face. I do see the corner of his mouth turn up after the sarcasm, a hint of glee hiding under a small smile.

Lola gets tugged out of my lap by Rebecca, Jo, and Emma, pulled into a corner to share the whole story. I glance at the guys around the table and find them all watching me.

"Sorry for lying." I run my hand through my hair and let out a laugh. "We knew you all were going to be dopes about this, so we wanted to surprise you."

"You're happy, right?" Neil asks, and the grin that touches my lips comes naturally as I think about the last week with Lola.

Early mornings cuddled under bedsheets. Curled up beside each other on the couch, her legs thrown across my lap while I do a crossword puzzle and she reads a book. Cooking in my kitchen, making sure she's eating three meals a day and taking her medicine.

I've always considered myself a positive person, the guy who finds the good in every day, but with her, I don't have to look for it. It's just *there*.

I see it as the sun sneaks through the curtains and I open my eyes, the sight of Lola draped across my chest. I feel it when she hugs me tight and tells me she loves me with her words, with her hands, with her actions.

That euphoria lasts a full twenty-four hours before starting anew. The desire to want to stretch out my time with her while simultaneously looking forward to sleep just so I can have a brand new day with her, fresh happiness sprouting up as every day on the calendar falls away.

"I've never been happier," I say. I glance at the love of my life from across the room and feel that warm embrace of elation wrap its arms around me just from the sight of her. "I've always thought I was happy. In my past relationships, it always seemed like everything was fine. But now... it's only been a week with Lola and—" I break off, cheesy hysteria shaking my shoulders. I steel myself and continue. "Now I realize how *wrong* those women were for me. They weren't bad people. They just weren't *her*. And she's all I want. She's all I'm ever going to want."

"Jesus." Henry shakes his head and scrubs his hands over his face. "You're making me emotional, man. I'm just glad you finally found what you were looking for, even if it was right in front of you this whole time."

"Me too," I say, watching Lola gesture animatedly with her hands before settling her palms over her heart and swaying side to side. I want to burst. I want to scream from the rooftops how much I love that woman. How much she means to me and how hard I'm going to work to show her that for the rest of our lives. "She was worth the wait."

"Did you tell her you loved her?" Noah asks, his chin in his hands as he waits for this vital piece of information.

"I did. After I shoved a piece of cake in her face."

"With you two, that seems like it would be the perfect moment," Henry says.

"It was. She told me she loves me too. Now we're two idiots in love, and we don't care who sees. I'll gladly be an idiot with her."

Jack sighs. He uncrosses his arms from his chest and reaches over, clasping my shoulder. "I'm happy for you. I know how badly it sucks to want something you don't think you can have. I hope you know we're all rooting for you two. We're always here for you if you ever need us."

"Thanks." I catch Lola's gaze and she grins, tapping her chest three times. *I love you*, she says, and I tap my chest three times back. "I'm not worried. Loving Lola is the easiest thing I've ever done."

FORTY-ONE
LOLA

"YOU LOOK GOOD IN A HARDHAT," Patrick says. "But you're holding that sledgehammer all wrong, sweetheart."

"Sorry." I grin and adjust my grip on the wooden base. "I'm just so excited."

He pulls out his phone and flips the camera to selfie mode, hitting record. "Lola Jones Designs, day one. We have a busy day today, starting with the first time we've been in here since you purchased the property a couple of weeks ago. After a few hours of work, we'll head to your magazine shoot and the interview. How are you feeling?"

"Excited. I can't wait to see what this place turns into. I'm also nervous I might burst a pipe and create a leak."

"That's why we went with the insurance," he jokes.

Life has been a whirlwind since we got back from our trip. I've spent my time reading resumes, tracking orders, and making sure I'm caught up on commission requests. I signed a loan for a shop on Newbury Street, right in the heart of Boston with heavy foot traffic and enthusiastic window shoppers.

Deciding between renting or buying was difficult, and Patrick and I weighed the pros and cons of both. The money from the contest made it possible to even consider purchasing outright, a luxury I wouldn't have if the results had turned out differently.

Long-term, I want to make this place *mine*, the creative liberty to do whatever I see fit with colors and layout. The previous owner was eager to sell, ready to move onto new things, and offered an outrageous deal on the property that used to be an art gallery.

I remember what it was like starting out, she told me, waving off my attempts to pay her the full price. *Just pay it forward one day.*

I plan to, my goal of selling clothes with a price tag anyone can afford at the forefront of my mind.

"I took lots of before photos so we can compare them when we're done. I really want to smash a wall down," I say, surveying the room a final time.

The building is in good condition and doesn't need a ton of renovating. It feels closed off though, with lots of walls sectioning off individual rooms and making the floor plan seem small and cramped. We're going to open things up and utilize the rectangular shape of the building, drawing attention in through the windows and creating a single sightline to the back of the store.

"And what are you going to wear for the magazine shoot? One of your own designs?" Patrick asks.

"The jumpsuit dress from the finale at the Florida Fashion Show, with the sequins and flashy colors and the cape. I love that piece so much. This sounds incredibly conceited, but it deserves some more recognition."

"Hell yeah it does. Okay, time to go smash some walls, folks. We'll see you soon." He waves to the camera and clicks it off.

"Are you waving to your fans?"

"More like your fans."

"Do people really care about how we're going to transform this place? I doubt it."

"That's where you're wrong, Lo," Patrick says. "There are comments on every one of your posts asking for an update on the store."

"You read the comments on my social media posts?"

"Of course I do. People want to know about the grand opening so they can plan a trip to come and visit. They're asking when your commissions will reopen. There's even a debate about what color you're going to paint the walls. So, yes. They do want to see how much we transform this place."

"Are you my social media manager now?"

"C'mon, honey. You know I can't even post an Instagram story correctly."

No, he can't. The photos are crooked and everyone's heads gets cut off. Yet here he is, a camera in hand, a tripod set up in the corner, ready to capture the renovation process from start to finish.

I stand on my toes and kiss him. "You are the best boyfriend ever."

Patrick slips his phone into the pocket of his oldest pair of jeans—he looks *so good* in jeans—and wraps his arms around my waist. "I want to talk to you about something before the gang gets here to help us tear this place to shreds. It involves spreadsheets."

I close my eyes and pretend to snore. "Is this the part where you start using numbers and data on me?"

"Yup, but I promise I won't bring it into the bedroom." He pulls out a piece of folded-up paper from his other pocket. "The check from the contest came through and it's been deposited in your account."

He might not be my social media manager, but I asked Patrick to oversee my finances. I trust him. I trust him to be honest with me about business decisions and what makes the most sense for my company long-term. He won't sugarcoat anything to protect my feelings, helping me reach solutions to problems that might be tough to hear but are the right ones to make.

"That's good news," I say. "I have a meeting lined up with someone tomorrow to talk about potentially investing in LJD. He's helped open some other boutiques across the country and he seems knowledgeable about the industry."

"About that," Patrick says. He blows out a breath and runs his hand through his hair. Flecks of sawdust fall from the dark waves to the concrete floor. "I want to invest the rest."

I blink, not sure I heard him correctly. "Pardon?"

"I want to invest. In you. In this dream of yours that you've had since we were kids, Lola."

"No." I slip out of his grasp. "No. Absolutely not, Patrick. I cannot ask you to do that."

"I'm going to invest in this space and your future—*our* future," he says firmly. "We're a team now, honey. You don't have to do this alone."

"An investment like this is worth thousands of dollars. I know what your salary is. You're not struggling, but—"

"Grams bought stock in Apple," he says. "Years ago, when they were a brand new company. Barely a household name. She claimed it was because she thought Steve Jobs was cute."

"God rest her soul. Grams was always a shameless flirt," I say.

Patrick rolls his eyes. He hooks his finger in my belt loop and pulls me back close to him. "She sold them the year before she passed. Turns out, it wasn't just *some* stock. It was *a lot* of stock. Thousands of shares. The money went to me and Isaac after her funeral, with a stipulation in place that we put it toward something that would set us up for financial success down the road."

"And you want to spend it on me."

"Yeah. I've been taking some online courses. I hired someone to run numbers with programs that are more professional than my spreadsheets. I've kept the money in my savings account until yesterday, when I withdrew fifty-five thousand dollars to give to you. I believe in this, Lola. I believe in *you*. Your designs. The classes you want to set up to teach young kids how to sew. The bigger dreams you have like opening an international location and being in New York Fashion Week one day. I'm going to support you every step of the way, and this is another opportunity to do that. Let me be a part of this, yeah? Let me be by your side."

A tear rolls down my cheek, and I wipe it away with the back of my hand. "I love you," I say. "I love you so much. How did I ever imagine a future for myself without you in it? You are the best thing to happen to me, Patrick, and I'm not just saying that because you're offering me thousands of dollars."

"It doesn't hurt though, right?"

I huff out a laugh. "I'd love you the same with nothing to your name. I'm saying it because it's true and I'm so lucky I get to do life with you."

He tips my chin up and I see his smile. Wide and bright. Crinkled nose. Wrinkles around his eyes. It's his Really, Really Happy smile.

It's also *my* smile. The one he only gives to me.

"Is that a yes? You'll let me invest in Lola Jones Designs?"

"I couldn't stop you even if I tried, could I?" I ask.

"No." His smile stretches wider and he brushes his lips over mine. "You couldn't. This is an argument you're going to lose."

"Okay," I relent, letting out another laugh. "Okay."

"Still not a yes," he murmurs in a teasing tone, wrapping his arms around my waist and dipping me to the ground.

"Yes!" I exclaim with enthusiasm. "Yes, yes, *yes*. Is that better?"

"There's no need to yell." Patrick backs me into the wall. He's careful to maneuver me away from the old nails sticking out of the plaster and drywall. "And I love you too, Lola Jones."

"Did you ever think you'd be here with me?" I loop my arms around his neck and tug him close. "Kissing me? Helping me knock the crap out of some walls so we can make a store full of my clothes?"

"Yeah," he says. He tucks his hands in my back pockets. "I did."

"Even when we were eleven and you thought girls were gross?"

"I never thought you were gross."

"And when we were fifteen and you started dating Gina Prince?"

"Yup."

"What about—"

"I'm going to stop you right there, honey." He folds his hand over my mouth, amusement dancing behind his eyes. "Every answer is going to be yes. I've thought about this for a while, Lola."

"And now?" I ask, my voice muffled by his warm palm. "Are you glad it happened?"

"Yeah." His forehead rests against mine. "More than glad. You and I are timeless. Written in the stars. Every moment it took for us to get here was well worth the wait."

"Thank you for being patient with me. Thank you for letting me figure myself out before figuring out my feelings for you. I never thought I'd be the person who counted down the minutes and seconds until tomorrow, but with you, I do. Every day with you is my new favorite."

"That's why we're inevitable, Lo. It's been twenty-four years of the best day of my life, every single day. Because you're there for all of them."

———

"THIS CANNOT BE the same place as five hours ago," Jo says, wiping sweat from her brow. "Look how big it is."

Our friends came to the store armed with coffee and donuts, ready to get to work. We've spent all morning knocking down walls and pulling up ratty pieces of carpet, taking them to the dumpster out back. It's laborious and far from glamorous, but it's the start of something special. The first shuffle toward a very big and very important step in making my dreams come true.

"The windows are my favorite part," I say. They're floor-to-ceiling glass on either side of the door, natural light flooding across the hardwood floors we discovered an hour ago.

"Are you going to keep the chandelier?" Rebecca asks, pointing at the crystal light fixture above our heads.

"I like it," Emma says. "It gives the room character."

"I think it's going to stay. Light is always a good thing. It'll look nice when we get furniture in here," I decide.

I glance over to the other end of the room where the guys are hard at work rolling paint onto the walls. Three sides are green, like the color of Patrick's eyes. The longest wall on the back side is a bright pink to match the exact shade of the Vivian Lee dress that kickstarted my dream.

It's going to take a few months to get the place fixed up and ready for customers. Add in the legal side of things, and I'll be happy to open by Christmas. Still, I can already see the vision coming to life.

I can't believe this place is *mine*, something I'm creating from the ground up with the best of friends—and the best partner—by my side.

Patrick looks at me over his shoulder and smiles, as if he senses me thinking about him. He tilts his head and lifts his eyebrow. I nod, one of our silent conversations passing between us.

You good? he asks.

Better than good, I answer. *I'm great.*

He sets down his paintbrush and walks over, dodging a tray of spilled nails and ducking under a ladder.

"You're going to have bad luck," I say.

"Oh well. This was fun while it lasted, right?"

"Right." I spin in a circle and put my hands on my hips. "What do you think?"

"About the room or the way your ass looks in those jeans? Spin again, but slower this time."

I flick his ear. "Can you be serious, please?"

"It already looks great."

"Are you sure you want to invest your money in me?" I ask. "Fashion is a fickle industry. There's no guarantee I'll be successful. I could go years without making a profit, and I don't want you to have any regrets about your decision."

"I'm always going to bet on you," Patrick says. "Win or lose. Money or no money. I don't care. You know what I *do* care about? Seeing you happy. This place makes you happy, so I'm all in. And I know, I just *know* you're going to be successful, Lola. A few years from now you'll be so busy you won't have time for your boyfriend, a principal who's pulling macaroni out of a kid's nose."

"You're not wrong about a lot of things, but you're wrong about that, Patrick Walker," I say. "I will always have time for you. No matter where I travel. No matter how long I'm gone. I'm always going to come back to you. You are my home."

"You can go away for as long as you need to. I want you to see the world. I want you to do everything you want to do, honey.

Take all the classes you can find and learn from every designer out there. I'm always going to be waiting for you with a light on whenever you get home."

It's an agreement, neither of us having to give up a part of ourselves to make the other happy. Maybe I'll get him to take that trip to Japan. Maybe I won't. It doesn't matter, because at the end of every day, Patrick will be there. Just like he's been there for the last twenty-four years.

"I'll always bring you a little souvenir," I promise.

"Lola Jones, you are too good to me."

Patrick kisses me and we ignore the cheers from our friends. The hoots and hollers and the unenthusiastic mumble of *finally* from Jack. I kiss him back with every fiber of my soul because he is the stitching of my entire being.

"You all didn't have to give up your Saturday to come help," I say to the group when we pull apart. "I'm sure there were more fun things to do with your day than pulling nails out of the wall."

"We wanted to be here," Jo says. She tugs me away from Patrick and slings her arm around my shoulder. "That's what friends do."

"It's really so you don't forget about us when you're famous," Emma adds.

"Can I have your spare ticket to the Met Gala?" Rebecca asks, and I laugh.

"If I get an invitation, I will take all of you to the Met Gala. Thank you so much for your help today. I appreciate it more than you know."

"I have an important charity event next year. Will you make a suit for me?" Noah asks.

"Of course I will, but only if you'll install some of the hanging lights for me. You're the tallest one of the bunch," I say.

"You've got yourself a deal. Lola Jones, designer extraordinaire," he says, kissing my hair in the most platonic way possible.

"Hey. Hands off my girl," Patrick says.

"Sorry. I thought this was the part of the afternoon where we all say how we've been in love with her a while now and—oh wait. That was just you."

I grin at my friends and the family we've created, feeling nothing but happiness and pride. I'm so thankful for everything in my life and everything that's yet to happen. I don't know what the future holds, but with all of them by my side, I know I can conquer anything.

FORTY-TWO
LOLA

"DO I HAVE PAINT ON ME?" I ask.

Patrick licks his thumb and wipes it across my forehead. He turns my cheek from side to side, inspecting my skin. "Not anymore. Problem solved."

"This is why I keep you around."

"Because I clean up your messes?"

"Exactly," I say.

We file into the elevator at the Mandarin Oriental Hotel and I press the button for the Presidential Suite where the shoot and interview will take place. Eight photographers and eight interviewers are waiting for me. Waiting to splash my clothes and name across the pages of magazines for thousands of people to see. Sitting on a coffee table or in a doctor's office waiting room. On someone's bedside table. There might be a kid out there who looks at *my* dresses and designs and uses them for motivation to chase their dreams.

The thought alone makes me want to burst into tears.

I expected to be more nervous as the elevator climbs higher and higher to the top floor, but I'm not. I'm oddly calm as Patrick taps his foot and holds my hand. I'm at ease as he runs his finger over my knuckles and kisses the top of my head. It almost feels like I've ascended over the point of a pyramid, the downward journey far easier than the rough climb it took to get here.

All those years of jammed sewing machines. Dresses with misplaced threads and incorrect sizing. Learning how to work with leather and chiffon, doing my best to not get frustrated or give up when I didn't grasp a concept right away.

When my name announced at the fashion show, it was the first time in my life I felt a true sense of belonging in this career. Art in any form—literature, clothing, music, dance, whatever— is subjective. It's hard to predict what someone will like, what trends will continue to be popular, and how different is *too* different.

Trusting the process and believing in yourself when you have ways to measure tangible success is *hard.* It's telling yourself you can even when you often truly believe you can't. It's trying again when something doesn't work, a second time then a third, until you see the positive result. Shutting down the voices that try to pull you in eighteen directions with eighteen ideas.

I've never thought I deserved success. I'd always hoped I'd achieve it; everyone does. Dreams are what keep us afloat. The reason we get out of bed in the morning and stay up late, putting hours and hours and hours of hard work into our craft. But now, as the doors of the elevator open and we file into the ornate entryway, I know I *do* deserve this.

I've worked my ass off to get here, and today, I'm going to enjoy it.

The foyer is bright with high ceilings and white paint. There's a long table with expensive vases and decorative bowls, and the marble floor is so pristine I can see my reflection in it. Chattering voices and the clicks of cameras echo down the hall and we follow the sound to the grand living room.

I've never been on this side of a photoshoot before. At the

few shoots I've been a part of, I'm the one fixing a last-minute outfit blunder off to the side, hidden away by strategic posing to capture someone's best angle.

"Lo." Patrick's fingers wrap around my wrist. His touch is warm, grounding, and I feel the buzz of energy and excitement in my chest calm to manageable with his gentle touch. "Are you okay?"

"Yeah." I glance at the room ahead, the dozens of people mulling around the large lights and backdrops. An entire window is covered in a white sheet and the furniture is neatly arranged. "The nerves just hit me."

"Want to turn around and leave? I can have the car pulled up outside in less than a minute."

I laugh, bursts of tension rolling off me in waves with his suggestion. "We can't just leave. These people are here for me. Okay, that sounds incredibly selfish. They're here for us, because I wouldn't be here without you." I roll my shoulders back and put on a brave face, determination outlining my features. "I'm okay. Really."

"You're never alone, Lola," he whispers in my ear, the assurance like a flower blooming amongst a patch of weeds.

"Never alone," I answer. I squeeze his hand and we march on.

———

MY CHEEKS HURT from grinning so much.

These are my people. A collection of individuals who love the fashion industry and enjoy sharing that love with anyone who will listen. The questions each magazine editor asks me are poignant and important, carefully thought out to show that our jobs aren't just about clothes.

It's so much deeper than a shirt and some pants or fabric

stitched together and thrown on a mannequin to make a profit. It's about inclusivity, creativity, and affordability. The power we have to shape style for generations down the road.

The conversation is unfiltered, raw and honest about the rise and fall of the economy and how we all prioritize different things to spend our hard-earned money on. We talk about the dark world of fast fashion, how companies are putting profits over people, and the toll it takes on smaller artists just trying to make a living.

When the heavy conversation shifts to lighter topics like my personal life and my plans for the future, Patrick joins me on the ottoman I'm perched on.

"You're doing great," he whispers. His hand rests on my knee and his thigh presses against mine. "A natural. Definitely not a blowhard."

"Shh," I whisper back. "You're going to distract me."

"I know other ways I could distract you," he says, trailing his hand up my leg before I swat him away.

I talk about the store, the knowledge that I could fail and go bankrupt in three years, but dammit, I'm going to try anyway. I pose for pictures with Patrick by my side. I rest my head on his shoulder. He holds my hand, and we smile so brightly, we could block out the sun.

"Did you make this dress?" Jeremiah, one of the photographers, asks. He kneels down and snaps an up-close photo of the sequined outfit.

I nearly hyperventilated when he introduced himself. He gained popularity a couple months back after his photoshoot with two strangers went viral. The pictures were *hot*, to say the least.

"Yeah," I say. "It's going to be the first dress I carry in the store."

"It's so unique." A flash goes off in my face, and I blink away dots from my vision. "A mix of vintage and modern. Genius."

I blush furiously at the praise, still not used to people seeing my designs out in the world and *liking* them.

I'm not sure I'll ever get used to it.

"I think that's a wrap," Janet says.

She flew in for the day, greeting me with a big hug and telling me how proud she was to hear my name as the up-and-coming winner of the show, adamant the Council of Fashion Designers made the right pick.

"This was fun," I admit. "I'm not sure I could make it my full-time gig, but for an afternoon? I had a blast."

"You have my card, right?" Janet asks. "Call me anytime. And let me know when you plan to open the store. Vivian and I want to be there for your big day."

Vivian's been a godsend in the weeks since the show, emailing me late into the night and letting me bounce ideas off of her. She's given me the contact information for her connections in the industry, and we have a call set up next month to strategize my next year as a business owner.

"Thank you," I say, pulling Janet into a hug. "I appreciate you."

Patrick waits for me on the other side of the room, his lips turning up into a smile as I approach him. He's leaning against the wall with his suit jacket draped over his shoulder.

That handsome man is *mine*.

I answer his smile with a grin of my own.

"Hey," he says.

"You're entirely too good-looking," I say. "Thank you for being here with me."

"As if there were anywhere else I'd rather be. Are you ready?"

"Take me home, sweet boyfriend of mine."

"Boyfriend," he repeats. His cheeks turn pink as he guides me to the elevator. "I'll never get tired of hearing that."

"I love you, Patrick Walker." I tip my head back and my eyes meet his. The green glows with pride and awe and a joy so expansive it wouldn't fit inside a football stadium. "None of this would have been possible without you. Thank you for taking a chance on me."

"I'm always going to choose you," he says with conviction, and I know it to be true.

His palm wraps around the back of my neck, skimming the sunburn tinging my skin after our park picnic yesterday afternoon.

"Remember when you didn't count our first kiss as a first kiss?" I ask. I swing our arms back and forth as we take the elevator to the ground floor, a lightness to my step.

"Remember when you meant to kiss my cheek and acciden-tally missed?" he says back. "I should've just kissed you for real then."

I drop his hand and grab his button-up shirt. He looks so smart and studious with the crisp collar and the tie around his neck. I want to undo the silk and watch it flutter to the floor. Revel in the way his eyes follow the bend of my hips and the twist of my back as I unzip my dress and let it flutter to the floor too, watching it land right beside the pink and green polka dotted tie.

Patrick's nose brushes against mine. He tugs me close, cradling me to his chest, and smiles with all his teeth and laugh lines on full display.

"How do you suggest we remedy that?" he whispers against my lips, pressing a soft kiss to the corner of my mouth.

"We should probably take another trip," I say. "Seems like we do our best work on the road."

Patrick hums, a low and deep sound full of agreement. "My bags are already packed, Jones. Just name the place."

"How about Japan to see the cherry blossoms next year? During your spring break? We won't stay long, and then we'll come home. Together."

He lifts me in his arms and spins me around. My heel falls off my foot and hits the tiled floor.

"I'm going to love you forever," he says. "And then I'm going to love you some more."

"How is that possible?"

"I'll make it possible. I'll make anything possible when it comes to you."

"Patrick? Can I tell you a secret?"

He chuckles into my shoulder, his breath warm on my skin. "You know you can tell me anything, Lola."

"No matter what happens down the road, no matter where we go in life—whether that's somewhere together or separate—I am very lucky to have found a friend like you."

Patrick cups my cheek and stares at me with so much love in his eyes, the love that you know is special. It's the kind you feel in your bones and in your soul, joining my heart to his for infinity.

"I am very lucky to have found a friend like you too, Lola."

"Who would've thought we'd be here, twenty-four years later, with silly matching bracelets on our wrists and tattoos on your body?"

"I thought it. I wished for it and hoped for it on every birthday and on every shooting star. But I think we're just getting started. The best is yet to come."

EPILOGUE

Patrick
Three years later

I BOUGHT the ring the morning after our first date.

Some people might consider spending money on a piece of jewelry a huge gamble when Lola and I had only been officially together for a few days. A jinx, a curse on the relationship before it even began.

I always knew Lola was the one for me, though.

The heart wants what the heart wants, and my heart wants her.

The ring is small. It's barely flashy enough to ward off potential suitors and announce she's taken, but Lola doesn't want flashy.

Simple, she told me one night over dinner as she raised her eyebrows and stabbed her green beans. I'd casually asked for her jewelry preferences, just to make sure I wasn't underestimating her tastes.

Simple, like our love.

Simple, like how easy it is to love *her*.

Simple, like how every day has been with her by my side.

I've kept the velvet box in my pocket for three years. It's traveled around the world with us to Australia and Edinburgh. The trip to England we finally took together, spending a day in Bath to see The Jane Austen Centre and buying a new edition of *Pride and Prejudice* for her bookshelves. At national parks here in the States and kayaking down the Charles River.

Every time we go somewhere new, I snap a photo of the diamond. Box open. Princess-cut stones catching in the sunlight. Lola's back turned as she ties her shoe or points to a flock of birds flying overhead. Walking down the side of the mountain ahead of me, oblivious to what's happening behind her.

The photos are all saved in a password-protected folder on my phone. LLF it's titled.

Love Lola Forever.

It's what I intend to do.

She's never asked me what it means, and I can't wait to show her what I've been hiding.

There have been plenty of opportunities to pop the question.

At the top of the Eiffel Tower when we were in Paris for Fashion Week last fall, sipping champagne and celebrating her success as a featured name on the runway.

Over dinner on a rainy Thursday night, the sky dark and the weather cool, sharing a slice of pizza on the couch in the quiet of our home. A walkup Brownstone off Newbury Street, a three-minute walk from her shop and a ten-minute train ride to my school. There's no porch or garage, but there is a rooftop terrace.

Compromise, I said to Lola when I handed her the keys. She gets the city. I get the house.

I also get her, which is all that really matters.

She kissed me real hard after that.

No time has felt like the perfect opportunity yet. It hasn't felt like *us*, two people who have known each other for eternity, long before her name ever appeared in glossy magazines and on the Academy Awards red carpet. Back before she had a million social media followers, a full inbox, and fan mail.

It's why I'm playing the long game. A plan that's taken close to nine hundred days to pull off, all ending today.

July 18th.

The same day I first met her twenty-seven years ago.

I carefully lay out a checkered blanket in the middle of a field outside the city, using four rocks to hold down the corners so the breeze doesn't pick up the tartan fabric and blow it away. I squint up at the sky and smile at the warmth on my face. The gray clouds from the morning have broken, giving way to bright sunshine and blue as far as the eye can see.

I spread out the books and make sure they're in the right order. I take a deep breath and fill my lungs with a nervous gulp of air. It feels like my heart is going to fall out of my chest and burrow in the dirt.

I don't know why I'm afraid. I know Lola is going to say yes.

We've talked about marriage dozens of times. I would've returned the ring if she had been totally against it, but she's not. Just the other day she looked at me over her bowl of cereal and asked if I wanted to go to the courthouse and make our relationship *legally binding*. I panicked and turned on the blender, drowning out her question so I didn't have to answer her.

This is worth the wait.

Satisfied with the setting, I jog back to the Jeep and open the passenger door. I make sure Lola's blindfold is in place and I slip her hand in mine. A current passes through me as our fingers thread around each other, a wave of electricity zapping me from just the squeeze of her palm.

Years later, and I still get butterflies when I touch her.

I wonder if that will ever end, and I really hope it doesn't.

"Okay," I say. "Ready?"

"For this big secret you're hiding?"

"I am not hiding anything."

"Yes, you are. Your voice got all high and squeaky in the car."

"I had a frog in my throat."

"You're a terrible liar, Patrick. The last time you blindfolded me we went to Disney World. What do you have up your sleeve this time?"

"Sorry to disappoint, but it's not an amusement park. Do you have the paper I asked you to bring?"

She waves the crisp sheet in the air. I smile at her handwriting, the loopy letters and the swoops of y's and g's. That piece of paper is crucial to my plan.

I lead her into the field, dandelions and unmowed grass coming up to our shins. It's beautiful out here, secluded away from noisy roads and towering skyscrapers. There are lines of blueberry bushes to our right and pine trees to our left, nothing but quiet air and a sense of peace surrounding us. It reminds me of the night we went camping in North Carolina where we felt like the only two people in the world.

When we reach the blanket, I tug Lola to the ground and pull off her blindfold.

"Should I know where we are?" she asks, plucking a flower from out of the earth and tucking it behind her ear.

"No." I reach over and squeeze her thigh, just under the hem of her dress. The green one she's been wearing all morning, a torturous outfit choice as I tried to make us eggs and bacon for breakfast. I burnt a piece of toast when she leaned over the counter to crack the kitchen window open, a smirk on her lips. "It's new."

"What's the occasion?"

"Our twenty-seventh anniversary."

"Patrick." She props herself up on her knees and her hands curl around my shirt collar. She tugs me close, lips almost pressed to mine. "I've told you this a hundred times. You can't count the years when our relationship was platonic."

"Doesn't matter." I kiss the tip of her nose. "You were always mine."

"Your former girlfriends would be appalled to hear that."

"So would Liam the bartender. I'm sure he misses you."

"Oh, I hope he graduated from college. I'll have to ask Henry what he's up to nowadays." Lola giggles when I narrow my eyes. She looks over my shoulder and brightens, visibly excited by what she sees. "More books?"

"More books."

She reaches past me for the one on the far left. "Does this have to do with the sheet of paper?"

"Yup," I say. "You know the drill."

"It's like Where's Waldo? I love it."

It's taken months to get to this point, handing over a book to her every day. Hidden somewhere in the pages of each one is a single word I've highlighted and underlined. I've asked Lola to find it and jot it down on the paper, sentences and paragraphs forming. I made her promise she wouldn't read ahead, waiting to put it together until the very end.

Which is today.

Lola kicks off her sandals and stretches out her legs. She flips through the pages of the book on the far left, a dark cover with flowers along the edges. Her eyes scan the lines until she grins. "Found it. The first word is will."

"Here. I'll help. You find, I'll write."

"You're too kind."

I add *will* to the bottom of the paper. "Next."

"Oh, I've been eying this one," she says, picking up the next book in the lineup. "Apparently there's a scene in it we need to try. At least that's what Jo told me."

"Yes, and Jack and Jo are also the people who defiled our

newly remodeled bathroom a month ago because they couldn't keep their hands to themselves during game night. I'm taking what she says with a grain of salt."

Lola looks up at me. She bites her bottom lip and her mouth stretches into a slow grin. "They have no idea you got me off under the blanket at movie night last week."

I pull her into my lap and settle my hands around her waist. "I'm a man of many talents."

"Yes," she agrees. She drops her head to my shoulder and lets out a content sigh. "You are. Humble too."

"Keep reading for me, love."

She takes her time, running her finger under the passages. I can tell when she's spotted the next word because she sits up straight. She wiggles against my thighs. "The second word is you."

"Great job." I press a kiss to her exposed shoulder, the cuffed sleeve of her dress dipping dangerously low on her arm to show off a patch of freckles.

They're new, sprouting up from weekends at the lake where her golden hair is a tangled mess and her happiness is free and unbridled.

She lets out a breathy sound and it takes every ounce of self-control to focus on the pen in my hand and not the other sounds I want to hear her make.

The groan in the back of her throat when I rub my thumb over her underwear. How she lets out a gasp when I drag my teeth down her neck and leave a pink mark. The way she whispers my name when her hands are in my hair, hips rocking into mine as a bead of sweat rolls down her chest.

"I love when you say that."

"What?" I ask. "Great job?"

"Yeah. I like when I make you proud."

"You make me proud every day, Lola. You are the most amazing person I've ever met."

"I love you so much," she says, spinning in my lap so her thighs bracket mine.

"I love you too. More than anything in this world. But I need you to be good and finish the books. Can you do that for me?"

"I like it when you beg though," she murmurs against my lips.

My cheeks flush and I dip my mouth to the hollow of her throat. I remember the rest of this morning when she was on the kitchen counter. I fell to my knees before her parted legs, asking her *please*. I burnt the second piece of toast and set off the smoke alarm, but neither of us cared.

"Please?" I whisper now. I kiss the spot below her ear she loves so much. The place that makes her shiver and arch her spine.

"Fine," she whispers. She opens the book and hides her smile. "But only because you asked so nicely."

The third word takes her longer to find.

To be fair, it took me longer to hide. I went through fifteen books until I found one that worked. I decorated this particular word with care. Hearts and squiggles and lots and lots of pink so it looks like it's jumping off the page.

It's impossible to miss.

"Well?" I ask.

"Hang on. I only see—"

Lola looks up at me. Her mouth parts and her pupils are blown wide. "Patrick."

"I don't think that's what it says. Do you want to try again?"

She lets out a slow breath. "It says marry."

I hum and jot it down, adding it to the page. "Marry... Interesting. Got it. Only two more to go."

"I don't want to."

"You don't? Why not?"

"Because this will be over, and I don't want it to end."

"Ah." I pull her close and rub my nose against hers. "That's the best part, honey. It's not an ending. It's just the beginning."

She finds the last two words at lightning speed, a newfound determination to her searching. I add the final punctuation mark, the last question mark on the page, and I hand the paper over to her.

"Start from the top," I say.

"Are you sure? I was going to start from the bottom."

I pinch her hip. "You're going to be the death of me, woman."

"Lola," she reads. "When I give you this, I will have spent almost three years on this project. Hopefully by now I've built you a library to fit all the romance books I've bought you, but books aren't why we're here. I've had this paper in my wallet since the night we first kissed, tucked right next to the photo of us at Disney World.

"You fell asleep with the cutest smile on your face. It was hard to leave you in bed, but I needed to start this note. It began on a napkin from the kitchen in our AirBnb, and it's ending with you here today, piecing every word together so they finally form something coherent.

"I don't know where to begin to describe the depth of the love I have for you. It's greater than the bottommost point of the ocean. More vast than the corners of the sky. I have loved you from the moment I first met you. I have loved you every second since, and I'm going to keep loving you for the rest of our lives.

"You mean everything to me. You are my entire world. Without you, I cease to exist. You once asked me how I was sure, how I knew you were the one, and it's pretty easy to answer. Even if you never picked me, even if you ended up with someone else down the road, there was no one else I would ever want. In every world, in every story, in every

405

CHELSEA CURTO

version of us, it was always you. Only you. I would always find you.

"I guess this is the time I should admit that I purposely forgot to remind you to grab your sweatshirt from the car when we were camping in North Carolina so you'd be forced to cuddle with me. I wanted to sleep beside you that night, and then every night after. I want to sleep beside you until we're ninety years old, looking back on a life well-lived together.

"I love you so much, pretty girl, which is why I'm going to wrap this up and ask you what I've wanted to ask you for thousands and thousands of days.

"Lola Jones. Will you marry me? Today?"

When she finishes, I reach into my pocket and pull out the box, opening it.

"I meant everything I said." I take Lola's hand in mine and kiss the tip of each of her fingers. She's shaking, and tears are falling down her cheeks. "Every syllable. Every word. Now I just need to know your answer."

"My answer?" She wraps her arms around my neck. "My answer is yes. Hell yes. Yes, yes, yes, *yes*. A million times over. I love you, Patrick. I love that you think of me all the time. I love how wonderful of a cheerleader you are. Most importantly, I love that you love me back. All of me. Even the imperfect parts. I cannot wait to be your wife."

"And my best friend forever," I add.

"And your best friend forever," she repeats. "Always."

"I'm a little late with the marriage pact." I slip the ring on her finger and rub my thumb over her knuckle. "By a couple of years."

"You had to be sure."

"With you, I've always been sure."

"Are we really doing this? Right now?"

"You told me you didn't want a wedding. Just something for

us. Here are your dandelions, sweetheart." I pluck a bunch from the ground and glance at the sky. Dark clouds have started to roll in, covering the sun, and I smile. "And I think you might get your rainstorm."

"Who's going to officiate? We're out here alone."

"The only person I could trust to be sworn to secrecy. A former non-believer but now a hopeless romantic who volunteered his services and promised to not tell the rest of our nosy friends until we're ready."

Jack steps out from behind a tree and smiles. He's wearing a suit, something I absolutely did not ask him to do, but I love him even more for it.

I tap Lola's backside and she stands, brushing blades of grass from her dress. I slip my hand through hers and nod to Jack as he approaches.

"I could have done without the blanket information," he says.

"And I could have done without you banging in my guest bathroom," I answer.

His smile stays in place. "Call it even?"

"Yeah." I pull Lola close. "But only because I want to marry this woman right this second."

"Wait. I don't have a ring for you." She frowns. "How can we get married without a ring?"

"We can figure it out later. If you want me to wear a ring, I will, but I think my new tattoo is a little more permanent than a piece of metal."

I carefully wiggle my left ring finger where I had an L inked on my skin this morning.

"You cannot keep getting these tattoos and hiding them from me," Lola says. She grabs my hand and studies the cursive, the letter matching her handwriting.

"Yeah? What are you going to do about it, wife?"

Lola kisses my palm and settles it over her heart. That *thump, thump, thump* calms me, brings me peace, and the rest of the world quiets. "I guess I have the rest of my life to be mad at you."

"Until we're stardust," I say. I brush a lock of hair out of her eyes. "Ready to do this?"

"I am. From now until forever, Pattycakes."

Jack goes through the cursory words. The *I do* part. The *to have and to hold* part. Our vows are quick, no different from what I tell Lola late at night in our bed when we're together, talking about our days.

It's a promise to her, to always strive to be a better man. To support her dreams and her goals in any way I can. To treat her with gentle kindness. To love her simply and simply love her through all the challenges of life, just like I've done for the last twenty-seven years. She says something similar, promising to keep working on herself and to keep filling my office with balloons. To always come home, never gone for too long.

"By the power vested in me by the state of Massachusetts and the website I used six months ago to get ordained, I now pronounce you husband and wife," Jack says. "You may kiss the bride."

I grin and tug Lola toward me, a thread around my heart pulling me to her. I put a hand on her lower back and dip her toward the ground. My lips brush against hers. "I should have made you my wife years ago."

"Wife. I like how that sounds." She tips her mouth toward mine and kisses me with delicate care. When I put her back on her feet, Jack's disappeared and we're all alone. "Where to now?"

"Don't care," I say. "Anywhere with you is my favorite place."

"Take me to the treehouse, Patrick," she whispers. "I think we should go back to the place where it all began."

ACKNOWLEDGMENTS

Thank you so much for reading Road Trip to Forever. Writing a book is never easy, and if you follow me on Instagram, you know I've been open and honest about how long this book has taken me to complete.

Months. It's taken *months*, and the hardest book I've ever written.

My brain made it so difficult to focus on Patrick and Lola's story. I was distracted. By work, by social media, by other stories I wanted to start. Finishing this 115,000 word book felt impossible. But I did it, and I'm so dang proud of myself.

This book wouldn't be possible without a few people.

Brooke: thank you for your help in getting this book edited. You are a lifesaver, and I'm so thankful for your patience and your grace.

To my beta readers: Alex, Amanda D, Kelsey, Morgan, Michelle, Dani, DeLayna, Haley, Katelin, Katie, Kelly, Kristen, Lily, Linna, Rhianna, Sarah, Skyler and Amanda W. You all saw this story at its worst and helped bring it to its best. Thank you for sticking with me. Thank you for your feedback. Thank you for your encouragement. You all are the best.

To Mikey: you are the best other half. Thank you for always supporting me. Thank you for believing in me. The next acknowledgments will be written from my desk in the home that we're buying together, which makes me so happy I could burst. I'm glad I get to do life with you. I love you and Riley so much.

To my family: thank you for being the best. I love y'all.

And to my momma: I promise the next one won't have as many spicy scenes.

If you read and loved Patrick and Lola's story, I would be grateful if you left a review on your preferred platform (Goodreads, Amazon, etc). Positive reviews help little authors like me much.

Thanks for being here. Kindness is the best personality trait one can have, and love always wins.

ABOUT THE AUTHOR

Chelsea lives in the Northeast with her partner and their dog. She's a flight attendant for a major U.S. airline. When she's not busy writing or reading romance novels, she loves to run, travel, spend time with her friends, and visit theme parks. She loves to meet new people, so make sure to follow her on social media!

instagram.com/authorchelseacurto

tiktok.com/@authorchelseacurto

amazon.com/author/chelseacurto